... as emotionally evocative and as grippingly compassionate as any this reviewer has ever read...
Pacific review

Compelling as fiction but potentially eye-opening in a spiritual sense, the peculiarities of this story fascinate the reader through every chapter
US Review

The author's creativity is commendable.
Hollywood Book Review

SO A MUKI
RECEIVING PROPHECY

by S L Bergen

A sequel to:

THE LAND OF THE BUTTERFLIES
– A PRELUDE TO PROPHECY

Primix Publishing
11620 Wilshire Blvd
Suite 900, West Wilshire Center, Los Angeles, CA, 90025
www.primixpublishing.com
Phone: 1-800-538-5788

Published by Primix Publishing   05/04/2022

ISBN: 978-1-955177-75-7(sc)
ISBN: 978-1-955177-76-4(hc)
ISBN: 978-1-955177-77-1(e)

Library of Congress Control Number: 2021924944

CONTENTS

DEDICATION

To my Grandchildren and all the foster children who lived with my daughter and touched my heart, in hopes they remember that all actions cause reactions. May they recognize that life contains errors and learn to forgive others, especially themselves. May they grant themselves the freedom to err and the courage to change and grow.

WARNING

SOME OF THE ACTIVITIES PARTAKEN by the characters in this novel are illegal and inherently dangerous. Attempting to mimic them likely will result in substantial fines and serious injury or death. Please, do not be foolish enough to try them.

PROLOGUE

March 21,1997,
Dear Friends,

I feel alien. Unintentionally created, my existence is a mystery. Unbound, I have no anchor to Earth. I belong to the universe. Without a doubt, I have no connection to time and space. I exist. Although it is my native tongue, I do not comprehend English. When I open my mouth, I speak only gibberish. Equally disconcerting, I do not comprehend what other people say to me. Their words, actions, and expressions clash. There is no meaning. Caught off guard, I am aware that what comes out will give the wrong impression and shut down communication.

When I was very young, I thought I was unique and nearly all others were ordinary. I conversed with God and played games among the stars. I loved everything and everyone. Innocent and naive, I danced in the rain and sunshine, delighting in the gifts surrounding me. Told I was not living in the real world, I rejected it, and thrived in the one that made my heart soar. I could reach the sky.

Once older and more cynical, I determined I was abnormal. I was too small, left-handed, spatially handicapped, and gullible. A misfit, I was simply born at the wrong time. I tried to figure out whether it was too late or too soon to no avail. Content to be abnormal, I preferred myself to the rest of the world. Does it matter if I did not belong? If I did not care, why should anyone else? Living in a world of association and acquaintance, I thrived within my comfort zone and gave the rest of normalcy a wide berth.

Wiser and approaching adulthood, I accepted a damaged label. My brain did not function similarly to other people. I was not normal. My central nervous system is improperly wired. The synapses of my brain lacked normal function. I was not alien; residual spermicidal chemicals and allergens from latex altered the working of my brain. In general, I chose to believe I was a forerunner of evolution. I allowed conceit to compensate for the efforts I needed to make to succeed using standards in which I held neither belief nor faith in their righteousness over what my essence offered. I grew defiant and stubborn. I would not conform. Instead, I fought. Brick walls became challenges. I was ready to stand up and call the world as I saw it.

I learned my lessons the hard way when I was very young. If you talk funny, people laugh and treat you as an imbecile. Recommendation: Do not speak. Moral: Life is a secret. If you are an original thinker, people shun and belittle you. Recommendation: Learn skills required to persuade and manipulate. Moral: Fight with fire. If you fail to conform to the accepted ecology and ethos, you risk failure and limited access to the future. Recommendation: Work harder. Moral: Believe in yourself; else, no one else will. If you are different, you will be isolated and alone. Recommendation: Befriend those who are also different and respect their differences. Moral: Seek kindred spirits, your soul will grow and thrive, and you will not be lonely. Thus, I grew up with the very best of friends—God.

I had human friends. They were few, but they were good friends. Deliciously, when God offers you a friend, the skies open, and it rains sunshine.

Thankfully, when God takes away a gift, He helps you find peace before shocking the system with a new demand, "My child, I have given you an apple. Now spit out the seed and savour the light."

Assuming God meant to tell my story, I tried. Reams of paper fell upon the floor. The words would not come. They hurt.

Thus, God laughed, saying, "Start in the middle. Tell the prophet York Sabastin's story. I will send you help."

True to His word, He sent me to church. Receiving lessons on love, I saw Christ in a church. He always arrived in a breath of wind, He sang to my heart, and I recognized him as Jarrock. They are the same. They are God. I rejoiced, and courage descended upon me. I told you "A Prelude to Prophecy", a tale from the Land of the Butterflies. I listened to God, searched for the signs, and endeavoured to follow destiny.

Although seeds are bitter and hard, they hold the promise of growth. With a seed, there can be a tomorrow. That truth is comforting. Whatever the wrapping, the tale is made of mud.

Sit back and make yourself comfortable. I will tell you a tale of receiving prophecy. Come, laugh and cry with me.

Sincerely, Tara

1

AN ENCOUNTER
WITH AN ANGEL

I WAS IN HIGH SCHOOL, THIRTEEN years old and in the eighth grade. I had the world by the tail! The school board did not know what they were doing when they had robbed me of a year of high school by putting grade seven back into the elementary school. Sure, I admit I was terrified on the first day of high school, but I was also extremely proud. I was among the big kids — young adults. I was probably the smallest kid in the school. My homeroom was in the converted eight-room primary school at the end of the lower field, with toilets so low to the floor that my knees sucked up into my face when I sat down on one. Even I had to kneel to use the drinking fountain. Proudly, I was one of the big kids.

It was a beautiful September day. Many leaves were still green. Summer was stretching far into autumn. The morning air had been crisp but not rainy, and I did not need to wear a coat. It was the kind of day when my steps were light, and joy filled my heart. Feeling wonderful on a Thursday afternoon, I was on my way home with a stack of books in my hand. Only one more day until the weekend, I thought with delight. Oh, life was so good. I was alive.

I was nearly home when God spoke to me again. I am afraid of God. He called my name. Now, God always got me into trouble. I did not have many friends. I was a shrimp, not athletic, or even very friendly, for that matter. It was not that I was unpopular. Others ignored me, and that suited me just fine. People were simply a bother to me. I find much more fun and satisfaction in doing my own thing alone than conforming to the blasé existence of ordinary people. I did not consider myself ordinary at all. I loved life. I loved questioning and arguing. I liked to take risks and be disobedient. I liked to shock my teachers and took a measure of satisfaction in the discomfort I caused them. A teacher called me an independent thinker. That term suited me!

However, I had my problems, too. My mouth got me into trouble with those I did know, including God. My friends thought I was crazy or unstable, and God was so bossy. The things God asked me to do were not that difficult, but they always involved doing something which did not come naturally to me. In general, they were outside the realm in which I defined my own character. They were things that I simply did not do. Often, God would ask that I interact with people more intimately than was comfortable. Naturally, God did not take no for an answer. Ignoring a call does not work either, but over the years, I had learned a few intricacies of answering God.

When you know for sure no flesh and blood person is talking to you, a call that comes out of the air around you, I have discovered, can be answered in three correct ways. It does not matter whether you say, God, my Lord, or Jesus. God does not care what you call Him. However, more is required.

If you say, "Yes, my Lord, I am yours!" you are asking for big, major trouble. This is the answer best given just before a truck runs you over or when a bolt of lightning strikes from the skies above. Either way, you are just as dead. If God does not have death in mind, such an answer seals your fate to be obedient. I did not want to be obedient then and doubt that I would ever have a smooth relationship with God; consistent, but certainly not perfect. God is my taskmaster, and I do indeed love God, but I also fear God. I do not like to disappoint God and feel quite incapable of living up to God's expectations.

If I felt up to it, a safer answer was, "Yes, my God, I hear you." It would set the tone for an incredible experience. Such an answer implied that I intended to devote my whole being to listen to whatever it was God wanted to tell me. It would take courage to say because I never knew just what God had in mind. If He asked me to do something I did not want to do, racked with horribly guilty feelings, I would be depressed for months to come. Of course, there was a challenge, too. If I could do as asked, I could be in seventh heaven for just as long. God rarely asked me what I could not succeed, with enough effort, in accomplishing.

The third answer, which I thought a real copout, but used most frequently, was to say, "Yes, God, I am here." This answer was simply noncommittal. It meant I was listening but not guaranteeing I would hear, without implying that I would heed His words.

In short, I was a quiet, unobtrusive brat whose thoughts and actions often went right over the heads of those around me, even if I could not fool God.

Do not get me wrong. I was not special. My grades were average, and I was not ugly, but petite and skinny, and maybe a bit homely. I was just a kid growing up in the sixties. That day was like the kind of day I got my glasses..."

I rode my bike to pick them up, and as I rode home, marvelling at the beauty of the world around me, a wave of awe and thanksgiving struck me. I shouted, "Oh God! Thank you for letting me be four-eyed!" In my heart, I knew that I would never have appreciated the fine intricacies of creation around me had I not experienced its loss. Birds were flying above me, and they had individual feathers along with their outstretched wings. The trees were no longer a blob of green but hundreds of clusters of smooth little needles extending from perfectly balanced branches. There were little pebbles on the pavement. If I had been careful how I aligned my front wheel, I could make them fly out across the street as I rode over them. That day, God had laughed and sent me peace with a simple, "You are welcome, my child." I had blushed, happily ridden the rest of the way home, and did not mind the teasing that my older brother and sister sent my way.

It was not fair. I had teased my older sisters about being four-eyed mercilessly some years before. I felt guilty and tried to be especially kind all week, which mostly meant, I stayed out of the way.

Anyway, it was that kind of day, and I answered in a clear, confident voice, "Yes, my Lord, I hear you."

"I am going to send you a friend. I want you to listen to him and learn what he must teach you." The answer came from the air around me like speech through a surround sound system. There was no vision, just the familiar warm feeling flowing through my veins. It was an unusual event. Usually, God told me that I was hurting my mother with my disobedience or needed to do a good deed for someone in my neighbourhood or some such thing. I was surprised and shocked that God would see fit to send me a friend.

"How will I know him?" I asked.

"You will recognize him."

The imp in me yawned and stretched, then giggled. "Okay. Whatever you say." Thinking quietly while imagining this friend, I wondered how I could evaluate just what it was for which God was setting me up. Everything had an angle, a purpose, an objective, and I was not sure whether I would need to scuttle the plans or not. Best to be prepared, I concluded.

As I walked up the hill of the back alley, I daydreamed about a knight in shining armour, a poor starving little orphan, and all things in between. Of course, I was the hero. I giggled as God chastised me, quickly opened my back door, and ran up to my room.

That night I had a wonderful dream. I met a man, a full-grown, honest to goodness he-man. He was tall, brown-skinned, had jet black hair, a little on the longish side, a very square face, and beautiful sparkling black eyes. His hands were huge and rough. Oh, I had a crush on him. His name was David.

I had had crushes before, mostly on boys in my class or at least attending my school. Usually, they were nasty little boys who called out to my heart for a hug and needed a little loving. However, this man was different. Maybe I was growing up. My dream was very clear. He did not need me; I needed him. Was this the friend God was sending me? I was so scared I woke up.

I had an awful time falling asleep again. After tossing and turning, I checked the hall to make sure my folks had gone to bed and then went to my closet and dragged out my big rubber doll. I held him close then tucked him under the covers so no one would see him if they walked into my room in the morning. Then, confident that I was not ready to grow up just yet, I snuggled under the covers close to my doll and went peacefully back to sleep. God and his friend could wait.

One cannot underestimate God. There is absolutely no truth greater than the word of God. God did not wait. The next day after school, I met David. I had joined the gym club, and it was late when I headed home. After crossing the field and entering the alley, I was upset to see a person on my pathway. Although surprised to encounter a stranger on the way, as I came closer, there was no doubt in my mind that the man standing at the corner across the street was the man I had seen in my dream the night before. It was drizzling just a bit. A hardhat and a steel lunch kit sat on the ground beside him. He probably worked at the mill. I could smell the sawdust on his clothes when I was halfway across the street. I love that smell. It is rich and reminds me of walking in the forest. I stared at him.

He laughed.

"What are you doing here?" I blurted as though he had no right to be standing at the corner.

Smiling, he half laughed. I blushed. He said, "I am waiting for a friend." Then, he winked. Not even purposely, I tripped and dropped my books. Kneeling, he helped me pick them up.

I looked into his beautiful eyes. Although completely out of character, I was overwhelmed with emotions. Feeling like an idiot and terribly inadequate, I struggled to gain the courage to speak to him again. I uttered, barely above a whisper, "I would like to be that friend."

Frowning, he looked at me very strangely. Neither of us moved for what seemed an eternity. Then David said, "You are a bit young for me, wouldn't you agree?" A great big smile spread across his face, and lights danced in his eyes. He laughed.

Shocked and embarrassed by his response, I pulled my books close and ran. When a few feet separated us, I turned back to him and yelled, "Not that kind of friend, David, a real friend." Then I ran and did not stop until I was at my own back door. I ignored his call. Thinking I had really messed up something important and special, I felt relieved when he shouted back, "How do you know my name? Do I know you?"

I prided myself that I had the last laugh. Suddenly, I was confident that I would see him the next Friday. After all, he was a gift from God. He would have to be my friend. He did not have any say in the matter whatsoever. Ah, I had power! I would find out a bit more about this game God had invited me to play. The only things that really bothered me were why I had offered to be his friend and just what I meant by not that kind of friend. Had I spoken to David, or had God intervened putting words into my mouth? God sometimes did that. God was setting up something big and exciting for me. I just knew it, but it really terrified me.

2

An Unusual Encounter

DAVID WATCHED AS THE GIRL ran up the hill as though glued in his position, unable to move. He could not even figure out for himself what he felt. This was a most unusual event for David. His friend, Mark, had often relayed stories about how forward and undisciplined these people were. Yet, this little kid had been adamant that she was not after sex. He wished he understood these aliens more clearly. Their culture was so different, so dishonest. Around them, David could never be completely confident that he interpreted them accurately. It seemed to him that their bodies and expressions said one thing and their words quite another. He had never felt this confused before by any of the people he had previously met. David has met many people in the last few months. He felt a shudder flow through him. A quiet filled him as he contemplated both crying and laughing yet felt both to be appropriate feelings for the occasion.

A beep of the horn of his truck brought him out of his trance. As David turned around, he met the laughing eyes of his friend, Mark, who was stepping out of the truck.

"What happened to you, David? You look as though you have seen a ghost," said Mark with a chuckle in his voice. David was a quiet, reserved sort and, therefore, Mark thought it odd and refreshing to see David look so out of control.

"I met someone."

"Oh no, David, you haven't been smitten by an Earthling! David, you surprise me. They're barely human, you know. Don't be revolting.

Yuck," teased Mark remembering his own heartaches for loving a forbidden woman on this planet. He felt sick for his friend. This was a sign of deep sorrow and pain to come. He did not wish to watch his friend suffer. He knew what such pain did to one's soul. This culture had no castles, their hearts were bare to react, and all the Muki (pronounced 'mucky') were vulnerable. Muki is the name they call themselves and their faith. It is a word with the same meaning as the word Christian.

On their home planet, the Land of the Butterflies, women were segregated from men until they ceased to be fertile. Castles were fortified complexes, housing an extended family of females and their children. Young boys left the castle at six years of age and, unless they earned a license to sire, would never meet or see fertile females, referred to as butterflies, throughout the rest of their lives. Growing up in a ridged culture where women held the upper hand, males, although protected and nurtured, were taught, by post-menopausal women, to fear fertile women as powerful beings who would fill them with lust, break their hearts, and ultimately, take their lives. The opportunity to mate, considered a holy occupation, had to be earned and was reserved only for the most righteous, respected, and distinguished males in their society. A license to sire was granted in recognition of honourable service to God, their families, and the Land of the Butterflies. If they became a sire, their duty was to protect their mates from all dangers and unhappiness with their lives.

"She was just a kid, looked about ten but must have been older. She would most certainly be a butterfly."

"Forget her, David. This planet is the Devil's domain. Hey, are you listening to me? Come back to the ground! Get in the truck." Laughing as David vacantly walked to the passenger side of the truck, Mark opened the door. "Get your lunch kit and hard hat. David, where are you?"

"In heaven, Mark," he whispered, then blushed as he retrieved his hat and lunch pail.

"Do not fall for a girl, David. Seriously, it would have no future." Then Mark began to laugh, and could not stop, as he watched David climb into the passenger seat. This was David's truck, and he always drove. After sitting behind the steering wheel, Mark dangled the keys in front of David's face. David shook his head, and Mark took a moment to stare in disbelief.

"I had better get you to Muma Horren because you've got love written all over you."

After nodding, David blushed and, laughing, said, "She's not that kind of friend." Then looked somewhat distant again as he strained to look up the back alley beyond the truck.

"There is no one there, David. Maybe you were hallucinating.

Do you want me to drive up the alley?"

"No," answered David emphatically.

Mark chuckled and drove away, worried that a tear was falling down David's cheek before they had gone a block. "Want to tell me about her?"

It was usually David soothing Mark's heartstrings. Describing Earth as a den of temptation, Mark had a weakness for anything resembling a female human and had to fight strong instincts to capture and carry off any that got within reach. This was a beautiful land, full of promise and opportunity. However, in Mark's eyes, it was also full of traps. It brought out the worst in him, and he regularly needed David to intervene on his behalf to prevent him from sinning. Just thinking about butterflies made him excited.

However, David falling for an alien was outside of character. David found women here amusing. They liked him, but David would laugh and push them all away. Having plans, he wanted to become a great judge and felt he had a destiny to fulfill. One of those oddball people who intended to become a sire someday, David was weird, but he was a good friend.

Although becoming a sire was holy, it was also a hazardous job to undertake. The duties, including fathering the next generation, ensuring the health of the women and children in his care, gaining the consent of the often-reluctant butterflies to impregnate them, keeping the peace between the various groups within the castle, and fighting any intruding males, were onerous and carried a heavy weight of responsibility. The women held the sire accountable for all mishaps and unhappiness. A castle could have a total population between two hundred and a thousand inhabitants, and there was rarely more than one male in the castle at a time. On top of that, virtually, the sire was a prisoner within his own quarters for health reasons. Because most sires died on the job, males usually did not exercise their licenses to sire until they were over fifty years of age. Typically, a position as sire lasted five to fifteen years, an absolute maximum of twenty. But if he displeased the women, it could end in his execution at a moment's notice.

Most men preferred the safer and more relaxed option of having sexual relations with older, infertile women even though losing their virginity terminated the option of ever becoming a sire. A male could only be a sire in a single castle and had to be a virgin to attain and maintain his license to sire. He also underwent extensive testing to ensure he would be genetically safe to breed in the castle accepting his application. On the Land of the Butterflies, the infertility rate for both men and women was extremely high (over one in three), while the genetic compatibility between individual castles was very low. Many men would not deny their sexual urges because it was not particularly likely that they would ever be an acceptable sire in the future anyway.

Mark was glad that David had joined this assignment because he was smart, and everyone knew that he held potential, as the professors called it. Mark thought David was too serious, but his own carefree attitude needed a little seriousness. David probably needed him for the opposite reason. Balancing each other in a good way, they were best friends. Still, Mark worried about David needing help in matters of the heart because he was not the kind of man who could take such things lightly. He hoped he would be able to keep David out of trouble.

While David appeared lost in thought, Mark waited for a few minutes in silence. Mildly amused, he began to let his own thoughts wander. Women, especially the young ones on this planet, were attractive. The only feature that Mark did not particularly like was that their skin was rather hairy. His own race had very few hair follicles other than on their heads, but other than that, they seemed much like women at home. All women held a mystery, and Mark much preferred to talk to women. He was better equipped to handle the emotional side of this culture. It was his specialty. He liked to know what made people tick, and David was always there to hold him back.

Their mission was a fact-finding assignment. Considered instruments of creation, his people policed oases of life in the known universe, carrying out the will of God as directed. They governed their actions by presenting their findings and interpretations of what God required of them to a group of highly respected religious leaders, called the Panel, who would listen, query, judge, and confirm recommendations prior to endorsing the authority to proceed with all actions. The Panel figured that Earth was dangerous and belonged to the dark side of life. Considering the people of Earth agents of the Devil, with the destruction of the Kingdom of God as their primary goal, Mark thought the Panel was probably correct, but had a feeling that there was something more to this remote solar system. The only way Mark could describe it was to use David's favourite description. David often said, "Earth is blessed in some way, Mark. I can feel it." David was more abstract in his thinking, but Judge Soronato, the expedition leader, recorded that statement. He hounded them over that comment. Frequently yelling, "Prove it," he put a lot of pressure on David for having said it.

Judge Soronato did not think Earth had any redeeming features at all, or, if he did, he kept them to himself. He endorsed that Earth is purely evil, and any kindness or righteousness found was a deception planned by the Devil. Mark figured Judge Soronato just wanted to keep them on their toes. Even if it was primitive in comparison to their home planet, an advanced civilization thrived here. Still, Mark and David both thought Earth an intriguing place and immensely enjoyed the times the Judge allowed them to interact with the natives.

Both David and Mark had joined the investigative team for personal growth. It was not every day that destruction assignments came up. Having been involved in such an assignment would put them in a good position for exciting tasks in the future. At their age, most assignments were boring and routine. They both felt blessed to be involved in such a serious endeavour as this current assignment but pleased that they were not in the position of issuing a final judgement either. The Panel had destruction assignments repeated ten times before accepting a recommendation, including destroying a planet, let alone carrying it out. Therefore, it was not as though they had to worry too much about the ramifications of their recommendations. This was only the sixth judgement. Overall, it was the best kind of assignment to have. It was unique and thereby held the possibility of a unique solution. Unique solutions invoked opportunities to meet with the Panel directly and often ended with the participants having their names in a chapter of one of the Great Books. Maybe it was a search for fame and fortune that attracted them to this assignment, but David and Mark had discussed applying mostly in career building. Besides, last year's university courses for Cultural Judges included curriculum on Earth; they had wanted to see it for themselves.

Since their arrival, their whole beings had been bombarded with the stark reality of being among aliens in a very alien environment. Both thrived on the excitement each day held. Although Mark had toyed with feelings of lust many times, even he did not relish the thought of leaving his offspring in this world. Muma Horren had been doing biological studies and had concluded that the races were genetically similar enough that conception would likely result from mating with Earthlings. That was enough to keep Mark's hands to himself, at least most of the time. Mark was not a saint by any stretch of the imagination, but he was still a virgin.

Treasuring the ordered and protected culture that the Muki enforced, David kept his distance from the females. On his home planet, called the Land of the Butterflies, women, although wielding the most power, confined themselves within fortified castles with armed guards patrolling its walls to ensure no one came or went without authorization. All premature and fertile females lived in isolated castles, and no males, other than infants and young boys under six years of age, and the authorized sire, entered. Attempts to gain access to fertile women generally resulted in the immediate execution of the offending male. In their culture, being around fertile women was simply dangerous, and submitting to unauthorized sexual desires was strongly prohibited. Therefore, David did not like to be around fertile women; Mark figured he did not trust himself not to fall in love. None of the women here had a castle, they were vulnerable, and David could not imagine a way to protect one if he loved her. Luckily, David had not been attracted to those he had met. Until today, that is.

What is it about the kid he met today? That was even taboo in this culture. Mark said a prayer asking God to ensure that whatever happened was according to Her will. Here, the will of man seemed more likely. Not wanting his friend to get hurt, Mark was not sure that David could handle forbidden love.

"Hey, David, snap out of it!" Mark called loudly. David jumped. "Tell me about this kid. Maybe it would help to talk."

"I will probably never see her again. There is not much to tell except, when I looked into her eyes, I saw a human being. She did not feel alien. I have never met anyone like her before, here or at home. Is there another team? Did anyone breed here on the last expeditions? There is something different about her. She might even belong to God."

"Have you lost it, David? We had better see Judge Soronato. Did you talk to her?"

"She knew I was alien. She demanded to know what right I had to be here, and her words, and everything about her, matched. There was nothing amiss like the other Earthlings. Without knowing what else to do, I laughed at her, Mark. It was so strange."

"Then what happened, David?"

"I told her I was waiting for a friend, and her eyes lit up. I felt God's presence within her. She said she wanted to be that friend."

"Are you sure you did not imagine it?"

"No, Mark. I searched her whole being and could not find any insincerity at all. She was genuine. However, that is not what has really frightened me, Mark. Listen. She knew my name. She ran away when I said she was too young for me. Then, as clear as a bell, she said, 'Not that kind of friend, David, a real friend.' Mark? What is a real friend? I have never come across that expression before. How did she know my name?"

I have heard that expression before, and I think I understand it vaguely, anyway. It means she wants you to be a friend, love her as herself, not necessarily as a woman, but not use her as an object or possession. She is not looking for a lustful relationship, but one like ours, David. She wants to be your soulmate."

"Ah, and now I am your soulmate, am I?" laughed David. "That's dumb. Why would she want me as a soulmate?"

"I don't know. It must be that smile of yours or your laugh. Remember the girl who wanted to haul you off into her den of ill repute last week? She told me the twinkle in your eye captivated her. Ache… women find you irresistible."

"Quit teasing me, Mark. It was not like that at all. She is different, I tell you."

"If she ran away, I do not know that she likes you. It would probably be best to stay away from her. You have fallen for her; there is no doubt of that! It is my turn to get you away from potential trouble, my friend. Dream while she is out of reach. Make sure you do not see her until you have come to your senses."

"Thank you, Mark. The table's turned, eh."

"Yeah, I guess it's my turn to see you wrench out your heart. I'm glad I am on this side for a change."

"I'm not, Mark. I'm scared and want to see her again, something awful, even just to find out how she knew my name. I'm sure I have never seen her before. She is not the kind I would forget or not notice. Something about her is special."

Mark almost replied but decided against it. David was head over heels in love with a little kid. Boy, when David flipped, he sure made it as hard on himself as possible. Relationships with Earthlings were taboo for all the Muki, Judge Soronato's orders. If the future held its destruction, it would not be comfortable having to sacrifice some of their own progeny—that made sense. No, poor old, serious David fell for a kid, not a woman by the standards and laws of this culture. A man had to be within two years of the same age as the girl if the relationship was to be acceptable if the girl is under twenty-one or nineteen anyway. How is a person supposed to tell a girl's age? You sure could not tell just by looking at them.

Mark glanced at David then shook his head while turning off onto the abandoned logging road leading to the transporter hideout. There was a landing about a mile up this trail unvisited by the natives since their arrival last spring. By the time they stopped, Doug and Loren were already raking their tire tracks. Mark looked at his watch. It took about twenty minutes to satisfy them that no one would see that a vehicle had come up here. Mark was glad. They would be early for dinner, and, therefore, likely have time to talk to the Judge. The Judge would reassign David to a new location, and no harm would come of David's heartache.

After David and he carefully removed the branches that camouflaged the transporter's hiding place, Mark sighed and grabbed the remote. Presently, the transporter floated out into view. The doors opened just as Doug and Loren came into view around the corner at the top of the trail. Quickly grabbing his shoulder, David whispered into his ear, "Mark, please don't say anything yet. Let me find out what she knows first. She might know more than my name. She might also be a key into a part of this culture that we have not seen before."

Shaking his head, Mark sighed again. David was not one to take the easy road away from potential trouble. He seemed to seek problems and delight in walking the line between safety and death. As usual, David was putting Mark into the hot seat. Common sense said run, and using common sense was always the right answer for Mark in situations involving the opposite sex. Mark always got over a girl faster the sooner he left her behind. It was acceptable to be friendly, and liking a person was not taboo or harmful. Caring and good feelings were valuable tools to learn to understand an alien culture. As always love was the root to the heart of any people the

Muki had ever come across. David was right; if he could control his emotions, this kid could be a treasure box of insight into humanity, as it existed on Earth. "One more visit, David. Then we've got to report to the Judge."

"Thanks. You are my soulmate, Mark. I appreciate it."

"No problem, David. You know I'm good for an adventure."

The two men laughed and fooled around. Doug and Loren knew something was up but knew better than to bother asking. Mark and David were secretive when they acted this goofy, and they would gain nothing. They would report the giddiness to Muma Horren, and she would keep an eye on the renegades of the expedition.

With everyone supporting each other's differing styles and methods, this expedition had a good crew. Although a rather motley crew, being the sixth expedition, they needed to be bolder and more critical than previous judgements. They also had to carry out the recommendations of five teams before them to confirm theories or test hypotheses.

They needed the diversity that Judge Soronato had put together in his team. He believed in using fresh minds and original thinkers, and many young judges benefited under his careful guidance and scrutiny. He had even endorsed the application of a university student. Brian, David's little brother, was a member of the crew, and because of him, Muma Horren had come along. It was wonderful to have a senior matron along because senior matrons were an exceptional and unique breed of women. All the men, especially the young ones, loved Muma Horren and trusted her judgement concerning matters of the heart.

The Miskenacks, David's family, had an excellent reputation as Cultural Judges. The family had produced several great judges, and Judge Soronato had taken both David and Brian under his wing as though he was their father. He envisioned bright futures for both these men. In fact, he took a particular interest in developing the skills of all the members of his team, just like a father to them all. Well respected, many of the panel considered Judge Soronato, a great judge. Everyone, especially the many young men like Doug, Loren, Brian, Mark, and David, felt very privileged to be working for him.

As Mark worked the transporter haze around them, Loren and Doug decided to keep a close eye on Mark and David themselves. Possibly, this week would be more exciting. There usually was not much fun on guard duty, but they would speculate on what David and Mark were up to. Then maybe they would get another opportunity to mingle with the natives themselves next week and carry-on whatever scheme these two were putting into motion.

One by one, the men disappeared into the sleek pencil-shaped transporter, and the door closed. There was a flash of soft yellow light, and the transporter, and its cargo, was gone.

3

THE GROUND
BENEATH MY FEET

IT WAS ALMOST OCTOBER. THE leaves were falling in droves. I hoped the rain would stay away for a while longer. I liked walking and shuffling through them. Stomp, stomp went my feet. Crunch, crunch answered the dry, brittle leaves amid rustles and snaps. It was Friday. The streetlights were already on because it was autumn, and the air was crisp and chilly. Without hurrying, I stopped and gathered some leaves into a pile, then jumped into them until they scattered again. I wanted David to be at the corner but did not want to get there just in case he was not. Besides, what was I going to say to him? If I were slow enough, maybe he would be gone already. Then I would not have to have these funny little flutters in my stomach. Seeing someone on the corner, I laughed at myself and hurried forward, wondering if he could be David. Trying to determine who was there, I stopped, then shrugged, and crossed the fingers on my left hand before calling, "Hi, David."

"Hi, friend," he called back, and my heart skipped a beat. After crossing the road, he fell into step beside me and started walking, but on the other side of the alley. Neither of us spoke until we were halfway up the alley at the bottom of the hill. David broke the silence. "Who told you my name?"

"God," I answered.

"God?" he asked, putting his hand on my shoulder and turning toward me.

"Yes, God," I repeated. I was not sure whether I should run at that moment, but something about the expression on his face made me feel safe.

He asked, "Why?"

"I don't know, David. God told me He would send me a friend, and you are he. You are supposed to teach me something, and I am to learn well," I answered in a matter-of-fact tone.

"You scare me, kid."

"So, what else is new? I scare lots of people," I said in self-defence.

We began to walk up the hill, very slowly. David looked at me strangely as though he was debating something in his mind.

Quite suddenly, he said, "What else do you know about me?"

"Not much. You can play the drums and dance and sing weird chants around a campfire. Are you a native?"

David trembled and went very pale. He did not even look like he had brown skin in the light of the streetlight shining on him from the street in front of my house. For a moment, I thought I might have the wrong person after all. He put his big hands on my cheeks and looked into my eyes. Although he was searching my very soul, I was not even frightened. Obviously special, maybe, he was an angel. He shook his head, "No, Littl'un. I am not a native. I am of the Muki."

"What is the Muki?" I asked, suddenly sorry that we were at my house.

"Bring me a cup of water, and I will show you," he answered. I went inside, dropped my books on the counter, grabbed a glass, and filled it. "I am going outside to play for a while, okay, Mom?" I called out as I opened the back door.

"Don't go far. Dinner is in three-quarters of an hour," came the answer.

"I'll just be outside. Bye," I said quickly before closing the back door.

At first, I did not see David and thought he had gone. "I'm up here," he called.

He was across the street and on the path that led up into the woods. A little voice inside me told me I did not know this man. He was a stranger, and my society had taught me to fear going into the woods with strangers. David might be a big bad wolf in disguise. He sensed my hesitation.

"I won't hurt you, Littl'un. I promise I won't touch you."

Having seen into his eyes, I believed him. I thought I was a good judge of character, even if I was just a kid. Besides, God had sent him to me. Praying my lesson would be pleasant, I ran over to him, careful not to spill the water. My hand shook as I held the glass out to him. Taking the glass, David said, "We won't go far," and then walked down the path into the trees. About fifty feet further, he stepped off the path, knelt, and started scraping away at the ground. While he worked, he quietly said, "Do not be afraid. Trust me. I am of the Muki. The Muki do not rape little girls."

I was curious to see what he was doing, and as my eyes adjusted to the scant light among the trees and bushes, I relaxed and knelt beside him. He had dug a hole in the soil and was picking up dirt and rubbing it between his fingers. This he did repeatedly until the soil was soft and granular. Then he pushed it all back into the hole, picked up the glass, dumped some water into it, and began stirring it with his big bare hands. "Join me," he said as he took my hands and rubbed mud all over them.

I laughed. "It is mucky alright! It is too cold to make mud pies!" I said sarcastically, but I did not pull my hands away. I liked the feel of the cold mud and his warm hands on mine.

David laughed too. "That's your fault. You could have brought hot water." David let my hands go and began forming the mud into things. One at a time, flowers, birds, and bugs appeared on the palm of his hand; he would show me an intricately designed model of some creature or plant, tell a strange story, then squish it again, and reform the mud into something else. He would not let me touch any of his creations, but we played in the mud, in the cold, at the end of September. Amid our laughter, I enjoyed listening to his tales while squishing mud between my fingers.

After forming a tiny mud person, he said, "I belong to the ground beneath my feet as do all of God's creatures. I am made of mud and shall return to mud."

"You mean ashes to ashes and dust to dust and all that."

"No. Ashes and dust are the very beginnings and the very endings, and only God can mould them into life. The Muki takes that which God has created and forms it to the will of God."

"Are you real?"

David put his hand on my cheek. "I am flesh and blood just like you. Look, you too can fashion mud."

Laughing, I squashed my feeble attempt at making a leaf and threw the mud in my hands into the hole. Suddenly feeling very strange, I wanted to run away. As I stood up, I said, "My hands are cold, and I should go home. Mom will be calling me soon."

Standing as well, David rubbed my hands to warm them up.

"Do you understand who the Muki are? Who I am?" he asked.

"Yeah, you are angels."

"No, we're not!" laughed David giving me a squeeze while being careful not to get mud on my clothes. "You've got a lot to learn."

"I guess you'll have to be my friend and teach me then, David." David laughed. "Good night, Littl'un." Then he walked away, following the path deeper into the trees.

I realized that he would be a special friend. Confidently concluding that any grown man who liked playing in the mud had to be okay, I decided I liked David of the Muki.

4

SOMETHING CAME
OVER ME

AT THE CREST OF A cliff some fifty feet further along the trail, there was a large tree. David allowed himself to collapse at its base. "What have I done?" he admonished to himself. He had told an alien his identity. It had simply felt the right thing to do, and he had enjoyed sharing his love of creation with the little smiler. David recognized God's will readily. There was no doubt in his mind that God had blessed what he had done. When she asked if he was a native, he had felt the warmth of God surround him. He had felt like bursting with the irony of her question.

David had felt a holy revelation at that moment. There really was something special about the land called Earth. It did have God's blessing. All shreds of doubt had drifted off into the night, and David had been confident in disclosing his race. David was a Cultural Judge. He was Muki. And strove with loyalty and dedication to serve the Lady as an honourable Instrument of Creation. In all seriousness, the little smiler had blessed him with a wonderful compliment.

David stared out into the river valley. Looking up into the starlit night, he followed the bright rays of moonlight across the heavens and along the silver sliver of the river below him. He stood, thrust his chest outward, raised his hands to the sky, and worshipped his God. With his eyes closed and head tilted back, David stood still, for only a few minutes, before a song rose in his throat, and he had to sing out, "Oh my God, I am yours!" The silence drifted around him, and in his own tongue, hands beating time against his thighs, David chanted the first verse of his favourite poem:

Jaca! Jaca! No a see.
Con moe a lay my,
Keshena a coat knee.
Jaca! Jaca! So a Muki!

He felt so good. Then in prayer, head bowed, David addressed the son of God. "Please, Jarrock," he whispered. "Help me become her angel. It is such a tall order, and I am ill-equipped to portray such an honour. However, I shall endeavour to love her and teach her according to your will. Dwell in me, Jarrock, whenever I am around her. Do not let me sin against her."

David then took a moment to be silent in creation. When he began to shiver, he quickly turned toward the streetlights and walked boldly out of the trees onto Vaughan Street, where he paused to glance at his watch. He had asked Mark to drive off if he was not there and come back an hour later. Mark had been picking him up between a quarter to six and six every day all week, and 'Littl'un' had not shown up until today. It was now nearly seven-thirty, and Mark would have been waiting for some time. Stepping up his pace, David whistled while he hurried down the hill. At Bowron Avenue, he turned toward the back alley, and there, parked at the side of the street, was his truck.

Mark was dozing behind the wheel. Instantly feeling impish, David snuck to the door, opened it suddenly, grabbed Mark by the shoulder, and demanded his keys. Mark awoke with a start and almost punched David before joining him in laughter. Mark slid across the seat and tried to assess his friend's state of mind. As the engine roared into life, Mark commented. "I take it you met your mystery girl tonight. Looks like your meeting went well."

"We can go home, Mark. We cannot blow up this planet. It is blessed, truly blessed."

"Oh, David, you've lost your mind.". With sorrow growing deep down in his gut, Mark shook his head, convinced that David was obviously over his head. Whoever this Earthling was, she must be incredibly powerful to induce David to make such a rash comment. Power was dangerous. He would have to find a way to shield David from diagnosis as certifiably crazy.

David headed straight out toward the transporter location, and while driving, told Mark the story.

Mark, and indeed all the Muki had strong faith. David's explanation soothed Mark's fears but did not entirely compensate for the sick feeling the lack of security created. Believing David had embarked on a challenging path, Mark concluded that it might be easier on all the expedition if Judge Soronato deemed him crazy. About halfway out, David suddenly became overwhelmed with the task he thought God had put before him. Mark took over driving and sat listening to his friend natter. Caught in the inner throws of self-doubt, David feared failure and was even terrified about the meaning of possible success. David did not rave like a madman; his reaction was textbook normal for having received instruction directly from God. Being human, he had to find comfort in living closer to God.

Mark, as is typical for the Muki, had had such experiences before, although nothing at quite the apparent scale of this intervention into the lives of ordinary people. Nevertheless, evidence of holy activity in David's encounter was concrete and terrified him.

This assignment had just stepped out into the realm of the unique and unorthodox. God was blessing the expedition. All the members of Judge Soronato's team would find themselves in the limelight back home. Their world would watch, drill, and scrutinize them for evidence of authenticity. If satisfied, the Panel would honour them. David was making history. Judge Soronato would have to open a new file and guide them all to produce a chapter, which might be worthy of entry into the Great Books. It was imperative that they gather tonight to perform a ritual of thanksgiving, purify themselves to work directly with Jarrock and prepare to wield the gifts of Koe

Sai Serena, the daughter of God, in a strange land very far away from home.

Mark did not need to make any explanation to Doug and Loren. One look at the soft glow emitting from David's flesh told all. After they each hugged David, they scurried to rake the tread marks off the half-grown over roadway.

A definite feel of winter in the air caused them to wonder whether this turn of events would force them to maintain guard here after the snow fell. With luck, the snow would be light, fluffy, and therefore, easy to blow over the tracks. Loren liked the remoteness of this landing. No one seemed to travel the main road during the weekdays, but occasional vehicles passed by on weekends. Whether they were mushroom pickers, hunters, or anglers, Loren did not know and did not care. If they continued to frequent the area enough to render the miles of road passable through the winter, he would not mind serving transporter guard duty here more often than once out of every six weeks.

He worried that the transporter might be stored closer to native establishments. Loren worried about security. The aliens gave him the creeps, and he was often sick to his stomach if he spent more than a few hours among them.

He tried hard to understand them, and Judge Soronato had wisely assigned him to gain familiarity with their worship rituals. The aliens worshipped God in buildings, once a week, and for only an hour or two at a time. Although their rituals shocked Loren, he did find a measure of comfort around natives on Sunday mornings. Some of the churches were large enough to blend into the congregation and be reasonably inconspicuous. Loren was wise enough to listen and ask questions; furthermore, he was skilled enough to avoid answering any himself that he was making good progress and even getting confident enough to make a few alien friends.

As they sat buckled in the seats of the transporter, the four of them chatted and laughed as though all was normal and nothing exciting had happened other than the natural fears that abound when your comrades are almost two hours late arriving at their rendezvous point.

By the time the transporter came to rest at their base camp, David's skin had lost its sheen. He was calm and peaceful. Mark was impressed with the confidence in which David was waiting for an audience with Judge Soronato. When the Judge summoned David into his office, Mark, Doug, and Loren gave him a nod of approval before heading to Muma Horren's office, where Mark would fill them in on what he knew of David's task.

Muma Horren would not let Mark begin until she had filled their cups a second time with hot cider, a favourite drink of the Muki. Then she sent Doug to the kitchen to fetch the remnants of the evening meal. Doug brought back not only food but also most of the residents of the camp, who were just as eager to hear about what was happening.

"David met an unusual native last week. She appeared to recognize that he did not belong to this world. Well informed, she knew his name. David thinks she is about thirteen years old and felt that she might be one of God's lambs."

"I witnessed evidence of the presence of God last Sunday myself, Mark. It was at St. John's after their worship. A woman took my hand and welcomed me. I felt that she, too, recognized my origin. I felt such a genuine comfort emanating from her that I truly felt welcome, and I heard God's voice in my heart telling me to reach out to his lambs," interjected Loren.

All eyes turned to Loren, and Muma Horren asked, "Why did you not tell us about this, Loren? Does Judge Soronato know?"

"I told the Judge right after it happened. He said he thought he felt a change in the wind and asked me to keep it to myself until more evidence showed up. He seemed quite excited, though. Go on, Mark. Tell us more of David's encounter."

"There is not much else to tell, except get this..." Mark smiled. Thoroughly enjoying the suspense, he said, "She told David that God sent him to her to teach her."

"Teach her what?" asked Doug in astonishment.

"David thinks he is to teach her to be Muki."

Silence fell. The group was shocked.

After a brief pause, Muma Horren stood up and began to bark orders. "Go all of you. Wash yourselves. Purify your thoughts. Judge Soronato will want us to worship. We will need God's guidance."

Rising immediately from their seats, they all did as directed. Muma Horren took Mark's hand to keep him back and gave him a big hug before telling him to finish eating first. Loren and Doug took that as a signal that they, too, could linger a while longer. Muma Horren spoke to them all but seemed to be directing her thoughts toward Mark, in particular. She spoke of the dangers of misinterpreting God and warned him of the need to protect and support David. Then Muma Horren excused herself to talk to Brian. Brian and David were much alike, and she wanted to drill him on the likelihood of David having lost his mind.

The camp was always ready for emergency evacuation. Before David came out of the meeting with Judge Soronato, rumours ran rampant about escape drills, relocation of headquarters, and even the possibility of abandoning the work already in progress to allocate resources to support David.

It was almost midnight when David and Judge Soronato emerged. Looking tired and uncomfortable, David went directly to the kitchen for a bite to eat. Judge Soronato addressed the men lingering outside Muma Horren's office.

"It is late. No more needs doing tonight. Go to bed. Sleep well." Then he summoned Brian, Mark, Muma Horren, and the expedition doctor, Natthia, to his office.

Everyone was quite disappointed in what the Judge had to say, but the rest went to bed assuming the Judge thought David crazy.

In his office, they went over David's credibility and his possible motives. Then they discussed what would be required to cause David to admit not only that he was Muki but to teach a basic cultural lesson to an Earthling. Mark was disappointed that David had not trusted him with the full story but was glad he was not in Judge Soronato's shoes tonight.

Thankfully, their meeting did not last long, and the Judge asked Mark to offer to celebrate a ritual of thanksgiving with David.

The Judge wanted information about the girl and had arranged to send scouts to track her and set up surveillance in all the places she frequented.

When Brian asked if he was planning to reassign David, the Judge replied, "No, Brian. However, David is on his own for the time being. We will protect the expedition. I have charged Mark with David's execution should that become necessary. Let us pray that David is right. We cannot ignore an act of God, Brian. Let us pray that God's will, will be done. Perhaps, we will be unscathed by this incident. God works in mysterious ways."

Mark was surprised that David was as cool and calm as he appeared when he joined him in the kitchen. David was pleased to worship and only asked that Mark permit him to use his own sacred chest. After worship, David cried. Saying he did not think he was strong enough, he prayed out loud for God's forgiveness.

"Oh, Mark," he wept, "Judge Soronato insists I be obedient to God. He says this is too unorthodox to risk any personal involvement except in investigating my Little Smiler. We must protect her. I think I have put her in danger. He will not have Natthia erase her memory, will he? Will you take me to town tomorrow? I want to keep an eye on her myself."

"Of course, I will. I am your soulmate, remember."

"Thanks, Mark. I will be careful. If I have made a mistake, I will fix it up myself; you trust me, don't you?"

"Yes, David."

"If I jeopardize the expedition, will you please stop me? That's what friends are for, Mark."

"I will protect our homeland. Don't worry, David. She is young. It really will not matter if she forgets you. Memory removal does not hurt, you know that."

"But my heart wants her to remember me, Mark. She is special. I'm going to try to teach her. Judge Soronato gave me the authorization to teach her about the ground beneath our feet, the sky above our heads, and the light of God. The only thing he asked was that I be sure that I am capable of being the kind of friend God told her I would be."

"Can you?"

"I do not know. However, I'm willing to try. God must have a plan in mind. I feel that it is imperative that I succeed."

"Then you will, David. I will help all I can."

"Thanks, Mark. I'll need your confidence."

Relieved David was okay, Mark laughed. Life was becoming exciting around here. It felt good to be part of God's plans.

5

THE SKY ABOVE MY HEAD

I T IS STRANGE THAT AN hour's encounter with an angel would have a profound effect on a thirteen-year-old girl. However, it did. Nothing could bother me that evening. I did the dishes without a fight and went to bed on time. I don't think I even dreamed all night. There was a strange peace in my heart. In the morning, while I did my chores, I thought about the ground beneath my feet. Even indoors, I knew it was there. Was David talking about roots? Maybe he really was Native American and just did not like the term or the popular connotations such a name invoked. He couldn't be an angel. You can put your hands right through an angel. David was real, not that angels are not. No, David had a body; he was a physical being, solid like Earth beneath my feet. The touch of his hand on my cheek had not been the touch of a spirit. Even I knew the difference between a spiritual experience and a physical one! At least, I thought I did.

It was drizzling just a little bit after lunch. I decided to drag out the stilts, perhaps for the last walk in the sky for the season. There was ice on the ground at the edge of the garage; it would soon be too cold for stilts because I did not like to use them with gloves or mittens. Slippery and heavy, one needed a good barehanded grip to lift them. Setting the two straight tree trunks, which I had inherited from my brother, against the garage, I climbed onto the fence, then the top of the garage door, and up onto the roof. To reach the footrests, I had to manoeuvre the poles further out. I stepped back a few steps, took a running leap, and grabbed both poles, swinging out into the air like pole vaulting, except there were two poles with footrests. On my first try, I was up and walking. Not bad! It often took me several attempts to free myself from the roof. The stilts were tall, my feet about thirteen and a half feet off the ground. As the poles were heavy, walking on them was strenuous. I headed for the telephone pole on the corner of the street, leaned my back against it, and rested. Although it was steep, I planned to venture down the street. Going downhill was unnerving, but the distance moved in a single step was awesome. Up on the stilts, I was powerful! Four and a half steps (I am exaggerating a little), and I would make it to the next pole.

Ever since my neighbour had thrown me up into the air when I was a little kid, I had been fascinated with height. When that big man threw me up, I was convinced that I could see all the way downtown before I would start the fall back to the ground, confident he would catch me safely in his strong arms. It was fun, but I soon got too big, and he did not even offer to throw me up. I had taken to climbing trees after that.

When I was just a dumb little kid, my sister and her friend had bet me a dime that I could not climb to the top of a big fir tree in the wood's kiddie corner to our house. I almost succeeded. Admiring the view, I stopped way up in the tree. My sister had become frightened; I was such a long way up and was yelling that I had earned the dime already.

I looked around me. I could see where the clear Quesnel River joined the muddy Fraser. I saw the bridges. I loved the bridges, the train tracks, the roofs of the stores, even that of my elementary school six whole blocks away. The branches were getting thin, but I was small too. Besides, I had a deal with God.

Having cracked my skull in a serious accident, I had died when I was five, but God sent me back, telling me He had other plans for me. I felt invincible. If I were aware of the dangers that faced me, I would survive, I wanted more and resumed climbing. Even my own house, less than a block away, looked tiny, like a dollhouse. Looking at the top of the tree, I thought that if I were to bend it over, I would be able to touch the top and really earn that dime. In my imagination, the dime became a key that would allow me to touch God. The top was just out of reach. Just a little higher, I told myself.

Of course, a branch broke under my weight, and I tumbled down, tossed from branch to branch like a rag doll. Every few feet throughout that slow-motion fall, I managed to grab hold of a branch only to have it torn out of my grasp until the last branch. My grip was secure, and my fall cheated once again. I dangled fifteen some odd feet in the air by one hand and yelled, "No, do not get Daddy!" I hated to be in trouble, and I figured I would get out of this mess somehow. I did not like upsetting my father.

Besides, I was immersed in the most incredible spiritual experience. I had felt God wrap around me while I was looking out at the world I loved. Loving God speaking to me, I felt incredibly secure. For some unexplainable reason, those moments also have always terrified me. I get overwhelmed. Huge defiance awakes in my soul. I will not become a puppet on a string. I will not obey, simply as a matter of principle.

One cannot really argue with God. I know I am a sinful fool. However, I also took God's promise of safety at face value. I was not testing God. I simply loved being immersed within God. If I climbed down out of the tree, I knew God would leave me. I would rather die and remain within the body of God.

Irrational, but I was just a child then. Part of me wants desperately to remain that child. It really was a slow-motion journey falling out of the tree. God giving commands, speaking of destiny and purpose, and me saying, 'take me with you.' I begged with all my being for God to free me from physical existence and take me home. All my fears of being alien and disconnected and all the lessons and gifts God had given so graciously absolutely terrified me far more than death.

I had concluded long ago that death was the greater gift. No matter how incredible, life would never come near to the ecstasy that I had experienced in death. Even though I had been dead for mere seconds, time had evaporated, and what I had experienced was indescribable. I wanted to be dead, desperately.

The imp within me also loved being disobedient. God was telling me precisely how to move, guiding my hands and every sense within me. Grab that branch. If I grabbed it, God would leave me. These moments were what life was about. They were the times when life was the fullest. I loved to live on the edge.

Thinking God found me amusing, in arrogance, I got angry. God could not make me grab a branch, and I would let one slip through my fingers. As I comprehended the stupidity I was demonstrating, shock coursed through my body. Hoping God would not send me to Hell, I closed my eyes. God took my arm, wrapped my fingers around a branch, and held me there.

I learned God could make me obey with absolute and incredible power. I had no weight. There was no strain on my muscles. I was comfortable in the arms of my maker.

Eyes open. Following the light up through the leaves as it shimmered and swayed, I recognized the arms of God. I knew the most precious, soft yellow glow of God held me. I was in Heaven and wanted to stay there. If my father came to rescue me, God would leave me again. That was a fact I did not want to experience.

Naturally, my father came running at my sister's frantic call that I was falling out of the tree, suspecting to find me in a heap at its base. God had other plans for me! I did not need anyone to tell me to hang on; my grip was like glue as my father approached. I had learned another lesson. Even if it would not kill me, a thrill could be terrifying. Embarrassed and ashamed, I thanked God as His arms withdrew.

Reality beckoned. I felt the strain of my own weight. Willing my fingers not to slip, I waited patiently, and teary-eyed, for my father to climb up to save me.

I only climbed to such heights once again, a few years later in another tree in my back yard. It was a difficult tree to climb, but I managed to gain a respectable height when I found two problems. First, the branches were getting too thin, and second, my mother had caught me; thus, I was prohibited from going any higher anyway. Coming down without falling was far more nerve-racking than going up, and it took a long time for my mother to talk me out of that tree. She had to guide the placement of my feet as the branches were far apart, and I had difficulty seeing the next branch while maintaining my hold to descend.

When I reached the ground again on that day, I thanked God for another lesson. I did not mind being punished either. God taught me that day that the past was behind me, and only the future and my own will to succeed would bring me the destiny that God preferred. Evincible, I had responsibilities. I was mortal. I did not really mind being mortal, but admitting it, and having it thrust in my face, bothered me. Therefore, I gave up reaching for the top of trees.

However, I still liked height, and the stilts let me see a long way. I still thought that if I got high enough, I would touch the future.

Resting at each telephone pole, I walked all the way to the bottom of the hill. "They were good for something besides birds, after all," I said, while I chuckled with a kind of pride in discovering that, yet again, I was succeeding in changing the definition of the things around me by invoking new uses for common things.

Such thoughts were a big part of my world. Being and thinking in unorthodox ways defined my uniqueness. For some unknown reason, I had an insatiable desire continually to prove to myself that I was unique, special, and very much alive.

I was on my way back up the hill when I saw David walking along the avenue leading to the water tower.

"Hi, Littl'un!" he called. "What are you doing?"

My immediate thought was one of disdain. What did it look like I was doing? I chuckled but said nothing. I did not want to insult David and hoped it was a rhetorical question. Something was said just because something needed saying. Such conversation I had long ago deemed a useless waste of breath and was terribly disappointed that my new friend would be so ordinary and unimaginative. I quickly forgave him, however, and returned my attention to walking on stilts.

It takes great concentration to maintain balance and still, lift each stilt one after the other to walk. Going uphill was hard, progress was slow, and I did not want to fall in front of David lest he thinks

I was dumb. I set my mind on getting to the next pole. Going uphill involved taking many pipsqueak steps. My knee at the top of such long stilts was highly ineffective in raising the bottom of the stilt far enough to swing it forward much more than an ordinary step because the hill was in the way. Out of breath and exhausted, I made my goal. David stared at me, scowling just a little.

Once safely leaning on the pole, I said hello, and asked where he was going.

"For a walk," he answered. "You are awfully close to the wires, Littl'un. It is dangerous."

I cringed. I did not want him to be a parent. "Friends do not boss each other around," I answered and hastily added, "Can I come?"

"Not on those!" David laughed.

Despite almost falling, I pushed off the telephone pole. Managing to regain my balance, I turned onto the avenue and confidently walked onward with my twenty-foot strides.

"Stand back, David. I will come down, but I must throw the stilts."

Standing beside my house, David watched. I was pleased that he did not tell me to be careful. I could see that he cared, and that was enough. After a few more steps, I carefully threw one stilt to the ground and hopped on the remaining stilt until the other pole lay silent and still on the dirt. If it was moving, and I landed on it, I could twist an ankle or worse. I liked to know everything was safe before falling.

I tried to hop at least four times before losing my balance. I was doing well that day and was proud of it as I managed seven hops. I felt it impressive even if I said it myself. Coming down, I let the stilt tip and rode it, then jumped while pushing the stilt in the opposite direction, hoping that it would not hit me. I landed with a thud. The stilt bounced and came to rest at a safe distance. I smiled. Although still feeling the impact in my calves and knees, I was not going to admit to David that getting off stilts was a bit jarring to the body.

David just laughed while I dragged the stilts to the fence, pushed them over, and lay them neatly against the side of the garage. Then, we walked up the trail into the bushes.

I asked, "Where are we going, David?"

"Anywhere you like, Littl'un. It does not matter," he answered. We continued walking down the trail, then over the cliff to the lower trails and the train tracks. Walking slowly, David talked about hundreds of things as he pointed out the different plants and animals that made an appearance. He even talked about the rocks, the clay, and naturally, the dirt. David had a thing about dirt and mud. Muki was a name that suited him.

Eventually, we ended up at Beaver Pond. The beavers were gone and had been for years, but the dam was still there. One of my favourite spots, the pond was deep and clear. Beaver Pond was not really a pond, but a channel of the Quesnel River, which the beavers had dammed. It cut deep into the bank, looked like an oval pond open to the river upstream, and damned with a massive tangle of trees, branches, and mud in a smooth curve from the downstream end of the island it created to the steep bank at the river's edge. The dam was not completely structurally sound; one could not walk upon it. In places, the water gurgled over or under it. Mud caked other spots in which grass and other vegetation grew, displaying splashes of green amid the brown and dark grays of the dam's wooden structure. I like to think it was seventy feet across, but it was somewhere between twenty and thirty feet. The surface of the pond was usually quite smooth and glassy looking. The current, though, was strong. Scoured clean, the bottom had the appearance of being a big deep bowl. It was rumoured to be twenty feet deep in the center, and I believed that to be true. You could see the bottom down to about ten feet; then, the water looked dark. Without a thought, I climbed up onto the trunk of a big old tree that had fallen across the pond. It gave me access to the island, and I liked the island. It gave me the sense that I was the King in the castle—I hated to be merely Queen, and it was my private domain. I was halfway across when David cried out, "Stop! It is too dangerous. I cannot cross this. It's slippery."

It was my turn to laugh. Stopping, I held on to one of many

stubs of the branch and said, "It is okay to crawl. There are lots of hand holds." Then I walked back, took his hand, and pulled with all my strength.

"I am not teaching you anything, am I?" he said as he pulled his hand away from mine and straddled the tree, inching forward using every convenient knot and branch as I backed away.

"Sure, you are. Every step I take, I am stepping on a million dollars. I am rich!"

"It is important to keep the ground under your feet," he retorted.

"It is, David. The tree is of Earth. It is not dead, and we're walking on it."

"I am afraid of heights, Littl'un. Let's go back."

"We're more than halfway across now, David. You will not fall. Can you swim?"

"Don't be nasty. Yes, I can, but I don't want to go for a swim!"

"Good thing, David. The current is strong. A boy drowned here a few years ago. The current pulls you under and holds you, tangled in the branches of the dam, until you drown. I cannot swim, so I do not fall. Understand?"

David grabbed my hand and held on until we stepped down onto the island. "No, I don't, Littl'un."

"You told me yourself. We are all part of Earth. Life connects us. It is a gift from God. Life is to be experienced. If I know the alternative and dislike it, living means conquering fear and all other obstacles God puts before me to challenge me."

"You do not have to die to live, Littl'un."

"Nothing risked, nothing gained, David. Life is for living. If all were safe, it wouldn't be any fun at all. Besides, everyone would come here. If that happened, it wouldn't be my place."

The island was less than a hundred feet long and quite narrow, about thirty feet across. Covered with tall trees, mostly fir, it had a dense tangle of undergrowth. Much of the island was not very high above the waterline, and parts were muddy and rather dangerous, but the far side was much like the regular riverbank. There was about a four-foot drop, then a narrow sand and gravel bar marred by fallen trees and old snags deposited each spring. Few people came onto the island, and there was not a clearly defined trail on it. However, I endeavoured to show David all its features.

There was an old grey dead tree, which still stood tall, as though it was a mighty soldier guarding the fortress around it. I pointed out the tooth marks of the beavers on the stumps of the trees that became the dam. I showed him tiny flecks of gold that glittered in the sand remaining in my fingers after holding a handful carefully in the river to wash away the dirt. Leading him to the seemingly out-of-place big boulder, I told him where I imagined great councils taking place when the moon was high in the sky. Lastly, I pointed out where I usually found lady-slippers when the season was ripe for the fairies to dance.

As I told him tales of great conflict and conquest that I imagined as the history of my little but grand kingdom, David started to laugh. Embarrassed and fearing that David thought me a silly child, I stopped talking. David was sharing his stories, and I had thought I was being very brave to share my own treasures with him. A nagging fear that David was not the friend I had hoped he would become awoke in the depths of my stomach. I felt suddenly uncomfortable.

We sat on the far side of the island, beside the rushing river. I told him stories about the sunken pickup truck in front of us that helped hold the island together even though it was now about ten feet out into the current of the river. After a short, uncomfortable silence, David said, "You are right in a way, Littl'un. It is beautiful here, especially because it is difficult to get here, but beauty is a state of mind. If you wanted it to be this beautiful and special, it would be, even if there were a paved highway right beside us. You do not need to be alone to be lonely."

"I am not lonely."

"You like lonely spots."

"Yes, I do," I answered truthfully. "David," I said nervously, hoping I was not about to make a fool of myself, "I am like this island. Each year, I know more of the island is travelling down the river than the river is leaving at the island to build it up into the great kingdom that I want it to become. In my heart, I know it is not merely that I am getting bigger that makes the island seem smaller with the passing of each season, although that is surely part of reality. Parts of this island will stretch all the way to the Pacific Ocean. In time, it will ride in the currents clear around the world.

"However, someday, it will no longer be here, and my world will be gone. I will become an adult and will not even remember what is important. I will become empty. Then, just like this island, I will be gone, used up, and forgotten. I do not want to change. I do not want to grow up. Adults do not know what is important; they just think they are important. I am afraid of becoming like them, ordinary and boring."

David smiled and said, "Go with your island, Littl'un. Let it take you with it. Let it grow along your horizon, and it will remain part of you."

Then, we sat quietly, enjoying the sights and sounds around us. The fear in my belly gave way as confidence in David's friendship grew once more. I did not have to change to be his friend. I would not even let God change me. Perhaps God's objective was to help me stay loyal to a world that time was hinting that I must leave behind to join the ranks of ordinary people.

After a while, I said, "There is gold here, David. There really is a million dollars under your feet right now." Again, David laughed. He looked at me and smiled a very special kind of smile that lit up his whole face, and his eyes glistened, saying something that I was not ready to admit was possible. Embarrassed, I looked away.

"We had better be getting back, Littl'un," he said, and we headed home. David even crossed the log on his feet almost all the way. I ran across without touching a single branch except for the one that you must grab because it is in the way and too big. You must hang on to it and pull yourself around it to continue in either direction—you cannot go over it. I watched David praying that he would not fall. Having a friend made one responsible for him, especially when you made him go where he did not want to. With a sigh, I concluded I would have to stop coming here. It was almost the end of the season anyway. The log would soon be too slippery... right? I shrugged, and David went on about the wealth of the ground under us. I guess I really did not get the significance of his lesson. He looked at me that funny way again when we were almost at the top of the cliff. Then he blushed and turned away.

"Sorry, Littl'un, let's get you home," he said quietly and even sadly.

I stopped on the trail, took his big hand, and said, "I have a name, it is..."

"No, Littl'un. I need to call you, Littl'un. It will remind me to remember what kind of friend I am supposed to be."

I felt devastated. Big tears formed in my eyes, and I let go of his hand and ran home. I went inside, up to my room, and cried on my bed. I was just a kid and wanted to be a grown-up, even if only for a second. I was confused and did not know God's intent when He sent me a friend.

Maybe I was beginning to understand. Maybe, I did need the ground to be safely beneath me, real close, touching the bottom of my foot. To embrace the unknown future I so desperately wanted, I had to ground my faith in the here and now, or I would lose it. With the conclusion that David would help me find the promised future held in the sky above my head, I smiled.

6

SEARCHING ONE'S SOUL

AFTER WATCHING THE LITTLE SMILER slip into the garage of the place she called home, David turned back to the trees and walked down to the tracks in silence. Feeling a deep sorrow, he headed north. He could not be the right kind of friend, and he knew it. His feelings of love for this woman were genuine. The Little Smiler had taken hold of his heart with her stories and enthusiasm. She displayed a wonderfully vivid imagination, yet her tales held truths stretching far out into the universe. David did not think he was reading more into the tales than she had intended to put into them, but somehow, this Earthling did not seem quite alien. David's heart ached to ask her to dance with him.

Smitten, that is what Mark called this feeling. However, David did not think his feelings were not genuine. This was not infatuation. He loved the little girl who was so elegant in the understanding of her world, even if she wrapped it in imagery. Furthermore, her faith was incredible. God was clearly protecting her. Blindly, excitedly, she was following God into the unknown.

She knew what she was doing to him, enjoyed teasing him, and was fully aware of the terror she invoked. Yet, her tales came from her heart. David did not think they were things she ordinarily shared. The Little Smiler was nervous. Carefully, she had searched his eyes before she would tell a story as though not sure he was worthy of hearing it. Breakable and frightened, she wanted him to understand the delicacy of her world. However, for her, there was no question or hesitation that he was a gift from God, a gift of friendship demanding fulfilment.

David needed only to close his eyes to see the tall gray sentry standing guard over her world. The sentry stood for righteousness. Littl'un said he simply refused to believe that he was losing the battle. Only he remained. The great champions of the past were nearly forgotten, yet still, the grey sentry had stood on. No sounds of battle came to his ears. No sight of replacement entered his horizons. He neither tired nor gave up. While the island lived, he would protect the kingdom. The snag would be the last to become of the past because hope would sustain him. Littl'un thought she could help her kingdom survive by remaining loyal to the standards of decency it represented. With her support, the island would be untouched by reality, cruelty, and disrespect.

"You see, David," she had said, "The world is fundamentally good. The good is only hidden by the heavy smog of evil." Littl'un had almost cried before she said, "Maybe the truck will carry the evil away, and the kingdom will thrive again. Probably not here, on this island, but it will grow further downstream. In the future, David, this will be a good place, not a sad place. It will thrive with life and outshine anything currently in the heavens. God will bless my world." Then she looked embarrassed as she tried to see whether David understood what she was talking about.

Her stories were all told with love and held a strong power that cut into David's soul. She seemed so innocent and vulnerable, acting as though she was not sure whether he was there to help her keep her world together or to break it. She was barring her heart to him because God had sent him to her as a friend. She trusted that God did not want him to destroy her world. With a painful pang within him, David suddenly wondered if she was begging him to defy his own God and embrace the world that she did not want to permit God to take away from her.

David tried to put the facts into perspective. He was now past the mills, and the world around him was quiet. Noting the sun getting lower in the sky, he realized he would have to cut back to the highway soon. The facts as David perceived them that day were that she knew he did not belong to her world and was an outsider, perhaps even like the truck carrying her world away. The second thing she knew was that he could determine the fate of her world. Without trying to deceive him, because she knew that he would see through it, she was opening her own soul to him in the hopes that he would love her and protect her world regardless of whether it was right or wrong. She was desperate, too. Obviously, Littl'un thought her world was running out of time.

David did not even go into Quesnel the next week. Judge Soronato had asked him to worship before God to find out whether the Little Smiler worshipped idols or a false God. David was afraid that God's answer might not be the one he wanted but was unsure what he wanted himself. The feelings he was experiencing were too new and frightening.

Surveillance had come up rather empty that first week. The girl did not talk much to other people. When she talked aloud to herself, she did not make a lot of sense as though they were hearing only one side of a conversation, laughter, and strange accusations that made the tracker uncomfortable. Yet none of the Muki assigned to watch her ever felt the presence of God around her. They had concluded that she was crazy or, at best, an outcast of the prominent society.

That analysis frightened David. He feared turning to God just in case she was a clever demon. David developed doubts. For now, at least, he decided to cling to the wonderful memories of a few hours with love. Longing to hold her close to him, he would rather love her than risk finding out what she really meant. Judge Soronato talked to him daily but was not insistent on taking the issue to God. He was concerned not only about the success of the expedition but genuinely interested in helping David to come to grips with what he was experiencing.

The structure of Muki society protected people from temptation. The love of a man for a woman was so holy that unless entering her castle to become sire, he would never be in a position that would open the possibility for him to fall into this kind of love. Such things as love were unpredictable, and God worked in such mysterious ways. The Judge was genuinely worried about losing an excellent young Cultural Judge.

As for David, he relaxed and returned to his duties in Quesnel, avoiding walking where he thought meeting the Little Smiler would be possible. He needed a comfort that only time could provide. Unable to trust himself to be the right kind of friend, David was not in the habit of remaining in the clutches of temptation and withdrew to teach his heart to be obedient to the will of God. The responsibility that God had bestowed upon him was to teach, not to propagate. He was feeling the wrong kind of love.

She was an alien. It was right to love her, but his love should be that of a man for his pet, not a woman, a mate. Barely human, most appeared to be spiritually dead, and it was blatantly clear that they did not serve the Lady. They were the living dead. As such, his culture would likely condemn them all.

It just was not right. His heart ached, and he could not remove the feeling that the Little Smiler belonged to God; she was different from the rest. The Little Smiler was alive, she was human, and he wanted to hold her, protect her, and love her as only a man can love his mate.

Being a scout for the expedition, his job entailed locating natives worthy of tracking. It was surprisingly easy to bug the homes and businesses of the small country town. Quesnel was an innocent, trusting place. The natives lived in very segregated groups determined not only by race but also by class. There were the upstanding so-called middle class of businesspeople, professionals, and political activists. The loggers kept to the loggers and the ranchers to themselves. The miners and prospectors, too, were a unique group. The town had character. There were town drunks, the wild youth groups interested in music, sex and drugs, and the law-abiding common folk. Many smoked; the language tended to be colourful; and tempers, as a rule, were quick.

Quesnel was a mid-sized town, too small to be a city, but too big, to have the sense of community and camaraderie that existed in a small town. It was set in a beautiful area of forests, lakes, and rivers in rolling hills of the interior of British Columbia on land known as the Caribou Plateau. The culture of its inhabitants was interesting. It was diverse enough to offer substantial insight into human life in the 'civilized' North Americas. Yet, it was not a hubbub of commerce, education, art, and industry. It was home to the ordinary. The backbone of the civilization on the west coast of the North Pacific. Quesnel was also remote. Thereby, it offered the kind of terrain and habitation that lent itself well for the team of Cultural Judges from the Land of the Butterflies to watch and examine in relative security and inconspicuousness.

David found Quesnel fascinating. Although he had only been here a few months, the peace he was able to find among the hills and river valleys of the Caribou Plateau reassured him that this planet was truly a Garden of Eden, and a creation to celebrate life. Earth had little natural violence of its own. Human civilization was at the root of most of the catastrophes that were evident. There were ever-present tell-tale signs that the future held a terrible sorrow. David wondered why. Why were these people so blind and destructive? Were they honestly unaware of the consequences of what they were doing?

David buried his concentration in searching out clues to the answer. Destroying this world would be a shame...a terrible pity. The thought hurt David very deeply. Furthermore, the grey sentry of the Little Smiler haunted him whenever he added evidence to his personal conviction that this world was doomed.

As he ventured among the people, his disgust at the arrogance and stupidity of Earthlings drove him away. Seeking refuge in quiet places, he walked while thinking and clearing his mind of his agony. When calm, he would once again listen and try to understand the culture of the many races of people making up the community of Quesnel. The trouble was that whenever he went for a walk, his mind awakened a vision of the Little Smiler. The island that was her kingdom would taunt him, calling, "Come back, here is the answer." Then his heart ached. He cried and had to struggle to return to the rendezvous point and the security of the base camp without stopping near the home and kingdom of the Little Smiler.

Regularly, he cried on Muma Horren's shoulder because the little smiler had captivated him with her smiles and her faith. She called to his heart, and his resolve to stay away melted like ice during a temperature storm.

A temperature storm was a weather phenomenon on his home planet. Like lightning strikes but more like microwaves or a ball of radiation, it was a cloud of highly charged particles that were lethal. These particles emitted bolts or waves, which caused temperature swings that could boil water and even melt metal instantly, and then refreeze them so quickly that slight motion would be evident. Striking during the autumn season, it could be described as a blast of incredibly hot air, like a laser beam of varying diameter and cross-section, which lasted for only milliseconds, but melted ice so fast it vaporized. There was a rebound incredible cold wave following the heatwave, which refroze any liquid before it had time to move more than a centimeter or two as the oscillating particles in the waves pulsed from exothermic to endothermic reactions attempting to regain some semblance of stability. As though a panicking living thing was fighting for life, it would eventually burn itself out. A dangerous weather condition, temperature storms caused many deaths, injuries, and damage to unprotected structures. Generally, a misty haze like rolling fog or the reverse of a shimmer of heat rising on a hot summer day preceded the touchdown of a temperature storm.

In his mind's eye, he kept seeing her smiling and hearing the tall grey sentry beckoning until his tears blinded him as he repeatedly turned his back to her kingdom to run away. She had power over him. However, it could not be evil. It was too innocent and touched him too profoundly to be anything less than holy. How could he teach her? What would she do with the knowledge? She could never become Muki.

Unfortunately, David could never become an Earthling. It was against the law. It was dangerous and contrary to the known will of God to remove or transplant alien life forms. Such things were taboo simply because they had the potential of destroying the foundation of the coming Kingdom of God. His feelings were wrong. They were sinful. He wanted to dance, wanted God to bind them together forever. David wanted God to bless his love and banish the empty, lonely feeling that filled him with pain and sorrow at being away from an alien. Oh, why was she not Muki?

7

A Pact of Friendship

I DID NOT SEE DAVID THE next Friday or even the Friday after that. It would soon be Halloween, and snow would fall. I had only talked to David a couple of times but missed him and wanted to see him again. Figuring I had frightened him away, I promised myself that I would not climb any trees, shinny up the soccer goal post, walk on stilts, or cross walky-talky trees if I could see David again. Walky-talky trees were half-fallen trees wedged against other trees, which were another of my favourite things to climb upon and defy God to take me on to the life I knew was beyond death. From the heights of walky-talky trees, I berated, chastised, and fought with the silent world below me to relieve my feelings of injustice and the anger I felt toward the real-world gnawing at my heels.

Perhaps another week later, I got into trouble with my mother, and at the first opportunity, I snuck out of the house, running away again as was my normal response to such trials of growing up. Heading for the bridges, I went down the alley, along the street to the railway tracks, and walked along them balancing on the rails. I climbed up the bank, crossed the highway, and started across the new Quesnel River Bridge. There were some people crossing it, coming toward me. As I did not like people because they made me feel vulnerable and scared, I slipped over the side and began making my way back under the bridge and along the shore. Hoping they would cross quickly, I was confident that soon I would have the pedestrian path to myself. I threw a few rocks into the river, and presently, the people were gone. When I climbed back up, I saw a lone man walking toward the bridge and just about gave up and headed back toward home before recognizing he was David. I waited for him.

"Hi Littl'un, where are you going?" he called out as though he was pleased to see me.

"For a walk, want to come?" I answered rather flatly. I knew he had been avoiding me, and I felt his shock of having encountered me in the way he greeted me. My anger very quickly focused on this friend. Braced to endure another of life's disappointments, I stiffened, fearing not even God could make this man be my friend. Regretfully, I remembered my dream. Although he did not need to be my friend, I needed him to teach me something God thought very important. I quickly settled for that nasty thought that seemed to sum up my anger: I hated the world and everything in it.

"No slippery trees on your route?" he asked. I shook my head. "Sure." Then David walked beside me, arms swinging freely at his sides. He was quiet.

So was I. I was still angry with my mom. I was angry with the people for being on the bridge and with David for being away for so long. Crossing the bridge, we slipped down the bank on the far side, made our way under the bridge, and up onto the grass at the little motel on the other side of the highway. Without a sound, David and I tramped along the trail and out onto the sand bars along the river. We had walked for about an hour when David broke the silence.

"Where are we going, Littl'un?"

"Round the bend," I answered.

"It is late. The sun will be going down soon."

"You go for a walk every day," I accused.

"Usually, sometimes my shift changes, then I miss my walk. Are you going to turn back now?"

Emphatically, I said, "No."

"I would like to go back."

"Go ahead. Go back. See if I care."

"Are you mad at me, Littl'un?"

"Yes," I answered rather curtly. David continued to walk beside me. I was hurt and angry. He was supposed to be my friend. I did not want to lose him, but I felt I would rather push him away now than try to hang on to prove myself worthy of friendship and risk failure. I felt failure somehow inevitable. Having friends was out of character. It did not fit with my world and me.

"Why?" he asked quietly as though he did not or did not want to know.

"You are avoiding me. You do not want to be my friend. You must be. God said so."

I turned a little bit of anger toward God, and that bucket of guilt swarmed over me awful fast. I had to ask forgiveness immediately. Sometimes I was afraid that God would strike me dead for being so defiant and ungrateful. I took strength in a sudden resurgence of the belief that David really did not have any more choice than I did. Whatever God had planned for David and me, neither of us could escape. In my experience, God never made things easy. Therefore, concluded I would have to botch my way through whatever the future held. There was no point in me fighting it. Deciding I could watch David suffer, and let him do the hard work, I watched him do the squirming for a while.

"I do not know how, Littl'un."

"I do not have any friends. If you let me, I will try to be a good friend. I will not get mad at you for calling me a kid. I will let you call me Littl'un. I won't mind," I said sincerely.

The little imp in me giggled as I threw caution to the wind and even contemplated the value of giving up some of my own world to conform to what he needed me to be. Feeling courageous, I crossed my fingers in hopes that I could change for David. Suddenly gaining confidence, I began to feel warm inside and proud that I could be obedient to God.

"Oh, kid. This is a dumb idea. I am of the Muki, and I am an adult. Our worlds are forever apart."

"We have a lot in common. We both like going for walks, and we both like lonely places. I like listening to you. I want to become of the Muki, too."

"You are asking me to play with fire, Littl'un. You are becoming a beautiful woman. Take advantage of being young. Stay a kid as long as you can. Play with other kids."

"God told me to learn from you. He sent you to me. Teach me to be Muki. I am a good learner and will remember to be a kid. Growing up is too scary anyway. Just remember not to tell me to grow up when I act like a kid, and everything will be okay."

As David shook his head, we stopped walking. Sighing, I turned around to head back to the bridge. David smiled. "I do like you, Littl'un. You are a good kid. I do not know what to think of little girls. When I look at you, I do not always see a little girl. Sometimes, I see a butterfly." The Muki identified females that were capable of bearing young as butterflies. Like butterflies on Earth, they considered these creatures extremely powerful and dangerous because they spun a hypnotic spell and captured males in a seduction that trapped them with heavy responsibility and a duty to ensure everlasting happiness and contentment.

I laughed, but tears still fogged my eyes, and I wanted David to be my friend. "Ask God about me, David. If God tells you to be my friend, promise me you will meet me after school. Maybe we could meet tomorrow. We will just go for a walk, and you can tell me about the Muki."

"I must go away for a while, Littl'un. When I come back, I will find you. We will go for another walk, and I will tell you my decision. Is that fair enough?"

"How long will you be away?"

"I am going north, about a month."

"You promise you'll come to see me when you get back?"

"I promise." Then David chuckled.

I figured he was a bit like me, part of him wanted to be a friend, but my age and the fact that I was female, bothered him just as everything about him awoke unfamiliar feelings within me. Our friendship would be taboo in both of our cultures.

We each returned to our silent worlds as we walked with a brisk step toward the bridge. It was late, and home was a long way away.

Strangely, I forgot what I was angry about with my mom. Suddenly, I felt very pleased to have been angry enough to go on a mad walk. When I was mad, it was the only time I took this route to the bridge. If I had not been angry, I would not have met David again. He would have gone away without saying goodbye.

I do not know exactly what it was about David that intrigued me. I just felt blessed and happy inside when I was near him. David made the whole world seem very alive and comforting. It might sound strange, but David made the ground beneath my feet come to life. With each step, I knew more life was seeping into my feet and flowing up into my heart.

As we continued across the bridge, I saw the first star of the evening. We turned along the tracks. David stopped to look out at the river, and I would have liked to take a picture of him. It was a perfect sight, and it was not lonely at all. David belonged to the world and knew where he belonged. Without needing to search out the future, he lived it.

I heard the rumble of a freight train pulling out of the station. Thinking that was my train, I ran up to the tracks. As the engine approached the far track, I smiled and uttered, "Perfect!" To David, I yelled, "Got to go, friend. See you next month. Goodbye," turned and ran along the train. Perfect for hitching a ride, it was nice and slow. Next car, I thought as I pushed myself, straining to gain more speed. Leaping and grabbing the ladder good and high, I let my feet stride along the ground, each stride growing ever longer as I prepared to swing my legs up onto the bottom rung. Finally, confidently, I swung upward, my foot landing safely on the bottom rung. I took a breath and placed the other foot securely onto the ladder, believing this was better than a roller coaster. I would only ride for about two blocks, but I loved riding the trains.

I looked back at David, who was staring at me in disbelief, and despite feeling terribly guilty, immediately proclaimed aloud that I was not giving up trains. It was too much fun. I turned my mind back to watching ahead of me. Very soon, I crouched down sideways to the train. My heart began to beat faster, and my muscles tensed. Getting on was easy. Jumping off a train, even though I had done so half a dozen times, remained terrifying. Earlier in the year, I had learned that fear caused the problem to become almost insurmountable.

If I stayed on past the mills, the train got up to full speed. It was still quite slow. I should be able to land on my feet. At full speed, I would be lucky to get away with minor cuts and bruises. I timed the clack of the wheels and counted ten nine… jump. Landing in a full run, I almost went head over heels but regained control. Quickly, I hid in the bushes because, sometimes, the guy in the caboose sees me and reams me out. It was safest to hide until the train passed by.

When the train was gone around the corner, I came out of the bushes and back onto the tracks. I could barely see David faraway down the tracks. I waved, sighed as he waved back, and smiled with confidence, knowing he was relieved. As I felt the tension dissipate in the air around me, I concluded David was special. With that thought, I started up the trail.

I would be home soon, and a month was not that long. If I felt lonely, I would only have to close my eyes, and I would see David looking out into my favourite river, knowing all was well and that I was not alone. I hoped that I had managed to get God to help me out by sending David to Him. I only felt a little guilty and decided that since I had not asked God for a friend, maybe God would feel obligated to tell David our friendship was according to His will. I chuckled as I thought about my arrogance in calling for God's intervention.

8

I Know Not What You Ask, My God

Judge Soronato had lost patience with David after that first week and had ordered him to return to his duties. He had called him, on the tenth day after David had last seen the Little Smiler, into his office as usual and began what turned out to be a very long lesson.

"Sit down, David. Make yourself comfortable."

Judge Soronato was smiling. He liked David and was confident that God would not be disappointed in this young man. After pouring two cups of fresh, hot cider out of the urn he had just filled, he sat down and watched David. The young Miskenack looked like his great-uncle, an old friend of the Judge. He often chuckled when he thought of his antics when they had been young friends like Mark and David now. David looked embarrassed by the audible chuckle that escaped his lips. "I was just thinking about your great uncle and me when we were your age, David."

David sat a little straighter in his chair and paid close attention to the Judge.

"Just a silly thought, David. I am not a great man. I believe that is because I made a mistake. I should have listened to your great- uncle. I might have been in the position you are today, but I could be wrong. It is hard to figure out the what-ifs of might have been scenarios."

The Judge laughed wholeheartedly, with the result that David became even more uncomfortable.

"At least I can laugh about it now, Judge Miskenack," he chuckled.

The Judge seemed to lose himself in thought again, and David finally summoned the nerve to say something.

"If you think your story might help me out, Sir, I would like to hear it," he said sincerely. Judge Soronato did not often talk about himself, and David hoped he was in for a treat.

Judge Soronato blushed, nodded, and then drank his cider and poured a refill into both their cups. David waited. When the second cup was also finished, the Judge sighed and said, "I was only a little older than you are now, David. It was just before my thirty-fifth birthday. I was on my first assignment as a leader. I was quite cocky; my supervisor believed in me and had given me a chance to prove my worth. My assignment was on Doleran. Tell me what you know of Doleran."

"There is not much to tell. Doleran blew up. Investigations showed no predictable cause and considered it an act of God." David went red in the face when the Judge motioned for him to continue. Hesitantly, he said, "The Panel accepted the conclusion that it was created to test our obedience, and we failed."

"Not we, David. Me. Josh Soronato."

The Judge looked about to cry. To err is to be human. The panel had honoured the Judge for having taught a very valuable lesson to all Cultural Judges. As a lesson in modesty, it reiterated that it is hard to wield the gifts of Koe Sai Serena and that great care was mandatory always to ensure the use of the gifts according to the will of God rather than to our own will. No one blamed the expedition on Doleran. The Judgement did not even name the Judges so that Cultural Judges and the Panel could not try to distance themselves from their own guilt. It was a lesson about being human and making errors. David hurt that Judge Soronato felt so personally responsible. "God needs to teach us, Sir. You should feel honoured that you were chosen for such an important lesson."

"You never saw Doleran, David. It was a violent world in a very subtle way, and I might have been able to save it, to mould it into something better and even more wonderful, a tool, David. Doleran could have become a tool to teach us all obedience firsthand from God."

The Judge sighed, took another swallow of his cider, and refilled the mugs.

"I have resigned my fate to your conclusion, David. Although I have used it as a lesson to guide my decisions and actions throughout my career, I still do not like it. It is also true that that error, my own disobedience, has helped many Cultural Judges and people in all occupations to trust in their own ability to be obedient to the Lady. Even when the thing God asks terrifies the soul or falls outside the realm of what custom dictates is the right thing to do. I can't help but think that the lesson would have been taught just as powerfully had I succeeded in obeying God."

"Success sometimes backfires, Sir. God may have chosen you with awareness you would have to disobey."

"Maybe you are correct, son. Thank you. Now let me tell you the story." The Judge paused for a moment, set his cup down upon the table, made himself comfortable in his chair, and let out a long deep sigh before continuing, "Doleran was almost featureless. The surface elevation varied no more than a couple of hundred feet pole to pole. The surface covering was a uniform layer of swamp-like water and vegetation on topsoil, which was generally twenty to two hundred feet thick, above a remarkably stable sphere of rock.

"Geologically, it was a masterpiece of perfection. Its creation had been unmarred by the expected forces of nature. It had never collided with another astronomical object, not even a small meteorite. It had neither volcanoes nor tectonic faults. It also had no rivers, lakes, hills, or valleys that survived more than a storm. Doleran did not have animal life that we could find other than viruses, bacteria, and tiny insect-type organisms, but it was very much alive with abundant vegetation. All life on Doleran had only one thing in common.

It lived for one revolution of the planet, then became extinct. A blanket of life stretched across the ground, like a swath of green covering a little more than a third of the planet from one end to the other in a migrating, roughly oval-shaped doughnut that followed the path of the sun. Each day, just before dawn, the surface erupted in rapid, even frantic, growth.

"By the time that the sun rose, flowers of every colour and design, and plants of every description and size, had burst forth from the ground seemingly barren and desolate during the hours of the long Doleran night. Then silence fell as the blooms opened, and growth stood still.

"The wind then picked up. The wind brought either hot, dry air or frigid ice blizzards, depending on the whimsical currents."

Typically, the air became heavy with humidity and hung like a wet blanket while the growth on the surface boiled into a mush typical of vegetables left in a steamer too long. Where the land dried, the vegetation turned black. As though placed in a broiler, complete with sporadic flames, the dry black land smouldered before literal acres of land spontaneously ignited. Thus, the heat of the sun generated massive fires and billows of smoke and ash. Even in the friendly regions of the wind, the plants withered and dried as the wind drew the moisture out of them. Alternatively, plants drowned as great thunderstorms dropped buckets of water upon them, like rain, hailstones the size of houses, or blizzards of snow such that the forces of the weather crushed all life over more than seventy percent of the day's growth. By noon, wherever there had been life, nothing lived unless a calm, overcast sky had left a patch of vegetation protected from both the heat of the sun and the ravages of the wind. Everywhere else, there were only the last wisps of smoke or steam rising in one area or another in a strange mosaic of snowfields, deserts, and charred earth.

"By the middle of the afternoon, the sky blackened, and thunder and lightning storms or monsoon rains would empty heavily laden skies. As the mists rose into the clearing skies, the ground erupted yet again with life. There was no semblance of order, rhyme, or reason for what grew forth. Things grew upon the shoots of other plants. Some lived only minutes before they faded starved of nourishment by an untimely wind, the growth of another species, an explosion of water and earth under their roots, wash away from above in raging torrents of water, or even freeze solid in a sudden draft of cold wind.

"Then an evening calm would descend. Growth slowed, and a special peace spread across the land. The evening could bring any kind of weather, but whatever it brought tended to bring destruction with it. The air usually grew cold, rained, or heavy dew settled onto the soil. In dry areas, hot winds once again caused fires. The net effect was that the life that had burst forth again had its habitat destroyed and died. Finally, the soil waited for whatever the skies cast down upon it until dawn promised life anew.

"The orbit of Doleran around its sun was stable, but the planet itself toppled frequently, but not quite rhythmically. Therefore, overall, life really did not get a chance to evolve into a predictable routine brought about by environmental stability.

"What got me, though, David, was the life that did exist. Doleran was beautiful and incredibly moving emotionally. A Doleran day was very long, let's see," the Judge did some silent mental arithmetic, before continuing, "about one hundred seventy-four of these Earth days. We could breathe the air. The pollens, varying microorganisms, and other life forms on Doleran were not harmful. We ventured from bases in relative safety during stable times. Very soon, we discovered that nowhere on Doleran could we touch anything. Our breath or a touch of a hand would kill literally acres of life within seconds. Doleran, as a world, was allergic to us. We had to wear specially designed space suits and filter the air we exhaled to enjoy being in the forests, fields, and gardens of Doleran. It was worth every bit of effort and discomfort. Doleran was very blessed. Touching my soul, it made me feel secure and close to God. I loved Doleran with my whole heart.

"We moved base camp continually to remain in one of the stable periods. The growth cycle did not permit anything to be on the surface. The growth was violent, David. The soil wreathed as it tilled the ground for depths up to thirty feet. Anything left behind was simply gone forever. The surface was unpredictable, predominantly either quicksand or like floating islands pockmarked with deep holes, but every conceivable terrain except outcrops of bare solid rock could be found. At the end of any growth period, the only predictable feature was the variety, beauty, and uniqueness of the vegetation that celebrated creation. For David, every cycle was a celebration.

"It was a terribly frustrating assignment in its own way. My scientists could only observe. The natural forces of the Doleran climate would permit plucking, crushing, or washing away growth without damage to the surrounding plant life, but we could not gather any samples without causing irreversible destruction of acres of land. We were aliens and did not belong.

"When we resolved ourselves to observing and appreciating Doleran, our whole team gradually attached to it emotionally. We all began having spiritual experiences. God began to speak to our hearts giving us visions of the growth, which would burst forth the following day or of things to come, not only on Doleran but also in our personal lives and other worlds. We kept diaries of the visions, and the Panel confirmed our belief that God was using Doleran to guide us. We were involved in a miracle of prophecy.

"The visions allowed us to begin to interact with the life on Doleran. Each day, we had a premonition showing how to obtain water and food from the surface without causing the accompanying destruction of the life around us. The visions described every detail about the location and method of retrieval. The method changed each day and only worked if we followed the directions precisely.

"It became clear that Doleran would teach us about obedience. We always had the equipment and capability to do the job, but simple errors, such as using the left hand when the vision specified using the right hand, resulted in disaster. We all concentrated on learning and gained great satisfaction from succeeding in collecting first a drink, a meal, and then supplies for a whole day without the terrible sadness of the guilt of dead patches in the otherwise lush surroundings on the surface of Doleran.

"Slowly, we lost all tolerance for excessive death caused by our need for food and water. We no longer thought the premature death of life on a swath of land surrounding our base was an unavoidable consequence of our own survival. As our confidence in trusting our visions soared, all of us began to realize that God was moulding Doleran to serve us; it was changing.

"The life that came forth began to take on a pattern. We could soon predict patterns of growth and plot locations of the right kinds of plants for our daily needs. Water left in a jug no longer became a foul and undrinkable liquid after sitting for more than an hour or so. Food could be stored for a day or two, and finally, seemingly forever. Our stores were filling for the journey home.

"Our health increased despite the challenges of being nomadic upon the surface and the frequent and highly complex ritualistic routines demanded in orbit. Our life was full of peace. Arguments and short tempers gave way to tolerance and quick forgiveness. Wounds healed without leaving scars. Death became very sporadic, and, finally, a rare occurrence, as we were nourished by the blessed food and holy waters of Doleran. We worshipped and celebrated life in the presence of God during our waking hours, and thoughts of God continually filled our dreams when we slept. We were sure that Doleran was not only a part of the Kingdom of God; it was a piece of Heaven and a celebration of the glory of God.

"The most precious gift Doleran gave me was the faith that challenge was a part of the Kingdom of God. When the Kingdom of God arrives upon us, we will still need to strive to follow our God, and we will still be able to lose the Kingdom if we stray from the path of righteousness. We will neither be bored nor lose the delight of feeling joy. We will still be able to experience sorrow and the disgust and shame of our own guilt and sin should we stray. Our lives will be full, and our hands never idle.

"Our learning took over two-thirds of our allotted expedition time. When we were beginning to prepare for our journey home, all of us were changed, and many of us did not want to leave this perfect creation of our God. Uncomfortable and unsettled, we began to receive visions telling us that our lessons were not yet complete. We spent months trying to understand what it was we were to do. It was a very frustrating time, and we began to error in our interpretation of the directions for obtaining food and water.

"Gradually, it became clear that we were to join with Doleran in a spiritual way and learn to be able to interact successfully without complete instructions. Plagued with fantasies about moulding Doleran into a world like our own Land of the Butterflies, we each knew God wanted us to do something when the visions stopped.

"Although we had only a short time left in the expedition, we could feel that something was wrong. Plagued by a terrible foreboding as though we needed to run away to escape a fear we could not justify, let alone fathom a cause, my team looked to me for guidance. I prayed before them.

"I became plagued with a re-occurring dream. I was on Doleran surrounded by a single species of a vine-type plant with a five-petal white flower. Three of the petals formed the back of the flower, creating a bowl at their base and extending up to the sky. The two lower petals curved upward to form the lower end of the bowl, levelled, and finally curved back toward the ground. The bowl was full of sweet nectar, and I dreamed it was holy water. In my dream, I undressed and bathed in the nectar—my head to the sky, my bottom against the lower curve, and my legs along the slope such that only my feet extended outside of the blossom. The nectar flowed down from the sky, splashing like a fountain around my head, flowing along my body, and immersing my toes as it washed over the tip of the bowl and fell like a waterfall to the ground below. The dream was full of ecstasy then always ended in a nightmare. The blossom closed over me, and I could not get out. The winds came. Ceasing to be human, I became part of Doleran.

"I would awake in a sweat, shaking in defiance. God wanted my life. I did not know why and did not understand. Becoming afraid to go to sleep, I spent days talking to the crew as we tried to understand what God wanted. We did not see the flower until I was very sick.

"One morning, the new growth burst forth in the plant of my dreams. I took a transporter to the surface and stood among the plants. David, they grew up to my knees, no higher. The flowers were tiny. I could not even put my whole thumb into the bowl of nectar. I did not disrobe. Seeking the courage to find a way to bathe in the nectar, I stood and wept. Until it was dangerously close to when the winds would arrive, I stayed.

"If I must die, I thought I should get it over with quickly. I had decided to pour the nectar into my protective suit. Thinking it would serve as the bowl, I planned to sit upon the empty blossoms so that they would surround me, but when I broke off a single blossom, the wind rose with a howl of anger, and the plant began to die.

"I realized that although this plant looked like the plant of my dreams, it was not. I was following my own will. I was making substitutions for God's instructions. The past visions of God had been explicit. Every detail was exact. Sometimes, we were to touch a specific single plant to gain our daily allowance of life-sustaining nourishment. On Doleran, I should have known that God gave exact instructions. Improvising was not necessary. Even as God had begun being less exact, the knowledge we had previously gained had always been enough.

"Overcome with grief and remorse; I struggled into my transporter. As I rose from the surface, I watched massive destruction spread out from the spot where I had stood. It kept spreading until the whole planet, not just a few acres, was dead.

"We waited, orbiting Doleran, praying that new life would grow forth again. A horrible sadness and loneliness filled us. No fire rose from Doleran. The wind continued to blow. Rain fell. Vapour rose again into the sky. Deep gouges appeared on the surface as the wind built huge dunes. Water began to gather into bigger lakes than we had ever seen before, and the momentum of the oscillations of Doleran's polar axis became more and more violent.

"The planet was out of balance as though it could not establish an equilibrium capable of keeping in step with the fluctuating distribution of mass tossed about by the winds and currents. For the first time, we saw bare outcrops and knew that I had destroyed the planet. Yet, I could not turn away and head for home.

"Your great-uncle was a good friend, David. He listened to hours of my ranting and raving. He encouraged me to seek God's help. However, I was angry. Turning away from God in shame, I felt an overwhelming inability to forgive myself, let alone seek the forgiveness of Jarrock. God poured love out upon me, but it hurt. I wanted to hide from the light, for it burnt me. I could not live with my own foolish audacity.

"I had thrown away all the knowledge that God had so patiently nurtured throughout the expedition. God had offered my expedition the opportunity to receive a grand and glorious gift. I felt ashamed and worthless. I was unworthy of redemption. Angry that God would not condemn me, I was unable to seek death for myself.

"My work was incomplete, and I knew it. Your great-uncle kept telling me to seek God's will and pray for guidance. I could not bring myself to follow his advice. Your great-uncle did not berate me. In silence, he stood beside me and prayed.

"We would be late returning to the Land of the Butterflies, but all the expedition agreed to stay, to wait, and to hope that Doleran would burst forth with life anew. The weeks passed, Doleran remained barren, but faith there was something we could do sustained us.

"None of us had any visions, but we all felt loved and knew God remained close to us. Slowly, each of us found a measure of peace and acceptance of both Doleran's death and our own humanity and imperfection. My own peace came through hard work. My crew and I began to examine the stores we had collected, intent on finding a spoor, a seed, anything which might contain a recipe for life that defied everything we knew about the science of botany.

"Your great-uncle came to me one day and said, "Let us ask the Lady to return life to Doleran through these plants and nectars we have collected. We do not know what made them grow forth nor what should come after them, but perhaps, with our faith and trust in God, a miracle will grow once more."

"That is what we did, David. It made no sense. Although we would all starve to death before we made it home if it did not work, we felt obligated to put our lives in God's hands. We loved Doleran. Consciously, we had decided that it would be only right to die with it if that was God's will. We transported the rich nectars to the surface and spilt it a drop at a time just before dawn and as the skies cleared in the late afternoon. We neither ate nor slept while we sacrificed our future for the future of Doleran, a world that defied logic but celebrated the very breath of God's love.

"Nothing happened, David, until our ship was empty of every sample of Doleran life that existed. Then like magic, full of peace and contentment, we slept. When we awoke, life was reborn on Doleran. We sang, danced, and shouted our joy and praise to God. We wept, slept well, and worked hard each day, taking only enough to sustain us, hoping that the nagging feeling within us that Doleran was still destined for death would leave us. Gradually, our thoughts turned toward home, and we began to gather stores. We collected only enough to sustain us on our journey.

"On our last day, David, we all went to the surface, and while we worshipped, a great vine grew in a huge circle around us. When they bloomed, the white blossoms of the plant reminded me of my dream. However, there was a red vein on the underside of the pedals, and I could not remember whether those in my dream had any colour upon them. The flowers grew on a single vine, unlike the numerous vines and blossoms covering the whole growth of the Doleran day of my dreams. The blossoms seemed to point at me and moved as I moved. I concluded that they were not the plant in which I was to bathe. We conferred as a team and decided among us that it was a gift of forgiveness. Feeling blessed, we returned to orbit.

"After eating dinner, I felt a sick feeling within me as your great uncle's words came into my head, 'Ask God for a sign, Josh. Let God guide your actions.'

"I realized that yet again I had turned to my fellow man for guidance rather than to God. I had not learned to trust the Lady, and my heart began to ache so that I found moving very difficult. Taking a transporter, I returned to the surface, again, delaying our journey.

"The winds were howling, and it was difficult to stay on my feet. Drops of rain began to fall upon me as I struggled to keep hold of the vine supporting the white blossoms while stripping myself of the protective clothing I wore. I prayed for forgiveness and the opportunity to carry out God's will the whole time. The rain stopped. The air was so thick and humid that it sucked my energy out of me. As I watched in anguish, the blossoms wilted, and the nectar poured out upon me. Like magic, energy filled me as the word of God sang out around me.

"God said, 'Only I, the one and only true God, have the power to guide you. My Kingdom needs your obedience. Trust me to lead you, my son.'

"I almost fell upon my knees. Instead, with a sudden realization, I stood tall in the mist. Wrapped in the security of God's love, I raised my arms to the sky, thrust out my bare chest, and yelled, 'Oh, my God, I am yours.' I fully expected death at that moment, but I heard only silence and felt God smile upon me.

"Moments later, in the voice of Jarrock, I heard, 'Go home, son. Serve me; there is much to do.'

"The transporter was only a few yards away, but it took over an hour to get to it. I struggled and fought both exhaustion and hopelessness with a growing staggering faith that God would show me the way to safety. God guided me, and I only progressed when I gave myself to obedience, even when God instructed me to turn my back to my goal and walk in the opposite direction. I lost every shred of doubt in the truth of God's wisdom.

"While I was on route to the ship and safe from danger, God remained with me, giving me strength. God even laughed. I felt such joy. Just before I fell into a deep sleep, God said, 'Gather my flock, Josh, and bring my children together! Be one of my shepherds.'

"David, I slept through docking with the ship, being transferred to my quarters and until we were leaving Doleran's solar system. When I looked back on Doleran when I awoke, I felt peace and took heart in the realization that Doleran was a gift of prophecy of the future that awaited us all. We were not ready. We still struggled with a need to be independent and human. We did not yet give ourselves freely to God. In silence, I said, 'I trust you, my Lady.'

"As Doleran exploded in a beautiful fire of colour and light, without sorrow, I watched full of hope and promise for the future.

"Perhaps, I was not destined to be great. God did not need me to be a prophet. My life was spent struggling to achieve humble obedience to God. God commanded me to do the little things. Often, I believe God merely sends me to places where another of God's children needs assistance: to follow God's will, to do what our culture forbids, to set the stage for change, and bring his flock together.

"I simply wait, David. Wait for guidance. I do not assume and then seek God's blessing upon what I have concluded is the right thing to do. No, I seek God's will and obey confidently blessed even when asked to do what my culture and friends condemn as unrighteous. God knows what is right. If you trust God, you will receive blessings.

"This young Earthling maybe your Doleran, David. Whenever your mind fights with your heart, go to God. Do not let pride, tradition, or man convince you not to do whatever God asks of you. The universe, as we know it, is changing. God is moulding it into something closer to Her. Do not be afraid and do not try to understand. Obey, David. Confidently, openly go wherever God is leading you."

As the office became quiet, David rose and stood before the Judge. He thought very carefully before saying, "Are you telling me that I should go and dance with the Little Smiler?"

"No, David. You love her. We all can see that truth. Love is good, but it is not always according to the will of God. You have taken an oath to uphold the universal laws of God. As a Cultural Judge of the Land of the Butterflies, you are forbidden from interfering with alien culture unless the Panel has approved your actions and been blessed by God. These are rules which history has shown will protect the Kingdom of God from being tailored to the will of man rather than to the will of God. There is much that we do not understand, David. It is very dangerous to wield the gifts of Koe Sai Serena. We must all be cautious.

"What I am telling you is that caution is not always right. We are becoming stale and set in our ways. We are not open to change or willing to accept new demands from God. As are most of the assignments that I am sent to lead, this assignment has stepped out of the pattern of the common. It is unique, and something unorthodox has occurred with the blessing of God.

"God is leading you. I can neither bless nor condemn your reaction to the position fate was put before you. Trust God, David. God alone can guide you. Open your heart to believing that God will not deceive you."

"But, Sir, God will tell me to walk away."

"The books we have tell you to walk away, David. You are writing a new book. God is dynamic. The Kingdom grows a spirit at a time. We have gained considerable proficiency in wielding the gifts of Koe Sai Serena. We are on the verge of receiving the next gift. Do not let fear, tradition, or experience keep us in the dark. Find your Doleran, and let it burst to the glory of God!"

That lecture gave David the strength to go to God. He felt strange that doubt would ever become part of his faith in God. It was not merely the written word defining righteousness. It was being willing to listen to the living words from above. David began to look to God. In fear of error, he asked that God give him a sign to guide him in dealing with the love he felt for the Little Smiler.

It was then that the Little Smiler had waited for him at the bridge. As they walked together, David had tried very hard to keep his mind open to hear the will of God. When the Little Smiler also sincerely sent him to seek God, David thought he already knew what God would tell him. He was going to have to be her friend, the right kind of friend. That thought terrified David. He needed time to get a firm hold on his emotions.

A friendship between a male and a fertile woman outside of a castle was a shocking concept and, oh, so very alien. He had told her he was leaving for a month. He would go far away, meditate, and seek God's guidance. With this friend, it was imperative that David followed the will of God, not the instinct of a young, possibly lustful man.

David did not want to be human. As a human, he did not stand a chance of success. To teach her, David needed to become Jarrock.

9

A LITTLE PEACE

JUDGE SORONATO WATCHED DAVID INTENTLY throughout dinner and the evening festivities when he arrived back at the base with a big smile spread across his face, a recognizable joy in his step, and a soft aura of God glistening around him. David's joy was infectious. The Judge decided to wait until bedtime before summoning him to his office so that all the members present at the base would benefit from David's mood.

At dinner, David took a generous portion. He ate it all. Not hurriedly, as though in a rush, but slowly while he laughed with his friends, teased Muma Horren or gazed out into space between mouthfuls. He savoured his food. Gone was the mechanical David of the last three weeks. The Judge decided that David had turned to God, and God had not disappointed Her young son. It was good to watch the effect David was having on the others. Depression took a terrible toll on them all. It was wonderful to feel the healing power of God among them tonight.

A crisis that none of them understood was now behind them. They felt good. They were loyal servants, lost in a strange land. However, something had happened to David, and he knew the path which lay before him. The Judge sighed. The will of God, as always, would be done. God was with them, and they would follow in obedience.

Customarily, the Muki sing after receiving direction from God. It was a way in which they could share the experience of being in

God's presence. Calming their nerves helped them avoid second-guessing the message received, as is the inclination of human nature, and helped to solidify God's will upon their souls. It was hard work being an Instrument of Creation. One's own individuality, thoughts, needs, desires, and experiences tend to interfere with understanding the whys and what-ifs of stepping upon the path of God, travelling forward not by one's own will but on God's beckoning.

As he listened to David sing after dinner, the Judge wondered what God had said to David. Where was God leading his expedition? Wanting to savour this moment of unity in the expedition, Judge Soronato let himself relax. Something deep within him told him that David was on his own. God was leading him beyond the written word. With a nagging feeling that tonight he would not sleep well, he feared David was going to frighten him.

"Oh my God," the Judge whispered, "grant me the strength to support David. Guide me to be his shepherd."

Afraid that his own foreboding would ruin the joy and open celebration of peace that seemed so alive in his team tonight, the Judge quietly slipped into his office. He stood at his window and looked out into the night. The sky was clear, the air crisp, and winter was in this land. Back home, at a time like this, one would watch the sky for the wavering haze of a temperature storm.

The Judge felt comfort that his team was all warm and cozy in their shelters. They would dance in the hall well into the night, growing sleepy, and eventually step out into the night air to say goodnight to all that they loved so far away in the heavens. They would feel the blessings of God upon them. Peace would settle into their hearts. Certainly, despite the flimsy construction of the camp, no temperature storm would fall upon them. God had blessed this land with peace. Then, they would go to bed and sleep wrapped in the arms of Jarrock, secure within the blanket of Koe Sai Serena.

They would sleep well, all except David and himself. David would speak to him, and Josh Soronato would find himself back on Doleran trying to understand what God wanted of him. It was always the same on every one of the Judge's assignments. God's will would not be clear. It would hurt him.

In the dark, the blossom would close over him until God showed him a new light that would jar him. The Judge never got used to the demands to guide one of God's sheep into the unknown. David would have to leave the flock to bring the flock closer to God further down the road. Feeling very old and tired, the Judge sat at his desk and prayed. "Please, Jarrock, do not make this assignment too difficult. I no longer have the strength of my youth. Forgive me." Then the Judge laid his head upon the desk and cried.

Moments later, a soft, gentle knock rapped upon his door. The Judge smiled. "Oh, my Natthia," he whispered before rising and heading to the door to invite her in. As he opened the door, he said, "Thank you, Jarrock. Natthia is exactly who I need."

Natthia stepped inside and closed the door behind her. Without saying a word, she put her arms around the Judge and hugged him. Natthia let him hold her until she knew he was calm. Then she lightly wiped the tearstains off his cheeks and smiled.

"God has moved fast this time, Josh. Take heart. I have a feeling David's quest will delight us."

"In the end, Natthia, it is always in the end when it is behind us. I wish I could see where it was God was leading us. Change is so frightening. I will never understand why God chose me, a stickler for tradition and constancy, to lead the universe into change."

"You will keep the pace manageable, Josh. With you as our spiritual shepherd, change will come in peace. Come, let us rest awhile." Natthia took his hand and led him into the adjoining room where often, she and Josh spent the nights together.

In the wee hours of the morning, David knocked on Judge Soronato's door. The Judge shouted for him to make a fresh urn of cider while he dressed, saying he would join him presently. David chuckled. There was no man in the team who did not envy the Judge's position with the team's doctor, Natthia. Women of the Muki rarely allowed men of their ages to share their beds. Women wanted the young to retain their virginity just in case they would choose a castle when they were old and mature enough to recognize their need to propagate. Natthia had worked with Judge Soronato for years. When asked about it, she would say, "He's as old as I am, and I was never able to entice him to exercise his license to sire. One day I realized that he really was serious. He loved God and me. He had no desire to sire. In his heart, there was no time to sire and planned to remain a Cultural Judge until he died. Then he gave me no choice. When I refused to go to his bed, he took another there to prove he could never be a sire. I am not a fool; there was no longer any reason to withhold my love for him."

While he watched the kettle, David yawned. He wanted the kind of relationship that Natthia and the Judge shared, but he was determined to become a sire someday. The Land of the Butterflies was dying for lack of children. All the work they did on behalf of God was useless if they all died and left no innocence to enjoy the Kingdom of God when it came upon them. As he pictured lying beside the Little Smiler, David smiled at himself. Scowling, he said aloud, "I sure hope the Judge can help me find peace in a platonic relationship. Is there a way to dream one world at night and live another by day without tearing one's soul apart?"

"No. David, there is not," answered the Judge. Then he laughed as David recovered from the shock of receiving an answer. "Your entire world will need to be in harmony, David. You will fail if you try to deceive her or yourself. Keep your emotions in check but do not try to disguise them."

David blushed and said, "I suppose you are going to tell me that dreaming is not free in this matter. Judge, I do not pretend to understand this culture. I do not believe we are equipped adequately to deal with other human races. We should stick to the primitive lands of the universe. We have not had a hand in the growth of this planet; I fear it is too advanced for us. God must have other instruments to use. Why did God send us?"

"Suffice to say that God works in mysterious ways, David. It is not our place to ask why of God. It is our duty to obey. What has God asked of you, David?"

"I do not know yet, Sir. I simply have a feeling that it will unfold, as it should. I am to be the right kind of friend to the Little Smiler and must go into the quiet lands to find my own inner peace. I told the Little Smiler that I was going north for a month, Sir. I had asked God for a sign to guide me. Our Lady put Littl'un before me. You will never guess what she did."

"Tell me, David."

"She sent me to God, just as you have been advising. She has no choice but to seek my friendship, and she believes that I have no choice either. She is right, Judge Soronato, God will demand that I be her friend, that I teach her to be Muki. Help me, Judge. Help me find a way to teach her to be what the law prohibits her from ever becoming."

"David, think of her as a piece of the Kingdom of God. We know that we cannot achieve the Kingdom of God until the time is right for God, not merely for ourselves. Teach her as though the future holds no doubt that you will succeed; believe there is a way to make a Muki of an alien. God will grant you a way. Proceed with the lessons of today confident that when the time is right, God will guide you."

"Go blindly into tomorrow? Judge, I am not like that. I like things laid out before me. If I know where I am going, I am both able and confident I will arrive. This is different. I know I cannot succeed. I cannot make water flow uphill; I can love this woman, but I cannot give her our ancestry. She is alien."

"David, it only takes a pump to make water go uphill. With God's will, all things are accomplishable. If you fail, David, God will send another and another until one has enough faith to obey."

After pouring cider into the two mugs on the desk, David sat down. Concluding, the Judge had to be right; the question was then how one teaches another to be something that was impossible. It was like asking a woman to become a man. Others could teach her to act and react spontaneously to stimulus in a certain way, but she would still be whoever or whatever her ancestry made her. To the Judge, David said, "I feel as though God has put a dog before me and is telling me to teach it to fly like a bird!"

They both roared with laughter.

"I think David, that is why God allowed you to be smitten by this Earthling. With love, David, all things are possible."

"Do you hear yourself, Sir? You are telling me to commit a crime. I could destroy her and break the Kingdom of God, for a piece of the Kingdom will be missing if I have tampered with her."

"I will have Natthia prepare to erase her memory should the need arise. We have tracked your Earthling for several weeks, David. God chose her well. She does not talk much to others. She has never mentioned you or the Muki. I believe the danger is minimal."

Disappointed and shocked, David uttered, "Not at all? Not even when talking to herself?"

Again, the Judge laughed. "She is wise, David. She recognizes the danger. Our presence here is unwelcomed. We are alien to them, too, David."

David blushed again. "Sorry, Sir, that thought was vain. I apologize. Please forgive me."

"Remember that this land, as are all lands, is part of God's creation. God has blessed the humans here with Great Books. (Great Books are accounts of events recorded as being messages, lessons, or demonstrations of the will of God, like the Bible, for example.) They are important to God. Remember that God will protect her as well as you. You have told me that her faith is strong. Build on it, David. Let your spirits grow. Let God lead you."

"Thank you, Sir. What would you recommend I do?"

"Obey, David. Obey God's instructions."

"I mean now."

The Judge laughed and drank a long gulp of cider to drain his cup. "What has God asked you to do?"

"I am not sure God asked me to do anything. It is just a feeling I have that I know what I should do.

"Then trust your feeling."

"Go north and think?"

"Yes."

"What about my duties?"

"Your duty is first to God, David. Obey God before you worry about obeying me. I am but a man. Now go to bed. Do not think about ways not to do as your spirit directs. Think about how to succeed. Rest with confidence and the security of God's love."

In comfort, David sat and thought, sipping slowly on his cider. Warmth settled over him. The Judge seemed so confident that all was well that David let his fears vanish with a long sigh. Then his thoughts turned to the celebration they had all enjoyed earlier in the evening, and his heart filled with gratitude. He liked Judge Soronato and hoped he would learn to lead like him.

"Good night, Sir. Thank you again for allowing us to celebrate this evening. We needed to let off a little steam," he said as he rose to leave when the urn of cider was empty.

"You are welcome, son. Goodnight. Sleep well."

When the door closed, the Judge quickly rinsed the dishes and returned to bed, surprised that he was not frightened but comforted. Love would be the key, and Natthia was right. This assignment was going to be pleasant for a change. It was not going to have a nightmare. His own job was to keep David focusing his love in the right direction. He needed to be his father, to help David keep his relationship with the Earthling innocent and holy. It should not be too difficult. David already planned to become a sire in the future. To fulfil his dream, he had to remain innocent. Contently smiling, the Judge went to sleep.

10

PREPARATIONS
FOR WORSHIP

IN THE MORNING, DAVID POURED over the maps, searching for the right place to go to meditate. Where he worshipped felt like a critical decision, which was odd. David generally felt comfortable worshipping almost anywhere. His personal preference was high in the mountains, in solitude among regions of land once torn with turmoil. It was as though the place of worship visually needed to complement the state of his inner self, his thoughts, and his fears... his whole soul.

As the morning went on, he became more and more frustrated. He could not find a location that called out to him. When he tried to ignore his feeling that location mattered, he would slowly acquire a dislike and even hatred for any location he began to triangulate into a transporter loop. Depressed, he picked at his lunch and began finding excuses to avoid returning to the survey room to continue his search. Natthia came and sat beside him, suggesting a very simple thing that changed his whole focus and let him find a place to meditate and worship before God.

Natthia said, "When you are dealing with genuine love between a man and a woman, David, the place that you should seek to go before God is a place that answers the vision of the one you love, not your own vision. When you are in love, you are no longer alone. You become a unity together. Apart you are broken, without peace and satisfaction." Natthia had rested one hand upon his shoulder, the other under his chin, and had spoken looking directly into his eyes. She smiled and then kissed his forehead. Calmed, as though Natthia had lifted a heavy blindfold and cast it aside, David watched Natthia, shining with the presence of God, leave the kitchen.

With a much lighter step, David returned to the task of finding a camp for a month-long meditation. He flipped through several maps, glancing at each, looking for a feeling that Littl'un would like this place and very soon enlarged one with growing confidence that he knew where the Little Smiler would go to worship. His finger slid across the screen and came to rest as though automatically. Looking at the spot, he smiled. Although far away, bitterly cold, even a little frightening, his heart knew that this alpine meadow overlooking a steep mountain valley was where he needed to go. He took coordinates and accessed the appropriate programs for advice on supplies for a temporary isolation camp capable of sustaining a single occupant for one month.

Just before dinner, he gathered all the pertinent details together and took them to the Judge. As a young judge, David had no authority to order provisions or to set up a transporter loop to get there. The Judge queried him and made suggestions to improve the safety of the camp, but any involving moving the camp, David flatly refused. Finally, the Judge laughed and said, "You have chosen a location that will consume most of your time and efforts in surviving, David. I hope you will have an opportunity to worship. Do not be a fool. Do not freeze to death. Proceed."

He entered the authorization and hugged David before saying, "You'll take a week on guard duty before you can leave, David. Think about where you are going and why while you guard the transporter. If you change your mind, I will be willing to change these orders."

David could not hide his disappointment but thanked the Judge and went to see if Mark would stand guard duty with him. It was a relatively boring week on guard duty, yet it was also comforting. He allowed a shadow of doubt into his thoughts about the safety of the location he had chosen. However, rather than make him look for another spot to worship, it sealed his resolve that it was indeed the best possible place. His worship would not be easy. It was not supposed to be easy. His task was a difficult one, almost impossible. Success would be like survival—basic, human, and primitive.

Canada was a special place. Here cultural differences were something to celebrate, but it remained uncelebrated. It was acknowledged, and to David, that was, in a sense, far better. If ever the Muki found acceptance as legitimate citizens or tourists anywhere upon Earth, Canada was where it would happen. In Canada, the Muki could retain their cultural identity, be proud of their ancestry, and refuse to assimilate the cultures of those around them. It would not be an easy life, surrounded by so much choice and freedom. Oh, the temptations that would abound...

"Mark!" David shouted, coming out of his private thoughts, "Mark, help me. I am losing my mind. I just acknowledged the fleeting thought of staying on Earth permanently. How can a mere woman have such power? How did you banish such thoughts when you were held in the clutches of forbidden love?"

Mark laughed and put down the console onto which he was recording environmental data. Motioning for David to accompany him, he returned to the small, heated tent they used to keep warm. They hung up their coats and put the equipment they were using in a drying unit to prevent damage by moisture from melting snow or condensation.

These sensitive instruments accumulated an incredible amount of data. If they damaged them, the Judge would be furious. With these instruments, they could run literally hundreds of programs to determine everything from the geological structures of Earth in a fifty-mile radius to depths exceeding ten miles to eavesdropping on a conversation in a single specified room within the same range. They did not need to be among the natives at all.

This was the first expedition to Earth where the Muki had permission to interact directly with the natives. This privilege came with the territory of being under the guidance of Judge Soronato. Some considered him dangerous. Others thought Judge Soronato holy. His greatness was always a subject of debate. Unorthodox, he followed his own vision, working with the blessings of God. The Judge was unique. Encouraged to take young judges with him, as the panel felt his wisdom enough for him to teach the young judges of tomorrow both the folly and reward of being different, unorthodox, or original thinkers. His assignments were always to places where the panel felt a look from a different angle would be advantageous.

Neither David nor Mark knew whether interaction with an alien culture was wise or foolhardy. Despite knowing it was dangerous and full of peril, they liked being so close to Earthlings. They were determined to reap a bounty of knowledge through interaction that eavesdropping could not possibly grant them.

While he waited for the cider Mark was preparing, David understood contact opened the door to the pain, sorrow, and thought that was plaguing his mind today, and he knew it would for many more months. Ever since they had arrived, Judge Soronato had hounded him to find evidence of the presence of God among these aliens.

The Littl'un had that special aura about her; he had to find out more about her. The only way was to teach her about his world. As he showed her his world, she would open the doors to her own. Convinced she was the key for which he had been searching, David could not run away. Even if it tore his own heart, he had to prove to the Judge that God had blessed this land and its destruction unacceptable. In the process, his future could be lost...

Handing him a steaming hot mug of cider, Mark said, "If you come back from wherever you are, David, I am ready to answer your questions now."

Self-consciously, David laughed. Sitting at the table warming his fingers on the mug, he gave Mark a serious expression that made Mark laugh and say, "I am not the Judge, and I am not Muma

Horren, but I will try to tell you what I have figured out through my own experiences."

It took a while before they could talk without bursting with laughter. The Muki were not stupid people; Mark and David were simply experiencing emotions and finding themselves in predicaments that their culture never permitted in young men. Unless licensed to sire and a man had walked through the front door of a castle, been accepted as an adequate dancer, and gained a key to the Sire's quarters, thoughts of love and sex were confined to dreams and fantasies. Being among fertile females was simply alien and outside of possibilities. As such, it made them feel very giddy and unsure of the righteousness of their thoughts and feelings.

Eventually, Mark began, "Love is the same here among these people as it is on the Land of the Butterflies. A woman judges a man by how he makes her feel. Being the sum of all that she has felt, she knows that a man is all he has seen. Therefore, to entice him, she uses imagery. She controls how she dresses and moves according to what she wants the man to feel. They are butterflies.

We are particularly vulnerable, for we expect all women to see us as young men needing nurturing and protection from the sins of lust and desire. Nurturing and protecting men are the last thing on female Earthlings' minds. Wanting to conquer, they trap men in seduction. They, too, are looking for a mate, but they use intimate feelings and their own reaction to raw sexual emotions and experiences to judge the acceptability of the males with whom they have access. Selfish, they offer little respect for age, their own desire to propagate, or any existing relationship in which she or the man may be involved. You have the kind of stuff that a castle would recognize as desirable in an interview or on your application papers, just as the women here recognize you as potentially pleasing. The difference is that these women assess all the men they see as potential sires or lovers without regard for their need for a sire. They have no boundaries. Wanting to experience whatever it is they think you have to offer, they accept the possibility that they may get hurt in the hopes of gaining something wonderful; a feeling of being loved and of having power over another's life."

"Littl'un is not like that."

"No, she is clever. She knows how to pull your strings. She uses her knowledge of our world to trap you into loving her and her world. You must learn that she is a demon. Believe with your whole heart that she wants to take you away from God. Only then will you be able to forget her and put your heart back together again.

"That, David, is how I escape being smitten. You fight back to banish forbidden love. You look for evidence that she is not sincere in looking for a lifelong relationship of love, including the intention of honouring you with children as their bible demands. Then you can teach yourself to recognize her kind of seduction and escape it in others.

"It is getting harder for women to deceive me, David. The first is the most painful. I have become a little cynical about my own heart's abilities to judge women and have learned to use the advice of my head before my heart skips a beat."

"Mark, if the Little Smiler did anything at all which hinted as insincerity, I would have picked it up the last time I saw her. Everything she did or said struck true in both my heart and my head. I looked for an excuse to run, any reason to grab to tell me that I should not trust my emotions. Yet, she continued to pull me in every direction.

"She needs protection. She might know that she is mortal but acts as though nothing could ever hurt her physically. All her pain is wrapped in fear for the future of the world, as she wants it to be. She lives in a fantasy world, which is delicate and vulnerable. If God had not demanded that she share her world with me, she would have ignored me and gone to the effort of avoiding possible contact if I had said hello. She is full of faith, and a blind acceptance, that God has ordained me to be her friend."

"Well, David, perhaps you were made for each other. I have never felt connected to those by whom I have been smitten. I have always known that they and I were aliens. It was something about them that I loved, perhaps not them at all. For all I know, I merely felt lust. If I be honest with myself, I did not get close enough to know them. When I did look more closely, I could see their sins and avoid further temptation.

"Maybe I can't help you, David, unless..." Mark paused and thought for a moment before he whispered, "Her God might be a false God, David. She might worship an idol. If she does, she would be sincere in her motives and actions. She could be innocently evil." Restraining a sudden urge to hit Mark, David rose, donned his coat, and headed back outside. He grabbed his console and faced the wind. He did not say anything. He could not. There was nothing to say. Mark could be right, and he hated him for voicing the possibility. It was time to worship. Maybe, tonight, he would ask the Judge to let him leave tomorrow.

No one else had seen the presence of God in the Little Smiler. Maybe there was a reason. Perhaps, the earthling did not know God after all. David forced himself to concentrate on his work, purposely rejecting all thought of worship, and banished the Little Smiler out of his head. He would talk to the Judge after supper, and there was nothing else to gain today.

11

HIGH ON A MOUNTAIN
OF THE NORTH

THE JUDGE LET HIM GO. Worship was hard. Temperatures dropped well below freezing, and the wind chill was horrendous. At night, the sky was clear but full of northern lights. Delighted by them, the northern lights reminded him of rainbows and temperature storms rolled together into a single phenomenon. The days were difficult. The snow was blinding in its brightness, and the wind was cruel in its furiousness. Furthermore, the day was too short to accomplishing anything at all.

Each day he spent not more than an hour all told outside of his tent. On the first day, when the temperature had been only ten below zero, he had built a snow house around the tent and thanked God that he had done so at least once every time he went outside. He did not stand and bare his chest before God during the day. Sleeping most of the day, he worshipped and prayed all night long. From within the safety of his tent, he only looked out at the sky, hoping to understand what God was saying in the northern lights. He thought, sang, and cried. However, what he mostly did was dream of teaching the Little Smiler and replacing the grey sentry as the guardian of her world.

David's thoughts roamed from the first moments that he had set his foot upon the soil of the land called Earth through the oaths he had taken to protect the coming Kingdom of God. He considered his promise to refrain from using the gifts of Koe Sai Serena for his own purposes. The ramifications of loving an alien also plagued him. With his thoughts full of worry, he even questioned the wisdom of God in having chosen him for this task. However, as the days passed, his thoughts became organized and followed a pattern, which comforted David. It began with his knowledge of this land.

The Muki did not know Earth because it was far out in the heavens and a long way from the heart of God. Perhaps born even before their Land of the Butterflies, it was an old world. For thousands of years, the Muki had had almost nothing to do with Earth. God did not send Her Cultural Judges or any Instrument of Creation from the ranks of the Muki. Yet, God was active there. Curiosity and a general belief that they had a responsibility to know the universe had drawn the Panel to endorse the occasional fly-by to keep an eye on Earth as they did millions of other oases of life in the universe.

It was true that over the centuries, a fear of the humans of Earth developed. Simply, the Muki did not know these people, and God was holding them separate. Earth was incomprehensible to the Muki. As such, it was only natural that they developed a fear of Earth and a worry over the Great Books that God had given them. There were so many similarities in their Great Books to those of the Muki. It was complicated to understand why God wanted to keep them separate rather than work together as other civilizations worked with the Muki.

God had many instruments spread across the universe, and each had a very clearly defined function. However, Earth's function was unclear. The information available worried the Muki. Created as a Garden of Eden, Earth physically appeared a peaceful land, yet everything but peace filled its people. It was blatantly apparent that Earth was not as God would have it. Therefore, the Muki feared Earth and its people. Had they lost the blessings of God? Were Earthlings completely blind to the will and light of God? Were they evil?

As civilization advanced upon Earth, reflecting less and less with each generation the picture of Godliness, terror began to fill the hearts of the Muki. Earth became a study for college students on how not to act and the hazards of turning your back on God. The Muki strove to be God-like. They tried to carry out their lives as Jarrock would have done. They could not succeed, for they were human even though they had always chosen to follow God when God tested them. Being human made them akin to the people of Earth. It was a scary thought.

"Be righteous, and think good thoughts, or you'll end up like the humans on Earth. You will become the living dead," said the lessons to all the youth of the Land of the Butterflies. "They are failing the Lady." For eons, the Muki and indeed many other civilizations had concluded that Earth was a symbol to them all on what not to be.

Only recently, God had brought Earth to the attention of the Muki. God told them to observe it and to prepare. For what were they to prepare? No one knew. However, the Muki had observed almost constantly for the last two hundred years and panicked at the knowledge that the people of Earth were preparing to enter the heavens. Judgements of returning expeditions began to hint and then to clearly endorse a belief that Earth becomes the subject of a destruction assignment. For some reason, known only to God, David had felt pain, sorrow, and even anger in his own belief that the fear of Earth would lead the Muki to destroy it.

After all, it was human nature to see the faults of others, and there were living dead wherever there were humans. Wanting to mould all of life to their own purposes, humans sought power and preferred being served rather than to serve. Even with the gifts of Koe Sai Serena, most people of the Land of the Butterflies would rather be blind to God's light and deaf to God's words. They did not want to feel with God's touch or give God their hands and tongues to do Her work. No! People wanted to have it all for themselves. They were content to create their own empire, leaving all the responsibilities with God, claiming innocence and independence.

They abhorred slavery and, with passion, tried to destroy it in defiance of the knowledge in the depths of their hearts that slavery to God was the only salvation for the Kingdom of God. They would rather be content with the knowledge that Jarrock had died for them and forgiven their sins as a freely given, unearned, and undeserved gift from God. They did not want the gift of Koe Sai Serena. Koe Sai Serena's gift only served to fill them with guilt.

Most people left the task of acquiring the Kingdom of God to the so-called holy, those drawn to serve as Instruments of Creation, people like himself who took on the task as Cultural Judges. They were revered and feared by their own people and all peoples in the heavens. Their own people followed them, not out of love but out of fear: fear for their own salvation. If God chose a member of the family, the family felt blessed but also sorrowful because serving God was neither natural nor safe. David did not feel superior, only thankful and proud that he could summon the strength to let God lead him. He knew he could obey God and that God would help him.

His heart told him that Earth was no eviler than were his own people. Perhaps they lived further away, but mostly, he believed their evil was simply more visible, their faith no different. His own heart had demanded that he join this expedition. He could not let fear destroy Earth because fear was the root of the coming destruction of the Kingdom of God. If Earth was to disappear from the heavens, David was sure the Kingdom of God would ultimately fail.

David had written his graduation thesis on Earth. Judge Soronato had read it and even given a copy to his supervisor at the Tower of the Panel in Shiacre. Although honoured, David was a little embarrassed at the questions fired at him when he had stood before the Panel. It was not common for the Panel to summon a graduating judge. When finally, David had admitted defeat and said that he found his basis for his paper only at the bottom depths of his own heart, the questions stopped, and the Panel dismissed him.

A few months later, David heard of the assignment of the sixth judgement to Judge Soronato. The Judge had laughed many times at the hearing, and David had been afraid to apply. His friend, Mark, had encouraged him, and finally, together, they had made an appointment to see Judge Soronato. Boy, had he put them through the wringer! However, he had accepted them both some weeks later. The first time he had stood before the Judge was at the panel inquiry into the ramifications of his thesis. Judge Soronato had accused him, quite rightly, of condemning his homeland as unholy because, unlike Earth, they hid from temptation rather than facing and overcoming it. His thesis postulated there were only two areas of life where the Muki allowed themselves to express their humanity. It was in their willingness to allow madmen to execute them and the indulgence of the dance of the Butterflies. In both situations, the Muki acted selfishly and openly admitted their sin before God. Ironically, both these activities people simultaneously thought were the holiest of everything that the Muki did in life. The Judge had told him that there would come a day when he would have to apologize for his words.

His thesis became a curse in that his applications to join expeditions were denied with the explanation that he was a rebel and likely to act on his own behalf to the detriment of the expeditions. David thought they were simply reacting to the truth of what he had written. They were avoiding the possibility that they were not as holy as they saw themselves by distancing themselves from him for thrusting their humanity in their faces. Simply, David made them nervous.

When Judge Soronato met with the expedition members before takeoff, he had singled David out for a lecture. He told David that he fully expected him to redeem himself on the mission and that he would be watching him very carefully. "It is your duty," he had said, "to prove that Earth is blessed. And I will hound you until you succeed, young man!"

The closer they had come to Earth, the better David felt about his thesis, and he no longer doubted his own feelings. Earth called out to him, and he felt blessed and confident that God had summoned him to prevent its destruction. From the moment they had entered orbit, David had felt the blessings of God upon this planet.

The Judge told him flatly that he had brought the blessings of God with him. He challenged David not to be a fool. True to his word, the Judge hounded David constantly, and everyone soon realized that the Judge expected David to find what he was seeking. Had he? Was the Little Smiler a gift from God? She filled him with terror, would tax his very being, draw out his humanity, and test his faith and obedience to God. She would tempt him. Yet, he could not believe her a demon. God had offered him as her teacher. She had sent him to God. Everyone seemed to have faith in him except himself. Perhaps, David was eating his words, and God was opening his eyes to see something that his heart would rather deny.

After seven days, his life fell into a routine, and his thoughts became a pattern repeated continuously. It was time to seek the will of God. As a man, he had run out of options. Warmly dressed, he stepped out about midday, faced south, and told God that he would watch the sun go down. He thrust out his chest, raised his arms to the heavens, and let them fall slowly to the horizon. He leaned his head back and watched his own breath freeze before his eyes. It was cold. Aware he would soon freeze to death, with determination, he closed his eyes and called, "Please Jarrock, speak to me. Guide me. I need your help."

Jarrock's voice came swiftly out of the wind. "Build a shelter, David. You are useless to me dead."

David laughed and felt a warm breeze around him that made him repeatedly glance at the sky, convinced that a temperature storm was reaching out to consume him. It took a little over an hour to build the shelter, but he did not get cold or tired because Jarrock was holding him, and the wind could not touch him. When he entered the shelter, it was bright with the presence of God. Obediently, David said, "I am here, my Lady, I am yours."

"Teach this child of mine, David. Teach her all that is dear to your heart."

"How?" David asked.

"Walk with her, tell her stories from your own heart, listen to her stories, give her your time, and be her friend. In time, David, you will understand and find comfort. You will know what to do, and I will be pleased. Trust me, David. I will not let you break her." Then God left David alone with a picture of the Little Smiler walking away from him. She turned and waved. He ran to her, held her, and laughing, she pointed to the sky.

"Yes, Littl'un," David said aloud, "the future is in the heavens." With the warmth gone from his hastily built snow shelter, David left and watched the sunset over the mountains. He looked down into the valley while the last rays of the sun warmed his cheeks. It was night already in the valley. It was time to go back to talk to the Judge. Jarrock and his friends would help him be the right kind of friend to the alien. The sun would rise each day, and his spirit would grow. God had blessed him, and he would not sin. David would obey and teach an alien to become of the Muki.

The Littl'un was right; the future would take care of itself. He had no more choice than had she.

12

THE WILL OF GOD, WILL COME TO BE

I LOOKED FOR DAVID NEITHER AFTER school nor when I went for walks. God kept me busy. A new family moved into the house behind ours, and a little girl needed a friend. She was only in grade three, but I played with her. It was not that hard to be a friend of someone half my age. I took great comfort in that thought. David was twice my age. She and I played school. I was the teacher. It was a very rewarding friendship. Her victories became my victories, and I felt very privileged. I thanked God for this lesson and hoped it meant that God was telling David it was okay to be my friend. I gained confidence that my big adult friend would agree to be my teacher.

Snow was on the ground. In only another week or two, David would be back. It was Friday. I had worked especially hard at gym class and, although needing one, did not want to shower. The showers in the girls' locker room were gross. I did not like the shower room. Closing my locker door, I decided to have a bath when I got home but was too hot and sweaty to put on my coat. Instead, I gathered my coat and books in one arm, picked up my boots in the other, and headed out the door. Feeling as though I had just stepped out of a sauna, I wanted to cool off in the snow. As the snow squished up between the toes of my bare feet, it felt heavenly. The crisp air on my cheeks and the sight of my breath freezing as I exhaled added to the delight of doing an unexpected thing. Although aware I was being naughty, I loved every moment of it and impishly wondered how far I could get before I would feel cold. If I ran, my feet felt only a delightfully hot stinging sensation while on the snow, but when I stood still, I would soon feel the chill seep in. This was living. I ran up the bank and began crossing the field. If I had not had my books and junk to carry, I would have done cartwheels or made snow angels. In my own little heaven, defying winter to slow me down, by the time I got to the alley and the corner, I had cooled down. I sat in the snow to pull on and lace up my boots. While I was busy with the laces, I heard a familiar voice, "Do not put them on on my behalf," followed by the full-hearted laugh of my friend.

Without even lifting my head, I retorted, "You are early. I did not expect to see you for at least another week!"

"Shall I continue on my way then?"

I looked up and smiled. David helped me with my coat and held my books while I did it up. I blushed. "I was hot when I left the gym. I am comfortable now. I am not cold. Besides, I did not run barefoot in the snow for you. You should try it. It feels wonderful," I said sarcastically while reaching for my books.

David just smiled and handed them to me, and together we walked up the alley. Although feeling silly for being caught being childish, I was somewhat glad too. I was just a kid, doing a kid thing, and I thought David understood that I was not trying to impress him or anyone else. I was doing my own thing because I always did my own thing and was a non-conformist. Probably, I went a little overboard with my antics, but a teenager is rebellious, right? One thing I was sure of is that I liked being who I was. I did things for myself and went to great pains to be unseen by others. I was not an exhibitionist. Creating my own world, I fought my own wars and loved the challenges life put in front of me every single moment of every day. So-called real life could not compete with the world I lived in.

"Was it not cold, Littl'un?"

"No! It was not cold, David. The snow feels like a stack of boiling needles sticking into your foot. I bet I would feel the same thing if I walked across a bed of red-hot coals."

"Make sure I am not around if you try that! You would burn your feet."

"How do you know? Have you tried it?"

"No. I love living too much."

"Well, I did not freeze or even get frostbite "I apologized silently to God for fibbing, I knew I had frostbite. "I feel wonderful, alive, and refreshed too. You are missing out on living."

"Who are you to judge my life, Littl'un?"

"You are afraid of life. You are even afraid of me, afraid to be my friend. David?"

"Yes."

"You are going to be my friend, aren't you?"

"Somebody has to keep you alive."

"Thanks, David. You won't regret it."

"Only one thing I ask, Littl'un."

Fearing the worst, I bit my lip and crossed my fingers. Again laughing, David rubbed his hand on my head. I had cut off all my hair. It was as short as boys' hair, and I loved it because it was freedom, but I got a strange feeling that David would have preferred that I would have left it long. Unsure of possible consequences, I stopped walking and gave David my full attention.

"You can do as you like when I am not around, but when I am, no climbing cliffs or trees, no jumping trains, no walking on ashes or anything else which will give me a heart attack. If there is any potential danger, you will ask me before you do something. Is that a deal?"

"You can get killed crossing the street, David. Breathing is dangerous," I answered before laughing. Then I smiled. "I can accept your terms," I said with a silly and kind of embarrassing giggle that I could not control.

"Good. Now tell me, what did you do to your hair? Burn it?"

"No, I had it cut off at the hairdressers. I paid for it myself."

"Why? You look like a boy!"

"Then you won't think I am a butterfly." I chuckled; I was teasing. I had not given David's thought on the matter any thought at all. "No, really, David. It is better this way. I do not have to comb it. It does not get in my way at gym. I just shake my head, and it is perfect. I like it like this."

"It suits you, Littl'un. May I ask that while you are my friend, you will not be anyone else's butterfly? You are special, Littl'un. Please, stay little, okay."

"I do not need a boyfriend. But someday, I will grow up, and maybe you'll want me to be your girl," I said without thinking, then blushed, unsure where to look.

"When your hair grows long again," answered David with a neat sound at the end which made me look at his smiling face.

"Deal," I replied, feeling as though I was on cloud nine.

The alley was too short today. I was back at home, and it was time to say goodbye to David. I asked, "When will I see you again?"

"Tomorrow afternoon, top of the hill, after lunch, say one o'clock."

"Sure. Thanks, David."

David asked, "What for?"

Laughing, I answered, "For coming back. You won't regret it."

"I am not so sure, Littl'un. However, I will teach you the best I can. Maybe I can make you of the Muki. It might be in our destinies."

That was how I became involved with the Muki. I could find nothing out about the Muki in the library. I read about cults and Indian tribes and still found nothing, but concluded that the only explanation for David was that he belonged to a religious cult of some kind, which had a Native American tone. I decided to see if my father knew anything about them. I liked discussions with my father but was not very impressed with his comments about cults. They were all useless traps to take the young and naive away from the mainstream of society. In short, they were bad things and something to avoid, like drugs and alcohol.

However, I was not about to stop walking with David. What he had to say was fascinating, and I spent every day waiting for the last bell so that I could meet him. I had made two very important oaths to myself. One, I was not going to introduce David to my folks or even talk about him or the Muki, and second, I would make it up to my folks by being especially good in all other matters. I hoped that would make me somewhat even. I knew until I was sixteen, a little more than two years away, I had no permission to date anyone. No matter what I wanted to call my walks with David, there were dates, even if we were not that kind of friends. He was a man, and I was a girl, and too young to spend time with such a person.

Keeping secrets from my family was not that hard. Since I was a very little child, I have frequently had religious visions and experiences, and speaking about them really upset my mother, who was afraid I was insane. Consequently, I had learned to keep these happenings to myself. After all, my association with David was clearly connected to God. God sent him as a friend, and I could not believe God would object to my disobedience, dishonesty, and disrespect of my parents' wishes and rules. I hoped my silence would not make me guilty of sinning big time. Being a loner also helped because none of my routines changed. As I had always searched out my own space, walking or biking at every opportunity and been gone from home for long periods of time, as long as I respected my curfews, did my chores, was not late for dinner, stayed out of trouble, and offered courtesies such as letting them know when to expect me home, my parents felt free time was my own. Although they wished I was more social, spent more time with friends, and was a little less of an oddball, they accepted me as I was, and I tried not to abuse their trust in all matters other than my association with David.

David seemed to understand. I think he, too, knew my culture forbade our relationship. In a way, David was no ordinary person either. He avoided other people just as I did, except that he often liked to watch people, which held no interest to me. David was a precious gift, and I held his friendship very dear. He quickly became a mentor, and I, an eager student in a school of far greater value than the one I spent most of my days attending. David taught me to see the world through an entirely different pair of eyes. He never took anything away from me. He gave me insight and challenged everything I believed in, my whole understanding of life, and my place in the universe. Yes, I came to love David in a very special and wonderful way. I loved him as a human being, not as a man.

This is David's and my story, and I want to share it. Read on, and perhaps you, too, will gain new faith and understanding of our place in the universe among the Muki.

13

A PLAN

JUDGE SORONATO WAS PLEASED, REASSURED, and relieved with the result of David's worship. God had not told David to break the known laws. He was to be a friend, not a mate to the alien. The plan was, therefore, simple. Constantly, David had to remind himself to be the kind of friend that God demanded. He had to give himself to Jarrock and conduct himself in the holy capacity of a teacher. Honoured, each member of the expedition wanted to help David. At the same time, they were afraid for him and guiltily glad he had the task rather than themselves. To represent God was simply too terrifying.

Mostly working with Judge Soronato, David developed a plan to determine where the little one was in her faith and build upon it, giving her the freedom to choose his faith or retain her own. He would not assume that she belonged to God. Only God wanted him to teach her about the Muki. God loved them both. Jarrock would protect her, so he did not need to fear his own actions, and his own confidence in the blessing of God upon his future convinced him that his future retained the opportunity to mate in a castle according to the traditions of the Land of the Butterflies. When he was with the Littl'un, he needed to be Jarrock, to love her as God loved her, not as a human.

David Miskenack, of the Muki, would obey his God, pray that Littl'un belonged to the same God, and do his duty as God's servant.

In the process, he might lose his humanity, even willingly. Yes, he would become a friend of an alien, a soulmate, and know that, in the end, he would cry, return to his own destiny, and she to hers.

14

THE LESSONS BEGIN

"IT IS FAITH THAT DEFINES people, Littl'un." began David on our next walk. "It would be very wrong of me if I destroyed your faith by promoting my faith, the faith of the Muki. Faith is not something that is right or wrong. It is a feeling, a sense of security, and comfort to the one who holds it dear to the heart. If what I say jars your faith, you must back away and be true to the faith that I see so strong within you. On the other hand, if the faith of the Muki feels comfortable and enhances your faith, embrace and assimilate it into your belief system. Littl'un, be cautious; I might lie to you, so be on guard, reject false words.

I will proceed to try to teach you on the basis that your God sent me to you, and my God advised me to rise to the challenge. Is my God and your God the same God?"

"There is only one God. They must be the same," I answered confidently.

"There is a better answer, Littl'un. Remember, you do not know whom I worship. Perhaps, I worship an idol. Do you know the better answer, Littl'un?"

I shook my head. "God would not call you a friend if you were evil."

"What if I tricked you into thinking that God was speaking to you and it was not God at all who introduced me to you?"

"I would have known. God talks to me all the time." More emphatically, I repeated, "I would have known. Besides, David, I saw you in a dream. You did not even know me! If you are a man, you could not plant dreams in my mind even if you could project your voice into the air around me."

"Well, Littl'un, you then have more faith than I, for my heart wants our God and our faith to be grounded in the same doctrine, but my being reminds me that you could be tricking me. My answer is maybe. Be on guard, Littl'un. Your destiny may not include the Muki. I could destroy who you are and who God wants you to become. Furthermore, you, Littl'un, have the power to destroy the Muki and me. I fear you. If you are wise, fear me, and weigh very carefully everything I tell you just as I will judge your answers."

David and I were tramping through fresh snow in no hurry to go anywhere, I listened. Thinking about David's lecture, I was even more convinced that we believed in the same God. Promising to think for myself, I said I would try to open the door to doubt.

"Good, Littl'un," he said and remained silent for a few minutes before he threw some snow in my face. He waited while I brushed it away before barking an order at me. "Define God, Littl'un."

"God just is, David. I cannot define God," I said after pausing for a few moments. Then David coached and prodded to get me to shed more light on what God was to me. I shrugged, and I scowled and eventually said, "God is the all-powerful creator who always was and always will be." David was still not satisfied.

Finally, I could take no more and demanded that David define his God to me. He laughed, and his eyes twinkled, and he gave me a look that confused me so much. Only he did not turn away and blush this time; he spoke clearly and confidently.

"God touches everything, but nothing can touch God. All of creation exists because of the will of God, and all that is or ever will be is because God ordained it to be so. All credit and all blame reside and originate in God. God is both nothing and everything. God has neither beginning nor end but is not static. God is dynamic, ever-changing, and ever-growing. Moreover, God is both powerless and powerful, independent and very dependent upon creation; and God is vulnerable. God's Kingdom could fail as easily as it could flourish."

I frowned and thought for a little while. "God is not powerless or weak. How can you say that?"

David's eyes twinkled, and smiling, he said, "Have you heard people say, 'you can lead a horse to water but cannot make him drink?'"

I nodded.

"Well, Littl'un, God can do no more than guide as well. If you refuse to follow God, God is powerless to make you. God could kill you, cajole you, plead, beg, and punish, but you are in control of what you are and of what you do."

I smiled. I understood. "My spirit is my own," I said and smiled.

"No, Littl'un, your spirit belongs to God. Your soul is your own."

I sighed, and David chuckled. "I won't go any farther today about souls and spirits. That is a whole other lesson. Tell me when you are ready for another definition of God."

"There is another?"

"Of course, there are many definitions, Littl'un."

"Okay, David, tell me another."

"All of creation is part of God. The sun in the sky and the planets revolving around it are integral and essential components of God. I shall give you an analogy to help you understand that God is dependent upon us as we are dependent upon God."

David talked, and I shamefully admit that I focused my attention on him rather than his words. He had shocked me, but for some reason, I figured that he was probably telling the truth. I began to think about other things that had shattered my world.

When I was a child, my whole world was close to home, and each year the boundaries seemed to stretch a little further afield. By the time I was in grade three, I had a vision of security in being Canadian, even North American. Trouble, pain, sorrow, and unrest were very far away from the world in which I lived. Then, the assassination of the President of the United States of America, John F. Kennedy, occurred. My whole sense of security died when my teacher announced the tragic event and followed it with a minute of silence. David's definition of God invoked the same feeling of terror and insecurity. I called these feelings, big people truths. I did not want to face the big world just yet. I wanted to think of God as all-powerful and always in control of every minute detail of everything in the universe, even if that sounded impossible.

Yet, I knew that God had rarely forced my hand. I had suffered for defying God, but God had always forgiven me, not invoked some magic to make me obedient. My obedience was my own. I did not want to be obedient, and that fact within my own relationship with God was blatantly clear at that moment. Forced to conclude David was not lying to me. The world was not as God would have it because most people were like me, independent and fiercely proud and protective of their independence, even from God.

I must admit that I did not hear most of David's lecture, but it was a story about how the solar system we lived in is an atom of God. The sun was the nucleus and the planets were electrons, positrons, or neutrons, which made up a physical component of God's body. The life, which existed on Earth, was akin to a chromosome of God. We were an imprint. We had a job and a duty to perform to sustain God and let the Kingdom of God grow and bloom. If we were not obedient to God, we risked becoming a cancer that could destroy our world and all of God's creation.

It was a very heavy and frightening analogy. It did frighten me. I wanted to think of being neither so powerful nor so insignificant. Seeking escape, I daydreamed, picturing David as a knight in shining armour protecting me from the real world. He stopped talking and laughed, before chuckling, "I have lost you, Littl'un."

I blushed. "Yes, David. I do not want to believe what you are saying. I am just a kid, and I like to feel secure and do not want to take a guilt trip. It is too depressing."

Pulling me close, David laughed while he hugged me. It felt so good that I would have stayed in his arms forever. I think David liked to hold me too, for he was in no hurry to back away. Internalizing the calm reassurance emanating from David, I felt a special kind of comfort restoring into my world. I was not alone, and the world did not rest on my shoulders.

After what seemed a very long time, David put his hands on my shoulders and kissed my forehead. "God will protect you, Littl'un. God asks from you no more than you can accomplish with ease. We need only to listen and be obedient to God. God is without neither compassion nor lacking in patience. Even if you were to fail in your obedience today or tomorrow, still in time, you will fulfil the destiny that God has set before you. God will guide you and protect you every step of your journey."

While looking deeply into my eyes, David waited a while longer in silence before, with both a serious expression and a no arguing tone, he said, "It is time to take you home."

We turned toward home, and David walked in silence beside me.

Often, we planned our meetings. However, sometimes our meeting seemed more like happenstance. David did not talk about the definition of God again all winter long. Instead, he returned to continue talking about the ground beneath my feet, the sky above my head, and the light. When freezing our walk was only a block long, from the corner where I had first met him to the top of the hill of the back alley where I lived, except on weekends. On weekends, David would take me somewhere in his truck. We would talk while he drove off into the bush, first one way and then another. Occasionally, we went snowmobiling but more often just watched the world of winter unfold, marvelling at the ground beneath our feet, the sky above our heads, and the light that let us experience it all.

I got very good at answering David's many questions. I knew that my wealth was in the ground beneath my feet, my security and my future were in the sky above me, and that my destiny and strength were in the light that God bathed me in every day of my life. Strangely, I felt I had always known these things to be true.

Before meeting David, I had faith in God and had always searched for my future in the heavens above me. If I got high enough, I was even more convinced that I would really be able to see the future. God had been teaching me lessons on firmly being grounded, and David's lectures filled me with pride, comfort, and security.

David had not kissed me again since I had told him I was not ready for his definition of God. He would rarely touch me in any way at all. If I said something that amused him, he might ruffle my hair or push me down into the snow and wash my face with a gloved hand full of cold snow. However, he kept his distance, and I respected his wish to ensure that we were the right kind of friends. I had turned fourteen, became a volunteer at the local hospital, and occasionally worked for my father, filing invoices once a week and helping with inventory when that job made its annual demand that every nut and bolt be counted. I was growing up and carving out a place in the world for myself. David seemed proud of me and often said something that hurt because I thought he was thinking of me as a daughter or frightened me because he loved me as a human being and maybe even a girlfriend.

As the snow melted, I tolerated David naming all the plants and animals that lived where we walked. Spring had come, and soon the mud dried. Our walks became very relaxed, and we, or at least I, forgot about learning and just enjoyed one another's company and the beautiful world in which we lived. We paddled a canoe in rivers and lakes, rode bicycles occasionally, but mostly walked close to my home or off in the wilderness, having driven to some spot an hour or two from Quesnel. David would go away for a while every couple of months, usually for a week or two but occasionally for a whole month.

After one such absence, I realized that David was much more serious about teaching me something valuable than merely sharing time together. One day, looking pleased and satisfied as we walked along the railway tracks out by the Cottonwood River Bridge on the highway north of Quesnel, he said, "I think we are ready to go on, Littl'un. I have a question for you. What do you need to survive?"

I did not give any thought to my answer. I had been answering this kind of question in school. I quickly said, "Food, water, and shelter."

Groaning, David stamped his feet. His face contorted in anger and frustration. Frightened, I had never seen David so upset before, and I started to cry. After apologizing, he remained quiet for some time. I was quiet, too. I was afraid of making matters worse and thought it best just to wait until David spoke again. I watched him. Slowly, he calmed down.

David could never hide his feelings from me. His face, and even his gate, gave away his inner thoughts. Gravely disappointed in me, he was composing his thoughts on how to proceed. David would never hurt me, and I knew that. However, he still knew he had frightened me and was angry with himself for doing so. Eventually, he stopped walking. Turning to me, he very calmly asked, "What have I been teaching you this last year?" Slowly shaking his head, he asked, "Nothing? What have you been doing all this time?" Again, he shook his head and stared at me.

I think I blushed for David blushed and looked very nervous. I whispered, "I think, David, that maybe, I have been falling in love with you."

David let tears fall down his cheek and uttered, "I am failing. I cannot even teach what is most dear to my heart." Then he looked away. I do not think David wanted me to know he was crying. I felt terrible, but I did not feel guilty. As we headed to his truck and back to town, there was a terrible tension and silence in the air. Neither of us spoke. When we arrived back in Quesnel, we stopped at the water tower and walked along the alley together. Very quietly, David said, "I will see you tomorrow, Littl'un. Maybe, I will know what to say then." Then he turned and walked quickly away.

As I watched him go, I regretted that I had opened my mouth at all. Then, I sat in the grass in my backyard and did nothing for a very long time. I had no idea why I had said that I loved him. I did and did not think there was anything wrong with loving David. He was my friend, and I thought I loved him as a friend. I did not dream about sex. That thought was gross. I liked to be near David and particularly liked to watch him while he talked because he was full of emotion. His words were alive. I could feel whatever he was feeling, and I was not on drugs. Sometimes, I giggled that I was high on life, but there was nothing artificial about David or dirty about our relationship. I was only fourteen.

I thought David might be thinking I wanted our relationship to change. Admittedly, part of me did. Part of me wanted David to touch me. Not to have sex, but I liked the memory of his first and only kiss. A shiver of ecstasy went through me whenever David's hand brushed against mine, and I longed for him to hold me in his arms. I did recognize that David needed me to be a kid and not a woman, but at that moment, out on the tracks earlier in the day, I guess I had wanted to be a woman and grown-up. Even I could not deny that. David knew the intent behind those words far better than I had when I said them. I was kidding myself. Unfortunately, I was growing up and had probably lost a very good friend by speaking without thinking of the consequences of my words before opening my mouth.

That night, I cried myself to sleep, but in the morning, I knew what I had to do. Gathering my money, I happily headed to school. At lunch, I ran over to Derbana's and had her chop off my hair as short as she dared. I did not want to lose my friend, and I rehearsed the right answer to David's question all afternoon. I prayed, too, that David would forgive me and remain my friend.

15

INNER STRUGGLES

THAT DAY OUT ON THE tracks marked a critical turning point in David and my relationship. If you allow me to regress a moment, I will tell it again from David's perspective and then carry on with its consequences.

It was early evening. The sun was staying up much longer than it had only weeks ago, but David and his Littl'un would have to head back toward town very soon. Having brought Littl'un out to the trails beyond the Cottonwood River Bridge, David had shown her the canyon from the east side. There were still patches of snow among the trees, and they talked about the hollows where a whole herd of deer had been spending nights. Littl'un had cried over the cougar kill on the other side of the highway just before the turn-off. Few people came here other than during hunting season, yet the trails were well marked and frequented by both man and beast. He had hoped they would spot the cougar.

Littl'un had a sad imbalance in her vision of the rights and wrongs of life. Neither evil nor cruel, the cougar had not wronged the deer. How could he explain the love of God for creation? Death is a gift the Muki held very dear because it released the spirit and meant freedom. There was something beyond death, something more glorious than physical life. Honoured by the cougar, the deer had sacrificed itself out of respect for God's creation. Thereby, it fulfilled its duty. The cougar had not toyed with it, death had been swift, and the deer had not suffered. A war of survival had been won, not lost; because of the sacrifice of the deer, both the cougar and the other deer would watch another sunset. This scene was an example of the beauty of creation. The balance of physical life in a dynamic environment ensured a future for all physical life upon Earth and movement down the line of an infinity of this world.

Arguing with him, Littl'un told him he would fight his own death, and David knew that was very true to a point at least. While there is a choice, one is bound to choose what he knows and is familiar with over the unknown. It is our nature. Before we step into the future, our spirit demands that we fulfill our destiny. Littl'un had fallen quiet for a while, and David had felt confident that God was guiding their conversation. It seemed the perfect time to move on in teaching the Little Smiler more of the Muki. They returned to the railway tracks and were about a mile north of the trail back to the truck.

Littl'un always walked on the rails, which David still had not mastered sufficiently to keep up with her, so he walked between them, constantly adjusting his gate to the uneven spacing of the ties. He had looked to the sky; the sun was bright, and he felt loved and, oh, so blessed. David sighed as he watched Littl'un walk without even looking at the rails. She was so confident yet so innocent. That old feeling welled up inside him, demanding that he protect her. Struck with the stark reality of being in an alien environment and overwhelmed by his need to carry out the responsibilities and duties his culture had taught him but forbidden him to express, he fought back his desire to hold her hand as she began to run. David had laughed, caught up with her, and said, "Let's start a new lesson." Like magic, she had stopped, turned back to him, and smiled up to him, obviously happy to listen.

It was a good day to begin teaching the philosophy of creation. David was confident that Littl'un now had the foundation to build upon, However, felt confirmation was the best place to begin.

Then Littl'un had shocked him so deeply. Becoming so angry and lost in frustration with his failure to succeed in giving her the foundation of the Muki, David believed he had failed miserably.

Although not aimed at her purposefully, expressing his anger had frightened her. David's whole world had tumbled down upon him. Overcome with sorrow for making his Tara cry; he could say nothing right. While he lashed out, she had not run. Instead, she had stood her ground and, as bravely and truthfully as Tara always spoke, announced that she loved him. David had known neither what to say nor what to do. Partly filled with joy, the other tore him apart with a terrible sense of guilt. Wanting to cry and hold his Tara, the Little Smiler, in his arms, he denied the impossibility of alien life forms becoming mates. He had done the only thing he could do. He had taken her home and said goodbye.

Believing Tara was wise and very powerful, David was sure that if she had light in her skin, like the Muki, she would have shone with the presence of God. Her whole being forbade him leaving, and she had given him no choice but to promise to think for the night and meet her again the next day. Could there be more to the foundation of his faith? Was there something besides the ground, the sky, and the light? Was it not true that love was even more sacred? Was Littl'un teaching him?

David knew it was true. He did not think of love as separate but integral to the formula. One cannot talk about the Muki without talking about love. David knew he had been expressing his own love. However, he had not considered that in the process, he had taught Tara to love him rather than creation. With great pain, David realized that his lessons had taught her to be his and captured her in his own web rather than giving her the faith of the Muki.

Without knowing right from wrong, good from bad, his whole being was torn. David was full of so many conflicting emotions that he felt about to explode. Feeling over his head, he was drowning in something that he had never felt before. His sight was full of visions of his Tara, smiling and beckoning. What she wanted of him was so wrong, so sinful. His guilt overwhelmed him.

Later, when Muma Horren had met him as usual when the transporter had arrived back at the base, she looked at him with such disgust that David broke down, sent Muma Horren away, and went directly to the Judge. Desperately, he had needed help. Despite all the efforts the Muki made to be God-like, they were still painfully human. David hated himself for wanting to sin, especially because, all these months, he had always tried so hard to behave respectfully toward the Little Smiler. He had followed Muma Horren's advice to refrain from even touching her hand in case that unleashed a flood of emotions, which could demand fulfillment. Failure stung David, and he needed to know that love awaited somewhere in his future.

The Judge was a man he respected. Without blaming him for exposing him to the dangers of interacting with an alien species, no matter how similarly human, David had known the risks and had taken them willingly. The understanding and depth of research gleaned from direct interaction with the aliens had benefited the expedition enormously. Judge Soronato had never demanded that he continue teaching the Little Smiler. Furthermore, it was also obvious that the Judge loved Natthia and would likely understand what was happening and possibly be able to direct him. Muma Horren only pitied him and was angry that the Judge had permitted this to happen. She could not help him today. David had also needed the protection of the security of Judge Soronato's office.

16

PLEASE SAY GOOD-BYE

"I HAVE TAUGHT HER NOTHING, NOTHING at all. I have failed miserably. I have tricked her into loving me as I love her. She does not see me as her angel. How could Littl'un have said that she loved me? I tried so hard to be the right kind of friend." David ranted as he paced in Judge Soronato's office on Thursday evening.

While he sipped on hot cider, the Judge let David spill his anguish. Soon David would cry, and then they would be able to talk a little more rationally. Thinking about all the little victories David had told him over the months, the Judge remembered Natthia had told him that the alien loved David long ago. They had worried a little about its meaning but assumed he realized it and was wisely holding it in check as he did his own love for the little alien and therefore did not bring it to his attention. In fact, He had spent so many hours crying over his own need to express his love for the Little Smiler so often that Muma Horren always met the transporter each evening David was to visit the alien.

Before meeting Judge Soronato each day, Muma Horren encouraged and helped David deal with his forbidden love. She always reminded him that loving Tara was natural and a blessing. Yet, God did not want him to express that love as a human because it could have no future and would destroy the coming Kingdom of God. She reminded him that he needed to recognize his own love as the love that God shared with all of creation.

Often David would glow with the presence of God, and the four of them (Muma Horren, Natthia, David, and the Judge) would talk together for an hour or more in the conscious presence of God. It had been a wonderful experience, but today, David had fallen apart when he saw Muma Horren and sent her away before running to Judge Soronato's office to pace, cry, and yell in the company of only another man.

David's talk of love made the Judge feel guilty. He knew what David was saying because he loved Natthia and did not think he could walk away from her even if God asked him. Amazed and pleased with the strength of David's faith and obedience to God, the Judge felt sick for David, who had been so strong up to now. Amazingly, David did not need the Judge to tell him it was time to say goodbye. That fact was blatantly clear as he ranted about hating his own humanity and how hard it had been to restrain himself from holding the Little Smiler, dancing with her, and claiming her as his own.

Because there was something special and endearing about the alien, her stories, and her island kingdom, the Judge had kept as many of the expedition as was feasible away from David. Like David, others privy to her had felt love for her and believed her a special woman, a child of God, and an instrument of change. They had come to call her Tara of Earth. By all accounts, she appeared to be an attentive student, and the faith of the Muki had not fought with her own faith. They had felt a kindred spirit, and it had frightened them all. David must have caught her off guard because she had demonstrated many times in the last weeks that, without any doubt, she knew what she needed to survive. Therefore, the Judge concluded her answer of food, water, and shelter must have been a signal from God.

Having argued well for permission to discuss the Muki philosophy about building the Kingdom of God, David had been prepared to teach the girl more of the Muki. The Judge had prayed for guidance, and God had only answered yesterday. The Judge smiled with the revelation that God was pleased and David's assignment complete. Through David and Tara, God had fulfilled the goal of the expedition. The Judge felt he could complete his judgement. It was the will of God for the Muki to love Earth. Simply to love them, and in time, Earthlings would contribute to building the Kingdom of God. Holding a different piece, this was where their worlds diverged.

Turning his attention back toward David, who was on the verge of tears, Judge Soronato figured it was time to snap him out of his self-pity and indulgence. "Enough, Judge Miskenack, sit down and drink your cider in silence," he said very coldly.

In shock at his harshness and lack of compassion for his anguish, David stopped and, for a moment, stared at Judge Soronato. Disappointed because he had thought the Judge would understand, he sat with an ashen face, realizing the Judge was not pleased with him either. Sighing, he picked up the mug of steaming cider the Judge had poured for him.

"Yesterday, God instructed me to let you proceed with your lessons, David. Although worried about the meaning and long-term ramifications of this task God has put before you, I believe that God is pleased, David. You have done what God asked, and now it is time for you to say goodbye to Tara of Earth. It is love, David, that God wanted the two of you to teach us all. We are to love Earth. Perhaps circumstance and fate have misled Earthlings, but they do know God, and their destiny holds a piece of the Kingdom of God. They are important, and we cannot destroy them, at least, not now."

David turned very pale. Despite valiantly trying, he could not hold his composure and cried out as though an arrow had pierced his heart.

Perhaps, he had found his Doleran. After all, the Judge had lived through this sense of failure and grown because of it. The Judge had permitted him to let off steam, hate being human, and even question the wisdom of God and the Judge in permitting his own pain. David felt privileged and blessed as his tears came even though his pain was great and the future bleak. The Judge had sat at his desk, patiently sipping cider and offering only his presence throughout it all. For some reason, which David could only call holy, it had worked, and he found inner peace. Grabbing it, the Judge had shocked him to realize that God had blessed, not condemned him.

Feeling ill-equipped to handle the situation and believing they would know how to comfort David, the Judge quietly left his office to fetch Muma Horren and Natthia. The Judge could not help but feel a twinge of anger that God would have needed to hurt David and Tara so much to teach such a simple basic message. Being human pained him. Even with the gifts of Koe Sai Serena, the Muki were still blind. They did not want to recognize these aliens as worthy of God's love. They and their customs were so vulgar, so disgusting that they were more evil than good. Yet, God forgave them and loved them as much as any of the Muki. God was so hard to understand.

Tears were in his own eyes as he found first Natthia then Muma Horren and returned with them to his office where David cried. By simply sitting beside him and holding his hand, Natthia supported the Judge while Muma Horren sat beside David and comforted him. Muma Horren began to sing, her voice soothing to them all. Tonight, all those most closely involved with Tara of Earth, even though only one had ever met her, openly acknowledged their love for her and the tiny world she wanted so desperately to save that she allowed God to give her a friend. A friendship sadly doomed by the very destinies of the two of them from the very beginning. As Muma Horren's voice soothed the Judge, the thought of hearing no more stories of Tara of Earth hurt him deep in his heart, and he knew David must be broken. Glancing at Natthia, he suddenly wondered if saying good-bye would kill David. Natthia's eyes seemed to be voicing the same fear. Unprepared for forbidden love, the Muki did not know what price God would extract.

When Muma Horren stopped singing, David took a deep breath and stood very tall before them. "Please, Sir. I do love my Tara. I do not know how to say goodbye to her, but I understand that I must. Please, could we celebrate a thanksgiving ritual? To be loved is holy, and I have been blessed."

"Eat first, David. We shall celebrate together after dinner. To prepare ourselves, we shall all eat in silence." After a brief pause, he stated, "Excellent thought, son. A thanksgiving ritual is appropriate."

David appeared wise and strong with this first positive thought of the last hour and a half, and in it, the Judge envisioned hope for

David Miskenack. He might be able to find a future without the alien and, to do so, needed strength, and this was the right note to pause on to get a meal into him. A thanksgiving ritual would probably leave him enlightened but too exhausted to eat. Natthia's smile confirmed that at least she saw the wisdom in getting David to eat first. That was a comfort. If this goes well, he might even consider letting the others resume interactions with more of the aliens.

The four of them sat together at a table in the kitchen. They all took generous portions, and David even managed to smile and laugh giddily. The only sign that something was amiss was the glassy look in his eyes, which betrayed his efforts to refrain from crying.

Mark walked over to the table near the end of their meal, and David immediately began to shake. Although the Judge quickly sent Mark away, David could not regain his hold on his emotions and quietly left the table. Natthia followed David and sat with him in his room.

The Judge explained the situation to the worried expedition members, and Muma Horren stayed to comfort the young judges who were afraid for the health of their comrade.

Natthia held David in her arms and let him cry on her shoulder. When he succeeded in banishing his tears, he suddenly laughed and smiled at Natthia. "Hey Doc, you are in my room! Will wonders ever cease, a Muki female entering the room of a young man... this world has taught us to break tradition. Please do not tell me we are losing sight of God!"

Natthia laughed and even blushed. As a doctor, it was her duty to comfort him, and she knew what was happening to him. She noticed David's skin had begun to glow. Standing back from him, she watched him carefully while analyzing the possible meaning of what he had just said.

The Mukis are spiritual people who live to serve and follow a visible God. Thousands of years before, they had been on the brink of extinction, and God had sent her daughter, Koe Sai Sarena, to save and teach them to be Instruments of Creation. Through the gifts Koe Sai Sarena gave them, they could perceive and understand God's will.

When God dwelled within them, their skin lit up, as do electric eels or fireflies and some other species do on Earth; they had something like a diode in their flesh. When God was directing or supportive of an individual's words, actions, or thoughts, that person would shine with a soft halo of light. God's will would be revealed and visible to all who God wished to witness the aura. God, with awesome power, dictated the direction and foretold future events or consequences. The aura had meaning, and it was God's will that would prevail. When Natthia observed David shining with the aura of God, she received visions of the future and instruction from God. While David glowed before her, Natthia understood that Judge Soronato and David's response, rooted in cultural traditions that demanded him to turn away from temptation and remain on a righteous path, was not according to the will of God. She realized that God would not allow David to walk away from Tara. His job was incomplete, and soon both David and the Judge would realize that the relationship begun according to God's will was not about to end, and David was not going to say goodbye to Tara. The expedition was going to step beyond known traditions, and under the direction of their dynamic visible God, they would follow into the unknown as loyal servants. God was taking this expedition beyond tradition, invoking new thoughts, ideas, responses, and truths that would permanently change the future and hold them on the path of God toward building the Kingdom of God. God worked in mysterious ways, and tradition could not stop them regardless of how unorthodox the demands of God were. As Instruments of Creation, the Muki was duty-bound to heed the will of God.

David may not realize it himself, but Natthia clearly understood that his relationship with the alien was not going to end, David would not say goodbye to Tara of Earth, and God approved. Judge Soronato was wrong. David's task was only beginning. God wanted more than the recognition that Earth held members of his flock and was to be loved. Natthia went very pale, and tears fell down her cheeks while David stood before her, held in the love of God.

She whispered, "Help me support him, Jarrock," then put her arms around David and kissed his forehead.

David whispered, "Thank you, Natthia." Then backed away from her and sat upon his bed.

Natthia turned to leave, "When you are ready to celebrate a ritual of thanksgiving with us, David, come to the Judge's office. There will be room there."

"I won't be long. I just need to take a shower." Then with a sense of urgency in his voice, he very quietly and sadly said, "Natthia, help me plan a way to say goodbye to Tara. I do not think I can do it, especially not alone."

"Certainly, David," Natthia calmly replied as she opened his door and walked out. To herself, she said, "I will make sure David does not lose his ray of sunshine. He may break every law in the book, but he will die happy, not broken. Love is more valuable than is anything else. I know. I love Josh." Her own light began to shine, and Natthia felt the eyes of the expedition watch her as she crossed the wide hall to Judge Soronato's office.

After the celebration, only Muma Horren scowled at Natthia when she supported David's plan to say good-bye on Tara's Island. If there had not been the remnants of a soft glow on both David and Natthia's skin throughout the ritual, which had lingered while they discussed a plan of action for the following day, Muma Horren would have objected. The Judge looked innocent. He did not know that the plan was doomed to failure, and with a sigh, Muma Horren said only, "Focus your mind on your destiny, David. Remember what you want for your own future. Someday, you will have the opportunity to enter a castle if you do what you know you must. Please, David, do not forget who you are."

"Thank you, Muma Horren. I will remember," answered David sincerely.

The thanksgiving ritual he performed with Natthia, Muma Horren, and the Judge finally eased his pain. David had been able to plan a special meeting with his Tara. She had given him a wonderful gift that he would carry with him the rest of his days. She was his, but he would not sin. David would summon the strength of the grey sentry for himself, and with the promise to protect the Island Kingdom, he would turn away from Tara of Earth and return to the security of the Muki. Littl'un was young. In time, she would forget him, and if she could not, David would bring her to Natthia, and Natthia would help her forget.

17

ALL I NEED

I WAS AFRAID THAT DAVID WOULD not show up to walk me home. It was Friday, and he usually met me at the corner after gym. When I did not see him, I almost gave up and walked home after kicking dirt for what had seemed a very long eternity. However, he came, took one look at my hair, and laughed. It felt good to hear that laugh. He rubbed my almost bald head and said, "Thank you, Littl'un."

"I know the right answer to your question, David. All I need to survive is the ground beneath my feet. For in the ground is my wealth and all the material I need to fill my belly, rest my head, and warm my bones. I need the sky above me, too. It provides the rain to quench my thirst and the air that sustains my life. The sky holds time for all things. In it, my destiny will unfold. And, David, to survive, I need one other thing, the light of God shining upon me, growing within me, and through me, such that all that is meant to be can come to pass."

David did not say a word. He smiled, and tears fell down his cheek. At the top of the alley, he kissed my forehead and said, "Goodbye, Littl'un."

In a panic, I grabbed hold of his hand, saying, "Promise me that I will see you again. I did answer correctly. I know I did. Please, David."

"You did answer very well. We are planning with fire, Littl'un. You've become a butterfly."

"I cut my hair, David. I will not let it grow. I will keep it short. I do not want to lose our friendship."

Looking as though he might hug me but would not allow himself to do so, he sighed and said, "I will see you tomorrow afternoon, Littl'un. I will think about it some more." As David turned away, I let a tear fall and heard a heart-wrenching sound escape my lips. My world was crumbling. Needing David, I would do anything to unsay what I had said the day before. However, it had not been a lie, and I could not deny my own feelings. As he walked away, I cried, wondering if David had taught me the lesson that God had sent him to teach. God was silent on the matter. I was alone. For the first time in my life, I felt lonely.

Fear began to dominate my thoughts, and I became angry with God and the whole world. I had nothing physical of David's, only memories. I remembered a conversation about pictures. David had become angry and said, "Life is to be lived, not recorded, Littl'un. All that matters will be held here." Making a fist, he had tapped it against the left side of his chest. Everything important, David kept in his heart.

I had a terrifying dream that night. I dreamt that David was an angel, and I would never see him again. Just like the day when God had told me that a friend was about to arrive, I found solace through the night holding a doll and clinging to childhood. God and His plans were simply too terrifying, and the world of make-believe had far greater security to offer that night.

Saturday afternoon took forever to arrive. I waited for David on the old trail. Since the construction of the new stairs that came out on the top of Kinchant Street, few people have used the old trail above the back alley. About halfway down, there was a crooked tree, which was comfortable to sit on. If you sat just right, you could see the river through the branches. It was close enough to the tracks that as a train whistled by, it would shake. I closed my eyes and pictured David. With gratitude, I realized he had left me something after all. He was safely stored in my own heart. He was a friend, and I began to tremble as a little voice inside me affirmed that he would not abandon me.

I heard him before I saw him. David often whistled or chanted lyrics in his own language. I smiled and waited to take a picture of him with the camera inside me to add to those stored in the album in my heart. David stopped singing when he came into view, took my hand, and led me to Beaver Pond. As David climbed up onto the big old log and began crossing to the island, I was shocked because he hated such things. The last twinge of fear that he was leaving faded away because I knew that David was telling me he was staying around. Our friendship was secure.

We sat by the river in my favourite spot and, in silence, watched the river flow by. With David holding my hand, I was in heaven. He was deep in thought, and I was never going to open my mouth or even move in case I destroyed the perfection that I felt just being there with him. While he cried, David looked at my hand without making a sound. His tears fell onto my hand, and he carefully wiped them away. He wanted to say goodbye, but I knew he could not and had confidence that David would soon realize that our God is the same and our destinies connected. Although I wanted to brush his tears away, I knew it would be wrong.

Slowly, David regained his composure and stared out into the river. He put an arm around me, and I felt a tremble go through my whole being when David shuddered, then sighed, let go of my hand, stood up, and headed toward the other side of the island. I quickly scrambled after him. I desperately needed him to say something.

David turned back toward me. He looked nervous and whispered, "Your hair grows slowly, Littl'un. Maybe, you could start to let it grow. I know I could not stay away even if I tried. I would miss you too much."

Turning very pale and falling onto his knees, he covered his face as though he realized what he had said. I walked over to him and touched his shoulder. My own tears clouded my vision, and I did not know what to say. All my fears of David leaving me behind and carrying on with his own life separate from my own came rushing back into my consciousness. Therefore, I said nothing. Silently, I prayed that God would guide us. I was just a child, and these feelings were far too grown-up for my fourteen years. David was twenty-seven and old enough to know that I was too young for him.

"Oh, Littl'un, my little Tara, I must seek guidance. I shall worship tomorrow," he said almost sadly.

"Please, David let me come with you," I begged. Nodding, David rose to his feet, then told me to meet him at the corner of Wilson Street and McNaughton Avenue early in the morning and bring a picnic lunch. In silence, we headed home. Walking near him seemed almost normal except that he was still upset and distant. I had questions awaking in my mind that I would have liked to ask but was afraid that I might cause David to change his mind and leave. We headed up the cliff, and he stopped at the top to say goodbye as I continued toward my house. Until I was at the garage door, I did not look back. David was just in sight. Before walking away, he smiled, raised his arms to the heavens, and then, in a blink of an eye, disappeared into the dark among the trees.

Mom would not expect me home for another hour, but I went inside anyway. I wished I could talk to her to gain some advice and guidance but knew that I would be slamming the door on ever seeing David again if I did so because I was a few years short of being allowed a boy-friend. Furthermore, I was beginning to contemplate running away with David, to wherever it was he went once a month, never to come back. My biggest concern was whether David would let me come. Worried that my parents would chase after me and have David sent to jail for kidnapping or something, I needed help from that imp who lived inside me. I was treading water and had too much to lose to risk error and had to remain silent.

Knowing there was more to the Muki than the ground, sky, and light, I still thought David was Native American. The way he talked and thought reminded me of stories and myths I had read. For David, everything was alive and had a spirit. Not in a hurry, David, like other Natives I knew, took the time to see and appreciate the environment around him and noticed everything within it. David recognized that living was a journey, not just a series of destinations. He looked native, too, especially in the sunlight.

My world was very different. Even the world that I created for myself was not like David's world. One thing was very clear. David and I were culturally alien to each other. I loved him, and I was convinced that David loved me, too. What we needed was a way to define the love that would protect our relationship and help us let it comfort us both without leading into the taboo and something too great to handle. Despite wanting to play with fire, I did not want either of us to burn.

18

LOVE IS GREATER THAN LAW

A S WITH ALL PLANS OF man, David had failed miserably. He could not deny his humanity. Tara had a hold over him. While beside Tara, watching the river flow over the old truck, he had realized how trapped he was. He had needed to run, and it was too late. If he opened his mouth, none of his words would have been goodbye. He had risen to run. Tara had stopped him. The words had tumbled out of his soul. She was his sunshine. He needed her as he needed God. His love was that great. Although he had tried and failed to say goodbye, he had felt very right in promising to take her to worship with him. At that moment, David had felt connected to the Littl'un. For now, their Lines of Infinity were joined, their destinies connected, and although terrifying, it had felt good, not sinful.

David had met his Tara and told her he could not leave her. Upon his return to the base, he had gone directly to Judge Soronato's office.

They met for only a short time. The Judge was terrified at what God might tell the two lovers, but his faith held him firmly. Forbidding David to break his promise to Tara, and regardless of how frightened David was, he ordered him to leave all thought of worship to God, get a good sleep, and prepare to stand, not alone or as two unique individuals but as a single entity before God. God would recognize them as one and guide their future. Whatever happened, God's blessings would be upon them both. Affirming David had found his Doleran, the Judge told David there was no turning away now. Only God could guide the expedition.

Determined not to give his people cause to shun him, David felt the Judge was right to banish his doubts and force him to be true to his word. Confident God would guide them, David and Littl'un would heed God, and all would be good and wonderful. As the Judge believed, his lessons were complete, Muma Horren would be relieved, and Natthia's words would ring true. It was better to have loved and lost than never to have known love. God would bless their love for one another, and if necessary, Natthia would ease their pain when the time was right.

If David had not told them that he would worship with Tara, Muma Horren would have accused Natthia of sin. As it was, both Natthia and the Judge saw the righteousness of the result, and Muma Horren struggled with her own heart to find forgiveness. Just maybe, Natthia did know what she was doing. Perhaps, her encouragement was righteous. Muma Horren prayed that it was so but could not help but fear the future. God might bless David and Tara. Then what would happen? Shuddering at the possibility, Muma Horren set off to her room.

Feeling a strong need to give her charge, Brian, a lecture, Muma Horren knew she could not protect David, but she would try to protect his little brother. Not for the first time, she worried about the wisdom of having come along on this assignment because Judge Soronato had a reputation for being unorthodox, and this was no place to train a boy. Brian should be safe in the security and constancy of the city, at home on the Land of the Butterflies. It had been wrong to let adventure lure her into bringing him into the heavens. There would be a price extracted, of that Muma Horren was now guiltily convinced.

19

TO WORSHIP WITH
A FRIEND

Astonishingly, I slept well until morning dawned with a clear blue sky. I liked the promise that I felt this Sunday. Although it was still very early in the morning, I ate breakfast. As no one else was up, I wrote a note to my mom telling her I was going for a bike ride, promised to be back by suppertime, packed a lunch, and quietly slipped out the back door. Confident that today would be special, I felt calm and ready to worship with my friend. God had sent David to be my friend, and I did not believe that God would intend for our friendship to end in pain and loneliness. As I rode down the alley and across the school grounds, I clung to that belief. David still had a lot to teach me, and I was willing to try to learn whatever lessons he could impart.

I had never seen anyone worshipping outside of a church. I thought of what happened in church as praying and thought there was something more to worship. I became excited as I neared my destination because my dad had built the little grey house on the corner around the time my brother was born. When I was three, we had moved, and I remembered very little about living on this street but had a strange sensation that meeting David near my old house somehow connected my path with his.

Having David walk on the ground holding my roots made me believe our futures would join as he guided me into the world of the

Muki. I was probably just crazy. After all, I did have a crack in my skull. However, since David told me about the ground beneath my feet, I had experienced tingling, like shivers, creeping up into the bottom of my feet and seeping up my legs to my heart as David and I walked over some special places. The grass around the tree my parents had planted in the front yard of the house that my father had built was one of those places. Waiting here for David felt wonderful. When David drove around the corner to pick me up, he stopped, hopped out, and came around the front of the truck to open the door for me, which made me feel special, but I always sat right by the window. Conscious we were not that kind of friends, he did not let me slide over to sit close to him. I wondered if that would change, then touched my head and did not worry about it. For today, and many days to follow, my short hair would remind us that I was just a kid spending time with a good friend and our relationship would remain innocent.

David set my bike in the back beside his snowmobile, and I wondered where we were going. It was late in May, and the snow was long gone. We headed to the highway. At the airport, he turned toward Barkerville. Barkerville was higher than Quesnel and tended to be cold even in the summer. I was glad I had worn a sweater. Today would be an adventure.

Although I tried not to, I watched David. Both of us were comfortably quiet. Driving and probably organizing his thoughts for worshipping, he was likely determining what it meant to have me along today. I simply could never get enough of just looking at him.

After crossing the Cottonwood River and driving up the first hill, David broke the silence. "I have never worshipped in the presence of any other than God, Littl'un. Please do not laugh. I am nervous and will need your help. This is very serious. I do love you, but I am terrified. You have become my ray of sunshine. You make me laugh, and you remind me of Deplukador. I will tell you about Deplukador someday. I think you belong to him."

"I have never worshipped. You will have to guide me, and you know how hard a time I have keeping a straight face. I cannot promise not to laugh, but I do not think worship is funny. It is holy. Probably, I will be speechless. God likes me to listen, and I think worship is about listening.”

“Something tells me that you have worshipped far more than I. I am glad you are with me.”

“David?” I asked, waiting to ensure I had his attention, “Why did you call me Tara yesterday?”

David’s face turned red. Slowing down, he pulled over to the side of the highway and stopped. He even turned the engine off. Looking into my eyes, he smiled before he put his arms around me and hugged me. “You will always be my Tara. Even if God tells me to leave you forever, remember that I am yours while I live or as long as you let me be part of your world. I love you, Littl’un.”

After returning his hug, I pushed him away. Sarcastically, I said, “You did not answer the question, David.” Then I blushed and touched my head.

“I know, Littl’un. I will wait. I will let you decide, but you must not tease me.”

“Who is teasing? I just asked you why you called me that name.” Laughing, I pointed down the highway.

David started the truck and laughed before saying, “Names are important, Littl’un. A name defines much of a person, both in character and personality. To me, there is no doubt that you are ‘Tara.’ To me, you’ll always be Tara.”

“Why not call me by my real name? I know you know it.”

“No, Tara. That name belongs to a world of which I can never be a part. I am Muki. Our worlds would condemn me for loving you, and I could not live in your world. My greatest fear, Tara, is that you will eventually choose your world over mine. The name Tara reminds me that you belong to yourself and will never be mine.”

“Then I do not like that name. Call me, Littl’un,” I said defiantly.

“Yes, Ma’am,” answered David.

Then David chuckled while I worried about this Tara that David saw in me. We talked as we continued down the highway. While I wondered what would have happened if I had not told David to drive on, I had to touch my own short hair many times to remind me that I was just a kid. I began to wonder if I really would marry David someday and thought I would like that very much.

We went into Barkerville and past the gate to cross at the rickety old bridge. On the far side, David stopped to turn the hubs to put the truck into four-wheel drive. The road was clear and dry, but he said it would not stay that way for long. He was right. The road went steadily uphill, only levelling occasionally. Soon there was snow in the ditches and then finally on the road itself. I worried that we would get the truck stuck every time David stopped to walk ahead into a snowdrift or assess the damage runoff had done to the road. Although David appreciated my concern, he laughed at my caution. "I want to get as close as possible in the truck. We will take the ski-doo when it is not safe. Snow-shoe Plateau is still a long way off. I would like to take the truck another twenty miles."

As I watched David throw a big rock into a creek bed, I laughed and began to enjoy this adventure. Work, perseverance, and struggles obviously were part of worship to David, or equally flattering, David wanted worship to include my world, where the effort in getting there added to the beauty and reverence of the spot where we would turn to God. He was making Snow-shoe Plateau holy. When we got back into the truck, I told him my thoughts, and David laughed with me.

"I won't put you in danger, Littl'un. I do not want to run out of snow with the ski-doo. We might not make it all the way. I came up here last summer, in August. There was still some snow even then, and I thought you would love the view. And besides, I just like to worship as high as possible because it makes me feel closer to God."

"I do, too. We are alike, you and me. No wonder God thought we would make good friends. Do you know what, David? I think you need me just as much as I need you, and that feels wonderful." It was the wrong thing to say, for tears formed in David's eyes again. He blushed and looked away, but I slid across the seat and put my hand on his knee. Once more, he stopped the truck. He held me close and let his fingers play in my hair.

"It is very short, Littl'un. You do not know what you are doing.

Please, you have no castle. I should not have brought you. Let us wait until we have worshipped. God will show me how to say goodbye. Stop fighting me." Then David put my hand back onto my own knee and pushed me away.

It was my turn to cry. Between sniffles, I said, "David, I already know that you could not walk away from me under any circumstances. I have learned more about you than you realize during these past nine months. I am sorry I frighten you, but God is not going to send you away. I know that. I can feel it. Furthermore, I am not going to hurt you. You must carry out your destiny just as I must carry out mine. When we worship, you will see. God wants us to love one another. I will wait, but I am your butterfly."

David turned very pale. He even shook and almost turned around to head back to town. He did not say anything until after he had offloaded the ski-doo an hour later.

Not purposely being nasty or taking advantage of him, at least not consciously, something inside me, like a dam, had simply broken, and I wanted David to admit that he could not leave me, that we belonged to each other. Wanting to grab all that life had to offer, perhaps, I was simply afraid that God might tell David that he had taught his lessons and encourage him to find a good way to say goodbye. I was desperate, almost fanatical, in a search to prevent the future from unfolding in a way that I did not want to consider as a possibility. However, David's reaction was clear. I had to back off, or I would push him away. Most definitely, I needed to know more about his culture. Why did I need a castle, and why was I a butterfly? What did these things mean to David of the Muki?

Sitting behind David on the snowmobile, I snuggled up against him. Wearing one of his sweaters over my own, I still felt chilly. Feeling very privileged, I laid my head against his back and held on as tightly as I dared. I still had an image of strength and fearlessness to uphold, and David would be aware that I was hugging him to be close rather than to be safe. I did not want to upset him more, but I wanted him to know that I needed him to be an active friend in my life, not a memory. Wishing I were older and wiser, I felt silly for wanting to grow up. Besides, growing up was out of character, but my feelings were grown up, and I thought my childish antics were what bothered David the most. I wanted to become whoever and whatever David would find enough comfort to continue our friendship. Yet, I remained confident that God was on my side in this matter. David needed guidance. I felt as though I was destined to frighten him regardless of what I did. If I was childish, he was afraid of taking away my childhood. If I acted like a woman trying to seduce her man, I terrified him because that was what he wanted, yet could not because he was Muki, and I was not. I needed something that I did not have. For some reason, I was taboo, even if I did not know exactly why.

We travelled by snowmobile for about an hour, continuing along the snow-covered roadway. Spring was here. The wind still held the bite of winter, but there was a freshness in the air from spring. There were patches of bare ground. Small, brave plants had pushed their way up and opened bright green leaves. Tufts of grass had found colour, too, and there was running water everywhere. The snowmobile was noisy. David hated it for being noisy and called it a primitive machine. It was not until we stopped that we realized how serene the place was, where we were to worship.

The sky was blue with little wisps of fluffy white clouds. Birds were singing, and even an eagle soared overhead. The ground beneath us was alive with the gurgles of water and glistened with a special light. The snow was hard and more like a big sheet of ice than what I would call snow. I ran around in the snow, sliding and giggling as I tried to maintain my balance while David watched me. Usually, he joined in games. Visions of other walks flashed through my thoughts, and I worried again. Walking back to him, I asked, "Whatever is the matter, David? You do not want to play, and you do not want me to grow up. How many times have you told me that the future would wait? Relax; I am not planning to kill you. It is beautiful here. You should be smiling and laughing. Please do not be afraid."

"You scare me, Tara."

"You are not allowed to call me Tara, remember? I scare many people, but I do not bite, David. Do not be so serious," I implored.

"Littl'un, I need to say goodbye. You are making it very hard. Yesterday, you would not let me when we went to your kingdom, and today, you have been pulling me apart with everything you do. I love you." Obviously fighting his desire to demonstrate his love, David clenched his hands and turned away but said, sadly and quietly, "You just are not part of my world. I need to run away before it is too late. I do not know how you managed to get me to bring you here. You are too powerful and frightening."

At a complete loss of comprehension why David would even think me powerful because I certainly did not feel it, and yet, I kind of liked the idea of being powerful, so I got confused, flustered, and blushed, before with indignation saying, "I am just a kid. I am not powerful. I just do not want to lose you. I will not let you go."

"I should not have brought you. I should have walked away when I met you."

"God would not let you walk away."

"I know. That is what frightens me. You have stolen my heart, and it is not right, Littl'un. You are just a child. I am old enough to be your father."

"In theory only, David. You are young enough to be my boyfriend. We do not have to be the wrong kind of friends. Yesterday, you promised to let God guide you... and us. I do not think our relationship is sinful or wrong. I think it is healthy and good… and that God approves. David, even if we became lovers, God would bless us."

"What makes you think that?"

"Simply because God sent you to me. God would not start something without knowing where it would lead. You will teach me, and I will become Muki. Then, your heart will be able to rest knowing that I have a place in your world."

David smiled and took my hand. "Come on, you little brat. Let us worship before you confuse me into believing I can teach you to be Muki. You are so innocent, and I am so guilty. It is wrong for me to love you as I do. We are playing with fire, little girl. If you do not run away soon, you will be burnt. I could never forgive myself if I hurt you. I am afraid."

I hit him. I was not even sure exactly why. I think he was acting superior, and it annoyed me. David was very surprised but gave me the look I loved so much.

He blushed, and tears welled in his eyes. Aware tears were falling from my own eyes, I told David to teach me how to worship.

Although nearby Yank's Peak was higher, Snow-shoe Plateau was nearly the highest point around. The view was breathtaking. While we walked to what appeared to be the highest point, David held my hand. Then giving me a wonderful hug, he promised, "Whatever happens, Littl'un, know that I love you. I always will." After wiping away my tears, he continued, "Now, let us face the sun and worship our God. They are the same. I, too, know so in my heart."

With a rush of confidence, I felt warmth grow in my own heart. Although I might be afraid of God, I trusted God immeasurably and silently prayed, after which I grew confident my lessons with David of the Muki were only beginning. We had forever ahead of us, and God was not going to end our relationship here. Snow-shoe Plateau was my kind of place and my kind of temple. David did not have a hope of enlisting God's help in walking away from our friendship because we were destined to be friends. Whole-heartedly, I believed God affirmed I was speaking the absolute truth.

Holding both of my hands in his, David stood behind me, and together, we turned toward the sun. The sun was not merely a ball of gas, a star, to David. The light emitted from the sun held power over David's thoughts and feelings. He described the light as holding life itself and believed it was God's arm reaching out to touch us, but he did not worship the sun. The light was a gift from God. God's words were in the light. The strength and power of God dwelt in the light as well. To David, the feel of a sunbeam upon his skin was the touch of God. We were standing in God's Kingdom, in His temple, and here, God would speak with us.

I never remembered having searched out God. If I needed help, I simply called out a prayer aloud or whispered one silently. God had always sent me some sort of comfort in such times. However, the most significant conversations with God came not at my bidding but in strange moments of tranquility, when I was not thinking of anything but feeling either nothing at all or very blessed. Gripped suddenly with fear and a feeling of inadequacy, I trembled.

David laughed and leaned against me. "The moment of truth, Littl'un, is shaking your fortress. The will of your determination is shattered, I feel. Perhaps, I am as strong as you, Tara."

Turning to look up at him, I scowled. He kissed me and smiled before just looking at me until I blushed. I shivered, thinking he just needed to be sure I knew we were meeting God on equal ground, I shivered. My teeth began to chatter, not because I was cold. It was because I was suddenly terrified. I had thought I had the upper hand, that I was loved and dear to God, and had not considered that David was just as important to God. He was strong-willed, too, and his relationship with God was better than was mine; David was obedient. Regretfully, I was a rebel, as apt to defy God as to listen to Him.

As David hugged me again, he said, "Ready?"

"That was not nice of you, David," I said through tears of anguish.

"I know, Littl'un," he answered and chuckled again, but I saw the tear in his eye before he resumed his position behind me. "Lean on me. We will stretch our arms out before God, tilt our heads back and view the heavens. Then we must close our eyes, clear all thoughts from our minds, and wait for God to surround us. When we feel God's presence, we can ask God to guide our future action."

As he raised them, I held on to David's arms and let my tears flow freely. I did not want this to be the last memory of David. Nevertheless, the sun was on my face, the wind was gentle, and I could not help feeling blessed and privileged. Every time I thought I was getting too warm, the wind soothed me, and the warmth of David behind me comforted me. After a few minutes, I sighed and felt at peace. I could hear David's heart beating, and content to listen to him, I let David become my strength. I do not know how long David and I stood like that, but I think it was at least an hour. My arms had ached to lower. My neck felt kinked. A few times, I thought I was going to pass out. However, an inner peace sustained me, and David held me on my feet.

I do not know how to describe the arrival of God into our little piece of heaven on the Snow-shoe Plateau. As the world seemed to swirl around, I suddenly felt very warm and secure. During a suspension of time, maybe lasting only a few seconds, but during those seconds, words and visions poured into me. Then all was quiet. The air that I breathed was sweet and full of life. Feeling as light as a feather, I thought I was floating in space, had become a star, and desperately wanted to dance. While feeling a sensation of being somewhere other than in my body on the ground, I held onto David. It was as though I was looking from above, at David and I standing before God, worshipping. Clinging to David, who was a star of light holding me, I watched our bodies in the distance and listened to the words of God.

The words were simple. God said, "To love is to be holy. Be patient, my children. Let your destinies unfold. There will come a time to express your love. Just wait and learn from each other."

Worship ended in a gust of wind that blew around us. We both felt cold and alone. I was not sure that I liked being that naked before God. I had never felt such scrutiny, and it had frightened me. Very tired, we sat down and held each other. Having trouble keeping my eyes open, I wanted to sleep. Simultaneously we both said, "I love you." It sounded right, and we felt blessed. David kissed my forehead, and I kissed his cheek. Then we giggled at one another. It was okay to love one another and just as okay to remain innocent. It was a wonderful feeling. As it grew, our energy returned. We played in the snow, running, falling, and sliding. We laughed. Then we returned to the snowmobile and ate our lunch, sitting beside each other on the seat.

David was more comfortable touching me. He wanted me close to him but acted morally, not sexually. He merely accepted I was more than a friend and that his love was blessed, natural, and good. To me, it was magic. God had changed me, too. I did not want to blush when David looked at me with unmistakable love in his eyes, but I had lost the sense of urgency to express love physically. I would savour him. Then run away as though compulsively aware that it was not yet time. When we arrived back at the truck, I hugged David and said, "God is totally and infinitely powerful. God changed me. I do not remember God asking for my obedience while we worshipped. Yet, I cannot defy the words God spoke. I am powerless."

"No, Tara. You offered your obedience when you stood to worship," countered David.

I did not mind David calling me Tara, and that frightened me. Knowing I had lost my independence, I realized I had lost a battle that day. I belonged to God and to my friend, David Miskenack, of the Muki. My destiny was not my own. It belonged to God, and I had no choice but to follow obediently wherever it was that tomorrow was going to take me. The name Tara took on a new meaning, promising that I was still unique, and somehow, somewhere down the road, I would be in control, even if only in my dreams. My world had grown. I was not a little girl anymore. I was a woman, and the whole meaning of love had changed. It would not be David running away from me. Now, I needed to do the running.

When David pulled me over to sit beside him in the truck before starting it up, I laughed, blushed, and pointed at my short hair. David put an arm around me and said, "I know, but now I can dream that it is long. Please stay close, sit beside me."

I did. I leaned against him, closed my eyes, and fell asleep.

20

REALIZATIONS AND RATIONALIZATIONS

THE JUDGE SPENT SUNDAY FEELING sick to his stomach. Nothing comforted him. He hated change. Once again, God had thrown him into the clutches of the taboo. David's quest was tearing the very fabric of their line of infinity. With God's blessing, David would destroy the world of the Muki. Was there a way to stop him? Did God want him stopped? Judge Soronato desperately needed to know whether his duty was to support or condemn what was happening high in the hills of this land called Earth. Shortly after lunch, he went out to worship himself. He felt such a deep terror.

Natthia and several others watched him leave. No one concentrated on work as they all watched the bushes for the return of the Judge. Nearly suppertime, when the Judge finally appeared back in camp, shining with an undeniable blue light, he was crying, went directly to his office, and closed the door behind him. God had terrified the Judge, and the rest felt even more uncomfortable.

When he arrived singing and giddy with overflowing joy, David confused everyone even more. Only Mark and Natthia sat with him in the kitchen. Everyone else snuck away to their own rooms or special spots to think and meditate. The happenings of the last few days confused them, and they were unsure of themselves and the righteousness of what was happening. Just in case the wills of men were luring them into sin, they hid from the Judge and David.

When David asked for an audience, The Judge sent him away, saying only, "I will talk to you tomorrow. I must think now. Enjoy your pleasure alone, tonight at least."

Obediently, David went to his room. He felt guilty because the Judge saw something wrong in his joy. David sighed and, as he showered, knew regardless of what the Judge thought now, God had blessed Tara and him just as the Judge had predicted.

Littl'un had not made any plans at all for worship before God. She had left all her hopes and fears with God, faithful that God would stand beside her and guide them to continue the friendship that God had ordained in the first place. As they approached their destination on Snowshoe Plateau, David had felt the power of her faith and struggled to remain focused on the righteousness of his own faith. Remaining steadfast in his own belief that God would neither permit him to sin nor encourage him to break the laws of his culture because, after all, the laws of God written in their Great Books were the foundation of his culture.

His human heart had continued to break. When they were ready to worship, he had purposely shattered the Little Smiler's confidence in a desperate step to meet God on equal ground.

When God blessed them, David had lost his pain. It no longer mattered whether his own people would shun him. He was a renegade, and God was leading him. He had Tara's love, and his future was in God's hands, where it belonged.

He could love her, and it was good. Tara was a woman, and it was her duty to run, not his to refuse to dance. Together, Tara of Earth and David Miskenack of the Muki would mould a piece of the Kingdom of God. David was honoured and thought Tara was as well. At least she was content. Admittedly, it had felt wonderful to have her sleep with her head against his shoulder today. Ah, to dream... what a glorious gift is the power of thought. No. His thoughts could not be wrong. He was not thinking of dancing with Tara, only holding her close. Their relationship was innocent, God would protect them so that neither of them would sin. The Judge had nothing about which to worry. David climbed onto his bed and, pulling his comforter around him, slept content with the knowledge God was in control.

21

THE HARSHNESS
OF THE MUKI

I REMEMBER LITTLE OF THE DRIVE back to Barkerville other than noticing the lack of bumps and jerks when we were back on the highway. Watching David rather than the road as we continued into Quesnel, I felt no shame in savouring him. He was indeed a very special sort of man. His seriousness and thoughtfulness reminded me of my father and his temper of my brother, but there was something especially unique in David. He was completely alive, and not afraid of grasping every shred of delight that the world had to offer without worrying about his image or what others might think of him. Perhaps, he was truly a free spirit. I found it very difficult to imagine David being less than perfect in every way and often had a feeling that being near David was akin to being with God. When I told him of such thoughts, David got furious because he was not a vain man and humbly apologized for misleading me. Then he chuckled or ruffled my hair and smiled that wonderful smile that lit up his whole face and said, "God is in all of creation. It is right to see God in everyone and everything around us. I see God in you too, Littl'un." In short, I loved everything about David… except his secrets.

I did not know where David lived, where he went when he was not with me or who his friends were. Yet, I knew there were other people in his life. Why my relationship with David was a secret, I understood. Some of the kids in my classes dated and hung around together outside of school, but I did not. Without belonging to a clique, I went to school, chatted with acquaintances, attended classes, and then escaped into my own world when the bell rang at the end of each day. After school, I went to my job to volunteer at the hospital as a candy striper, home to do homework or meet David to go for a walk. I did not associate with people from at school outside of school. If my parents had known about David, I would not be able to continue my relationship with him. It was that simple.

David did not seem to have a valid reason for keeping me a secret from his family and friends. Yet, other than occasionally mentioning doing something with his brother, Brian, or friend, Mark, or laughing about something Muma Horren had told him, I had never met them. Before we worshipped, it had not seemed important, but now I wanted desperately to become part of David's world. I thought his friends were of the Muki, and I wanted to become of the Muki.

Besides, David's responses to my questions intrigued me. He said his friends and indeed all the Muki would not accept my presence and that I would not be safe around them because I was not Muki and our relationship was taboo. Moreover, that was always the end of the conversation. The weeks passed. We went for walks. I continued to learn more and more about the Muki from David as he continued to teach me lessons as we shared our lives and thoughts.

We were not exactly angels. Some of the things we did were wrong. David liked to watch people. We often spied on unsuspecting souls, trailing them or standing hidden around a corner or behind bushes. David had very good hearing and an excellent memory. Later, we would talk about conversations collected while eavesdropping. If people were just chattering about idle gossip, David did not bother to track them. However, if they talked about something he considered 'cultural importance,' he became quite obsessed with remaining within earshot. Much to my dismay, occasionally David would interrupt a conversation and say something strange or ask a leading question. Usually beat red, I hid behind him on those occasions. Some people would only look at him funny and walk away, but others would engage him in a lengthy conversation. David mostly listened, and I never said anything.

I could not fault David for this behaviour, though. His interest was genuine, and he was not out to put people down or hurt them. I had concluded that David was merely a spy. I often played a spy game with imaginary characters, and even David would join in the antics of capturing the bad guys. Therefore, in a sense, his game was just an extension of a game I played myself. There was an element of risk, and it certainly was an exciting pastime. I thought it was innocent and unlikely to cause any damage. David was after information and liked people. Even if oddly, people watching was more like a game than anything else. David was not ordinary. When we were together, I always had fun. Everything we did seemed to lead to a lesson on how to judge the world, distinguish between right and wrong, and formulate a feeling for how it should be.

I often thought about the God connection, as I called it, to our friendship. I wanted to figure out God's intent. Our worship had changed something in David. We no longer talked only about the ground beneath our feet, the sky above our heads, and the light. Instead, David embarked on what I called the philosophy of life.

I concluded David's world was harsh. There was sadness in a fundamental belief of the Muki that life was a gift, but living was harsh and unpredictable. Whenever we listened to conversations about rights, David came very agitated and even angry. Yet, he would listen intently, trying to comprehend how people could even contemplate the existence of inherent rights. I think our conversations about rights led David to teach me more about the Muki.

The foundation of the Muki philosophy of life was that God was in total control of the birth, death, and wealth of all of creation. There exists no birthright. From conception, all creatures have an ordained and limited future. They contain all that is required to dictate a life span and have all the survival instincts they will ever need. They have a soul and the genetic strength that their ancestry provides. God controls the spirit but not necessarily ancestry. All life has the capacity to hold the spirit of God, but it is not essential to their existence. One can be born with it and lose it or gain it later. Belonging primarily to the realm of science, growth, and reproduction are laws or facts of existence. In a sense, both your chromosomes and ability to survive in the environment you emerge dictate survival. Environments are dynamic, they constantly change, and the survival of a species is dependent on its ability to evolve with its ecosystem. Willfully denying the necessities of life through a lack of thought or care is wrong, but David told me the Muki believe that it is equally wrong to defy death, which is also a gift from God and best left in the hands of the Lord. Both birth and death are holy. Both are expressions of God's grace and love. They are celebrations. While birth is the opportunity to serve the Lord in creating the Kingdom of God, death is a reward for fulfilling one's duty or serving one's purpose. It can even be an escape from pain and suffering because God is compassionate.

Another element of the faith of the Muki, which jarred my young soul, was the idea that God believed in redundancy and did not have a lot of faith in His servants. Therefore, literally, thousands could have the destiny to perform some minuscule task on God's behalf. Although most failed, God's Kingdom would remain safe. For God needs only one servant to succeed. The body is a machine and subject to failure, damage, and accident. Imprisoning a spirit within a malfunctioning body would be cruel.

This was where the concept of a dynamic God came into play for the Muki. They believe God cannot control creation. After setting it in motion, God only guides it, thus encouraging it to endorse and enable the growth of the Kingdom of God. David said this did not imply that God had no power, for God's power is unbound. As easily as we can grow a new cell, be it a flake of skin, a strand of hair, or a single blood cell, God can replace a world. If we fail to please God, God could destroy us in less than a blink of an eye. The catch is that we could be like a piece of rough fingernail. Smoothing the whole nail necessitates cutting away more than the rough spot. Some of the healthy, smooth, and beautiful nail must be lost to make the whole finger attractive and pleasing to God. Therefore, God's task of bringing about His Kingdom is extremely complex and difficult. God requires obedience. In general, God will not destroy those who are not obedient. To do so would also destroy that which is obedient or at least holds the promise of becoming obedient. Another comment David made concerned not knowing what part of God the world made up. It may be an essential component. In which case, God's efforts to bring about obedience might be of far greater importance than showing might and wrath. In an odd fashion, God could be at our mercy. Our errors and search for control and power could be destroying God, rather than only our world and ourselves.

Although still uncomfortable with David's insistence that I have a lot of Deplukador in me, I found these lessons about his culture fascinating.

According to the Muki, all of life and God's role reduces to an expression of a single word: yearning. This is a completely unstoppable raw emotion that demands expression. It is God's passion and the reason that God created life.

The Muki believed that the yearning was composed of three parts entwined within our spirits in varying degrees, amounts, or strengths. They are called The Voice of Life, the Lines of Infinity, and Deplukador.

The Voice of Life is that undeniable instinct to survive. Creation is the result of God's need to be expressive, and as such, all of creation is good according to God. The Voice of Life celebrates that goodness. Living is worth all the pain and sorrow we endure to experience life. It is joy and wonder.

Life is full of peril. It is dangerous. Everything we see and all that we do matters tremendously. Our lives exist on Lines of Infinity. A reasonable analogy is to say that the Lines of Infinity are threads of a tapestry of life. Every choice we make in life affects the future of not only ourselves but of all life. Therefore, we must be responsible and choose well. Only God provides the right choices. We need to live in the will of God, and to do that; we need to be obedient.

Deplukador, the last component of life, is akin to the imp in the formula. Deplukador is not evil. It is simply the force within us pushing the limits of life. To live is to experience, to challenge, and to defy limits.

To put it another way, the Voice of Life is the static component of life, a need to keep things the same, comfortable, and secure. Deplukador is the dynamics of life: change, growth, and discovery. It is the challenge that God puts before us to entice us to reach for the Kingdom of God. The Lines of Infinity are the threads that hold life together in a balance of ceaseless opportunities to grow and develop.

Always new and exciting, God loves all of creation. Extremely well ordered, God's creation is not chaos. However, it contains freedom of expression and the opportunity to grow through trial and error. It can be infinitely satisfying. It contains all that is necessary to bring about the Kingdom of God.

God, too, is patient. It is acceptable to God that we err and take wrong paths. The Lines of Infinity cross and are woven in countless different patterns such that there is always a way to redeem creation. Infinitely forgiving, God takes immense delight in witnessing growth. There is a catch to life, though. The more one obeys God or gives life to create the Kingdom of God, the wealthier the person is. There is more of everything good given to the servants of the Lord. This is not about longevity or lack of suffering. It is more about a feeling of grace, a strength that fills one's soul with elation, thanksgiving, and freedom. Simply, the truth is being good feels good.

I had a lot of trouble with this concept of God. Certainly, there was truth to the lessons David was teaching me, but... I had difficulty accepting that slavery was the route to incredible freedom. I wanted to control my own future, be myself, and I did not want God or anyone else shaping me. Yet, I freely admitted David was shaping me. Furthermore, I was sure that it was according to the will of God. Unable to escape, slowly, I forgot to try to run away from God. I felt privileged and began pondering my actions and why I did them and discovered that it was true. When I knew that I was doing the right thing, I felt wonderfully warm and incredibly blessed.

Day to day life held literally thousands of little things that one could do to make the world a better place. I liked to smile, and it was easy to smile everywhere I went. However, I retained a discomfort with being among people. Increasingly, I found that the world held a sadness that almost overwhelmed me.

David told me that I needed to be aware of the faults of the world to understand the need for change and to summon the strength to work toward bringing change about. Experiences were to teach. The things I saw in life mostly frightened me, and I did not want to be part of the world. Instead, I wanted to create my own little shelter, my own niche, where I could live in peace. David insisted that was wrong and evil and destroyed the very fabric of the Kingdom of God.

For example, there were many duties as a candy striper that I was very uncomfortable doing. I could barely handle filling water jugs. Most patients appreciated my efforts even though I was not aware of it at times. Although knowing it was a service to humanity, I did not feel good about doing it and felt like an intruder. Hating to wake anyone up or interrupt a conversation to ask if I could fetch the flask, especially in the chronic care ward, I felt like a snoop or a thief when I had to move things to find the lid or prevent something from falling onto the floor. It sounds like a simple task, but I hated doing it, and patients often gave me the creeps. Many of the old folks had lost their ability to talk coherently and had most definitely lost their dignity. They were often rude and acted as though they no longer needed to act decently. I was very uncomfortable.

Delivering meals was not as hard. Most people understood why I cleared their tray or appreciated me cranking up their bed to make them as comfortable as possible to eat supper. Occasionally, I laughed with them about the frequent lack of attractiveness of the meal I served and felt I was doing something good. I prided myself on giving out smiles and providing meals efficiently. There was a catch occasionally. Some of the patients could not feed themselves. Although I tried to be comfortable feeding an elderly patient, I could not escape feeling very embarrassed and clumsy. I had no problem feeding children, but feeding adults terrified me. If no one was in the candy striper room to direct me, I always went to the pediatric ward. I walked by the nursery window in maternity to see the new babies but generally avoided the rest of the hospital.

David did not approve of my avoidance, but he did not argue with my lack of compassion for many of the patients. In fact, he supported my feelings about some of the patients as a result of injustice. David said the spirit of many of these people had already left life behind, and that man had wrongly prevented the death of a worn-out carcass. Human arrogance forced these people to suffer and degenerate until their bodies could fail in a way the doctors could not compensate. It was cruelty I was witnessing and should feel as I did. "But sometimes, Littl'un," he would say, "the spirit lives on in a body racked with pain and suffering because they still have a duty to perform. These people you should search out and try to learn what they need to teach to find peace and go on to God and heaven."

Saying I was focusing on the wrong things, David challenged me to discover the holiness of the water I delivered until I understood to ignore my own feelings and alienation from the sick. However, the more I tried, the more I hated the job. It was not holy. It was empty and pretentious, and I could not explain why. David just smiled and told me I was beginning to understand. That only confused me more because I did not get it at all.

When I cried and told him I could not do it, he ruffled my hair and said, "Just try, Littl'un. Start with saying hello to only one patient every time you go to the hospital, nothing more unless you feel comfortable. Then go to pediatrics. Children need love too. There you can freely give your love. Use your gift with children, but you need to grow and expand your love to encompass all people. If you do not try, in the end, you lose out. You must not be content to use only the gifts you are aware of and comfortable exercising. Reach out for all that life can give you! Live, and you will be blessed!" He made me feel very guilty, and by the time summer holidays rolled around, I had started stopping in to see an old lady. After saying hello a few times, she would smile when I arrived without looking at me quite so suspiciously. Just when I had started to like her and feel comfortable visiting with her or even reading to her, she died. David said I had helped her let go. I felt sad and missed her. David replied that no one wanted to feel forgotten and said I should endeavour to remember her as every life is important and valuable. That little, withered-up old lady had indeed taught me something. She had taught me that everyone needed to feel a ray of sunshine against their bare skin. I did not want to face reality and admit that the world was a cold and lonely place to be. I withdrew to pediatrics where there was hope at the end of a smile.

When I told David that I would not try to make a friend in the chronic care ward again, he ruffled my hair and said, "Perhaps you have learned your lesson, Littl'un. Someday, you will know what to do with it."

I did not understand him, but I did not feel guilty anymore when I went to pediatrics. I had a feeling growing inside me that a little old lady had blessed me. Her love would sustain me until I could do something about the cold reality of living. While I fell in love with all the little sick children, David and I talked about our infinite capacity to love one another and the importance of accepting God's love, including death. I began appreciating that death was a gift even more precious than life. More importantly, I began to grasp that life was greater when death was in God's hands.

As it was summertime, and I was too young for a full-time job, I started to go to the hospital every day at eight-thirty in the morning and stayed until five in the evening. I concentrated on learning and spent hours talking to David about what I thought God was teaching me.

I learned two things very quickly. One was that no one could grow and thrive without love. Although I could love, feel loved, and know it was good and right to love these children, I understood they were not mine, and I could not keep them for myself. The second thing that I learned was that loving sometimes hurts very much.

There are children whose pictures I still carry around in my heart. They are in my heart not because I loved them but because they loved me and helped me grow. It was a bit of a revelation to me that everything that happened in life happened for a reason. God was in control. If I opened my eyes and thought very carefully, I could recognize innumerable opportunities to learn and contribute to building the Kingdom of God. It was a satisfying revelation. Young, I had time to learn and had a duty and responsibility to serve God. The world was not on my shoulders, at least not yet, and if I let God teach me, then perhaps, I would be able to make a valuable contribution.

One of the dearest children in the whole world was a young boy. He was two years old and had spent most of his life in foster care homes. People said that he was developmentally disabled, a victim of fetal alcohol syndrome. Disagreeing, I thought he was just unloved. Recovering from pneumonia when I met him, he was listless, and his eyes were dull. All he did was sit and share vacantly into the space around him. As though by a magnet, he drew me to him. While I played with him, he slowly began to look forward to my arrival, smiled, and made noises. I worked with him during playtimes, and he soon learned how to walk and feed himself. Although I begged my parents to bring him home and adopt him, they refused and lectured me about how we could not solve all the problems of the world.

I felt disgusted at the women who occasionally visited that young child. They said that they had had him for a few months and that he was no trouble at all. He just sat and did nothing all day long. I thought they were starving him, and I hated them for abusing him far greater than had they beat him. He needed love, encouragement, and someone to appreciate his accomplishments to find the strength to come out of his shell and embrace a life that had let him down since the day of his birth or even since his conception. I remember his smile and his first step and treasure them. I am thankful that I knew him and pray that life has been good to him. In our friendship, I was not the hero. He was the hero, and I love him still. No child should ever feel unloved.

Another child very special to me was ten days old when I met her. I never knew any of her family. She had straight pitch-black hair that looked blue in the sunshine. She was cuddly and liked me holding her as much as I liked holding her. She was tiny and delicate. I wanted to take her home as well. I fantasized about being her mother, having the boy as her big brother, David as their father, and being a happy family. These two children made me feel needed.

They also made me very resentful of hospitals and the lack of care that some nurses showed to the children. They fed one child at a time, so only the first child got a hot meal. The rest got meals that had sat around getting cold and unappetizing. Nurses gave none of the babies a spoon and treated the patients as mechanically as possible. It was as though these nurses resented having to care for them. I fed as many children as there were highchairs, up to five at a time. I let them try to feed themselves and used extra spoons to fill each little mouth with a spoon full in a quick rotation from one child to the next. I admit that meals were a little messier and made twice as many dirty dishes and spoons, but I know the children were happier. It is with fondness that I remember our laughter and their messy fingers and faces.

Perhaps, I was unfairly judging the nurses. Our society demanded recording everything they did. Making out reports consumed much of their time. Still, I witnessed a lot of time spent on idol gossip, drinking coffee, and reading paperbacks. It was probably natural that some nurses grew to resent my presence. The late sixties were a time of unrest. People were unhappy and unsatisfied, and the labour movement was in full force. I believed that unionization fed on malcontent and slowly robbed members of the pleasures of doing their jobs well. Unions took away more than smiles. Employees stopped caring and lost their dignity and dedication, loyalty, and pride. Their work was no longer honourable. They worked for a pay-cheque that no longer held any satisfaction. David said I should pity them because they had lost their spirits and were worshipping false gods: money and self-indulgence. However, I did not pity them. I tried to compensate for their lack of care toward the sick, frightened, and lonely children in their care. I cleaned the playroom and stocked the laundry room while the children slept after lunch. As they woke, I changed their diapers and played with them. I had a routine and enjoyed it, and most of the nurses appreciated my presence because I did make their jobs easier. The union did not like me at all. I was taking away jobs, not that what I did would justify hiring another employee. It was the principle of the thing I was told. The head nurse called me into her office and told me that I could not come anymore. It was not justice, nor was it rational, but it was typical of the 'real' world. It was wrong in my mind, and, ever since, I have hated unions with a passion and believed them to be nothing more than the work of the devil.

David agreed with me rather than try to console me. He frightened me with other examples of the wrongs of my culture. David believed that time had no intrinsic value. The value of time came from what one did with it. He believed in slavery and that we were all born to be servants. As we grow, elders should teach us to serve as slaves to one another so that we would know our destiny and appreciate the responsibilities of power when we are old enough to wield it ourselves. Democracy was evil as well, for it could only breed contempt and corruption because democracy was designed on the idea that righteousness was popular, which was far from correct, according to David. "What is popular, Littl'un," he would say, "is rarely good, and what is good is never popular." David began to make me feel very depressed about my own culture. I felt doomed.

Try as hard as I could, I never satisfactorily answered David's many challenges. Based on the values contained in our Books of God, what is a valid response to the question, what is a wage if it is not profit? If work needs to be done, why should our culture not support the concept that those needed to work are brothers and sisters and, as such, require our love, a place to live, a kitchen to eat in, and as many pleasures as we ourselves enjoy? Yet, David did not mean communism, for he was even harsher in his condemnation of communists, for they denied the Laws of God and destroyed the spirit. When I asked about what form government should take, he laughed and said, "You need no government, Tara, only the laws of God."

22

UNAUTHORIZED INTERFERENCE

DIVULGING THE FUNDAMENTAL BELIEF SYSTEM on which the Muki conducted their lives did not take very long. Doing so left David with a guilty feeling. He was using the Little Smiler, moulding her for his own benefit. It was a human thing to do. His homeland, the Land of the Butterflies, was a long way away, yet it pulled on his consciousness, reminding him that his love for the alien was condemned.

For the expedition, it was sometimes hard to understand why God had blessed David's love. Judge Soronato was equally nervous about the future. All approved of what David was gaining, an immense storehouse of information on the soul of an ordinary citizen of an alien culture. However, they felt David was sinning to get it. Promising her a future that did not exist, he lied and misled the alien.

David criticized his own culture. His work was resented for it did show that these aliens, as primitive as they were, worried about the same things and struggled with their efforts to live up to a standard only attainable by God. Simply, the members of the expedition did not like the constant reminder that they, too, were human and sinful in the eyes of God. As discomfort rose, Judge Soronato isolated David even more by stopping all contact with aliens other than the Little Smiler. Strangely, only Loren and Mark felt any resentment. Mark because he enjoyed his time with the aliens even if all his acquaintances were superficial. Loren had become accustomed to spending Sunday mornings with the congregation of St. John's and resented giving up what had taken him months to find comfort doing. Besides, Loren thought that God had spoken to him as well. Maybe, he was slightly jealous. The rest of the expedition members seemed relieved to leave the temptations to David.

There was immense comfort in isolation. It was not perfect, for some arguments did occasionally break out over the righteousness of David's relationship. While some offered encouragement and support, others would have nothing to do with him. Overall, the expedition seemed content to carry on with gathering information on which to judge Earth. Although no longer sure of their conclusion, they did not doubt that Earth was full of evil and sinful people. It was blatantly clear that Earthlings worshipped idols, put themselves upon high pedestals, and their worship of God was superficial and often insincere. Yet, they grasped with the horrible guilt that Earthlings were not unlike themselves. They tried to know right from wrong, at least in general terms. The expedition slowly concluded that eventually, they would need to destroy Earth because it was not as God would have it. They were beginning to fear that the Land of the Butterflies was just as guilty in the process. It was a terrifying thought.

Increasingly, David felt guilty and ashamed of himself for misleading Tara of Earth. She wanted desperately to become of the Muki, and David knew it could not happen. He felt as though he was teasing her, leading her on a path that was doomed to come to a dead end. Even more than before he had worshipped with his Tara, he loved her and did not want her to get hurt. The more time he spent with her, the more he feared that he could not protect her from reality. The real world was poised to shatter her island kingdom just as she had long known. David felt powerless to prevent her loss and feared that ultimately, he would become responsible for its demise.

The summer had changed David. Enjoying feeling close to God as Jarrock guided his conversations with Tara, he was learning along with her and felt extremely blessed. For a time, he felt redeemed of the controversy over his thesis and discussed it again with Judge Soronato, saying that he wished he could swallow his words and was sorry he had ever said them. The thesis was proving its truth. Only now did David realize the depth of its ramifications.

While Tara pushed him to introduce her to his friends, David became increasingly depressed. Losing faith in the future, he hated what it seemed to hold and became convinced that he would break his promise to Tara. He would not be able to remain the grey sentry standing guard over this world. Just as guilty, he began to see himself as the instrument of destruction and hated himself for it.

As David's health began to fail, the Judge increasingly sent him to God. David would return from worship calm but unrelieved. God remained firm in instructing David to love Tara, teach her, and continue to learn from her. Telling him to have faith that God had plans to make Tara of Earth, of the Muki, the Judge continued to encourage and support David. All things were possible, and David needed only to trust the Lady.

David had begun to feel a stabbing pain in his chest several times each day. Often, the Judge had to summon Natthia to his office when he and David were discussing encounters with the alien. Although there was no physical reason for his pain, David was sick. Natthia told the Judge that David needed help as he was too young and inexperienced in walking alone on a new and unfamiliar path as directed by God. Overwhelmed, David may fail if the Judge did not assist him. As Natthia spoke, and David gave the Judge a look which begged him to be his shepherd, the Judge went very pale.

"I know not how to help you, David. I am unauthorized to interfere. This is your Doleran, David. You must have faith. Walk with Jarrock and let him guide you."

David cried in agony and fell to the floor. Muma Horren began to chastise the Judge, accusing him of failing his expedition, imploring him to do something which would give David the faith he needed to carry on.

"Do not hide behind Doleran, Judge Soronato. I beg you. Give David what you needed but were afraid to reach out to grab. Learn from your mistake by preventing David from erring as you erred so long ago."

The Judge turned blue with rage and sorrow. Never had anyone insulted his ability to lead. After he assisted in taking David to his bed and asked Natthia to stay with him, Judge Soronato returned to his office and paced back and forth, trying to discover whether there was something that he could do. Jarrock told him to follow his heart, but the Judge cried in frustration at not knowing what it was in his heart that needed action. Nothing came to him. Tossing and turning on his bed, unable to sleep, he missed Natthia and worried about David. He remembered the pain he had suffered when he knew neither how to obey God nor understand what he was to do or why God wanted his life.

Did God want David's life? The Judge neither wanted David to lose his Doleran nor his company. Ever since he had read David's thesis and queried him before the Panel, the Judge had loved David and known his destiny included something important. The Panel had ordered him to take David along on the expedition and had been angry that he had refused to send the boy another summons. He had talked for many days to the Panel, convincing them that it was necessary for David to offer himself because one should never drag another into potential danger, and attempting to work directly under God's guidance was dangerous. Few mortal men can give themselves totally to the Lady. A task, such as his own Doleran, or defying the known laws of God on alien soil as David was instructed to do, was terrifying both from fear of failure and of losing one's humanity. It was easy to say, even to think, but almost impossible to give one's life to the Lady to do only that which God commands.

How do you support an alien concept that defies your own culture's teaching? How could the Judge prove to David that Tara of Earth could and, if God willed it, would become of the Muki? The idea was simply preposterous. He did not believe it himself, so how could he help David believe it?

Around midnight, the Judge dressed and went to David's room. He knocked softly on the door and heard Natthia stir. When she let him in, Natthia looked tired, and although he slept, David looked feverish and uncomfortable. Judge Soronato said, "Natthia, I once looked like he does now. He needs to find comfort in God when God has frightened him. It is not easy to face a destiny that is not the one he has grown up believing to be his own. As I cannot sleep anyway, I will sit with him."

While she held Josh's hand in one hand and dabbed the sweat off David's forehead with her other, Natthia whispered, "Thank you, Josh. I think you will help him much more than I can. As Muma Horren said, Josh, you know what it is like and what is happening to him. You are one of God's shepherds and can guide him if you believe in yourself. I trust you and your lessons on Doleran, Josh. You won't fail." When she saw the tears in the Judge's eyes, she added, "Share your anguish. It, too, will help. He will know he is not alone. Being among friends who understand will strengthen him."

The Judge hugged Natthia then sat in the chair Natthia had set beside David's bed. When Natthia left, closing the door with an ominous click as she let go of the knob, he felt very alone. Judge Soronato held David's hand or rubbed his back as he searched for a way to relieve his pain. How can he give David the support that he needed when he knew that David could not succeed in making Tara of the Muki? He had to teach him to believe. But how?

Judge Soronato thought about his own struggles on Doleran and remembered the elation he had felt when he accepted his destiny. He had not understood it, still did not, but he had grown in his faith that God knew what She was doing. Confident Her plan was good, he sincerely believed that, in the end, all would work out for the betterment of the Kingdom of God. The Judge had dedicated his whole life to change in thought and tradition. This assignment was about changing attitudes, extending the definition of who they were to include the universe rather than only the Land of the Butterflies and the life they had a hand in developing. All of God's creation was connected.

Emitting the steel blue colour of fear and anguish which reflected off the walls of the darkened room, the Judge began to shine as he thought about the words God had told him while David and Tara were worshipping on Snow-shoe Plateau. Slowly, his colour changed into the comfort of white light, and the Judge smiled. With satisfaction, he confidently told David, "Tara will become of the Muki, David. It will be as God-ordained. You will succeed, son. You have the blood of your great-uncle within you, and just as he supported me, I shall support you. Pray that God has chosen the Little Smiler well and knows what God intends. She has been telling us what to do all along. We need only to trust her ourselves. She belongs to God, David, and God knows her ancestry. If God says, she is Muki, who are we to dispute it. Bring her home, David. She is one of us."

The Judge felt giddy and alive. Bursting into song, he banished his anguish.

As he sang of Deplukador, he was thrilled with his own revelation. They needed a ritual to 'adopt' the Little Smiler and to formally name her. Even if accused of acting without authorization, the Judge would take her to the Land of the Butterflies, and there, her destiny would unfold. Deciding he would let the Panel worry about the law, he would follow his heart, as God had instructed.

David's fever ebbed, and he slept peacefully. Comfortable that Jarrock would hold him the rest of the night, the Judge symbolically spread his own light across David. With dull skin, he went to his own room to hold Natthia and tell her all was well because he knew how to support David.

In the morning, the Judge assembled his expedition and said, "Fellow judges, God needs your trust and obedience. We must support David to give him the strength to do all that God asks of him. Please prepare yourselves for a thanksgiving ritual. We must cleanse ourselves and prepare to welcome Tara of Earth into our mist as one of the Muki."

The members of the expedition stared in shocked silence for a few seconds before beginning to talk among themselves. They were worried about the sanity of their leader. In tears, David fell to his knees, thanking the Judge. Later they heard him yell, "Praise the

Lady! I have salvation! Jarrock, please guide us into this unknown future." Unable to argue with the wisdom of their leader, they felt unity that gave them strength as David began to shine with the presence of God. Calmly they went to prepare their bodies and souls to stand before God in thanksgiving. They were unsure what would happen next but were confident that it would frighten them all as God had frightened David. They were not entirely individuals. They were connected, were of the Muki, chosen by God as Instruments of Creation.

23

LITTLE MESSAGES

As summer and fall unfolded, David and I spent many hours talking about culture and the will of God. He wanted me to tell him about things that happened in the time between our visits, and we discussed my life with the intent of discovering what God was teaching or guiding me to do. I often found things overwhelming and would rant and rave about the need to change the world radically with a power I neither had nor was likely ever to accumulate. David listened and even laughed at me sometimes, which really aggravated me. After such occasions, David always was able to change the topic and make me laugh and relax. Then he would work our conversation back into a discussion of my everyday life with a firm demand that I look for little things. "Little things, Littl'un, create momentum and growth, big things not much more than shock," said David many times that summer.

Whenever David did not approve of my ideas, he called me Littl'un, and when he did, he called me Tara. I laughed when I figured that out and began trying to make sure that he called me by each name equally often to satisfy my need to please him and be independent. I do not think I fooled him, but I certainly could wrap him around my fingers. I continued to think of David as a gift and felt somehow powerful around him. I liked feeling powerful.

David did not want me to lose that feeling of power. He just wanted to direct it into something worthwhile. Calling me his challenge, he was as determined to shape me to the will of God as

I was to maintain a sense of control over my destiny. Often a mule, David would offer me water and knowing that I was thirsty, I would purposely turn away. I do not know what it is in my own soul that causes me to run away from God besides fear. I knew what was required and that I could do as directed. However, it required that I change and give up something that I could not let myself do.

It was not only my independence at risk. My character and self-image were threatened. In all that I did, I needed to be sure that I was acting, not a robot. Learning was easy; however, working on what I had learned was immensely difficult. My life became a battlefield of wills, but I thrived on it. Even when I clearly lost, I liked to do battle. The aggravating part was, unfortunately, the realization that David was correct. Losing a battle with the Almighty was far more rewarding and satisfying than winning because winning was empty. Nothing would ever be the same again. David had shaped me, God would continue to shape the rest of my life, and because it was part of my nature, I would simply do everything the hard way.

After I had been 'fired' from candy striping, I never returned to the hospital except for a few years later when invited to come to receive a reward for voluntary service. However, with David's help, I continued to learn from the experience. Tiny single events do have far-reaching implications for the future. One of my treasures was David's affirmation that I did not own my experiences. As small and insignificant as they were, they did help to shape the world. For better or for worse, I was involved in change. It boggled my mind that God would use each of us to initiate change and growth.

I discovered the meaning of hope that summer and developed confidence that righteousness would eventually win in God's creation. After all, God made us the way we are, and even God loved my defiance. There was also satisfaction in my knowledge that the Mukis were not perfect either. Even David had faults. I became a little more content in being human and part of humanity. Sharing such thoughts with David usually resulted in laughter, teasing, and, if I was lucky, a kiss on the forehead. I often got a lecture reminding me not to be content and apathetic. David would say, "Strive for perfection, Littl'un. Know and be comforted that you cannot achieve it but demand it anyway!" I loved David.

My big picture was that hospitals were very lacking. The sick and the dying belonged in the comfort of their own beds with the care of their families ever present, not in sterile hospital wards. It was ironic that a desire to reduce pain and suffering drew people into the health profession, yet society strangled their efforts through unrealistic expectations and accusations of malpractice. These noble people were so afraid of doing something wrong that they could not do what they knew were the right things to do. The priorities were wrong. Our medical oath was to sustain life regardless of its quality because we, as mere humans, should not play God and judge who should or should not live. In our society, death means failure.

The Muki thought of death as the reward for completing service and experiencing life. Death is the highest honour that God grants creation. Muki doctors had a different oath entirely. They concentrated efforts on the prevention of lack of health and agonized over interfering with the will of God whenever they treated the sick. The Muki concentrated on maintaining the spirit. Without the spirit of God, a person was dead in their eyes and not worthy of life. However, they did not appear to condemn lightly. David would laugh as he said, "A spark is sufficient. Often Littl'un, one finds whatever they are looking for. Make sure you look for the good in all around you."

Then I would ask, "Are the Muki good, David?" Depending on his mood, he would laugh or cry before saying, "For all our sakes, I hope so, Littl'un. Let us remember always to ask for God's guidance in all that we do. Only then can we claim to be good."

"I think you are good, David. I know you. However, I do not know the Muki. Please introduce me to your friends. Take me home."

His answer was always, "I can't, Tara. I am afraid." That question consistently resulted in David shedding tears and saying it was time to take me home where I belonged, in the house at the top of Kinchant Street.

Every time that happened, I would spend hours praying that

someday David would accept me as worthy of being a part of his world. Then, I would run away with him forever. David had become my future, and I would try even harder to prove to him that I had learned my lessons well. I could become Muki because I had to. God said so.

24

PREPARATIONS

THERE WAS A DEFINITE FEELING of fall in the air as the members of the sixth expedition of the destruction assignment to Earth sat around a campfire after dinner. In the morning, they had each cleansed themselves and, either alone or with close friends, had celebrated the most common ritual of the Muki, the thanksgiving ritual. The ritual had left them calm. On this day, they did not worry about the questions and fears that had dominated their thoughts before the ritual. They focused on God, listening for guidance, accepting the unorthodox as though it was not strange, sinful, and dangerous. Tomorrow, they would let the worries come. Today was totally in God's hands.

The day had passed quietly. Judge Soronato had wandered at will into all the rooms of the base camp, offering hugs and silent support. He was pleased there was little tension in the air, save a hint of resignation. As each had long expected, their walk had taken a turn embarking on a path guided only by God and Her chosen shepherd. Painfully aware that he could be embarking on the will of man and that his decision to support David and Tara openly was unauthorized, the Judge was looking for more than acceptance and hoped that he would see signs of God's presence. If God did not give him a sign, he would have to back down and accept that David had to remain on his own.

God had been with his people. Natthia shone most of the day. The Judge saw that as a good sign even though Natthia was apt to shine at one time or another every day. Muma Horren shone as well, but the Judge had only seen Muma Horren shine with messages of caution, and he was throwing caution to the wind. Oddly, David had not shone. Instead, he had slept the day away. The Judge sighed. David needed rest and strength because the burden upon him was heavy. The presence of God was witnessed in Mark and Brian at lunchtime but not in Loren. The Judge would have been far more confident if God had been with Loren, for God had talked to Loren almost a year ago about gathering the flock together.

Again, the Judge sighed as he looked around the circle of his crew. He reached for the hand of David on his left and Natthia on his right. Simultaneously, all joined hands.

"Guide us, oh my Lady. Hold our tempers and our fears at bay so that we may hear you and embark upon your chosen path," prayed Judge Soronato aloud.

Several minutes of silence followed, but the Judge waited. Someone would speak. Although tension was rising among them, he needed only patience because someone would speak. Aware whoever spoke first would set the mood, he watched Muma Horren guiltily, hoping that she would remain quiet, but all heads remained bowed. As he turned his focus onto David, he knew instantly that David would be silent all evening. Surveying his people yet again, he wondered whom God would direct to speak. As his tension rose, he repeatedly prayed, "Speak to us, Jarrock, do not let me lead us astray. Guide me, and I shall be obedient. I feel David needs our help, please, Jarrock. I am yours. Use me."

"Be patient, Josh. The one to speak is young and afraid. Give him time. Support him," were the words that awoke in his consciousness. He put David's hand into Natthia's and stepped out of the circle. He began with David, setting his hands on his shoulders, and silently blessed him before moving on to the next. The Judge could feel a sense of calm restored as he progressed around the circle. David let tears fall down his cheeks. Many sighed and watched him progress around the circle. However, the Judge still did not know who would speak when he arrived back at his starting point. He was beginning to think he was asking too much of his young judges. He asked them to break all the rules about maintaining security, and accept an alien among them, not because they wanted to, but because he thought God was directing the alien to expect them to welcome her into their midst.

Only another minute passed before Doug raised his head and stared at the Judge. He fidgeted, and the Judge could not restrain a smile, but when Doug looked about to nod his head again, in desperation, the Judge motioned him to speak. Then he worried that he had interfered in the work of God, yet again.

Obviously not wanting to be the first to speak, Doug blushed and took a deep breath before speaking, "Sir, we must maintain as much security as we can. David's time with the alien is constrained. The only way to bring her here, have some time to do anything, and then to get her back before her curfew is by using the transporter. It would not be right to introduce her to our technology. I do not think it would be wise to drug her either, for she would recognize the deception, just as she recognizes that we do not belong to Earth. May I suggest that we disguise the transporter as an airplane? I think I could create a simulation that would do the trick."

"Would it not be safer to use an airplane?" asked Mark.

"No. Doug is right, Mark. Their laws require filing flight plans. Even if we trust Tara, repeated flights to the middle of nowhere will raise suspicion and curiosity. Others may follow to find out what is going on here. We would lose all security," interjected Brian, "Besides, their airplanes are too slow, and their range is too short!" Then, he laughed.

The Judge smiled. Everyone began talking, exchanging visions of advertising the location of their base camp with the flashing lights of the cities and a good year blimp announcing, "Come see the alien invaders!"

"Stop it!" yelled Muma Horren. "This is not funny. They would not come to gawk. Earthlings would come to kill us all. Doug is right. If we must bring her here, disguising a transporter so that the alien is comfortable would be wise."

The Judge detected fear in Muma Horren's voice and made a mental note that she was trying very hard to be brave and trust his reputation and authority to lead them into the taboo. As he listened to the conversation focused on their security, Judge Soronato relaxed. None questioned the righteousness of bringing Tara of Earth among them. They were acting as though they completely accepted it as inevitable.

The thought that they were blindly following him worried the Judge, but he also felt relief. David did need help, and sharing the duty of educating the alien could not be bad. However, Judge Soronato still desperately needed self-confidence and to feel the presence of God in these conversations. The only evidence was the tears and expression on the face of young David Miskenack, and he could be displaying gratitude rather than holiness.

After they had sung praise to God at sunset and then to the heavens as the stars awoke above them, one by one, the Cultural Judges from the Land of the Butterflies went to bed. They were secure in the belief that whether right or wrong, they could follow their leader, confident that they had the technology to retain their secrecy.

They planned a visit over the next weeks and intended it to be special. However, Jarrock remained silent, and Judge Soronato worried. Although the others trusted him implicitly, without the grace of God visible before him, Judge Soronato felt like he was back on Doleran, alone. One night, Jarrock spoke to him in a dream saying, "Will you ever trust me, my son?" and the Judge did not understand. Did Jarrock mean that he was on the right path and should feel righteous? Did Jarrock approve of the plans or condemn them because he was interfering without an authorization? The Judge cried and then hugged Natthia. Comforting him, Natthia had confidence that he was doing the right thing, complete with the blessings of Jarrock and Koe Sai Serena. The Judge wished he had Natthia's faith.

The leaves had changed colour, dried, and fallen from the few coniferous trees near the base camp. The green undergrowth was gone. It would snow soon. David had continued to meet regularly with Tara. She had threatened to hide in the back of his truck, and both he and Mark had taken to checking before they drove out of town.

One day, they had found her hidden under a tarp. David had promised that he would bring her home, and to prove it, he introduced her to Mark, who was with him at the time. Staring at him, she walked around him and was downright rude to Mark. Then she looked at David. With the same authority that she had used when she first met David, she demanded that he prove Mark was Muki.

Mark had blushed and scowled, then looked to David and said, "Help me, David. She is deaf, blind, and too stubborn to feel the truth. I do not like her."

Before David could respond, Tara jumped back into the truck box, put her hands on her hips, turned back to Mark, and said, "Mark, I have only seen David's family and friends in a vision I had a long time ago. It is hard to remember. If you beat time on your knees and hum a tune, I think I will recognize the sound of a Muki. If you make your skin glisten as David's skin glistens, I will see a Muki, and if you look at me as David did when I met him, I will feel the touch of a Muki through your eyes." Then she had stood silently glaring at Mark, who glared right back.

David said, "Go home, Littl'un. Do not insult Mark. He has as much right as I to be here. He needs to prove nothing."

"You have no right to be here either, David. This is my world. God sent you as a friend, my friend. I do not recognize this man."

It was a standoff. Tara would not budge from where she sat in the back of the truck. Mark continued to stare, and David fretted. When Mark looked away, the little alien clapped her hands. "Look at me, Mark. You feel like danger, and you even smell like danger. David told me I would not be safe among his people. Come closer. David, protect me."

David stared at Littl'un with disapproval, but she stared right back. She was terrified, and Mark was the cause. As he lifted her out of the truck and set her down between himself and Mark, she clung to his hands and stared again at Mark.

"He is my friend, Tara. He would not hurt you. I won't let him." David tried to assure her.

Still Littl'un trembled. David did not know what to do. Feeling like a fool, Mark was looking to David for a way out of this situation, decided that he did not want this alien anywhere near him and definitely not in the base camp.

Eventually, Littl'un turned to David and cried uncontrollably on his shoulder. David patted her back, confused with what she felt in his best friend. Mark did not have a mean streak in him. Kind and gentle, he had a wonderful sense of humour and spent his time exploring all that life offered him with gusto. Wondering what frightened his little alien, David looked into Mark's eyes himself but saw only an angry, confused friend.

Littl'un whispered to David, "He thinks I am nothing. In his eyes, I do not deserve life. He hates me, David. Will all the Muki hate me so? Are no others like you? Tell me he is not Muki. Please, David."

Despite her softly spoken words, Mark heard her, and when he touched her shoulder, she winced. "I am sorry, Tara. Perhaps you are seeing my fear of what you can do to my friend. I neither trust you nor see God around you either. May we call a truce, for David's sake?"

Littl'un brushed the back of her hand on Mark's cheek and whispered, "Please Mark, look at me."

They stood in one of the many parking lots out on Two Mile Flat and stared at one another for what seemed an eternity. Quite suddenly, both David and Mark felt the presence of God surround the little alien. David glanced from his treasure to his friend Mark and saw a transformation. Like magic, Mark's features relaxed, and a smile awoke in his eyes. Mark fixed his eyes on David, and Littl'un looked at David.

"I apologize, Mark. You are Muki. I can see that now, and I will prove my worth.

David? I understand now why you are afraid to take me home with you. However, you must, David. I must learn to be Muki, or your people will destroy all I love and me. With your help, I can be brave. Teach me, David, before it is too late.

"Mark, I have no choice. God demands that I learn. I am as vulnerable as you are. Maybe if you try, God will guide you, too. David has no choice. Maybe, you do not either. Peace, brother."

Littl'un held up her hand, palm forward. Mark looked again at her and slowly nodded before he, too, raised his hand in peace.

"David, please take me home, now. I will not try to deceive you again. I will wait until you are ready to take me home with you. Mark, tell the Muki that I do not bite, and I will prepare to come and learn among you. Perhaps God will tell us both why I must become Muki. I, too, wish God had chosen another, yet I have no choice. I love David and think he holds my future. God said so."

Together they climbed into the truck. David drove, and Littl'un sat in the middle, as close to David as she could, so there was a vacant space between her and Mark. She did not look at Mark again. She watched David. David drove into the parking lot of the Catholic Church and stopped close to the trail up to the water tower site. Littl'un climbed out after him, still clinging to her fear of Mark and having angered David. "I needed you to know I was serious, David. Please forgive me," she said sincerely.

David kissed her, and she ran away. David and Mark watched her climb up the bank to disappear beyond it. Then David got back into the truck and drove away in silence. Neither had known what to say, but the Judge took it as his sign that God approved their plans.

They revamped their plans again, leaving the activity very loosely arranged because they were sure the little alien would not conform to their agenda. They were all more afraid now. God had sent them to this land and had told them to pass judgement on Earth. Without a doubt, it was an evil place. The people clearly did not live up to the standards of their own Great Books of God. The little alien was the most terrifying creature alive. Yet, she had met a second person of the Muki, and like the first, God was present around her. She used sin as a weapon, and God defended her. What was she going to do to them? Was she so powerful a demon that she could trick them into seeing a false God?

Throughout the discussions, Natthia continually repeated, "The blanket of Koe Sai Serena protects us. We can see with the eyes of God. We hear with the ears of God. Our touch can be the touch of God, our words, God's words, and our hands can and will do the work of God. Tara of Earth is a test, perhaps a demon, but we are to teach her the ways of the Muki. Through her, we will see the will of God."

On the Land of the Butterflies, the rigid social order endured by its citizens produced a phenomenon whereby otherwise sane and socially normal individuals would suddenly turn mad and expose their own and others' sins for all to witness and publicly beg God to deliver justice upon their own flesh rather than asking Jarrock to carry the burden of their sins through forgiveness. In the most severe cases, although shining with the light of God, they purposely either killed themselves (by completely ignoring safety, such as walking off the edge of a cliff or diving into turbulent water,) or draw people to them, like a powerful magnet, to be executed like lambs to the slaughter. Without fear or hesitation, normal people would step up to be slaughtered. The Muki called all these individuals madmen. They, too, were thought to be Instruments of Creation and holy. Only those considered to have stone hearts can stop madmen. Despite the carnage and blatant sacrifice caused, the Muki did not hate or blame either the executor or those who were executed. Rather than holding on to the horror of madmen's actions, the Muki honoured them for paying restitution for their own sins and those of all citizens in their homeland once they had been stopped. Their actions carried out God's justice, honoured God, and prevented Jarrock, who, like Earth's Jesus, died for the forgiveness of sins, from suffering the consequences needed to make restitution for their sins. By demonstrating their willingness to carry the weight of their sins, these people cleansed the Land of the Butterflies of sins. They reminded others of the pain and sorrow sins heaped upon God and led them to strive to be less sinful and more righteous, constantly seeking God's will and reflecting it in all thoughts, words, and deeds. The Muki believed these madmen served God and were destined to carry out God's will, on God's schedule, when they were conceived. Muma Horren concluded that the little alien was a madman, and many others agreed, except David, who just cried more and more often. Having never seen the side of Tara that she had shown to Mark, the base camp was the last place he wanted to bring her. To David, Tara of Earth was sweet, lovable, and innocent, but to Mark, she was a very powerful Cultural Judge directed by God to judge the Land of the Butterflies. Judge Soronato recorded Mark's feelings and used them as evidence that they were indeed working with a very dangerous madman. He reminded his expedition that madmen were holy even on the Land of the Butterflies. Madmen were very powerful tools of God whose duty was to expose the guilt of sin with blatant honesty.

"Be clean. Make this base a holy place! Through Mark's words, God has sent a message, reminding us not to take God's word lightly. This is the sixth judgement of a destruction assignment. Think, ladies and gentlemen. We cannot take a destruction assignment lightly. This land belongs to God, is part of God's creation, and all of creation is good in the eyes of God. As David long ago proclaimed, look for the good. This land is blessed! Get off your self-righteous pedestals and look with God's eyes at this land! Become Jarrock! Do not for a moment allow yourselves to believe in your own superiority. Be humble. You are slaves. Work for your master with a humble, grateful heart. Wear the gifts of Koe Sai Serena lest we condemn ourselves."

Judge Soronato lectured, and it was a subdued and frightened group of Cultural Judges who completed the preparations for the arrival of a young woman into their midst. They worshipped and cleansed their bodies and souls. They did not want to fail.

25

PLEASE TAKE ME HOME

A NEW YEAR OF SCHOOL HAD begun. I had some excellent teachers, and my world seemed to have come alive. I had learned so much in the last year that I felt incredibly powerful. Gradually David had been proving to me that slavery was indeed the route to incredible freedom. I no longer tried to live in the 'real world.' I refused to conform and began looking for ways to demonstrate more to myself than to others that I could be unique and succeed. The catch was that the world was not mine, and to succeed as an individual, I had to be ten times better at everything of consequence than was anybody else to get half the mark. That was the cost of being a non-conformist.

I took delight in my English class. I liked my teacher. He demanded quality and rationale for my insistent conviction that I interpret the work of authors with my own eyes rather than regurgitate his own or the popularly held interpretation. Often succeeding that year, I was a free spirit and determined to stay that way. An A or B paper was a victory, and I began to see that my world could grow with time and without my having to give up anything that was very dear to me. Although I would have to struggle, my island could take me into the future. David would help me. As my guardian angel, he was becoming the grey sentry.

I began to believe sincerely in the power of the grey sentry. All I needed to do was believe that righteousness would always win in the end, and I could make the world into my island. David and the things of the Muki, which he taught me, gave me confidence. God was not in my life for nothing. I did have a purpose, and I was of value. I had to represent the way of life that the grey sentry represented because the real world was not as it should be and ignore its beckoning calls for it was wrong, and my island kingdom righteous. I needed to make my kingdom grow and slowly accepted that my duty was to rock the boat and to challenge everything and everyone. Yes, I did everything the hard way, but it was worth it, for slowly, I saw a change come about. The shades of life in my world changed. Although I would forever bash my head against brick walls, I would expose the world, and it would begin to crumble. I knew I would not see my kingdom rise in glory, but I found overwhelming faith that it was growing and moving, not to death but rebirth. I wanted more.

David seemed content to spend time with me. The table was turned again. I needed him to teach me and somehow knew that the pace David was setting was not fast enough. I did not have time because time was running out. Desperate to be among the Muki, I became obsessed with a need to have David take me home. I angered him and spent many hours crying because I could not make him understand how important it was for me to become Muki. I did not even know the reason myself and began repeating over and over, "God said so," as though that explained it all. To me, it did. I had no choice but to be obedient. God controlled me. I did not believe I could disobey even if David said my obedience was my own. My obedience that fall simply was not a choice, at least not as far as becoming Muki was concerned.

I told David that I would find his truck and hide in it one day. When he arrived home, I would be with him, and he would not be able to stall any longer. "Danger is a challenge," I said. "The longer you wait, the more frightening it will become. The danger is growing. It will get too strong. Sooner is better. Please, David, I must become Muki! You must take me home."

Then, like many things in my relationship with David, like happenstance, I decided to walk out of town on the railway tracks toward the Cottonwood River. I was on Two Mile Flat savouring the smell of the lumber mills, letting the sounds of the saws lure me into believing the mills were alive when I glanced at the cars in the parking lot in front of me and spied David's truck. I giggled and, feeling very mischievous, walked up to it satisfying myself that it really was David's truck. Maybe David did work at one of the mills! I had begun to think David was a bum and did not really work at all because his routine was so odd and irregular. The idea that David really worked was scrumptious. He would be able to support me when I married him. Believing this was an incredible discovery, I hopped into the back feeling blessed with the opportunity to discover more of David's secrets. I hid under a tarp and worried about how long David would be. I was not comfortable; even if I was happy, I did feel very guilty. Learning about the Muki had made me far more conscious of sin. However, I told myself that God had brought me here and must have a plan. I tried to think about the whistles, wondering whether shift change was a long way off when I heard David's voice. He was laughing and joking with someone, and I became full of fear. David would be angry and disappointed in me for hiding in his truck. He always said, "You would not dare spy on me, Littl'un. I would be very angry with you."

By then, they were right up to the truck, and David said, "Check for Tara, please, Mark. I have a feeling that one day she will be in the truck. She is apt to do what she says she will!" Then to my mortification, they both laughed. Before he lifted the tarp, my guilty feelings vanished. How dare he laugh?

Then his friend terrified me.

Have you ever watched a child investigate a fly? I am talking about the situation where the fly has the undivided attention and even holds all the child's fascination. However, that fascination offers no respect or regard to the life of the fly. It is not a meal but just a toy or object with which to play. Holding the fly captive, the child gets bored and then meticulously tears off its limbs, one at a time to watch it suffer and make feeble attempts to escape, before out of pity, but not shame, the child squashes the twitching torso with his thumb and is disgusted with the ugly goop that has smeared on his thumb.

Seeing Mark glaring at me in the back of the truck made me think it would only be moments before Mark reached out to dissect me., I saw myself as the fly in Mark's features, not dying to feed or serve any purpose, just to be disposed of when my buzzing no longer captured his amusement as though I was worthless, useless, and undeserving of further attention. It was horrible. I whispered, "Please God, help me." Then I tried to stare down Mark. Inside I cried, "He could not be Muki. Mukis are angels like David." Then I made a fool of myself, and David took me back home.

After that, I was quiet about going home with him. Believing him, I realized it was unacceptable to go among the Muki and felt totally defeated. David would never marry me because I did not belong in his world. Needing to be anchored firmly to the ground beneath my feet, I told myself to be content with his friendship, learn what he was willing to teach, and trust that the future would unfold according to God's will and on God's schedule. If I had had a choice, I would have stopped time altogether and stayed out in the forest, walking with David forevermore, just walking, going nowhere, and savouring the light that shone in David.

Who was I to think I was worthy of such love? I wanted to bask in the knowledge of being loved by someone as wonderful and special as my friend, who forgave every one of my faults, was patient, and oh, so confident in the future. Wanting to make up for insulting his friend and for trying to trap him, I did not want to lose him. Yet a nagging conviction within me repeated, "David is not yours to keep. He has responsibilities. When my lessons are completed, he will go to another to work his magic on God's behalf. David is the future." I no longer wanted to learn about the Muki. The end was drawing near, and I wanted to keep it at bay.

26

THE FUTURE DOES NOT WAIT

DAVID GROANED AS HE CLIMBED out of a transporter at the base camp. "Doug!" he shouted. "How could you do this to a transporter? It is horrible... noisy, bumpy, and the vibrations are apt to break a person up into tiny pieces. Have you no respect for the class of a transporter?"

Doug burst out laughing. "So, you think it will pass as an earthling's airplane? Pretty gross, isn't it?"

"I don't know how you did it, Doug, but yes, this is all too much like the primitive machines of these people. Oh! You don't realize how I hate being bashed. Could you turn the noise down? It gives me a headache. Littl'un will know something is not right if I throw up. Just tame it a little, will you?"

"I really don't think I should, David. We have built false innards. It would be a real job to soften the vibrations. Besides, I am very proud of my effort. Judge Soronato told me to make it as real as I could. It uses five times the normal energy consumption, but it has all the bells and whistles."

"Are the readings on the dials realistic? She will notice."

"As accurate as those in a small aircraft," answered Doug, still laughing at David's disapproval. "I set it up with four seats. I will fly it, and you can sit in the back with the alien. I do not think the visibility will be good enough for her to see the speed. I worry about her reaction to our speed, but I did not dare put the speedometer in a less visible place. It would cause suspicion. The outside is a holograph, except the sleeve attached around the doors. You will have to be ingenious in helping her into the transporter. I cannot get the shield any lower, David. She will still feel a jerk when she enters and exits. I suggest you toss her in, get out before her, and I will toss her back. If we do not put in a ladder, it will seem appropriate."

"What about visibility?"

"The hologram blocks out almost all visibility from the back seat. If she keeps her seatbelt fastened, she should not see much besides sky."

"Has the Judge given us landing and take-off locations?"

"I could not get the pontoons to sit in the water, so I removed them and have left them as holograms. You cannot let her try to touch the plane. You will take off from Fish Lake, about an hour southwest of Quesnel. We have the directions, all logging road access in the survey room. I suggest you familiarize yourself with the route. Sorry, it is so far, but it was hard to find an area unfrequented but big enough to pass as a legitimate seaplane site. Fish Lake at least comes close to legitimate. The Judge wants the transporter exposure minimized. Upon arrival, you will radio us, and we will land, pick you up, and get out of there as quickly as possible."

"I do not like it, Doug. If I bring her out on a Saturday, we have only about six hours. Littl'un would be suspicious about going so far to take a plane. Seaplanes are common on Dragon Lake, only three miles south of town. Is the transporter noise just inside or from the outside as well?"

"Primarily, it is inside, David. Why?"

"Make it look like a boat from above, Doug, and we can get on board at the bottom of Bowron Avenue, right in the Quesnel River, taxi around the corner upstream, just past her island kingdom, and take-off out of sight. I think there would be less risk. We should be able to fly down the power line to get back on course, rejoin the standard loop, and return the same way."

"Why don't I just make it invisible? Hide in Beaver Pond. When you make some noise, I'll change the hologram to a plane. You get onboard. I'll make us invisible again, and we'll take off around the corner. If anyone sees anything, it'll be no more than a haze in the air," laughed Doug.

"Turn down the noise, and it would work, Doug," answered David seriously.

"David, you can't be serious. It is against the law to land in the river."

"Littl'un won't mind. In fact, it may work to our advantage. She likes taking risks. It isn't impossible for a good pilot to land or take off there, which would explain why we stay so close to the ground. If you have landed illegally, you have to stay out of radar range."

Doug laughed and promised to talk to Judge Soronato. David was being very gutsy, but he did know the alien. It just might be a more plausible plan. I'll put a fade into the vibrations for you while I'm at it, David. Who would you like me to bring as the co-pilot? Mark?"

"No, she's afraid of Mark. I will ask Brian if he would like to come."

"It is fine by me if the Judge approves. Let's plan this for Saturday."

"Sure," answered David before he choked. "I really have to bring her then?"

"Yeah, it will be alright. We'll be polite. Don't worry."

It was time for lunch, so they headed to the kitchen. Frightened because the Little Smiler had reacted so badly to Mark, David really did not want to bring her to the base camp. Furthermore, Mark was the least of his concerns. If she is afraid of Mark, what will she think of Doug, who vocally despises Earthlings? Or how will she react to Muma Horren? Muma Horren never hides her disgust for fertile females wandering at will outside a castle. She had often told him that she did not approve of his relationship with Tara. David sighed. Tara was right. The sooner he got the introductions over with, the better. Still, he picked at his dinner.

After talking to Doug, Judge Soronato came to sit with David, who explained his reasoning again, and the Judge laughed and laughed. Then he said, "David, make it at night, and I will let you try it once. I will have the base on alert, and we will evacuate at any hint of trouble.

You had better prepare the alien for a visit, David. What explanation will you give for us being so far away?"

"That's easy. I'm an adult. Adults rarely live with their folks, Sir. She will think we are strange, but she knows that already. That is the least of my concerns."

"Do you have any instructions for us?"

"No. Nothing that we have not already discussed, Sir. I will feel better when it is over. Maybe she will decide she does not want to be Muki after all."

"I hope not, David. You need help teaching her. Trust God. Put your faith where it belongs. Looking forward to meeting her, I feel as though I know her already. Take heart and relax. It will go well. This crew is good, and they will act appropriately."

"I think I will surprise her, Sir."

"Your choice, do what you think is best," said the Judge with a smile as he stood and left the kitchen.

Everyone else let David be alone with his thoughts. The news of the impending arrival of the alien into their base camp spread throughout the camp quickly, and David could feel both the resulting excitement and apprehension. Many were treating the visit as an inspection, and he felt honoured that they wanted to impress his friend.

David made a point of seeing Tara early in the week and asked her if she would arrange to be late on the following Friday evening. Sometimes, Littl'un told her parents she had a babysitting job, and David just paid her what she would have made if she really were babysitting. It worked very well. That was how he managed to have the last three Friday evenings with her without worrying about explanations or early curfews. It was sinful. David felt guilty about it and did not mention it to anyone. Earth was teaching him to do things that were far from right, but he treasured his time with the Little Smiler. He did not allow himself to think about the deception he was asking her to live. It seemed a normal component of her culture, and she did not feel upset about lying. She told him that she compensated for her tricks by doing extra chores or buying her mother flowers. His whole relationship with the alien was a deception, so there was no point in letting a little convenience upset him. Besides, it allowed him to contact her by phone without raising suspicions. She always babysat on Saturday evenings for the same people and often once during the week, so it was not hard to have an almost steady Friday evening job. The new apartment building, only a block and a bit away, was full of families with young children. David and Tara doubted that her parents were in the least concerned. She walked over after supper. David picked her up in the lobby or on the way and delivered her back home around eleven in the evening. David usually took Tara for a drive and never went anywhere where there were other people.

David had asked the Judge earlier to set up an exploration camp for the meeting. However, the Judge refused and told him that the alien already knew the Muki were not ordinary people, and they would not compromise their own culture for her sake. They would retain the laws and let her reach whatever conclusion she wanted. If a problem became evident, Natthia would erase her memory of the visit. He said, "She thinks we are a strange group of Native Americans who never gave up the old ways of a nomadic lifestyle. I think our base camp will support that theory. God will know what to allow the alien to understand. We need only be ourselves, David. God will protect us."

Shocked by the Judge's faith, David, wondered if Earth and its evil ways were rubbing off on him again. After that conversation, he cleansed and prayed for Jarrock to protect them all. Since she had reacted so strongly to Mark, he was not as confident of her trustworthiness and feared she was too powerful.

27

AT HOME WITH THE MUKI

I NOTICED THE EXCITEMENT IN DAVID the moment I saw him. He was everything but calm, and something was up because David never glanced at his watch during the first half of our visits. He only worried about getting me home on time. I stayed out of sight and watched him for a while. Usually, I found him sitting on a log when we met on this trail below the water tower. He knew I particularly loved the walky-talky tree just before him and would stare at it, wondering why I never fell. After laughing, he would sing the Deplukador song. It had a neat tune. I tried to learn it in Muki; the translation was not nearly as grand as the real thing. During the summer, I had grown proud of being akin to Deplukador, more so because the Muki considered it a masculine trait. Women tended to be connected heavily to the Voice of Life aspect of God. You know, concerned with nurturing, safety, security, and constancy. Not me. I was the bull in the china shop. Wanting control and power, I pushed at the limits with full-hearted tears, frustration, anger, and defiance. The world was mine to mould and shape into something, which fulfilled me. Yes, I was openly selfish and defined everything on my own terms. David laughed at me. He could burst my bubbles anytime he wanted, but he rarely did. He would turn them around, and I would burst them myself... this was God's world, not mine, no matter how hard I fought. Giving up was not an option. I had to push. Pushing fed my soul, keeping me alive. It was not evil; it was the Deplukador in me. I was confident God loved me, even needed me to be exactly who and how I was.

However, today, David was not singing at all, not even sitting. He was pacing back and forth under the walky-talky tree, glancing at his watch and then at the underside of the tree above him. I waited, wondering why he did not climb onto it and use it properly. "David," I yelled suddenly and laughed as he jumped and went very red. David seemed to blush easily, and he went red all over. He literally shone with red! I climbed onto the walky-talky tree and continued until I was high enough that the trunk swayed with each step. "Come on up, David. I guarantee that speaking your mind up here will banish your frustration. I am not late. In fact, I am early, at least a quarter of an hour."

While shaking his head, David laughed and then, as seriously as he always spoke, said, "One day you will fall, Littl'un. I worry that I might not be here to catch you. Come on down, Tara."

Yup, something was up. I came down, and David put his arms around me and held me close. Then he whispered, "I love you."

"You are taking me home," I whispered back. Knowing I had guessed right, I laughed at the shocked look he gave me. Suddenly, I was full of questions. As I jabbered on, getting more and more nervous myself, David seemed to relax.

"Just be yourself, Littl'un. You will do okay," he said so many times in the next minutes that I was not sure who he was trying to convince, him or me.

I did not want to embarrass him and made a silent vow to myself to do everything within my power to make David proud of me and hoped I would be capable of displaying the appropriate respect to the Muki. That was not as easy as it sounds. The Muki honour honesty very highly, and to be insincere is a worse crime than being rude, justifiably rude. The standards of the Muki were very different from the culture in which I worked and played. To be acceptable, I had to be myself, and I was antisocial by nature. David's friend, Mark, had terrified me, quite literally. I wished God had not told me to become Muki. I would be on display and felt certain that the Muki would find me lacking. Whatever it meant, it was true; I did not have a castle. I was lacking, and they would see all that I lacked. David overlooked my deficiencies and tried to build upon my soul whatever was missing as though he was my guardian angel. However, the Muki did not love me. They hated me. At least if they were like Mark, they did. David had always said I would not be safe around the Muki, and I did not feel safe around Mark. He was so creepy. I did not want even to brush close to him. He oozed hatred. David hugged me; I was trembling so badly that I could barely stand up.

"You do not have to come, Tara. You do not have to meet anyone. We can go on, just you and I, for as long as you need."

I pulled myself together. Giving me confidence, David was my strength. Without any options, I had to succeed in becoming Muki because God had said so. As David held me, I said a silent prayer, "Please, protect me."

Such calm drifted over me that I knew David was right. It would be as it should be. My future was in God's hands. I had no choices and no options. Regardless of how I felt or how hard I tried, whatever was supposed to happen would unfold according to God's will. I would just be myself and enjoy this time with David. I felt comfort in anticipating the unravelling of David's secrets.

I was nothing more than a bystander caught in the theatre, playing the part that God ordained me to play. This evening, I was to be the spy. With that thought, I laughed. My laughter frightened David, and I felt powerful again. David would carry the heat, so I really did not need to worry, but I squeezed his hand, and he too relaxed. I hoped we would not have far to go because distance and time can shatter the best of confidence.

David continued to watch the time. I giggled every time he looked at his watch, and he blushed every time he looked at me. Finally, he said, "We can go now. I will protect you, Tara. My friends won't hurt you. I promise."

"You'll bring me back any time I ask, right?"

"Just say the word."

"Thanks, David. I really want to meet the Muki. I'll try to be brave."

"You will do all right. We have talked about you. You already have some friends."

I cringed. "I hope you haven't built up expectations that I cannot live up to. I am just a kid, David."

David said nothing but ruffled my short hair and smiled. I let out a deep sigh and took his hand. Together we walked down the path. I asked, "Where are we going?"

"We are going to Beaver Pond. Ever flown before?"

"That's not a good place to leave the truck, David. No. I've never flown, but I'd like to. I love heights. A plane would take me ever so high."

We had crossed the tracks, but I still could not see the truck. I looked curiously at David, but he just smiled, which caused me to feel wonderful. David clapped his hands, suddenly making a deafening clap that made me jump. Although very nervous, I could not see anyone as we continued through the bushes, and then I saw the weirdest looking plane I have ever seen sitting in the middle of Beaver Pond. It was deathly still. I was sure the engine was not on, but it did not move. As I could not see a rope holding it, it should have floated up against the log in front of the dam. The door opened with an audible hiss. I was terrified. Nothing seemed right; even the air was foggy in the pond but not outside it.

Who was David? Who were the Muki? As I concentrated on David's touch, I rubbed his fingers. He was real and human. I told myself repeatedly; the Muki were Native Americans. They lived like the tribes of the past. Only they were modern. They used the culture of the world most of us lived in but kept themselves separate. We were corrupt. They needed to know what we were up to for their own security. David was a spy. White man was still the enemy. Their planes were different because the Mukis were different. A plane was sitting in Beaver Pond because I was going somewhere secret. I was the enemy, but David had opened his world up to me because God had told him to teach me. I was here because God had brought me here. Maybe I was dying. Maybe David was an angel. Maybe... no, do not go there! Calm down. David just is not ordinary. The Mukis are not ordinary. Cults are weird. They have weird airplanes.

The plane had pontoons, but it was very low in the water. The plane's body sat steeply uphill as though it was a rocket or a missile about to take off. It was narrow and had an odd curve, and the wings looked designed for a different machine. Poised to flap, they looked almost like a real bird's wing.

I pinched myself, but I was not dreaming. Something was making the plane move. Hoping someone was reeling in an anchor line, I crossed my fingers. There were two shadows in the doorway, one sitting at the controls and the other waving at David. The whole scene was eerie, yet I felt relief and comfort when David waved back.

This was an adventure. I was part of it and realized something special was happening, especially for me. David was about to give me a gift, the gift of the Muki. A feeling of honour elated me. "Please, God, do not let me let them down. Guide me. I do not know why, but I feel that you are nearer than usual. Please stay with me. I want to be obedient."

David looked at me. I could tell that he loved me. He asked if I was ready to get on board, and I nodded but did not move. Lifting me up, David threw me to the man in the doorway. Something had kicked me or sucked me forward, but I felt a funny sensation. I was trying to figure out which, while a stranger held on to me and motioned for me to sit in a seat on the other side of the plane. David jumped in, too. I wondered why there was not a ladder but did not say anything. I was trying to figure out how I felt about the man who still held me. Did he think I would fall out? I did not feel frightened by this man. I quickly decided he must be David's brother. It simply felt right. "Hello, Brian," I said, and he set me down immediately.

David laughed and introduced me. "Brian, this is Tara. Tara, my brother, Brian, but I guess you knew that already. Told you she was special, Brian."

Brian glanced at me, said, "Pleased to meet you." Then he quickly clambered into the front seat and sat beside the pilot.

While he helped me hook up the seatbelt, David said, in a calm steady voice, "The pilot is my friend, Doug. Doug, Tara."

Hastily, Doug glanced back at me, said, "Hello," turned back to the controls, and must have pressed a button to close the door, for it slammed shut and clicked into place. Then I heard the same odd sucking sound as it apparently sealed itself. David said it was a pressurized cockpit, but I was not entirely sure I believed him. I was too excited about flying to worry about how coldly the pilot had greeted me or why I felt so safe when Brian had caught me and helped me into my seat. When David asked if I was ready, I nodded, then he spoke to the pilot, and the engines roared into life. I thought the whole thing would jiggle apart, and it was horribly noisy. I pushed my head against the window as we taxied out of the pond into the open river, and suddenly, my concern was for David.

"We're too noisy, David. Someone will see us. I've put you in danger. I am so sorry. You should have told me how dangerous it was for you to take me to your home." Then I cried uncontrollably over the enormity of what it was David had sacrificed to teach me to be of the Muki.

David just held me while I prayed for safety and security for David and the Muki. I felt terribly guilty, but it was too late to turn back. We turned around the bend. As I could not really see anything out the window, I stopped straining my eyes and tried instead to concentrate all my efforts on making God protect David. "Don't let anyone see us. Don't let anyone hear us. Make us quieter, please." I thought it did get quieter as we rose from the water. Feeling pushed into my chair for a moment, we climbed straight up for a second then levelled off again. "Oh my God, the radar," then aloud I screamed, "David!" Everyone stared at me, even Doug. I felt very silly.

"It is okay, Tara. We are safe. Stop worrying," soothed David. The others returned their attention to flying the plane. I hugged David and closed my eyes. It was dark, and I could not see anything anyway, and being close to David comforted me. As I calmed down, the tension in the plane seemed to dissipate. I thought we must be out of the range of the radar at the airport. David leaned over, kissed my forehead, and I went to sleep. Vibration can do that to me; the plane had lulled me to sleep in only minutes. I woke up when it went quiet. We had landed, the engines were off, and it was dark. We had been in the air an hour.

David jumped out, and Brian grabbed me to toss me to him. I felt insulted. Something about how I had to get out gave me the creeps. My stomach tied itself up, and I thought I would be sick, so I did not complain. Besides, there was something special about David's little brother. He made me feel safe. I did not feel hatred from Doug, just indifference or maybe curiosity but mostly a need to have me outside his space. I wondered if I would get such strong feelings from each Muki. They were not like anybody I had ever met before, like open books. I could feel their presence and even their thoughts within me. I must be crazy; I thought as we walked along a trail leading away from the lake or river where we had landed. I could not tell. It was too dark. I was glad David was holding my hand.

Presently, I saw movement in the trees in front of us. There were people moving about, but they must have been wearing camouflage clothing. I could see someone one second, and then he would disappear. The Mukis were private people was the thought that kept running through my mind. Invading their world, I was alien and did not belong. Realizing they were frightened as well, I prayed, "Do not let me frighten them. Help me show them that I am one of them, just another human who will not hurt them."

I think God laughed, but I felt warm inside. David was with me, and everything was going to be the way it was supposed to be. I took a few deep breaths. The air here was cold and crisp. We must have gone north. It felt north, like Barkerville, only I did not think we were high up rather in a valley. I could not see much in the darkness, but I trusted my imagination. The trees around us were small, and I was sure we were in a forest. It felt right. I was at home and not even afraid anymore. I was incredibly safe. Furthermore, I knew I belonged.

We walked out into a clearing. A few people disappeared into the trees on the opposite side of the clearing. A fire flickered in the center, and I knew I had seen this place before. It was the campfire of my dream over a year ago before I had met David. Closing my eyes, I raised my arms and even let go of David's hand. I do not know why I did, but I stood there listening to the breeze until I heard the chants of my dream calling me onward. I tilted my head back and opened my eyes to look at the stars. Concluding this was a holy spot; I felt very blessed, especially because God had brought me here.

A cool wind brushed past me. I looked around and blushed. David and his two friends were staring at me, and I felt embarrassed. David took my hand and told me he loved me, and then Doug said, "She is special, David. Come on, Brian, let's go get changed."

I watched them walk away. They, too, disappeared into the woods beyond the fire. I wondered where they were going: to tents or tepees?

I jumped when David said, "I have got to change, too, Tara. I have told you a little about Natthia. She will look after you while I am gone."

At first, I felt panic, but then a wave of calm swept over me. I would be fine. Natthia was nice and would be my friend. Smiling, I nodded with confidence that these people were special, and it was a privilege to be here among them. They were all angels. I do not know what they saw in me, but I sure wanted to be one of them. Although young and naive, God was honouring me. I did not know why. But I was thrilled, despite knowing I did not deserve to be among such noble people as the Muki. Silently, I promised God I would do my very best to be all He wanted me to be tonight. It was an unreal place but very real at the same time. This place was good. I could feel the blessings of God all around me. Pondering what to do, I debated the appropriateness of both falling on my knees and praying or dancing and singing for joy. But before I had made a choice, Natthia appeared, and David began to introduce her to me. I liked her instantly.

Natthia wore Egyptian-type sandals with laces braided up her legs to her knees and a plain but dignified and expensive-looking dress that came down to her knees. I think it was leather. See, they were Native Americans. Her hair was long and silver. She was old, incredibly old, yet not weak or feeble looking. Although she only said hello, I loved the sound of her voice. It was full of love and respect, and even wisdom. After following a trail along a cliff, we walked behind a rock and entered a door into the hill. As the door behind us closed, everything went very dark. Then David opened another door and bright lights blinded us. It took a moment for my eyes to adjust, I felt like I had stepped into a cathedral when they did. It was just a hall with many closed doors on both sides. It was wide, at least twenty feet, and the ceiling curved like a dome. I am sure it was a rock. The walls and doors looked old and constructed from untreated wood. I do not know why I felt like I was in a church. It struck me with the same kind of awe that fancy churches invoke. I said nothing until David stopped more than halfway down the hall.

"Go with Natthia, Tara. I am not far away. Natthia, please keep her happy and entertained while I change," instructed David. I chuckled as I realized he did not want to leave me. I liked David wanting me close to him and, especially, the protection that his eyes promised. After watching him walk across to a door, open it, and disappear as he shut the door behind him, I spoke to Natthia. "He's going to put on traditional clothes, is he not? Should I change also?"

Natthia searched my eyes carefully before she answered, "If you would be more comfortable, I am sure we can arrange something. Come, Muma Horren and I set up a room for you, just in case you did not want to wait out here in an empty hall. It does not seem right."

"I think I like this hall. It makes me want to dance," I said happily.

Natthia gasped. "This is not a castle, child. You cannot dance here. Come quickly." She grabbed my arm and made a fast beeline for a door further down the hallway. I knew I had said something wrong but was not sure why I needed that castle or what was wrong with wanting to dance. It just felt like a big ballroom: the hardwood floor, the high vaulted ceiling, and the holiness of the place just filled me with joy and excitement. I decided to keep my mouth shut and follow instructions. We entered a rather bare room, and Natthia closed the door. A stranger faced me. Natthia introduced the woman as Muma Horren.

Muma Horren was a small woman. I had pictured her as a round jolly woman about fifty. I could not have been more wrong. She was skinny as a rail, old, and even frail. Her hair was wispy and grey with some pure white mixed in here and there. She wore it in a small bun at the back of her head. Like Natthia, she had wrinkles, but her skin was paler, almost white. She, too, looked wise. After looking me over, she grunted and said, "How can you wear such garments? You must be uncomfortable."

"I would like to change, Muma Horren. I have always worn clothes like these. I have never dressed as a Muki. I would like to, please."

Muma Horren laughed. I sighed, believing I had said the right thing. Muma Horren looked at Natthia and scowled. "How can we dress her? What would be appropriate?"

I said, "David says I am a butterfly. Do butterflies dress a particular way?"

Muma Horren and Natthia both gasped. Muma Horren said, "I warned you, Natthia. She knows more than she is letting on. This is no castle, Tara. You should not be here. You belong in a castle. Nothing good can come of this."

"Calm down, Muma. We have no stinger. Relax. We cannot make her into a butterfly. Let's do the best we can."

"That's right, Natthia. If there is no stinger, there is not a butterfly. We will put her in brown. Come with me, dear; get out of those clothes. Muma Horren can make you respectable."

I was not sure I liked the sly snickers that Natthia and Muma Horren were exchanging, but I did not dare object when they each knelt and started undoing the laces on my runners. It felt funny, though, so I sat down on the floor and took my shoes and socks off. "You probably want a shower, Tara. Just undress. We will measure you and make the necessary adjustments while you clean up," laughed Natthia while she helped me to my feet.

Embarrassed, I did not think my feet smelt that bad. When I lifted a foot to smell it, they howled in laughter. Honest, it really did not stink. Then they offered to help me undress. I sighed, saying it was not necessary, and began undressing. They watched, and I felt very awkward. As I removed an article of clothing, Muma Horren would grab it, fold it neatly, and place it in the bottom of the closet by the door.

The room was small, at most seven by eight or nine feet. It had a window for I could see the fire outside and a couple of stars. Natthia assured me that no one could see in, and they both laughed at my modesty. Although everything I did and said made them laugh, I could not seem to get mad at them. I just felt silly and out of place. Because I wanted to belong and be acceptable, I just reminded myself that I was an outsider, and they meant nothing by their laughter. It was normal because I was stupid and did not know anything. Feeling dumb standing naked before them, I asked to use the bathroom even though I could see neither a door nor shower stall. They laughed and laughed, apologizing whenever they caught their breath. I did not know what was so funny. Finally, Natthia said she was finished. I sighed too. I did not know why they needed so many measurements for a dress.

"You go get the dress, Muma. I will teach her how to use the facilities." Natthia chuckled. "I am sorry, Tara. This is just so unusual for us. You are a treat. It reminds me of when I was a girl. Your first dress; this will be a celebration."

Muma Horren scowled at Natthia. "Be careful, Natthia. There are young men and even a boy here. It is not right. She is beautiful. She knows what she is." Muma Horren then pointed a finger at me before continuing, "And you, young lady, be careful. This is no place for a butterfly. Watch your step. I am going to take my bow."

"Muma Horren!" shouted Natthia, but Muma Horren just left.

I felt alone, and Natthia just shook her head. Then smiling, she laughed. "She likes you, Tara. She will act like your senior mother. Take some advice, get Muma Horren's approval before you do anything, even before looking at David." Then Natthia laughed again, and I blushed.

Natthia pointed at a weird bowl mounted on a pedestal near the wall by the closet. It looked like a low fountain. "That's our style of toilet," she said, "Come, I will show you how to use it."

It was the strangest toilet I have ever used, but it was also the neatest. You stand over the bowl and pull a string hanging on the wall. The bowl rises to fit snugly up against your skin, moulds to your shape and it is not obvious what you are doing. Luckily, Natthia warned me, or I might have been frightened that first time I used one. A warm spray of water flows from the front and back of the toilet, you do what you are there for, and when you are done, you pull the string again. After the water stops, a warm wind blows you dry, and the whole thing lowers again, only it retains its shape. Set up just for the occupant of the room; it is private. Natthia says it is faster when already shaped to your bottom. Fascinated by the toilet, I would like one because there is no paper, no mess, and it feels wonderful. When you wear typical Muki clothing, you do not even have to undress. You just step over it and look like you are just standing around!

The shower was right there in the room, too. What I thought was a fire sprinkler was the nozzle. A drain was on the floor, and there was a curtain to pull around it. I had assumed it was a drape for the window. You step in, push a button on the wall, and the water pours out. Natthia helped me adjust the temperature and offered to scrub me down. You will never guess what she used instead of soap. She used salt. Boy, did it hurt! Although I felt very clean when she was finished, I thought she would scrape off all my skin. I discovered that the Muki simply do not hear 'no thank you'. I am glad because I would have missed something special if I had not let her bathe me. I really felt loved and special. I was a guest, and this was how the Muki welcomed a guest.

By the time I was dry, Muma Horren was back with a brown cloth draped over her arm. She laughed as Natthia told her about all the silly things I had said about the facilities. As Natthia was already my friend, I laughed with her, realizing that I really liked everything about her. Somehow or another, her presence gave me confidence and a strange sense of freedom that completely delighted me.

They dressed me, and I just stood there enjoying their attention. The dress was very soft and light. Made in panels with various strips of chocolate brown material overlapping and joining at the shoulders, it had a front and a back but no side seams. Some straps wrapped around my breasts and my waist to hold them together. Taking an arm each, Muma Horren and Natthia braided a multitude of overlapping straps, attached at the shoulder and around the edge of material to my underarm, into intricately woven sleeves. It felt wonderfully comfortable. They laughed, then joined me for a few minutes as I twirled around until Muma Horren said, "Let's get the tights and shoes onto her. She's acting too lively, Natthia."

The tights were tan, surprisingly heavy, and looked like nylons gartered to a waistband. I pulled them on and sat on the bench under the window while they each laced up a sandal like their own onto my feet. I felt a little silly as Muma Horren gave me a good look, sighed, and told Natthia that I would be perfect if my hair were longer.

I still felt a little naked. The Muki does not wear underwear. I thought I was wearing a nightgown. I would feel silly going outdoors dressed like this but somehow knew that I would not be cold despite the lightweight. Besides, other than the fact that this dress looked a deep chocolate brown while theirs were a pale tan, I felt that I was dressed appropriately.

Natthia said, "Walk around a bit, Tara. Let us get a good look at you." I walked. Muma Horren started to cry.

"Oh, Natthia," she said, "We have made her into a butterfly, stinger or not. She cannot leave this room."

Natthia looked at me very closely before she nodded. "You are right, Muma. She is exactly herself. She is a butterfly. We cannot hide it. Nor should we try to disguise her. Maybe she is supposed to dance."

"Natthia!" scolded Muma Horren. "This is not a castle. I will not let her near Brian. You know better. This world is an evil place. Do not forget who we are. We must protect this woman. And, Natthia, we must protect David and all the others."

Natthia sighed and nodded. "But she is so beautiful, Muma."

Silence descended that was quickly broken by a rap on the door. "May I come in?"

It was David's voice, and I quickly said yes. David stepped in. Natthia rushed to close the door behind him. Muma Horren grabbed a bow, fitted an arrow in the blink of an eye, and pointed it at David while Natthia held me behind her. She was strong for an old lady. Her grip on my arm hurt. It was that tight. David stood very still. Natthia talked calmly to Muma Horren.

Muma Horren loosened her grip and backed away, still aiming the arrow at David but not saying anything. David stared at me. Then he trembled, covered his eyes, and cried. Natthia stepped between us and took his hand. David uncovered his eyes and said, "Oh, my Tara. You are a beautiful butterfly. How can I protect you? I want so badly to ask you to..."

"No, David. You must not. Go quickly. You should not be here. These are not your quarters. Go before I shoot you, David. Not here, not now, never David. She is not Muki. Your eyes are deceiving you," said Muma Horren, very calmly.

I had never seen David look so handsome. He wore a light yellow shirt beneath a tan leather vest, much like the dress I was wearing. A broad leather belt wrapped around his waist, and the tassels hung down to his knees. I struggled against a desire to run into his arms.

"David, we were just deciding that I needed to change. This dress makes me feel funny, kind of like I think I would feel if I was a bride. You are missing something, David. You are not dressed as a groom. I do not want to look like a butterfly; my hair is too short." Despite the strength in my voice, I inwardly shuddered and filled with foreboding and an incomprehensible desire to escape – to anywhere but here – but could no longer find a voice to use, and my feet felt glued to the floor and would not respond.

Natthia held David firmly, and Muma Horren said, "You are right, Tara. David has no sword. He is not authorized. He has no license. Send him away."

Recovering my voice, I quickly answered, "Do you have another of those tunics, David? Please bring me one."

Immediately, David turned and left. Natthia and Muma Horren looked at me curiously but did not move at all, except Muma Horren lowered the bow. A moment later, David rapped on the door. Natthia opened it just enough to take the clothes he had brought from him. As soon as the door closed, Muma Horren began undoing my dress.

As Natthia took it away, I cried. That dress was special, because it told David that I was his, and we all knew it. I kept touching my hair to remind me that loving was good and right, but David was my teacher, not my lover, and I knew we had to remain innocent. I grabbed David's clothes with an odd mixture of regret and defiance. Muma Horren and Natthia just stood back and watched as I put on David's shirt and struggled to tie up his tunic.

Natthia came to my rescue, straightened, and adjusted the tunic. Finally, she tied the leather belt to her satisfaction. She asked me to turn around, and then we all laughed, as with a sad voice, Muma Horren said, "She looks like a young man now, Natthia," and sighed. There were tears in all our eyes.

As she hugged me, Natthia said, "You've done well, Tara. You are very wise. I am proud of you."

"I do not know, Natthia. Please, David knows. Bring your bow, Natthia. We will sit her between us."

Natthia wiped my tears and asked if I felt ready to meet the Muki. I nodded, and Muma Horren held my hand while Natthia fetched her bow. I do not know exactly how I felt. Honoured is the only word that seems even close. Feeling very nervous, I did not think I wanted to meet anyone else. However, I had to fulfill my duty. Again, I nodded. Natthia opened the door.

The hall was not empty now. There were two rows of men lined up on either side of the hall. They all looked handsome, but I was only looking for one person, and I could not see him. As confidence ebbed like the changing tide, I shrunk into my shell, gritted my teeth, and affirmed my identity by whispering to God that I do not like meeting people. Wanting this over quickly, I took several deep breaths and entered the hallway.

Everyone stared at me. I hated it. Blushing, I was shaking

uncontrollably. If Natthia and Muma Horren had not held onto me, I think I would have collapsed. You have no idea how scary it was to be paraded down rows of strangers in a holy place. I had searched all the faces, twice all the way around, and David was not there. Thoroughly panicked, I sat down, hid my face, and screamed.

"David!" I yelled repeatedly, and people started to move and then stopped so suddenly that I had to look up to see what was happening. Natthia and Muma Horren were standing over me, bows raised, arrows pulled taunt. No one dared to move. I felt terribly guilty and let tears fall freely into my hands. The silence was deafening. My voice broke across it and sounded wrong and out of place. "Do not shoot anyone. I will be okay. I just need David," I said quietly.

"Muma Horren?" rang out in a loud stern voice.

"Yes, Judge Soronato," Muma Horren answered back in a voice that said unmistakably that she had authority.

"May I please release, David?"

"He loves her. It is not safe for either of them to be in contact with each other."

"He has been seeing Tara for a year, Muma. He has acted appropriately."

"He is a man. He has seen her as a butterfly. It would be immoral."

"We all know she is a butterfly, Muma. David needs our help, yes. But, he needs our support and trust, perhaps more so."

"I shall hold you responsible, Judge Soronato," returned Muma Horren as she aimed her arrow directly at him.

I wondered if an arrow would kill him that far away and shuddered as I concluded it likely. Looking around at the faces of all the people, standing so still, I knew this was not a game. It was very serious, and someone could be dead if anything went wrong. Clearly, the Mukis were very serious people and not putting on a show for me. David was right. It was not safe to be among the Muki. I was a cause of extreme danger and not supposed to be here. Whatever it meant, I was supposed to be in a castle, not here in this place in the presence of these incredible, strict, frightening, and powerful beings. Honestly, I was overwhelmed with conflicting emotions, some screaming of the honour and privilege of being among them and others warning that they were foreign and dangerous. Furthermore, they lived by standards that I could not comprehend.

"Muma Horren," called someone. It was a voice like David's, and I began to search the crowd for Brian. "I will guard David for you. I will not let him err."

Muma Horren let out a heart-wrenching squeal. She sighed as many more voices offered to stand guard duty. "Judge Soronato, let David out; guard him yourself, and I will relent."

A tall, dignified man stepped out of the rows of men and went to a door at the end of the hall. It was not David's room, and I wondered what had become of David. The Judge came back a moment later with a sword at his side. The men moved away from David's door. The Judge opened it. Both he and David returned. The Judge drew his sword and walked behind David, who cautiously approached me.

David kept his eyes on Muma Horren, and I suddenly remembered Natthia's instruction to seek Muma Horren's approval before even looking at David. Therefore, I quickly turned toward her and stared into her eyes. "May I hold David's hand? I am frightened, Muma Horren."

She smiled and sighed. "You be a good girl, young lady. I am sorry. I am over-reacting. You simply look so Muki. I forget that you are not. Go ahead, David, comfort her."

David quickly helped me to my feet and put an arm around me. I was fine as soon as he touched me. Muma Horren lowered her bow, and Natthia followed suit.

Tension in the air dissipated as everyone seemed to relax. With a bit of fanfare, the Judge sheathed his sword and smiled. "Welcome home, Tara. We will find you a castle, do not worry." Then the Judge laughed, and David blushed, causing Muma Horren to scowl.

"Tara, this is Judge Soronato, our leader."

"Hello, Sir. Thank you, Sir," I answered. I wondered if I should curtsy but decided against doing so.

Tightly holding my hand, with Natthia and Muma Horren following us, David introduced me to everyone present. Sometimes,

I felt vaguely comfortable as they looked me over, but mostly, I was embarrassed.

Each member of the Muki was as unique and different as David and his friend, Mark. There was a similarity, though. Each of these people expected something from me. I did not know what, but I had a distinct impression that my presence invoked strong emotions. The sting of incredible hatred burnt into me from about a third of the group, like how Mark had made me feel when I first met him. However, I also felt a guarded love from Brian and even Muma Horren, although Muma also regarded me with fear and likely disgust at my ignorance. I do not know how the Judge felt about me. He had an aura about him that spoke of vast authority, wisdom, and acceptance. Of all the Muki, Judge Soronato seemed undecided toward me. I was welcome. I belonged, but… I was a disappointment and a threat, too. When the introductions were finished, I was very relieved and proud that I had remained polite. Other than panicking when I could not locate David, I thought I had conducted myself reasonably well and had no need to be embarrassed or ashamed.

I felt relief as everyone headed outside. David told me that it was time to sing to the heavens, thanking God for another day of life. We all sat around a fire. Surprisingly, it was not cold at all. The cold did not cut through my tights, and David's shirt and tunic made me feel slightly too warm and overdressed. My garments caused quite a stir. I was not appropriately dressed was whispered many times, before loud laughter, while we were being seated. However, I felt I was more correct than I would have been in my blue jeans.

True to her word, Muma Horren sat beside me and instructed Natthia to sit on the other side. Both had bows and two arrows each sat across their laps, arrows pointed toward me. David laughed when I asked if I was in danger.

"No, Littl'un," he whispered, "you are safer than you have ever been in your life. Those arrows mean that any false move made toward you by anyone will result in their immediate execution. You have made a friend in Muma Horren. She will protect you with her own life. Feel honoured, Tara. Muma Horren knows you belong."

Harshly, Muma Horren ordered David to take his spot in the circle, leaving me there. However, I never lost sight of him or felt afraid the rest of the evening. I was not Muki in most of their eyes, but I did command respect because God had told them that I was to become Muki.

Being with the Mukis was a treat, which I will never forget. Drum rolls started the activities. The obviously native dances and the beat of the songs they chanted were like an enactment of the scenes God had shown me the year before, in a dream of prophecy—the promise of a coming friendship. I stopped worrying about who the Mukis were, as I preferred to believe they were a people with a strict culture, blending the old ways within a very modern society. Furthermore, without a shred of doubt, they were a holy people. In a sense, I knew that they did not belong in the common world. Their clothing was a mixture of cultures within our past: the Egyptians, the Native Americans, and the swordsmen of the Middle Ages, but the materials could only be space-age fabrics, light but incredibly warm. I swear that the dancers had a light of their own, changing the hue of their skin with the beat and emotion of the songs they chanted and danced. Perhaps I was merely losing my mind and hallucinating but was powerless to do anything other than savour the privilege of being among these people. I witnessed a celebration.

Technologically advanced, their home was nothing I thought possible within Earth technology. Carved out of solid rock and completely camouflaged, the only evidence of habitation remained the remnants of ashes within a circle of rocks in the clearing. There were windows that I had looked out of to see the fire before me, but despite the bright indoor lights, I could not even imagine where the windows were from outside. I was sitting before a bare rock outcrop, neither smooth nor artificial. The campfire itself was not an ordinary campfire. It reminded me of gas fires, but I saw no evidence of a gas line or switches or valves to control it. The fir trees waved in the wind around us, but I did not feel a cold draft brush across my face even once. Yet, all my senses told me that I was indeed outdoors. There was even something abnormal about the plane in which we had arrived. I could not put my finger on exactly what was not right. However, I knew it was not quite real. Somehow, it was an illusion.

Several times, I touched Muma Horren, my clothes, the smooth texture of the arrow, and the deadly reality of the bow on Natthia's lap to confirm that they were real. David's home was alive and holy was the only conclusion to which I could come. I wanted to stay forever. Sadly, the songs ended. The Mukis, except David, Natthia, Muma Horren, and I, quietly lined up and filed into the crack in the rock. Muma Horren let David kiss my forehead, and then we entered the rock.

I wanted to ask questions, but Muma Horren told me not to ask what they could not answer. This was their home. It was how it was meant to be. They lived according to their own traditions and customs. I was to enjoy being among them according to the will of God, learning, and teaching as commanded. Then, I was to return to the world where I was born. When she told me that, Muma Horren was completely calm and sincere. Unmistakably stating that I did not belong, her words cut me very deeply. Only a guest, I cried and kept on crying as Natthia and Muma Horren took away my clothes of the Muki and handed me my own blue jeans, T-shirt, jacket, and now terribly uncomfortable underwear. Even my running shoes seemed to hurt my feet!

Just before David threw me up to Brian standing in the plane, I said, "But David, my clothes are dead!" I had really meant it. I felt as though I was dead myself. Leaving this place held fear and horror. To my annoyance David, Brain, and Doug burst out laughing.

David tried to comfort me, but Doug whispered to Brian, saying, "At least she knows she's dead. Maybe that was what she was to learn, and we can get on with our assignment."

Again, I slept going home to Quesnel, to be among ordinary people, in an ordinary town... When the engine noise died, I woke up back in Beaver Pond. I managed to say thank you and goodbye to Brian and Doug.

In the dark, David walked me up the hill and to the edge of the woods. He hugged me and said he would see me the following afternoon. Convinced my world had lost something tonight, I clung to him. "Please, David, help me become a Muki. I do not want to be dead." I begged him as he gently told me it was time to go.

Then David cried, and I ran indoors, knowing my world and I were doomed. Nothing would change that fact. Letting myself into the house, I locked the door, made a glass of warm milk, drank it, rinsed the cup and the saucepan in the sink, and then, with a heavy heart, went upstairs, undressed, and crawled, naked, into my bed. Unable to sleep, I tossed and turned, struggling to find direction and contentment. Finally, in desperation, I cried, "Oh Lord, I need a hug."

That had always been my favourite prayer, and I think it always will be. Immediately, I felt the warmth of God around me and remembered that God had been close to me all evening. God never wastes words. He said, "You control what and who you are."

I knew then that I wanted the light of the Muki, I wanted to be alive, and nothing was going to stop me from finding out how to become Muki. I needed David and the Muki to teach me, and I would continue to demand to be taught.

28

A PRIVATE CULTURAL WAR

DAVID HAD MET WITH HIS Tara more often in the weeks following Tara's visit to the base camp. A subtle change in the Little Smiler bothered him. In her eyes, the unmistakable evidence often appeared that she viewed him not only with love, trust, and adoration but also with terror. She had very mixed feelings about the bows and arrows that played an important part in Muki rituals. They both terrified and comforted her. She could not grasp an understanding of why.

Since he had met her, David had worked hard to build upon her culture, to mould her slowly into the image of one of the Muki. That had become impossible now. Their conversations were about differences and comparisons. Indeed, a cultural war had begun to take shape between them. David knew neither what to answer nor what to reveal. It frightened him. He was afraid of losing her love.

Rather than helping, the visit had opened a can of concepts, which would not empty. Often David worried that they had embarked on the path of man and lost touch with the path of God. When he worshiped, God seemed supportive, yet the direction God aimed him was so unclear and alien. The Mukis never engaged in conversation defending their existence, faith, or culture. They were leaders! They moulded the universe! Who was this woman to question their righteousness?

It was with such thoughts that David waited in Judge Soronato's office.

Judge Soronato was incredibly pleased with the first visit that Earthling had made into the base camp. He did not think anything could have gone better. The Judge had long ago developed special feelings toward the woman he had met that evening. She was everything he had expected her to be and much more. There was no doubt that God had sent her blindly into the affairs of the universe, but she was up to the challenge. She was learning more than from David, too. Her spirit was strong, and despite her incredibly young age, she displayed uncanny wisdom. Obviously, she conversed with God.

The thing that intrigued the Judge most of all was that despite her relationship with God, she did not appear holy in any way at all. It seemed a contradiction. Those of the Muki with a close relationship with God were always holy in appearance and essence. The Judge had concluded that, as David had always proclaimed, Earth had the blessing of God. However, God had blessed it in a strange way, which the Judge was intrigued with trying to unravel. Encouraging David to throw out all the rules and to talk about the differences in the Muki books of God to those of Earthlings rather than only the similarities, Judge Soronato was ready for an argument! A special argument would give him the solution to his assignment: does the civilization on Earth have any redeeming features?

A mere child, an outcast of her own world, was a tool of God's. For better or worse, Tara would expose the will of God.

As he set a steaming hot urn of cider onto the table and took his seat, Judge Soronato glanced at David and noted he was in such pain. The Judge knew he could not help him find peace, but he would do all he could to ease the burden. David smiled as the Judge poured the cider. With the feeling that this was going to be an important conversation, the Judge settled into relishing the cider while freeing his mind to receive the will of God. There was no doubt in the Judge's mind that the assignment was on track. God was guiding it with both pleasure and delight. The Judge thought that God had waited a long time for this day. The Judge knew he had himself.

Before either the Judge or David felt comfortable enough to

talk, they emptied the whole urn. David searched very carefully for words, and the Judge listened in mild shock to the honesty with which David struggled.

"Bringing Tara to the base camp was a mistake, Judge Soronato. Tara has learned to fear me. Although she does not want to believe it, she understands that we are aliens. There are questions she wants to ask but is more afraid of the answer than the question. She now sees me as an executioner. She has brought Earth's Great Books of God before me, and she trembles at the words written there. One moment, she is begging me to take her home with me, to live with the Muki, and the next, she is defying our right and responsibility to carry out the Judgement ordained by God. She wants to live, but not at the expense of Earth as she knows and understands it, even if it is evil and ungodly.

"Sometimes, I fear that she hates me. I need her love, Judge Soronato. However, we are now at war. Without destroying her culture, I cannot defend ours. Now totally lost, I fear breaking her spirit. God demanded that I love her and forbade me from harming her. Yet, her insistent arguing makes me want to tell her to rot in hell. Often, I fear wanting to never go near her again.

"Teaching, I can no longer accomplish without lashing out against her culture. Therefore, I must turn training the Little Smiler over to you. You want to argue. She loves to argue. She does not love you, and she can dismiss the truth from you. However, Judge, to learn from me, she must give up her love for me. Instead, she must hate me and despise what she knows in her heart, that which the Muki will ultimately do to her island kingdom."

While digesting David's words, Judge Soronato filled the urn with fresh cider. He kept having visions of the terror he had seen while worshipping before God while Tara and David sought God's blessing upon their love. He knew that Tara and David's love for each other were critical. Without love, they would never find the will of God. Aware David was neither a warrior nor a fighter; he had to find a way to put David back on God's path.

If David failed God now, all would be lost. The Judge had to make David understand that he could not run away now. He had to find a way to turn a cultural war into a display of harmony, glory, and love.

Sitting in silence once more, the Judge offered David a cup of cider. Although David was broken and ready to bolt, to run away from his own culture to embrace forbidden love rather than destroy what God entrusted him to protect, Judge Soronato could not let him do that. It would prove that Earth was doomed, and the Judge now desperately wanted to redeem this land.

They eyed each other across the table. Both David and the Judge lit up as God surrounded them. The nightmare was beginning, and he could not stop it. The Judge suddenly stood and took hold of David's shoulders. "David, my son, this is your Doleran. It is too late to run. You must dance with Tara." Then the Judge cried in his own agony and retreated from his office.

David sank into his chair. It *was* his Doleran. God wanted his future. While Tara lived, he would never see the Land of the Butterflies again. He would never receive a license to sire. He would never enter the front door of a castle because his destiny was to redeem Earth and give it a new ancestry by moulding it into the image of the Muki, one small step closer to the image of God. His task was nothing great, nothing spectacular, just sin and death for the sake of righteousness. David cried. Then, he threw up.

Time slowly passed while David sat in the dim light of an office of authority and slowly realized there was no shame in what the Judge had ordered him to do. It was right. God had laid out his path clearly before him. He knew it was true. The order had not come from the Judge but God. Eventually, David would learn to use love as a weapon—the greatest weapon ever granted by God. Love would soothe the pains of a bitter struggle. Worse than war, this was a struggle for identity, faith, and position in the Kingdom of God. If he failed to teach the Little Smiler well, all of Earth would pay. Earth would have no redemption. The tenth judgement would conclude in favour of destruction.

One young woman of Earth and one inexperienced, naive Cultural

Judge from the Land of the Butterflies would lay bare their united vision of the Kingdom of God. If God approved, blessings would fall upon them all. If they failed, their line of infinity would fail along with them. It was no longer a question of the redemption of the Land called Earth but of testing the ability of the Muki to be Instruments of Creation.

Yes. David needed all the help the Judge and the expedition could give him. Leaving the office, he walked out among the stars. The moon was bright, and the snow glistened around him. Miraculously, the skies seemed to open above him, and he suddenly knew he would succeed. He would serve the Lady because Jarrock was with him and leading the way. It was a path full of promise, full of light, and love. David felt blessed. He could break the Laws, his people would never again accept him as a fit sire, but he would sire, not for a castle, but for a whole world... God was honouring him, and it mattered not that his own people would shun him.

Understanding his position, the Judge would protect him with his authority until the expedition returned home. Then, it was up to the Panel to determine his fate. If God were leading him, the Panel would recognize him and even honour him. If he strayed, he would die. David simply concluded he had to succeed. He had no other choice. It was not worth worrying about. God introduced him to the Little Smiler to guide and lead her along God's chosen path. David belonged to God. He would do all in his power to serve the will of God with strength, determination, and grace.

Again, David cried. Tara of Earth was so young, so vulnerable. She had not the teaching of the Muki to give her strength. As all Earthlings did, she lacked the gifts of Koe Sai Serena and, consequently, had to walk blindly with only faith to guide her. She had only her two small books of God, her island kingdom, and a friend in an alien, himself. More than ever before, David needed to be her sentry. Bathing her with a blanket of Koe Sai Serena's love, he was her guardian angel ordained to give her the strength and will to survive. Just as the Judge needed to fight and argue with Tara, David needed to stand beside her, holding and strengthening her according to the will of God. He was her friend and would protect and love her as not only an Instrument of Creation but as a man, a human, and a mate. Furthermore, the Judge would support his decision.

29

TO SHOOT AN ARROW

AFTER MY FIRST VISIT TO the base camp, David and I went through some miserable times. Often acting as though I was something indefensible, he would not answer my questions. He reminded me of the way I felt about Mark. I could not allow the Muki to tell me they were superior, and so perfect that their culture and standards were beyond reproach. I would yell at David, "Only one thing is beyond reproach, and that is God!" Then although admitting that I was correct, David would cry, and I would feel awful. Unsatisfied, we would part to meet again another day.

I was guilty. An arrow, and whether David could shoot it for me, was not worth the destruction of a friendship. Yet, the discussion concerning such matters began arguments between an angel and me. For alien or not, there was a connection to God that I could never deny. The Mukis were holy. That was an undeniable fact.

I asked David to bring a bow and a quiver of arrows to a visit. I wanted him to shoot it for me. Used according to the will of God, not man, they were sacred weapons, and David said they belonged in the camp among his own people, the Muki.

"Then, David," I said, "Show me your skills at the camp." I simply needed to understand how a holy people could kill or threaten to kill with such calm and belief in their righteousness. Craving understanding, I could not explain to David just how much the bows and arrows frightened yet comforted me. I deemed David's explanation that the bows belonged to God, were holy, and that they could only be used correctly as a copout answer. They were deadly weapons and did not fit in my view of a loving God. Finally, David had relented. Refusing to bring such weapons away from the base, he had arranged for me to make a second visit to his home.

Natthia had told me that all sin is equally wrong. To kill, even in error, was no more sinful than to take the name of God in vain. "Besides, Tara," Natthia would continue, "We are all guilty of sin and deserve to die. No one is free of sin. Death is always just!"

I found that idea very frightening!

"Where are we going, David?" I asked once we had arrived after David opened my door at the base camp. He was dressed traditionally, and I was again wearing his clothes.

"To target practice, Tara, as requested," David answered with a tone of sadness and, perhaps, disappointment.

It was early afternoon on a Saturday. The sun was shining, but it was still cold, and there was fresh snow on the ground. We stood out in the clearing near the site of the evening campfire. A few people, including Natthia and Muma Horren, stood behind David and me to watch, and I thought judge how I reacted to wielding a holy instrument. Their continence terrified me, and I was afraid to touch the bow David held out to me.

"Tara, you have been chastising me, and my people, about the discipline and ritual meaning of this deadly weapon as you call our bow and arrows. Yet, now you are afraid to touch it. Perhaps, you are unclean. Let us cleanse first, and then you will be confident enough to wield a weapon of God's."

I cried. I had touched Natthia's bow last time I was at the base camp and had loved the feel of its power. Although only a piece of wood, it had offered me immense comfort and security. I could fathom neither how it could contain power nor how it could belong to God. However, David was correct. I could not touch it. I tried. I really tried hard, but my hand could not reach it because something held me back. Tears fell, and I continued to struggle against an unseen and unknown power restraining me.

Again, the questions that had begun to haunt me awoke in my mind. Who was David? Who were the Muki? Just who was God?

I felt terribly dirty. Part of me wanted to ask David to take me home, and the other part wanted to seize that bow and prove that it was only a man-made primitive tool. I did not want it to be holy. Clearly, I did not understand holy things.

David's words filtered into my consciousness, and I felt anger and terror before slowly relaxing and nodding. David lowered the bow and took my hand. While he held me close, a comfort flowed through me, confirming my conviction that David was holy. Regardless of whether he was an angel, he was a gift from God, and I was safe.

In the time it took my tension to dissipate, not much more than a second, again, the strange reality of being among the Muki shocked me. I heard the distinctive sounds of people snapping to attention, arrows being drawn from quivers on their backs, loaded, and by the feel of heat on my back, I knew arrows were being aimed at us. Until Muma Horren broke the silence, neither David nor I moved.

"David, Tara, turn around."

Obediently and without fear or hesitation, we turned.

"This is not a castle, David. Tara is not Muki and cannot handle the holy symbol of God's power in her evil hands. She has failed. Take her home," commanded Muma Horren.

"No, Muma Horren. Tara is not evil. She needs to cleanse. It is her reverence for God that holds her back. She is holy. Had she been evil, she would have grabbed hold of the bow, and it would have crumbled to dust in her grip. She is wise, recognizes her humanity, and will not despoil the grace of God."

I stared at David in disbelief. Simply terrified to touch the bow, I did not know what he was talking about. I was not holy; I was defiant. The bow had a power that I was unfit to touch. I did not belong to God. I was human and clung to my humanity with fierce determination.

Did I need to take another bath? Puzzled and unsure, I looked into David's eyes. Reassuringly, he smiled and squeezed my hand. Without knowing what was happening, I trusted David would protect me, and a strong will welled up inside me, promising that I would find a way to prove to Muma Horren that I could become a Muki.

David said, "Come, Tara. We will use my sacred chest."

Muma Horren gasped. Immediately, Natthia and several others redirected their arrows toward Muma Horren. She lowered her bow and ran crying toward the strange entrance to the hall.

Loudly, Natthia shouted, "Muma Horren, I will cleanse with them. I will not permit them to sin."

Muma Horren stopped for a moment, then nodded to Natthia and said, "Thank you, Natthia. God bless you. This is just too new for me. I shall pray in my room for God to protect you all. Do not sin, Natthia. Do not let Tara or David sin. Oh, Jarrock, hold them in your arms. God save us!" With loud wails, Muma Horren turned away and disappeared into the rock.

We stood in the clearing and waited until Judge Soronato came outside. As he walked toward us, I clung even tighter to David. The Judge was the kind of person who commanded respect. When David introduced me to him, I felt I needed to acknowledge his authority, but curtsying still did not feel appropriate. Therefore, again, I did nothing. He stood before us, while I blushed and waited, gazing in silence for several minutes. The Judge seemed to be able to penetrate my mind, and I felt naked before him. Finally, he smiled.

"With Natthia's presence, David, I approve. Be careful, though, son. Do not sin," he stated calmly and firmly.

David blushed. I wondered about cleansing, and I glanced at Natthia.

She smiled and said, "Come."

David said, "It is alright, Tara. I will not touch you. Let us cleanse before God."

As a voice within me reassured me, I followed, realizing they were offering me a blessing.

When we arrived at David's room, Natthia raised her bow. David chuckled, then stated, "I will fetch my sacred chest, Natthia, and meet you in Tara's room."

When David let go of my hand, I trembled. As Natthia patted

my back to reassure me, I tried to be brave, and with a phony, forced laugh, I whispered, "I guess I should have believed David when he told me a bow could be holy."

"A bow is holy, Tara."

"I want to understand, Natthia. The Muki seem so impossibly unreal, but I love you with all my heart, even Mark, Natthia. Help me do this thing. Help me become Muki, too."

Natthia just smiled and dragged me to my room. Once inside, she hugged me and said, "Just be yourself, I will pray now for you." Natthia knelt on her knees and touched my tunic before continuing, "Jarrock, you have asked David to teach this woman to be of the Muki. You have asked us all to trust her and let her lead the way. We are afraid. We are afraid for David. When Tara has no castle, and David loves her so dearly, to cleanse is courting disaster. Give David strength and hold his humanity at bay. Protect us. Let me stand between them and die in their stead should I permit them to sin. Help us, Jarrock! Spread the blanket of Koe Sai Serena over us all that we will carry out this ritual according to the will of God!"

Feeling warmth enter the room, I felt safe, and as the imp inside me awoke, my desire to run left me. I had come here only to learn to wield and understand the meaning of a bow and arrow and was being given something much greater. Too proud and too frightened by this culture that God had told me to seek, to turn away, I decided that I would enjoy the events that were to follow because I was not afraid of David, and I loved and trusted Natthia. Knowing I was safe, I began to dance.

Natthia raised her bow and pointed an arrow at me.

"No, Tara. You must not dance. Please, do not dance."

Tears began to fall again, and I remembered Muma Horren telling me I could not dance. However, the pent-up energy created by my tension demanded release, and I began to hum the Deplukador song.

Natthia put a stop to that, too. "Stay here, Tara. I am not strong enough. I am going to ask the Judge to join us."

Loneliness descended upon me as Natthia left my room.

She said, "Mark, please come and guard this door. Let no one pass through it until I return."

Before she closed it, her glare toward me ensured that I understood the seriousness of what was about to happen.

I did not hear Mark answer, but I felt his presence. When that door closed, I was clearly under guard. I was not safe. The Muki were not safe with me either. I sat on the bed in silence, which I had never slept in, and watched out the window. Too frightened to cry and too honoured to object, I tried not to think at all. There was no doubt that whatever a cleansing was, it was also a kind of test.

Rather suddenly, I blurted at the window, "Only God has the right to judge me!" Then I let tears fall as a calm, reassuring voice from deep within me said, "God will be judging you, this day."

It is hard to fathom the emotions which then filled me. I was sure that today might be the last day of my life. Although aware I could die in the next hours; the thought was more comforting than terrifying. I felt loved and knew with my whole soul that God would forgive all my sins. Taking comfort in the existence of my own faith, I wondered if the ritual had already begun. Had they left me alone to figure out the meaning of what I had agreed to do for myself? Sighing, I concluded that the wisdom of the Muki would demand that I understand and see for myself what I had agreed to do. I felt stupid and gullible for taking David's warnings and explanations as a challenge to reach out to the Muki rather than at their face value.

To follow God, go where God directed me, and seek knowledge of and union with the Muki, I had to make decisions that would forever change my life. I would have to give up my own identity and become a slave. Committed and trapped, not by God, but because of God, and who it was that God wanted me to become, I had no other options, and it was too late to back away.

Resigned to be an actress, I played a part as commanded by my own destiny and realized I would die readily. Believing fully that life was nothing more than a dream, I had confidence I would awaken tomorrow to dream again, in a new world, no matter what happened this afternoon. With a smile and an impish chuckle, I spread my arms wide before me. Between my own giggles, I began my part. Proudly, I addressed my director, the powerful controller of the strings attached to my being, theatrically bowed, and said, "Guide me, oh my God, and let the show begin!"

Getting up, I danced with a sense of freedom and independence. Whatever followed, I was completely innocent. I had become a puppet on a string and intended to enjoy it fully. After all, everything I did with David had always had an element of fantasy attached to it. The Muki were not quite real... I was dreaming and wanted the show to go on!

Quite out of breath when I heard movement in the hall, I blushed and affirmed that although I was being a fool, I no longer cared what the Muki thought of me. God had trapped them, too! I sighed.

The door opened. Shocked by her glance toward me, Natthia looked frightened, and, when I smiled to set her at ease, she went pale. The Muki were afraid of me! Oh, how I loved the feeling of power that enveloped me!

Then when I looked at David, I realized I wanted to please him and needed his love and respect. I blushed as I discovered to gain his respect, I had to respect both him and the ritual in which he had invited me to participate. Again, I felt guilty and dirty. Embarrassed, I stopped looking at David, turned to Judge Soronato, and giggled again as I told myself that here was a man to fear. If God ever walked before me, Judge Soronato would be how he looked.

As I watched the Judge, I saw a cartoon play within me as I watched the Judge. I imagined him as a four-star general. He said, "Jump," and I said, "How high, Sir?" I must have said it aloud because questions appeared on all their faces. I blushed and laughed before curtsying, as formally and slowly as possible. Despite my natural shyness, I began playing my part with mischievous glee and satisfaction. Please do not think I was being rude, for I felt sincere. I did not feel that I was behaving inappropriately, at worst, only immaturely. As I was only a kid, I told myself that it was not a crime to be immature.

The Judge smiled, and I said, "Please, your Honour, guide me." Judge Soronato only nodded and regained his straight face.

Again, we all held hands and waited in silence for something eluding me. Sometimes, I found the Muki frustratingly slow! Then, I again felt that strange warmth within me as that voice of authority reminded me that these incredible and powerful people were trying to catch up with me! Oh, I loved the power that God used me to display. A nothing like me took them aback. It felt so good. I could have begun to dance once more. However, I did have to admit that I also felt great honour and wanted desperately to perform well for their sake and the sake of all people on Earth.

"Tara," the Judge began, "A cleansing is a ritual performed to make you clean and pure before God. Every single move you make matters. You must make all you do live with indisputable meaning. You can hide nothing. Use no deception, for it will surely kill you as swiftly as the arrow you could not touch. There can be no sin in the proceedings, and it is your own responsibility to ensure that you do not succumb to temptation. This, Tara, is a holy activity. Are you ready to proceed?"

I nodded.

"Good, then let us stand naked before our God, with no secrets hidden."

"Me, undress? Stand naked?" I thought, "In front of David? Oh, my God, how can I?" I wanted to cry.

The Judge laughed. "Listen, Tara. We, of the Muki, wish you no harm. We will help you keep temptation at bay."

I listened. Sounds coming from the hall, and people were moving and shuffling about. Then a short silence fell, followed by a loud "Boom!" I jumped. "Dum, dum, dump," began filtering through the wall as the drums began a rhythmic beat that raised and lowered while I listened. It was a heartbeat, steady and strong. I was safe in my mother's womb. Chants, like moans and groans, joined the drums, and I frowned.

"David tells us that you believe us to be a tribe of Native Americans. They are banishing evil and filling the air with a powerful spirit, our Mother, our God. We will let no temptation enter this room. Stand naked before God, Tara. We will support you. Use your faith to give you strength. Discard your thoughts, your emotions, and very being as you discard the character behind which you hide. We are with you and will also stand naked before God."

They began to undress. I noticed something very special, which gave me courage. Not merely disrobing, the Judge, David, and Natthia were discarding, symbolically getting rid of inhibitions before surrendering themselves to God with each other as a witness.

Perhaps embarrassment produced my own giddiness. However, I needed something dramatic to focus on to allow myself to let go and face God. I grabbed the long belt, which held my tunic around my waist. I literally fought it before I untied it. I screamed and called it my fear and let it become my fear. I was not crazy, and it was symbolic, but my fears flowed through my body and into that belt. I whipped it through the air before me and, with sudden anguish, thanked God that it struck no one. It was leather. Had it touched any of my friends, it would have produced a huge ugly welt. I dropped it. I could not afford fear.

With great care and love, I solemnly and slowly removed my sandals. I let tears flow freely as the laces became looser, falling freely with each twist around my legs. I was trying with every ounce of strength I could muster to put all of myself into those sandals. I shudder even remembering that struggle. I did love myself. Yes, you are correct. I was then and remain extremely vain. It was a symbolic quest having no real meaning in a physical sense. One cannot remove their own character, and I did not try to pretend that I truly believed myself capable of separating my essence from my body to cast it aside to become what another demanded of me. It did not matter that someone was the God of us all and all of creation. However, my quest was not without meaning. My struggle was real— almost too real.

My thoughts filled with the memory of the day I had died, almost ten years earlier. Then, I was too young to be afraid. When the angel had said, "leave that behind," I knew what he meant. My character was as mortal as my body, and I did not need it. Superficial and meaningless to God, it was a human attribute, evolved from genetic material, and it separated me from God. It was not enough to want to give myself to God. God demanded that I demonstrate that willingness sincerely, even if only symbolically. Yet, I could not bring myself to the point of complete belief in my own ability to do so without giving up existence as a living being. To succeed in my quest, I had to admit that I was dead. It had been easy when I was young, for I truly was dead. However, in a base camp of a special people, I felt very alive, and I did not want to die. I wanted to dance and live to the fullest that physical life permitted.

When I sat on the floor and pulled off the sandals, I felt a terrible sense of loss. I wept openly but sought no condolence from my friends. I felt guilty for wanting to hang onto my own values and my own laws, regardless of their emptiness and sinfulness. I felt pain as I laid them neatly beside my belt and pushed them away. Even as I sighed and tried to turn my attention toward removing my tights, I felt a tug from those shoes. I giggled as I realized there was an invisible thread running from my feet across the floor and into that, which defined me as a human being, and I realized that I would never completely belong to God until I died. I was dirty and sinful. Simply, I was human. I blushed and dared not look upon my friends, convinced they would know that I still hung on to my own sense of reality. I was not, and would never be, completely naked before God.

I heard God laugh.

Several minutes passed as I tried to establish meaning and symbolism to my tights. They were warm; they were David's, and eventually, I determined that they represented my strength. Feeling weak and suddenly calm, I determined the tights held no power. They were insignificant, and I removed them without remorse because I knew I was safe.

The dum, dum, dump of the beat of the drums filled my ears. There was strength in the chants and the breath of my friends around me. God was holding me. Delighted with the realization I was being blessed, not stripped, was an enlightening feeling. I really was safe within the womb of my Mother. Strange, I thought. God is my Father, but He is the Mother of the Muki. With glee, I smiled. I was becoming Muki!

I did not know exactly what symbolic meaning the removal of my tunic signified. I simply removed it, folded it neatly, and set it over the other discarded definitions of myself. Before turning back to my friends, I thought about that tunic for a long time. Proceeding was impossible until I understood its significance. Finally, I smiled, confident that it was my ancestry, my connection to a place in the universe, to Earth.

All that separated me from God was sitting in a pile, discarded yet not lost. As I cried, I took confidence in the tingling in the bottom of my feet, which promised that I would be able to retrieve everything that I had set aside. Drained of defiance and the will to resist, I turned to my friends, painfully aware that I had no shield and was naked before them and before God. I could feel my own filth and sin. I knew I was not clean. However, I did not need to run. I needed to bathe, cleanse myself, and feel the mercy and love of God upon my soul, or perhaps, only upon my spirit.

As I stared at the nakedness of Natthia, I felt blessed and comforted. Natthia was beautiful. I could not see the dirt upon her that I saw upon myself. Natthia was already clean. Then, I forced my gaze upon Judge Soronato. I had never seen a naked man. The closest I had been to a naked male were infants under my supervision in a bathtub. The Judge made me feel very young. Thankfully, he was a supervisor, and his honesty and sincere desire to protect kept me from harm.

As I looked at David, the sound of the drums became my anchor. The sight of David filled me with ecstasy, and I wanted to hold him. His maleness had no power to frighten me because he loved me, and I felt as though I was in heaven. I wanted desperately to dance openly and naked before God, appreciating the wonderful gift He had given me when He had offered David as a friend. My feet tingled as I felt myself pulling the power out of my shoes and physically kicked against them to prevent temptation from destroying the holiness of the activity that I was participating in. Every cell in my body was active. God was blessing me. As gratitude filled me, I had to express it. I knew only one way to give myself to the Lord, and that was from the memory of having worshipped with David a long time ago on the top of the world, on Snow-shoe Plateau. I raised my arms high above my head. Slowly, I let them fall to the horizon. I kept my eyes on David's eyes and let go. Not even a thread remained to connect me to all that I valued. I belonged to David. Empty and naked, but dirty, I would stand before God and ask to be cleansed, forgiven, and shown holiness. David's eyes filled with tears, and they began to roll down his cheek. I wanted him to stand with me. Smiling to realize that David was indeed very much with me, I giggled. I felt that special warmth in the air, which always comforted me. God was with us and filled us with love. Confident that I had done the right thing and delighted Judge Soronato was smiling, I lowered my hands very slowly and nodded to the Judge.

With obvious pleasure, the Judge said, "Let us proceed. David, it is your chest. Please, open it for us."

Natthia lifted the chest from the desk in the corner of the room and held it out to David. He took it without stopping his gaze into my eyes. Although honoured, I could not maintain my own gaze because I wanted to see what was within that beautifully carved wooden chest. It suddenly shocked me... I recognized it. God had told me to build one like it when I was about ten.

David set it on the floor before all of us. As he unlatched it, I could not resist putting my hand on his when he lifted the lid. Natthia gasped, but when I glanced, the Judge held her and told her not to worry. With great authority, the Judge assured Natthia that I would not sin.

Having not meant to worry Natthia, I stood and backed away from David. I had acted spontaneously and been unaware my motion would result in sin. "Forgive me, Natthia," I said barely above a whisper.

She smiled, and David lifted a silk-like cloth out of the crest, spread it out on the floor, and carefully lifted the chest and set it upon it.

The Judge began speaking, explaining the significance of the cloth. I could feel it was holy, but I listened carefully as, without reservation, they handed more of the world of the Muki to me.

"Tara, this is the blanket of Koe Sai Serena. She is the daughter of God, but she is not God and remains human even after death. She will never die, for she left part of herself among us and can never again become whole until the Kingdom of God fills the universe.

"Koe Sai Serena was born an ordinary child, but she was silent until she was old. Then she said, 'Please God, take away my eyes that I will see only with your eyes.' Lightening came down from above and struck Koe Sai Serena, where she stood in a field with her family standing around. She was cleansing before the Lady, and they were her witness. Koe Sai Serena covered her eyes. She cried, and then she sang. 'Oh, my Lady, you are so precious, please give my eyes to my people, that they may use them to see what you have given us.' Song broke the silence in the skies, and God smiled. Koe Sai Serena was blind, but she rejoiced. Her people were afraid of her yet drawn to her. When they touched her and walked with her, they could only see what God saw. Their own guilt filled them with sorrow, and only those brave souls who sought the wisdom and sight of God dared to guide Koe Sai Serena through the streets to preach to her people. A short while later, Koe Sai Serena went again to cleanse before the Lady. 'My Lady,' she cried, 'I do not wish to hear the sins of my people. The noise prevents me from hearing your voice. Please, take my ears, and let my people use them to hear your will.' God smiled upon her people. Koe Sai Serena laughed, and her people writhed in shame while they watched the agony that Koe Sai Serena expressed at the loss of the voice of God within her. She said, 'Thank you, my Lady, my people will listen, and they shall be able to hear your will with your gift.'

"Again, her people were afraid. When they came near Koe Sai Serena, they could hear God, and God's words frightened them, for they felt dirty and sinful. God's words were free, but to heed them required action and change. Many more were afraid to walk with Koe Sai Serena. They began to recognize that they had to give up a little of themselves to hear and see the will of God. They clung to Jarrock and began to shun Koe Sai Serena and call her a madman. Her people wanted to argue and fight with her, for she frightened them. She was blind and deaf, yet still, she worshipped God and felt only blessed.

"Koe Sai Serena was saddened, and she cried, for her people did not appreciate her gifts. She went out into the field again and worshipped for many days. Her people began to gather around her in both fear and gratitude. She shone with the sight of God, and any who came near heard singing angels and God speak directly to them through the ears that she had freely given up for them. Her people were dying, and they needed the gifts of Koe Sai Serena to see and hear God and knew that when they were with Koe Sai Serena, God could guide them.

"Suddenly, one night, Koe Sai Serena screamed to the heavens. All camped around her awoke to hear her say, 'Oh Jarrock, my people want your love and forgiveness, but they cannot feel your presence. Take my sense of touch and give it to them, that they will know your comfort as I know it. I cannot bear to leave my people in the cold.'

"The voice of Jarrock thundered down from the sky, 'Did I not show them the way?'

"Koe Sai Serena answered, 'Oh yes, Jarrock, they do indeed know the way You showed them. They love You, and they honour You. They have become lost and do not know how to follow you. They can see the path through my eyes and hear your voice with my ears, but they cannot feel your presence. You seem impossibly far away, and they are frightened. Please, Jarrock, give them my sense of touch. Then, through me, they will know how to walk along Your path and know You are with them!'

"While they watched, a cloud descended upon Koe Sai Serena. She screamed in pain, praising and thanking the Lady as her skin was torn off. It lay like a dully shining blanket around her, and she wept for her people to come and gather close to her and carry it away with them as a gift from her to her people.

"Few dared to go before her, but those who did took water and kept her flesh warm and moist.

"Koe Sai Serena never again left the field. Everyone knew that the journey toward Jarrock began in that field, and everyone who left the field knew that they would take some of Koe Sai Serena with them when they left. They feared that she would die if they took too much of her. Without believing their own eyes, they saw that the more of Koe Sai Serena's flesh stretched out among those who touched her, the larger became the blanket of the feel of God lying around her. Her people cared for her out in the field for many more years. She sought no cover from the rain, the snow, or the wind. They marvelled that she did not die. Coming to the field gave them strength and healed them all. They felt blessed and realized that Koe Sai Serena was holy.

"Yet still, her people did not follow God when they left the field. They strayed into temptation, and once again, Koe Sai Serena cried. She lived in terrible pain for their sakes, but she had still failed to give them what she had discovered was the truth. To the Lady, she cried, 'My Lady, why am I failing? What is it that keeps them away from You? Why are my gifts not enough?'

"The Lady replied, 'Your people are evil, Koe Sai Serena. They do not want your gifts.'

"Koe Sai Serena shook her head and said, 'It is not so, my Lady, they simply cannot smell your glory. Give them my sense of smell, so they know you are here for them, not only when they are in need, but always.'

"The people cried out, 'No, Koe Sai Serena! No! Keep your sense of smell for yourself. We want to see your smile when you smell the roses that we bring to you. We need you to smile.'

"Koe Sai Serena answered, 'I will smile for you always. Take this gift that I have offered. Use it, and you too will smile upon God, and God will smile upon you. You will know that the smell of righteousness is greater than all the smells of evil rolled up together!'

"With that, Koe Sai Serena tore her nose from her face and laid it gently on her skin. It dissolved and blended into her skin, and the blanket grew brighter. It hurt her people to look upon Koe Sai Serena. Every breath laboured and gurgled in her throat.

"Her people were ashamed. They wanted to protect her. She was dying, but she could not be done with it. She gave them strength. She always wore a smile: a smile, in a blind, mutilated face that offered nothing but love for them. They cried because they could see the pain of her sacrifice. They could see, hear, and touch God because she gave the gifts to do so, and they knew the glory of righteousness.

"Still, they did not want her gifts. Now they could feel the safety of their own souls when they went to the field. It did comfort them, but they still wanted to be their own masters.

"Koe Sai Serena continued to cry behind her smiling face. Many of her people tried to accept her gifts. Her blanket grew even larger and brighter. Her people finally recognized that they wanted what Koe Sai Serena was offering. They wanted desperately to belong to God.

"In spring, when the grass turned green the next year, Koe Sai Serena reached down to the ground and gathered a handful of soil. She rubbed it between her fingers, unfeeling, yet somehow knowing that she held it and did not drop it. She kissed the dirt, and she blessed it. Then Koe Sai Serena laughed. All thought she was dying, but she spoke to them.

"'My people, I have little left to give you, but all that I have I give willingly. You belong to God, and She needs your help to build Her Kingdom. Go out into the heavens and spread my gifts. Work for God. I give you my hands so that all your work will be God's work.' She took a sword and raised it high over her own head. 'You will need to be able to taste the goodness of God. Therefore, I give you my sense of taste, for I taste only the goodness and righteousness of God's grace. My friends, I give you my words that you will not have any power to do work against the will of God! I will have nothing left but my life, which I place in your hands.'

"Her people then watched in fascination and horror as Koe Sai Serena cut her tongue out of her mouth. They could see her agony and saw that God loved her for her sacrifice. She opened her throat and removed her vocal cords. She cut off her right hand and placed the sword between her knees. She used the bloodied, ugly stub of her right arm to sever her left hand.

"Her people wanted to stop her, but they could not go onto the blanket surrounding her. She writhed in an agony, which she did not feel except in her heart. Her people cried. As though they were one, together, they prayed to God. The blanket around Koe Sai Serena changed from pastel reds through the colours of the rainbow, and they felt the love of Koe Sai Serena touch them. They did not dream even for a moment that they could lift and wield the gifts Koe Sai Serena had given them, but they could not stand and watch her suffer. Together, using the strength of unity, they lifted and held the blanket of Koe Sai Serena, promising to God that they would use it as Jarrock would have used it.

"Angels sang. The air around them was fresh and clean. They felt loved. They accepted the gifts of Koe Sai Serena. The blanket turned a brilliant white. God blessed them, and Koe Sai Serena could give them no more. God told them that she would suffer forever in darkness for their sake and asked them to show her their love.

"Her people cried. They tried to wield her gifts, and then they looked upon her brokenness. They heard her rasping breaths and raised their swords and bows, and just as they had killed Jarrock in fear and hate, they ended Koe Sai Serena with love and mercy.

"Tara, this cloth is of Koe Sai Serena's blanket, all that she offered us and left behind for our sake. She stands behind God, in total darkness waiting for the Kingdom of God! We are the descendants of Koe Sai Serena's people. She made us of the Muki. We owe our salvation to Jarrock and our duty to Koe Sai Serena. We cannot let her rot in darkness. We must serve God!"

"Who is Jarrock?" I asked.

"Jarrock, Tara, is the Son of God, and he was God, walking among us, guiding us as a shepherd of all of God's creation. Your people call him Jesus. Let us continue. Please, continue, David."

I fell silent again. David lifted a small bowl filled with liquid and a stone shaped like a heart. The stone had been pierced twice, and a wooden arrow still stuck through it. It reminded me of Cupid's arrow, and I felt love emanating from it. David set it upon the blanket. He took a pair of porcelain hands, one cupped in the other out of the chest. They were tiny, like a child's hands. These he also placed on the blanket in front of the bowl. Next were removed two miniature swords, which were crossed and set beside the hands so that the hands were between the hilts of the two swords. Then, David took out a candle, which he placed between the blades of the swords. Last, David removed three vials, closed the lid of the chest, and set them on it.

Judge Soronato began to explain the ritual to me. "Tara, now we must bless the oils so that all our filth, guilt, and sin will be washed away when we wash with them. David prayed aloud in his own tongue. Although I did not understand the words, I felt a special kind of warmth grow within me and was sure that the oil had changed. It appeared to be alive. It swirled and bubbled as though speaking to us from within the small glass vial.

David hesitated, the Judge nodded to him, and he opened the vial and spilt a drop of oil into Natthia's outstretched hand. Natthia turned to the Judge and began to rub it over his body. I was amazed that a single drop would spread so far. I could see that there was more than symbolism involved for the Judge seemed to shine and sparkle with newness. Astonished, I perceived that he was more alive and stood straighter and taller than before. Yes, I concluded, everything about him spoke of cleanliness, not only skin deep, but totally pure in thought, word, and expression.

David gave a drop of oil to the Judge, and he proceeded to rub it into Natthia's flesh. My turn was next, and I felt very honoured and nervous. Again, David hesitated when the Judge was finished. Natthia held her hand out to him, and he looked as though he was going to let her wash him. I felt hurt and cheated. I let an odd sound escape my lips, and David turned to me. I held out my hand. David blushed and looked frightened. Natthia gasped and shook her head. I turned to the Judge and stared with all my strength into his eyes, defying him to exclude me from doing what I felt was my duty and mine alone. The Judge went pale and looked like a steel statue. I was frightened but did not back down.

After several minutes, Judge Soronato nodded ever so slightly. Natthia picked up her bow. With trembling hands, David handed the vial to the Judge, and he, also trembling, spilt a single drop into my outstretched hand. The oil was warm and comforting. I waited a moment to savour its purity and evident holiness.

I felt guilty and silently prayed that I could do my duty to God without sin. As I rubbed the oil onto David's flesh, I felt incredibly loved. Tears rolled unhindered down my face as I tried to comprehend why God would have sent such a precious gift to a vain, sinful nothing like me. I felt so blessed and thankful. By the time I was finished, David had shone like a candle. He was pure. David was an angel. I stood back admiring him and then trembled to realize that I really was among holy people. They all were so much greater than me, and I knew I did not belong. Too stubborn and too defiant, I could never be like them.

David looked to the Judge with fear and trepidation. He was afraid to wash me with holy oil. I fell to my knees and prayed aloud, "Please, God. Give David strength. Help him wash me. Please."

David stared at me as though I was being exceedingly cruel. I bit my lip and said, "It is all right, David. I will understand if you cannot. Let Natthia put the oil on me if what I ask is not appropriate for the Muki. I know I do not have a castle, and that matters to your people."

Natthia shook her head as the Judge held out the vial to her. David cried, and the Judge hugged him. Then with a sigh, David held out his hand for the precious drop of cleansing oil.

I closed my eyes and savoured the touch of David's hands on my body. I wanted to grab hold of him and never let go. He filled me with love and security. I felt my sins flash before my eyes and then dissolve away with every rub. I blushed many times. Often, I had to think about when I had committed these sins and felt terribly guilty that I had not even thought of them as sinful.

I really was dirty and began to worry that I was making David's hands dirty by having him wash me. I imagined his hands getting muddier and blacker with every movement. Mud, David loved mud! He was reshaping me, making me closer to the image that God had intended for me. Oh, how lucky I was! I was being freed, reborn, and I prayed to become a better, more worthy being.

When David stopped, I opened my eyes. I did not shine. When I looked at all the others, they all shone. I felt alien. Natthia put her arm around me and soothed me with a quiet hum.

"But Natthia, why do I not shine? I feel clean. I want to look like you." I wept in shame.

Natthia shook her head slowly. "Oh Tara, you are not Muki. The gift of Koe Sai Serena has not been given to your people.

Perhaps, the gift of creation is not this land's special gift. Perhaps, Tara, you need only ask for it. Let's continue."

"Yes, Tara," continued the Judge, "Now we light the candle and prepare ourselves to stand before the Lady."

Ask for the gift of Koe Sai Serena? I shuddered. I could not. Someone had to die to give us the close connection to God with which the Mukis were endowed. I could not imagine the self-torture that Judge Soronato had described to me. It sounded vaguely like something, which could come out of the Old Testament, but terribly unchristian and cruel for the teaching of the New Testament. I examined the blanket on the floor. It was just a small piece of fabric, but I choked as I realized that it was not fabric. A synthetic, I hoped. Could it really be a piece of human hide? I cringed at the thought. I knelt beside it and reached out toward it. It was holy. Like the bow outside earlier that day, I could feel its power, and I could not touch it. It was a gift too precious for my hands. I stood up again and nodded to the Judge.

He smiled at me. After leading us in a prayer that sounded much like the confession, David passed out a handful of seeds from another vial and then poured water into the bowl containing the stone. We ate the seeds in remembrance of Jarrock and drank of his life-giving water. The stone represented Jarrock's heart, he told me, and the arrows were the ones used to kill him. The Muki had not crucified their Jesus. They had shot him through the heart with the first one and then a second arrow. The bow, therefore, had the same symbolic meaning as the cross has for Christians. Like Jesus, Jarrock had risen from the dead, walked among his people, and still is seen walking among them from time to time. The Muki recognize Him as God.

The light emitting from my companions was the reflection of godliness provided by the senses of the prophet Koe Sai Serena, who they consider part human and part God. When someone of the Muki is following and working for God, they shine with Koe Sai Serena's gifts. It is how God shows the Muki pleasure and blessing. Silently, I tried to figure out whether I really wanted to wield such a gift. My guilt would be so obvious! I was sure that I would rarely be able to shine. With a chuckle, I realized that I would want to shine. My desire might be enough to make me strive harder to follow Jesus, for holiness and righteousness would always be so vividly visible to all. A visible God, that was what it was all about, seeing God among us, recognizing God.

In the depths of my mind, I thought the Bible said we had lost the gift and privilege of experiencing a visible God. Perhaps the gift we lost was the gift that Koe Sai Serena managed to give back to the Muki. We were condemned until the end of time. Were the Muki? I did not know that answer. However, I did not dare hope or pray that I would begin to glow after this ceremony—a ritual of cleansing and renewal.

David lit the candle. The flame did not burn our flesh as we each, in turn, passed our hands into it to capture the light of Koe Sai Serena. We did it five times. The first we released against our eyes, pledging to see only with God's will. The second handful of light was released over our ears, first the left and then the right, so that we would hear only the words of God. The third we released over our hearts that we would feel only with God's love and compassion. The fourth handful of light from the candle, we clenched tightly in our hands that we would do only the work of God. Finally, we released the last handful into our mouths that we would speak and echo only God's words.

It was a very moving ceremony, and I took it very seriously. I felt clean and ready to serve the Lord and thought that just maybe, with the help of the Muki, I could learn to do exactly that, become a servant of God, and make the world a better place, not for myself but for God and His Creation. I wanted the world to be as God wanted it. Feeling as though God had washed me clean, like baptisms, yet not merely saved, I had been empowered to contribute to the building of the Kingdom of God. I liked the way I felt at that moment.

"Are you ready to join us again, Tara?" laughed the Judge as he waved his hand in front of my face.

I blushed and apologized for being far away daydreaming. We all laughed.

"Tara, the next part of the ceremony is very personal. Stand before God and ask Her will for you. I shall warn you. You are now pure. You have no inhibitions. If God tells you to die, you will obey. You have put yourself completely in God's hands. If you are afraid of obeying, stop now. You are already clean and could return with David to try again to handle a sacred bow."

I hesitated and then said, "Today is a good day to die, Judge Soronato, and I would willingly do so if that is the pleasure of God." I was not even afraid. Besides, I thought I had stolen the last nine years of my life from God anyway. I had nothing to lose and was sure I had everything to gain. David took my hand. Despite Natthia's look of disapproval, he did not let go, and Natthia did not raise her bow. I did not know what Natthia and the rest of the Muki were afraid of, but they were very stuck-up about the moral correctness of young men and women. I liked that. Something about their attitude made me feel valued.

I experienced something like when David and I worshipped together on Snow-shoe Plateau. God asked nothing of me, but I felt incredibly blessed and loved. It was a wonderful experience. When our spirits returned to our bodies, David and I struggled incredibly hard not to put our arms around each other and sin.

Both Natthia and the Judge intervened, literally holding David and me apart as we wept. I was not Muki and knew that I never could be, but still clung to a belief that sometime, somehow, God would make it possible in our futures. I began to feel that I was a tool. A tool used to open the way into the future that God wanted between the Muki and ordinary people like me. I would have no glory, but God's Kingdom was not about the glory of man. It was about the glory of God. I laughed, and the tensions dissolved. I realized I had changed. God was alive inside me, and I liked that feeling.

I said, "I can dream, and that is sufficient for now. God knows what is right and has promised that David and I will belong together in time." The Judge and Natthia clapped, and I blushed.

As he began to dress, David asked, "Do you want to do some target practice, Tara?"

I giggled. "I think you'd better take me home, David. I need some gifts which I do not have to wield the weapons of God. When I can feel the blanket of Koe Sai Serena surround me, then I will be able to touch a bow of the Muki. Without God's explicit guidance, I am apt to destroy what God is building."

They all smiled. Before David took me home, I put on my own clothes. I did not want to revert to the things that I had discarded when I removed the clothes of the Muki. I would do a lot of soul searching before wearing David's clothes again. There were not merely coverings for our bodies. They were symbols of who we were and what we stood for and tolerated as a culture. I was confident that I was more Muki than I had been the day before. I wanted to blend our cultures, make my own clothing and actions reflect their belief and culture even if I could never truly be of the Muki.

30

NATTHIA

I WENT HOME WITH DAVID AT least twice every month after turning fifteen. While I was there, I always felt I was in heaven, in the holiest of locations in the whole world. Leaving each time left me depressed and was a cruel reminder that I did indeed lack something critical. I was dead in their eyes, I had no castle, and more importantly, I did not have a light of my own. Yet, they treated me like royalty. Provided my questions related to the culture and meaning of being Muki, I would receive answers. They simply left unheard of any question about technology or how they did things. Muma Horren was correct. I had to be Muki to know the intricacies of their culture. I was not, and there was no use in arguing. While at the base, as they called their settlement, I had permission to walk through the hall to my room and to join in the celebrations outside. I neither ate a meal with them nor saw the kitchen or any other part of the base. However, I did not complain. I spent hours and hours with Natthia, sitting in my room and talking. Natthia became a very special friend. It did not matter that she was far older than was my own grandmother. Our difference in ages seemed irrelevant. We talked about love, friendship, and religion. She taught me so much about the Muki!

David had shown me the results of the customs that governed the Muki. He was an angel. He was confident, happy, and excited about being alive and about growing, and learning. David and the Muki were indisputably alive! Life gave them satisfaction. From Natthia,

I continued to get the impression that, according to the Muki, my world was not alive. Our customs taught us to be dead and seek to die rather than to live. We simply put in the time, making up our own rules, and creating a fantasy in which to dwell while waiting for the end in the hopes that heaven was better than earth. As a rule, we neither thought of Earth as part of heaven itself, life being holy and sacred, nor God being around us and in us all the time. We had our own kingdoms, and I guiltily admit that my own world was an escape and a fabrication to satisfy my own needs and desires.

However, when I allowed myself to question what was wrong with my world, I found myself involved in conversations leading to cultural genocide and felt obligated to defend it. By the laws and standards of the peoples of Earth, the Muki were savage and cruel. To gain what was necessary to be alive, they locked up children, especially women, without freedom and forced them to work as slaves. A man was not an adult until he was twenty-five years old! A woman did not gain her freedom to go and to do as she pleased until she could no longer bear young, sometimes over sixty years old!

On the one hand, the Muki abhorred murder but held arrows pulled taut against any who may try to take individual action against another. If he did not back down, the Muki would, without sorrow, shame, or guilt, kill him and not even consider that, in our world, they had committed murder. Natthia laughed very long and hard when I used our refusal to kill even murderers in revenge as a point in favour of the righteousness of our culture. Natthia asked, "How can the dead be murdered? A heartbeat or a brainwave does not define life. It only exists as a biological machine. Living requires light. Only God provides the light. If one does not have any light, they are not alive. If they do not seek the guidance of God in the things that they do, then they are agents of darkness, demons to be destroyed. They are merely malfunctioning robots!"

How could I argue? Even I, a child, had little wisdom and openly admitted that Earth was not as God would have it. It was corrupt, and priorities were very likely mixed up and irrational. However, we were not God. Only God should stand in judgement of us. I often blurted out in defeat. Natthia would change the subject, usually to something supporting the concept that slavery was good, not bad. It was much better to count one's blessings than to tally one's miseries.

Natthia loved her childhood. She loved her castle and assured me that she never felt wrongly enslaved by her culture. "Slavery was the route to incredible freedom, greater freedom than we can even imagine. Learning patience, self-discipline, respect, working hard and always giving our best does not come naturally to human beings. Choosing such attributes is not automatic. We must learn them. They are best learned through bondage, where there is no alternative other than embracing them." Natthia told me repeatedly, "Only when one has learned to think will he recognize that serving God as an enslaved servant grants him the freedom and rewards that he seeks."

Natthia said no one ever abused her, either physically or mentally. She simply learned that if she did not work, she did not eat. She learned to be patient by discovering the fault of idleness and the joys and satisfaction of innumerable successes gleaned through waiting, practice and proving that she was ready to tackle the next step. Natthia was proud to give examples of how she learned that if she did not respect herself and those around her, she could neither gain the respect of another nor would she ever truly respect God. Without respect for God, one can neither achieve freedom nor earn any rights or privileges.

"Tara," she would say, "When it was time for me to leave my castle, the prison as you want to call it, I was sad. I was ready to go, but I did not want to go. To leave, I had to say that another was ready to take over my work there, admit that I was no longer needed. There is always more that I could have done, more than I could have taught my sisters. However, it was their turn. I had had mine. I needed to take all that I learned out into the bigger world, use it, and continue to grow myself. I was afraid that I would be unnecessary in the cities. And that I was no longer useful. Change, Tara, is frightening but it was like a rebirth, giving me back the enthusiasm your culture associates only with adolescence. I discovered I had a lot to offer, and others were willing to listen and learn from me, just as I was willing to learn and see new things. I took courses, met Judge Soronato, and through him, I have met you. My life is always new; I took the time to let God give it to me. I did not try to take it all at once in a way which I could not appreciate even a millionth of it. I take a little at a time, always secure yet challenged. I gained life and freedom, which continue to grow. My days are full of promise and ever-increasing freedom. I freely, graciously admit that I try very hard to be God's slave. I am not perfect, for I remain human and sinful, but I know when I feel blessed. I am willing to do anything that God asks of me to continue to feel that wonderful ecstasy within me. I want to be a servant. I desire nothing more than to be recognized as a slave of God."

I had never met another older person like Natthia. Natthia had few regrets. She treasured every memory. I know many older people, and they all had regrets. Sometimes they wanted to go back to their youth and live it all over again as though given a second chance, they were sure they would do a better job of enjoying, savouring, and experiencing life. They would warn me not to be in a hurry, not to wish my life away.

Until I had spent time with Natthia, I had not really understood what they were talking about. Natthia knew exactly what they meant. Much of life is a series of habits, one following the other throughout each day. We become robots, sliding through life on automatic pilot. When we grow old, we pause to look upon our lives and realise that we have missed so very much. It makes us sad, and we try without believing in our own ability to succeed to warn our children, especially our grandchildren, not to make the same mistakes. However, it is too late. Time only goes forward, and the damage is already done. Our children had already learned how to operate on automatic pilot and were teaching their own children to do the same.

I suggested to Natthia that we only need to have good habits, and all should work out right. She laughed. "A good habit is better than a bad one, but that is all, Tara. Life, other than remembering to breathe, eat, and sleep is not habitual. Life is dynamic. If you do not strive to keep up with it, you will lose your life, your will to experience, and become overwhelmed. You will do as you have done, Tara. Build a fantasy and live in it."

"But my Island Kingdom is good!" I cried.

"Not really, Tara. It may represent how things ought to be. It is very noble, but it is a fantasy. It will not make the 'real' world any better. It may even make it worse for it lacks what you should be contributing to it. You are taking, but you are not giving back. You are contributing to the death of your own world. You are absorbing life but not giving life away."

Sometimes, I really did not like Natthia because she was never wrong. The truth might make her cry, but it would not ever make her lie or avoid answering a question as honestly as she could. Like David, she was not trying to hurt me. She was teaching me, hoping that I would change and begin to live, shine, as they both assured me God meant me to shine. God meant for me to have light, and as I tried to follow the examples of the Muki, I did change and soon discovered that I had no world to comfort me.

The real world grew ever more distant in my effort to capture the essence of life that the Muki experienced. My heart ached to become Muki. I desperately wanted to capture the will of God and let it shine forever, in me, around me, and through me. It could not happen because I was human and could not let go of the freedom and control that I treasured so dearly yet was incapable of rationalizing. Natthia said it was my ancestry. I was of the world of my birth and could not escape it. Then she would cry as I begged her to help me become Muki. I did not want to go back to that other world that had always beckoned, pulling on my heels telling me that I could not escape, that I had no choice but to grow up into the world I was destined to inherit, like it or not.

Spring came, then summer. I lived a double life. I spent most of my life dreaming my way through the days and hours alone. Sometimes I tried to experiment with ideas that Natthia or David had discussed with me. However, I mostly hid from the world that

I could no longer call my own and struggled with learning to see myself as one of the Muki.

I did not have very much time anymore. Fortunately, I had an afterschool job. I was very proud to have my job, and I loved it. I always tried to remember to smile, for my smiling was a gift that the Muki recognized as being from God. The Muki liked my strength of character, so I did not try to curb my sense of justice and knowledge of right and wrong. I continued to fight conformity at school, speak out on matters of principle, and get myself into a good share of trouble by doing so. My mother often lost patience with my father and me, as we spent hours each evening arguing about almost everything. Dad and I preferred to call them discussions.

That year the stilts never moved from beside the garage. Walky-talky trees did not get an earful of my complaints and admonishments. I only put my chin over the highest point of the upper post of the goalposts in the field once. When I had, I had learned something very important. I did not have to go up high to see the future.

Nearly always, at least once a week, I saw my future. A friend promised and freely sent from God, David Miskenack, of the Muki, held my future. Slowly, he and Natthia, and even Muma Horren and the others, helped me bring it into focus. I felt special. I knew I was special. God loved me. And I would develop the faith that come what may; I would become one of the Muki. It was never too late to find my own light. It was my destiny, and I walked among those I wanted to emanate.

Yes, our world was corrupt, and the world of the Muki was frightening, often cruel, and extremely harsh. Yet, I wanted David's world for myself. I wanted the freedom and the pleasures he took while he lived. Slowly, I understood that it was their upbringing — hard love, which gave them their strength and sent them to God, into the light that I would not accept although I craved.

I liked the feeling that I was self-sufficient and capable of surviving all alone without any help from anyone. My independence was at the very core of my character. My soul had no reason to believe that

I needed God's love and light to live. I figured that to have it was a bonus rather than a necessity.

I decided to strive to maintain my humanity, as Natthia called it, and superimpose a sense of godliness on top of my character. I know it sounds silly, but you must remember that I was young, very opinionated, and defiant. I was also among radically different people. During the summer, I began to accept that the Muki were not merely a lost tribe of Native Americans, but to entertain the possibility that they really were alien beings and not from Earth.

I felt pressure to redeem Earth, to prove somehow that neither it nor I were dead even by the definitions of the Muki. I believed it imperative that I do so. The Muki thought nothing of terminating malfunctioning robots!

The year was not all struggle and sadness. It was full of laughter and joy. David remained my teacher, always building upon my soul, taking me ever closer to the light of God, and ever giving me more of the Muki to call my own. Natthia seemed to take a dual role: providing stark reality and taking pleasure in every opportunity to enjoy and experience the mysteries life presented. I treasured Natthia's laugh and our shared giggles, our secret dances, and her letting me wear the brown dress, which turned me into a butterfly in the eyes of every single Muki. Natthia and I giggled and laughed while we acted out silly fantasies in the privacy of a room dedicated as my very own, whether I was in camp or not. I am totally convinced that there is no more holy activity than being present and even participating in the worship rituals around an open campfire, real or not, among the Muki.

By late fall of 1970, I once more became obsessed with the idea of remaining with David, at the base camp, never to return to Quesnel, my family, and outside life. When I dressed up as a butterfly and danced with Natthia, I soon longed to be dancing with David. I did not like them telling me that the law prohibited me from dancing with David. I hated when Muma Horren would catch Natthia, and I dressed 'inappropriately,' as she called it. "Natthia, you are not a butterfly! Stop acting like you are!" Muma would yell very loudly after slamming the door. "She will get ideas. Tara is not Muki. She cannot dance. To let her think that she could and teach her how to dance like a butterfly opens her heart to despair. You are being cruel, Natthia. There is so much you could teach her about our culture. Why teach her what can only harm her?"

Natthia answered, "Oh, Muma Horren, she wants to dance. She belongs to David. We all know that is true. Perhaps it would be wiser if she knew what dancing meant in our culture. Perhaps if she understands the significance of a dance, she will understand why she cannot."

Then Muma Horren left only to return with a bow and quiver of arrows. She aimed an arrow at me and said, "If you dance here, Tara, you will die. This is not a castle. David has no license to dance, so he, too, will be shot." Then turning to Natthia, say, "Go ahead, Natthia, teach her to dance. Do not forget to teach her that dancing will signal not only David's death but also hers. Their deaths will leave us neither teacher nor student to teach us that Earth is blessed. Do not forget that it is David who believes in this woman." Natthia cried, and then we changed and no longer danced.

After Muma Horren left, she would wipe her tears and my own and say, "If God wills it, my child; there will be a way for you and David to dance. Be patient, child. God will show the way when the time is right, as God ordained on the mountain. In a castle, Tara, you would enter the Great Hall. You would use your body in dance to lure the Sire into wanting to dance with you. If he were willing, he would call out, "Tara, dance with me!" and then you would dance. If he frightened you, you would try to run away to hide in your room where he could not follow, but if you let him catch you, you would become his mate and live with him in his quarters. You would let him father your child and serve him until the child walked. Then you would return to the Great Hall and choose whether to return to your room or dance yet again.

I learned about castles and finally discovered that in a fashion, I did have a castle. A castle is not just a building where you live. It is much more than that. With satisfaction, I determined that my Island

Kingdom was my castle. It nurtured, taught, and held promise for my future and a world that was right in the eyes of the Muki and me and in God's eyes. Yes, my island kingdom was how the world was supposed to be but was not and could never become.

31

ACCEPTING FATE

SOMETIMES I GOT VERY DEPRESSED. I felt powerless and incapable of playing the role that God was asking me to play. I had absolutely nothing to give to Earth or the Muki. I was arrogant. I was disrespectful. My school friends were correct. Crazy and full of blasphemy, my destiny was to rot in hell. I did not want to be in the position in which I found myself. If I tried to confide in another outside of the Muki, either the words would not come out coherently at all, or I would get frightened that I would be locked up as insane where I would never see David again. The worst was thinking I would say the wrong thing, and Earth would kill the Muki. I felt very alone when not with David. Clinging to my island kingdom, I feared the coming seasons, for I knew my island kingdom was slowly disappearing, a grain at a time.

I decided that I was indeed insane. Sane people heard no voices in their heads. Normal people had dreams, not visions. God belonged locked securely inside the Bible. My culture told me I could not touch God and that God did not laugh and play games with an outcast dead kid who wanted to be an alien, living in the light of the Muki.

With each visit, leaving base camp had been increasingly difficult. Usually, I cried, tears running down my cheeks, shaking, and even sometimes throwing up before I would let David pick me up to throw me into the plane. I wanted to stay with the Muki. Subtle little changes occurred, causing me to fear each visit might be my last opportunity to stay.

Convinced my friends were preparing to leave, I panicked one day shortly before my sixteenth birthday. I ran away from David at the base camp. We were at the plane. David was frustrated with me, and he had raised his voice.

"Tara, you cannot stay. I will not bring you here if I must put up with any more temper tantrums. I am tired of them. It wrenches my soul to take you back, too. I want…" David went pale and stiffened as those accompanying us aimed arrows at David. After several moments of absolute silence, while David and I stood motionless staring into each other's eyes, David whispered, "Grow up, Littl'un." I was shocked.

Suddenly, I heard echoes of Muma Horren telling me that if I danced, David would die. David had never asked me to grow up. He had almost asked me to dance. I was terrified. I turned to Doug and calmly said, "Doug, stop pretending. Either shoot me right now or put down that arrow. I know who the Muki are. You are from the Land of the Butterflies, up there." I pointed to the sky. "This is Earth. You are alien. You do not belong here. Face facts. I do not belong here either. Get rid of that crap on the plane. I need no more tiptoeing around who and what we are. Get real. Be real. I will wait in my room."

I turned back to David. "David, I love you. I cannot dance. Your people would kill you, and my people would imprison you if I did. Our love is forbidden. You are my teacher. I am not going to dream anymore. Teach me how to worship. Finish your lessons. Then go home." I pointed to the sky again. "Unless you intend to take me with you, we will have to say goodbye. I do not want to be guilty of killing you. I love you. You are an instrument of God's. Go report to your people. Tell them Earth says…"

I was at a loss for words. Tears fell down my cheek, and I sobbed, "We are not malfunctioning robots. You cannot kill us. God would be unhappy." Addressing Doug again, I said, "Doug, I am going to my room now. Come get me when that plane looks right. Shoot me if you must." With that, I walked up the path back to camp. No one stopped me.

As I neared the hall entrance, I felt other arrows pointing at me. I pointed at each person holding a bow with an arrow pulled tautly and aimed at my heart. The bows literally fell out of their arms as I did so. Hysterical, I started to laugh. Once in my room, I fell onto the bed and cried. I did not know what to do. I began to wish they had shot me. I felt dead. I did not know who I was. Why did I have the power to make them drop their holy weapons? I stopped crying, sat up, and stared out the window. In absolute terror, I said to the window, "What have I done?"

I had never felt so lost and empty as I did then. I closed my eyes. Thinking of all the lessons David had been teaching me, I became unnaturally calm. I stood, faced the window, and worshipped.

Natthia came into my room a few minutes later. Touching the waist of my blue jeans, she knelt beside me to support my prayer. I looked down. She was deathly pale. In agony, I collapsed. Natthia put her arms around me and began humming a soothing tune.

Wiping my eyes, I started pouring out my woes. "It isn't fair, Natthia. I am lost. I do not understand why anything is happening. Nothing makes sense. Why did you not shoot me? Why did you drop your bow? I do not want any power. I am afraid but I want to dance with David. Why is dancing forbidden? What does God want from me?"

"We will figure this out together, Tara. Rest assured that God has a plan. It is not always easy to understand what God wants of us."

Like a baby, I let Natthia rock me. Wishing I was dreaming, I watched her while her skin changed as the seconds ticked by. The paleness first went blue which darkened until I thought she must be dead. I wondered if she was having a stroke or heart attack. However, she kept humming very softly. I did not feel cold. Her touch against me was warm and comforting. I felt my pain, sorrow, and confusion drifting away into thin air. For some inexplicable reason, I could almost see it doing so, like a fog lifting off me, swirling before us and rising into the room around us. As it slowly vanished with a shimmer of colour, I imagined thought as strands of light.

Totally convinced she was a guardian angel, I hugged Natthia.

The blue in her flesh seemed to dance as it changed into a dazzling shimmer of light as I did so. Natthia's light was warm and breezy. Touching sunlight was how the touch of Natthia felt. Losing all awareness of my own agony, I saw my fears wash away in a fountain before my own eyes. I had no concept of what was happening. I simply concluded that Natthia was an angel, and I was in the presence of God, safe, secure, and nothing was going to go wrong. Everything was as God ordained.

Natthia said, "Tara, let go. Become a puppet on a string. Let David teach you. All will be as it should be in time. Now wipe your tears. Go home. David will bring you back again. The Muki will remain here. Have faith in God. Learn to worship, and you shall become of the Muki."

Natthia stood. Offering me her hand, she smiled at me and nodded. Feeling calm, I took her hand. Together, holding hands, we walked back to the plane. Natthia was so bright I could not look at her.

Before letting go of Natthia's hand, I took David's hand. "I will be coming back," smiled at David and said, "Let's go."

David hugged me a moment before he tossed me up into the plane. No one was there to grab me. Although I felt dizzy, I did not fall. Calmly, I sat in my seat and did up the seatbelt.

Because they were staring with stunned looks on their faces, I laughed. "David, Brian, and Doug get in. Natthia's right. I'll be late. It is time to go. I apologize for my outburst. I will try not to let it happen again." I watched David do that strange dance that the Muki did before they got into the plane. I wondered why they waved their arms around like that. They did not appear to be superstitious in other ways. When I squinted, I thought I could see a funny haze in the air. I closed my eyes because I did not want to believe any evidence that confirmed my belief that David and his friends were, in fact, aliens.

I was shocked that no one had disputed my outburst. Saying a silent prayer, I whispered, "Please God, do not let them really be aliens. They must think I am crazy. Tell them I am just a stupid kid with a big imagination." God laughed. I blushed. "Then I will figure out their technology," I said in defiance.

David jumped through the door, kissed my forehead, and sat down. I watched Brian and Doug. They kept glancing at Natthia and then at us but did not move. Judge Soronato joined the group of people standing in the clearing. Calmly, and without saying a word, he took Natthia's hand and nodded to Brian. Brian jumped onboard. The Judge shone beside Natthia.

Doug asked, "What am I to do, Sir?"

The Judge laughed. "Just take her home, as usual, Doug. She will not object."

Looking confused, Doug shrugged and jumped into the plane, took his seat, and, almost immediately, the door closed with the same audible hiss as always.

Overcome with exhaustion, I held David's hand, leaned my head on his shoulder, and slept.

The sense of peace that Natthia had imparted to me before David took me home that day lasted until I went to bed. However, as I settled into bed and tried to sleep, the enormity of what I had done and experienced overwhelmed me, and I felt the weight of the world fall upon my shoulders. I do not know whether it was after-shock or total terror at having no answers to the multitude of questions and possibilities that refused to stop plaguing my thoughts, I could not function and perhaps suffered a mini nervous breakdown that emotionally paralyzed me.

All week I walked around like a zombie. I do not believe I even thought at all. Not upset or frightened, no emotion at all registered in my being. I simply existed in a calm blank stupor. At the end of the week, I went to bed and laid on it until the early hours of the morning. Then I cried. Completely uncontrollably, I sobbed. What was real? Why on earth did I exist? Why did God do these things to me? How could I have a part in any scheme of God?

I began remembering spiritual experiences. Visions, fears, words, and odd experiences from the past played in my thoughts like reruns without commercials. I could not deny a God connection. I could assume I was crazy. However, I could neither remove physical evidence that they had indeed occurred, nor could I forget the messages or the lessons I learned through them. I only understood that I did not want to be in a predicament I found myself in. Experience had taught me that there was nothing I could do to make reality other than what it was. I was lost. However, I had no choice whatsoever.

Fate had put me here as it had every other time I had spoken with God. Nothing is ever as it first appears. There is always a catch. God is not exactly forthright. God eases you into circumstances. Letting you believe whatever you like until you figure it out for yourself. Usually, you understand after committing to a course of action or reflecting on the consequences of actions already taken. As memories surfaced, I tried to find the connection to the present.

I was only four years old. It was Halloween. Being an odd child, I had funny ideas about Halloween. Although excited about candy, I was not keen to go because the whole concept of Halloween made me feel guilty and evil. Mom made me an angel costume. When she put it on me, I wanted to be an angel and agreed to go trick or treating with my sisters and brother.

Being shy, I found speaking to strangers difficult. My sisters had to drag me to the doors. I liked receiving the candy, walking between the houses, the jack-o-lanterns, and even the scary costumes of others in the street, but often, my big sister would take the treat from the person at the door and put it in my bag because I would not go up the steps or step forward for my treat. I cannot remember if I even said thank you loud enough for anyone to hear me. My sisters were losing patience with me.

Mom had done a good job on the costume. I was little and cute. People made a fuss over me. I did not like it, and it annoyed my sisters, too. At a house about a block away from home, a man came outside saying, "What have we here? A little angel is it." He shouted down the hall, "You've got to see this!" He picked me up and carried me inside. He held me around the waist, facing ahead. I was terrified. He took me into a kitchen full of people and set me down on the table. God spoke to me, saying, "Be an angel. Smile." I felt giddy and honestly believed that God was in the room with us. Eerie smoke accompanying the hiss from an oxygen tank cleared, and the colour of everything changed. The Holy Spirit bathed the room in soft golden light. God directed my gaze to a person in a wheelchair. This person was old and sickly, probably deaf, too, because the man holding on to me was talking very loudly.

I was overwhelmed with the feeling that I really was an angel and was going to heal this person. All I had to do was smile and touch him, and like Jesus, I would cure him. I willingly followed all the instructions God gave me. Knowing something had passed between us as we looked at one another, I felt incredibly calm. No longer frightened, I felt quite comfortable as the man picked me up again and returned me to my sisters outside. When the door closed, I was asked what had happened. I replied, "I was a real angel."

Then, I tried to tell them what happened, and they responded, "You are lying. You are not an angel."

I retorted, "Am so. I'm going home."

My oldest sister was furious. I would not cooperate, and she eventually gave up trying to convince me and followed me home, berating me all the way for spoiling Halloween for her. While she left to rejoin the others, I sat contentedly on the floor in the living room and sorted my candy.

Early in November, I enquired why so many cars were parked outside the house where I had been a real angel. It was because of a funeral. With shock and disappointment, I realized I had been an angel of death and had not healed anyone. Confirming my fear was true, God spoke to me while I cried. God told me I had taken his fears and helped him let go. Feeling deceived and used, it took me a long time to forgive God. Despite God telling me that what I had done was good, I honestly thought I had committed murder. It did not matter that he was old; I wanted to have removed his suffering and made him well, healthy, and happy. Maybe, even young again.

I was supposed to have delivered a miracle. Beyond my understanding of miracles, God told me that was exactly what I had done. Death was not good. It was bad. God laughed. I felt small and stupid. Henceforth, I always tried to figure out the angle behind all further requests God gave me. I always answered God with trepidation.

Taking a deep breath, I relaxed and followed the advice of words appearing in my consciousness. I gradually understood that the answers to my questions were in the lessons David had been teaching me and those God had taught me throughout my life.

David and Natthia also considered death a gift. I think the memory of being an angel for God when I was little was haunting me because I was somehow in the same position again. I wanted to dance with David. Dancing with David would unleash miracles. This I did not doubt. However, Muma Horren was adamant that dancing would result in David and my deaths. I had no problem with my own death. I awaited death. There was absolutely no doubt in my mind that God had on numerous occasions proven death was a gift whether I wanted to believe it or not.

When I was five, I had died. My brother had screwed a round of firewood onto the end of the swing chain in the basement. He twisted the chain round and round, sat on the log, and let it unwind. It was a fantastic ride. Spinning at an incredible speed, the chain unwound. Then it continued to wind up again until it had consumed all the momentum. Rather than let it unwind again, it was my turn. I climbed on, and my brother wound it even more before letting me go with a good push. Back and forth, round and round, laughing and leaning my head back, I enjoyed my ride. Unfortunately, the screw was undoing as I turned. The log fell off the chain, and I slammed onto the cement floor.

That was the first time I had an out-of-body experience. I knew I was dead. I looked upon my still form on the floor while I held the hand of an angel and listened to instructions. I saw the path of golden light and understood what the angel was telling me to leave behind. I also remember the powerful voice and the emphatic denial of passage down that glorious path. "Go back. I have work for you." I remember my reluctance to return to my body, pride, and oath to be obedient. In anticipation of something wonderful awaiting me in the future, I allowed the angel to return me to my body. Confused, I could neither breathe nor cry, and I did not remember how I got onto the stairs or where I had been. I crawled, gasping for a breath that I could not figure out how to take. I think I passed out.

The next thing I remember, I was in my mother's arms. I began throwing up. I had incredible visions in the hospital, and the angel stayed with me. Even as young as I was, I felt both ecstasy and terror. Like the lady in the chronic care ward, whom David had insisted I befriend, I was alive only because I had something to teach or learn before earning my ticket to the next world.

Applying that memory to the questions I had while lying upon my bed, I determined that my friendship with David was connected to why I was alive. He was part of my destiny. I feared I was going to be responsible for his death. I began to pray that we would die together. I childishly hoped that David's home was at the other end of the path beyond death's door. Desperately, I needed to believe with my whole being that death was all God had promised.

Sighing, I would do as Natthia said. I would learn how to worship. I would become a puppet on a string, and David and I would touch the future.

Although I slept the remainder of that night in peace and comfort, when I awoke, I also felt strange that the idea of dying with David did not feel sinful. I certainly did not think of loving him as a suicide pact. I neither wanted to end my life nor intended to end his. It was more of acceptance that destiny included death. Lessons... I loved how lessons grew.

When David had said life was a sentence, and death, the period at the end, I had laughed. However, as time progressed, I also learned that that period was incredibly important. I did want control. Sometimes I wanted to end with an exclamation mark. I definitely did not want to leave life behind with a question mark. I wanted to understand my lessons thoroughly. When the time came, I wanted to have done exactly the ultimate that my destiny held. Daydreaming about my epitaph, I wanted my tombstone to read, "I lived, loved, and was loved." What could be more perfect and absolutely portray my satisfaction with having a successful life? I would love David. Someday, the time would be right, and it would be worth all the consequences.

David had tried to teach me about time, too. I admit I did not understand precisely what he meant. Understanding that God was unconstrained by time was not a hard concept. I liked that time was dynamic rather than static. The analogy of time as an elastic band was intriguing. Experiences had taught me that the perception of the passage of time was dependent on attitude and emotions. It always takes longer to get somewhere than it does to come back. Boredom and anxiety make time drag. Concentration, focus, and regret speed the passage of time. Falling out of a tree was an event occurring in slow motion. I had felt time suspended.

When held in God, time does do strange things, like skip, pulse, and bounce forward and backward. I imagine creation as a timeless tray upon which God pulled strings here and there to align past, present, and future. When the stage is set, God lets go, and time unfolds. All things are possible. After death, perhaps I will discover that my period was really a semicolon at the end of my life! I remember David laughing when I said that.

That morning I had accepted my own mortality. I had also determined that there was time to change our destiny. I would work at securing a future for David and me. Somehow, with God's help, I would render dancing benign. I would prove I was Muki, had a castle, and could legitimately dance with David. The Muki would not be justified to shoot either of us. The time would be right. Everyone would know it was true. God would smile upon us all. The arrows demanded by tradition would fall harmlessly out of their arms just as they did on my last visit. God ordained David and my friendship. I honestly believed God would grant me all the power I needed to have the future unfold according to His will. God would keep David safe. I did not need to worry. I needed to become a puppet on a string.

With that objective in mind, I waited for David at our rendezvous. He was late. It was cold. Just as I began to think that David would not show up, I heard his truck. Without waiting for him to open the passenger door for me, I hopped in and slid over beside him.

Smiling, rather than saying hello, I said, "I am sorry I caused so much trouble on my last visit, David. Will you forgive me?"

David sighed, "Littl'un, you need no forgiveness. Although you terrify me, I am proud of you. Unfortunately, I do not believe I can protect you, and it is time for me to go home and for us to say goodbye. However, the Judge has told me I must complete my lessons before we can leave. I am afraid of hurting you, Tara. When I worshipped after taking you home last week, God told me to remain the right kind of friend. I am afraid I will sin against you."

"We must talk about the future then, David. There must be a way to make the future safe for all of us. I will go home with you if you let me. You know that. I will run away with you. You can take me to the sky with you." With my voice cracking and sounding too desperate, I was begging, and even I did not like the sound of my own voice.

David pulled over and hugged me close. "You cannot come home with us, Tara. It would be illegal. I have no license, and you have no castle. My people would slaughter us within minutes. I love you too much to be willing to risk your life. The whole idea gives me nightmares. You were correct when you spoke to us at the base. Our relationship is taboo in both our cultures. It is time we both admitted it and honestly accepted that you and I have no future."

I thought silently for a while. I looked at David, trying to come to terms with his admission that he really was an alien. When his skin did not glow, he did not look alien. I started to shake. Somehow, it was easier to believe the Muki were angels than aliens. Wishing again that I had not spoken so stupidly at the base, I tried to calm my rising panic. As an Earthling, did I not have a responsibility to protect Earth? Should I tell someone? Whom could I tell? Who would believe me? How dare David say we had no future? Our friendship was, for some reason, imperative to the future. I did not even know why that was true. However, I believed it deep in my soul. I truly thought the world would end if David ceased being my friend.

Why could David have not laughed and said I had a vivid imagination? Why did he not lie to me? He is teasing me. He must be teasing me. He cannot really be an alien. The Muki are angels. Please, God, let the Muki be a religious cult. I closed my eyes and leaned against David. He felt so wonderful. I was always safe with him. I pinched him.

"Ouch. What did you do that for, Littl'un?" David's scowl turned quickly to laughter.

"Just making sure you are real, David. I could not be imagining you, could I?"

"Do you think you are powerful enough to conjure me up from your subconsciousness?" Chuckling, David added, "I am flattered, Littl'un. I am human just like you." Having pulled over and parked the truck, he held me and played with my hair.

Like the fool I tended to be, I reached out to wipe a tear off his cheek. With a gasp, David grabbed my hand then pushed me away.

"It is time to take you home," he said very factually.

I burst out laughing. Then I told him I loved him. He would not look at me all the way home. Contentedly savouring David, I concluded I could not possibly have dreamed up someone as wonderful as David. He was not like anyone I had ever known. He was incredibly handsome, horribly serious, and made me feel irresistible and safe. David would protect me with his life, even from himself.

Parking the truck by the Catholic Church, David walked me home. We always met in secret except when he walked me home up the back alley after gym. My mother had only caught me talking to him once. I did not even lie to her. I told her we had just talked, which was true. She gave me a lecture on boys, and I admit I sadly told her we were not that kind of friends. Although I think she believed me, she gave me an odd look and told me that I was not a little girl anymore and that his intentions would not necessarily be as innocent as I thought. Silently, I chuckled at the irony of her comments. I love my mom.

That event had happened when I was almost fifteen, and after my mom's comments, I had started to think about David seriously as having a valid potential of becoming my boyfriend. At the same time, I went to my room embarrassed and excited. I remember wondering if there would ever come a day when I could introduce David to my family. My folks would say he was too old. My brother would call him a sissy because he cried so easily. I would not like my sisters to dislike him, but I was not very confident when I thought of introducing David as my boyfriend. I do not think they would want to take him away from me, but I certainly thought my sisters had more to offer a boyfriend than I did. I was clueless.

Besides, we were not that kind of friends, not even in my dreams. Just like in real life, when I acted inappropriately, David ran even in my dreams. I might cry but wanting David to treat me like a girlfriend made me feel wrong. I liked that he would run. There was a God connection to my relationship with David. I never could escape the guilty feelings or the firmness of the powerful voice that spoke inside my head whenever I thought or acted inappropriately. I needed David for some reason that I could not fathom.

God did not explain why I had been offered a friend. I did not want to risk ruining the future that God promised would result from me learning the lessons that David was teaching. Yet, I was human enough to understand that I wanted God to let me marry David eventually. When we worshiped on Snowshoe Plateau, I hoped that was what God had meant. I needed time to grow up, and there was time.

We walked down into the bushes so that David could walk me almost all the way home. In Quesnel, January can be exceedingly cold. Both David and I were well bundled up against the cold. However, it was still beautiful walking in the woods with David. Our breath froze as we breathed. The crunch of our steps on the snow was loud and alive—the wind bit into us. I could feel the tingle of the cold seeping up my legs and arms. If we stopped and sat down, we would likely freeze to death within a very short time.

As we climbed up the hill, my big toe throbbed. It had frozen while I had been dancing in the snow the year before, and it always let me know when it was too cold. I wish I could have stood in the trees with David forever. Although I did not dare to, I wanted to kiss him goodbye.

Instead, I said, "David, I do not trust myself either. Let us meet with Judge Soronato, Natthia, and even Muma Horren. They will be able to guide us. I will try very hard to remember that God sent you to me as a friend. Please do not leave me yet, because I need you to be part of my life. I promise to remain a little girl." Suddenly playing the part, I said, "I hereby pledge to remain a child forevermore! I will be a student and call you, Sir."

I giggled and ran home. David said nothing. As I listened, I smiled because he laughed. Before I was out of hearing range, I heard him singing in his own language and waited until I could no longer hear him before continuing home. As I headed home, I daydreamed about learning to speak their language. They had a strong accent, like the French roll their r's, the Muki did something to their k's, and I tried practicing rolling my "k's" but was not sure that I was not supposed to choke on them instead. Try as hard as I could, and I could not imitate the sounds they used in their speech. They laughed at all my attempts to mimic their words when I was at the base. I felt that they did not want me to learn their language because whenever I came upon any of the Muki, they always immediately stopped talking or switched to speaking English. I loved listening to their language and felt very privileged when they used it when singing praises to God around the campfire or when David would burst into song as he had after saying goodbye. Their language seemed to be alive and spoke to the soul, and its meaning seemed to awaken in one's heart and spirit a feeling of peace that stayed with me for a long time after silence fell.

By the time I entered the garage at home, I had regained confidence in the future again. God would indeed give me all the power I needed to protect David, the Muki, Earth, and myself. I went to my room feeling better than I had all week. Confidently, I would wait for the next weekend.

32

SEEKING APPROVAL

JUDGE SORONATO PACED IN HIS office while awaiting the arrival of David and the Little Smiler. As pictures of her directing Brian and Doug last week flashed through his thoughts, the Judge wondered what the future held. Then he smiled because Tara was such a joy. Full of mischief, anger, and determination, she did indeed have power. She was also terrifying. Therefore, the Judge had the base on full alert. Even he no longer had confidence in their safety because it was hard to trust that she would not betray them.

Assuming she had not understood the ramifications, let alone the truth in her own words, he hoped her love for David was strong enough to prevent her from exposing them. She was such an imp and told such fanciful stories; the Judge hoped that they would not believe her even if she told the right authority. Thinking he was a good judge of the character of Earthlings, he thought it probable that the authorities would laugh her right out of their office. The poor child did not deserve the reception she would receive. Besides, she would not have a clue as to where to tell them to find the base. She could not expose them. The worst she could do was cause David danger. She would not do that.

The Judge sighed. Concluding God had chosen her well, he stopped pacing and went to fetch Natthia. With all the unrest, it would be advisable to meet the transporter.

Everyone had met in the morning to discuss today's meeting. All had agreed to let it unfold according to her agenda. It was impossible to do otherwise. The Judge thought they were in for a treat. God had sent clear approval of his plan. Furthermore, God had told the Judge that today the child belonged to Her.

In Muki culture, power was directly connected to God. Using the gifts of Koe Sai Serena, they readily recognized the will of God in all their conversations and activities. A person earned their position in society based upon their reputation. All they did and all that one's senses told them had to remain true to maintain their position and authority. Yet, the granting of authority and power was dynamic and adjusted to suit the will of God. Regardless of position within society, if a person was recognized as proceeding under the direction and authority of God, they were readily given the respect, authority, and power necessary to carry out their duties as commanded by God. The Muki recognized Tara of Earth's request for this meeting as a command from God and therefore had no options except granting her all the power and authority she needed to carry out her obedience to God, for God speaks through all Her servants and orchestrates events to guide the building of the Kingdom of God.

Tara looked nervous when she and David disembarked. She nodded to Natthia and the Judge but said nothing. Keeping her eyes on the path, she went straight to her room. After opening the door, she said, "Natthia and Muma Horren, I need your help. Please come with me."

The Judge nodded his approval. Natthia and Muma Horren entered the room and closed the door. David, Brian, and Doug accompanied the Judge to his office, and the rest dispersed to their duties.

After sitting down, the Judge asked Doug to make an urn of cider and David to tell him what he knew of Tara's plan.

"I don't have a clue, Judge Soronato. Other than cutting off the circulation in my hand by holding it so tightly all the way here, other than it frightens her, she gave no hint of what she had in mind. I do not think she has uttered more than two words since I picked her up. She has not looked at me. I might be going crazy or imagining it, but I thought she was shining several times on the way here. It only happened when I glanced at her. When I focused on her, there was nothing. I did not feel the conscious presence of God with us."

"It is true, Judge Soronato," added Brian, "Doug and I also saw the presence of God around her. Only for brief moments, though. Is she becoming Muki, Sir? Is that possible?"

"All things are possible. Has God spoken to any of you?"

David answered, "No, Sir, yet I feel calm. I am not frightened, but I think I need to change. I am not dressed properly. May I be excused?"

"He has been a zombie all day, Sir. However, I do not feel any danger either. I am confident she will not demand David dance," laughed Brian.

Turning beet red, David stared at Brian with shock. "I will not dance, Judge Soronato! I am a Cultural Judge. I take my oath to uphold the law seriously. I will not succumb to temptation. I will conduct myself honourably." David's eyes pleaded with the Judge to believe him.

The Judge laughed. "Relax, David. Trust God. I trust you to behave in an exemplary manner. However, David, I agree with you. This meeting is formal. Please dress accordingly but join us for a cider. There will be enough time to change later."

The Judge began talking quietly about the assignment and the judgement they were building. Doug brought the cider to the table, and they all sat silently, processing their thoughts while drinking the cider.

Tara leaned against the side of the platform and took off her shoes. Placing them neatly in the bottom of the closet, she addressed Muma Horren. "I must prove that I am of the Muki, Muma. I must act as though I am. Without knowing how to do so, I need your help. I do not have any choice. Please help me put on my dress. I know it frightens you. However, it is not really a butterfly dress. Therefore, you can relax. I am not going to demand David dance. I will act appropriately. God told me to trust my heart. He said I was in control of who I was. The best way to help you recognize me is to dress traditionally."

While Tara took the dress out of the closet, Muma Horren stared at Natthia. After a few moments, she said, "Tara, this dress will not make you Muki. It will put you and all of us, especially the males here, in extreme danger."

Tara held a hand, outward, palm forward. Although tears formed in her eyes, emphatically, Tara said, "Stop, Muma Horren. Be silent. We will talk after I am dressed." She stared at Muma Horren. Like a pair of angry cats, they stared each other down. Natthia put a hand on their shoulders to calm them. Eventually, Muma sighed, grabbed the dress, put it over Tara's head, and began fastening the straps. She was none too gentle. Uncomfortable and reluctant, Muma Horren had recognized Tara's authority as being according to the will of God and could not deny her request even though it terrified her and knew it would have far-reaching consequences. Muma Horren's thoughts were racing to determine how to proceed to maintain the laws of the Muki when her request if proven true, demanded her execution as it was illegal for a butterfly to be outside of the confines of her castle and to protect the males here from execution should Tara demand the base to be recognized as her castle as none of the Muki residing at the base had the authorization to enter a castle. Tara's request cut at the very core of their culture and broke sacred traditions. Muma Horren was desperate to find an appropriate simulation that would keep everyone, including Tara, safe and alive.

With tears in her eyes, she walked around Tara when she finished. Putting a hand under Tara's chin, she said, "I wish your hair were longer." She chuckled as she gave Tara another good looking over. "Perhaps you could pass as Muki."

All three laughed, and the tension in the room dissolved. Natthia handed Tara her tights. While Tara put them on, Natthia and Muma Horren each picked up one of her sandals. In silence, they lovingly laced them onto Tara's feet. The job complete, they stood back as though waiting for further instructions. Tara sat on the edge of her bed like a stone statue. She looked from one to the other and began shaking. Muma Horren immediately sat beside her, held her hand, and began humming. Natthia, too, sat beside Tara putting her arm around her shoulder. They remained thus until Tara shuddered, sighed, and smiled at her friends.

Tara whispered, "Thank you." Jumping up, she turned to face them, "Natthia, Muma, I want to dance. May I dance? Just in here?"

Natthia nodded. Muma Horren stepped over to the door. Her stance clearly said she was on guard.

Closing her eyes, Tara swayed and waved her arms. She walked back and forth in the small room, trying to find a feeling of peace in her soul. After a few minutes, she stopped in front of Muma Horren, opened her eyes very wide, and giggled, "Muma Horren, I need wings to be a butterfly."

Muma Horren laughed. "And you need a stinger, child. You are correct. You are not dressed to dance. You are a young lady. Furthermore, a butterfly does not dance in brown.

"I need to meet with the Judge and David, too. How am I supposed to act? Do I invite them here? Dressed like this, where will you allow me to go? I want no one to get hurt. Do I need to carry a bow?"

"So many questions you ask of us, child. Sit with us. We will help you work it out." Muma Horren then led a serious conversation about appropriate conduct. She very sincerely assumed the role of a Senior Mother. Soon there was no question about her intention to protect everyone, even Tara of Earth, as innocent and naive as she was, as though she really was Muki.

Tara was very flattered. Natthia was pleased that fate had led Muma Horren to be here. Marvelling at the wisdom and foresight of God, Natthia began to glow. Muma Horren stopped talking and smiled toward Natthia. She sighed and began to glow also. Tara felt incredibly calm watching her friends shine with the presence of God. Silently wishing she could shine as well, Tara held hands with them.

Feeling the presence of God, Tara had visions and faith filled her. Then God terrified her. Falling to the floor, she cried. God was asking the impossible. The room went dark as she became dizzy. Sweating and gasping for breath, Tara clung to Natthia and Muma Horren. Although they no longer shone, their skin maintained a soft glow. Tara looked at her own hands in a strange realization that the same hazy glow was on her own skin. Nearing hysteria, she shouted to the others, "Look at me. I am Muki, too!" then she passed out.

When she awoke, Tara found herself lying on her bed under a comforter. Natthia was standing guard at the door with an arrow held across her heart and a bow in the other hand, and Muma Horren was sitting on her bed. Eyes closed and softly humming, Muma was pale. There was no longer any hint of light upon any of them. Yet, Tara did not even for a moment question whether she had been hallucinating. Sitting up, she looked at Natthia and said, "If I err, Natthia, stop me."

Getting up, Tara hugged Muma Horren. "Temporarily, this base is my castle. Please, Muma Horren, protect and guide me."

Muma Horren stopped humming. She gave Tara a very serious expression then nodded. "Natthia, the Judge's office is our backdoor. Inform him. Allow none into the hall. Ask the Judge to lock those needed to be protected in their rooms or workstation." Muma took a deep breath. "Have I forgotten anything, Natthia?"

Natthia took some deep breaths as well before answering. "Brian... Muma Horren, is just a boy. Do we need to lock up Brian?"

"I trust the Judge, Natthia. Besides, I think Brian is safe. Why is that? I must be insane. Let us trust God. Tara is going to grant us a blessing. We are safe. So are Brian, David, and the others. However, I believe I have forgotten something." Muma paused, surveying Tara. Smiling, she said, "Tara needs a bow. At a castle, she would be a guard at her age and must go to the foyer. That is right. We have company." Muma Horren, lost in thought, silently paced the room. "Ready, Natthia. Now go inform the Judge. Bring back a bow. Put three arrows in the quiver." Muma nodded to Natthia.

Without a comment, Natthia opened the door and left.

It was with some trepidation that Natthia knocked on Judge Soronato's door. Stepping in, the men in the office slightly shocked her. They were dressed very formally, and there was the lingering aura of the presence of God surrounding them. The Judge stood and came around the table to hug Natthia. She smiled and commented on how good he looked. He blushed, and she laughed.

"It is a good thing that you have your sword, Josh. The Littl'un has informed us that the base is her castle. Muma Horren has told me that this office is on the foray at its backdoor. She suggests that you protect all those needing protection by locking them in other rooms. None must enter the hall, especially when Tara is outside of this room or her own room."

"Natthia, do you know why we are guests? Can we prepare for her arrival?" asked the Judge.

"No, Josh. I do not know anything more myself except Muma has asked me to bring a bow to Tara."

David stood up and said, "Tara does not know how to handle a bow. I must teach her."

All stared at David. He blushed.

Natthia said, "Give him a sword, Josh. I will inform Muma and Tara."

"I cannot dance. Natthia, what is going on? I did not mean..."

"Calm down, David. Tara will not let you dance."

"Why won't she?" David asked indignantly. Then he did not know where to look. Everyone laughed. David smiled sheepishly.

"Relax, David. Both of you know you cannot dance. However, David, take some advice. Make sure Tara knows you want to dance with her." Natthia patted David's back and headed to the door.

David asked, "What do you mean, Natthia?" However, Natthia had left, and the door shut before him.

The Judge chuckled and said, "I guess I had better get you a sword, David. Just remember, son, you have no authorization to dance and no license. Consider it an examination while you teach her to handle a bow. Err not."

David sat down, looking confused.

The Judge addressed the others, "Young judges, take care of David. Keep him here. This door is not to open for anyone other than me. I must inspect the base. I should not be long and will bring David a sword."

Having locked only a few doors, Judge Soronato returned a short time later. He made a show of presenting David with a sword and helped him put it on.

Natthia returned to Tara's room and told her the Judge would inform them when all the preparations were made. She held out a bow and quiver to Tara.

Hands shaking, Tara very carefully picked up the bow. She drew an arrow out of the quiver and asked Muma to help her put the quiver on properly. Muma showed her how to adjust the quiver strap to fit comfortably. Then, although obviously nervous, Tara sat on the edge of the bed holding the bow and the arrow carefully on her lap while she watched the door. Natthia and Muma Horren sat on either side of her. Silently, all waited.

When a brisk knock on the door broke the silence, Tara stood and, shaking only slightly, nodded for Natthia to answer it.

The Judge said, "All is ready. Give me five minutes to return to the foyer." Turning to Tara, he said, "Make us all proud of you, young lady. Let the show go on." He clicked his heels, nodded, and pulled the door shut.

Without knocking, Tara opened the door to Judge Soronato's office. When she nodded, Natthia and Muma Horren both put arrows against their bows but aimed at the floor. They stood on either side of Tara. Feeling silly with her bow clutched in one hand and an arrow in the other, Tara addressed the Judge.

"Welcome to my castle, Judge Soronato. I must apologize for the delay. I need to borrow David for a while. He must teach me how to use this bow. Then I will be able to meet with you here. I do not think I will be very long and hope this delay will not waste too much of your time. Please feel at home and do whatever you should be doing if I was not here." Tara's face went red with her embarrassment. Everyone smiled at her. "Um, I would like Mark to guard David against me, just in case I act inappropriately. But please do not act rashly, okay, Mark? I intend to act with due respect and honour. I am not dressed to dance and want everyone to be aware of that fact. Brian, would you please guard me against David while we are outside?"

Both answered that they felt honoured to perform guard duty as requested.

"Muma Horren will observe. Clear action through her before carrying out your duties."

Brian and Mark nodded, rose, and fetched bows and quivers of arrows. Judge Soronato nodded, and all went out into the hall.

David stood beside Tara and, smiling, said, "I see you can hold the weapons of God. Do they no longer terrify you?"

Tara looked at David and faltered. Taking a deep breath, she sighed. Without taking her eyes off David, she instructed, "Brian, protect me."

Immediately, Brian aimed an arrow pulled taught against his bow toward his brother. David nodded. "Tara, may I please show you how to hold the bow?"

Tara nodded.

"I will need to touch you. Do I have your permission to do so?

Again, Tara nodded.

"Brian, I have no intention of acting inappropriately toward

Tara. May I have your permission to teach her how to use a bow of the Muki?

"Yes, David. However, I will hold you accountable if she cries," answered Brian very formally.

Tara stepped beside Mark, "I am frightened, and you know I love David. He is so handsome... I want to... but I really want to act appropriately. I do not want to put him in danger or hurt him. Why is he wearing a sword? Do I have to refuse to let him touch me? I want him to teach me, Mark."

Mark laughed. "Under the circumstances, it is appropriate for David to be wearing a sword, Tara. He is not supposed to be at a castle. If caught here by a castle guard, he risks execution. His sword is his only means of defence. I think my own safety demands that I permit you to allow him to teach you. Otherwise, you cannot do your duty. Therefore, I must permit you to allow him to touch you. If his actions are consistent with him teaching you how to use the bow, and your actions are also consistent with learning to handle a bow correctly, I am honour bound to protect you both."

"Do you trust me, David? Please, if you think I might err, refuse to teach me now."

"I trust you, Tara. Upon my honour, I will endeavour to teach you and only touch you accordingly. I have no intention of acting inappropriately."

"Muma Horren, are you satisfied that neither David nor I will do anything inappropriate? May we proceed with your blessings?"

Smiling, Muma Horren nodded.

Standing behind Tara, David instructed Tara. He showed her how to hold the bow, retrieve an arrow from the quiver on her back, and position the arrow. He helped her gain comfort in drawing the bow and aiming the arrow. "Okay, Tara, I must fetch a target now. We will do a little target practice, and then it will be legitimate to call you a castle guard." He smiled at Tara, and for a moment, their eyes locked. Both Brian and Mark drew arrows and aimed them at their hearts. Yet, when Tara and David faced them, both were smiling.

Blushing, Tara and David stepped apart. Even Muma Horren was smiling while Mark and David left the hall.

They returned with a curtain, stand, and a target. Oddly, as they set it up, Tara got very nervous. She began trembling and felt the terror that had prevented her from touching the bow so long ago. Convinced she would drop the bow, she called out with desperation. "Help me!" Thrusting the bow into Muma Horren's hand, she bolted for her room and threw up. David ran after her, but Brian tackled him at her door. Mark aimed an arrow at the two of them. It became incredibly quiet.

Natthia and Muma Horren asked to enter the room with Tara. Mark nodded. Brian and David stood and cautiously moved to the side, keeping their eyes on Mark. The door closed. With it, the tension in the hall calmed. Brian was upset. The Judge took Brian and David to his room. Mark took guard position at the door.

"Judge, I should be supporting David. This is wrong. It is unnatural. I might have shot my brother. Why did she tell me to protect her?"

"She is wise, Brian. She chose guards who would protect David. David, you are a fortunate man. Never doubt her love for you. You did very well, Brian. I am proud of your action. Although unorthodox, they were effective. We need to support Tara because I believe she is beginning to understand the ramifications of what she is trying to prove. David, how can we ease her pain?"

"Sir, Natthia told me to ensure Tara knew I wanted to dance with her. I do want to and am trying to trust myself to act appropriately. Without any intent of sinning, I would have held Tara if Brian had not stopped me. However, I wanted to fight Brian, Sir. This land is dangerous. I think Tara understood that this kind of thing could happen. I think she chose the guards to protect Brian, Mark, and me. She is acting like a Cultural Judge, Sir. She is under God's guidance. I am not sure that she needs our help. God will not let us err against her, nor will God allow her to err against us. The blanket of Koe Sai Serena protects us all." David began to shine. "Allow me to hug her, please. It will reassure her, and her aim will prove true."

The Judge opened his door and, with the young judges, headed to Tara's room.

He knocked, and Natthia answered. "Tara needs David to hug her, bring the bow. I will hold it for her."

Pale, nervous, and unhappy, Tara came out of the room. She watched Muma Horren give her bow and arrow to the Judge. Nervously, she asked Muma Horren permission to hug David. Muma Horren said, "I trust you, Tara. Let him hold you." Tara looked at Brian and Mark. Both immediately turned their backs, faced the wall, and set their arrows symbolically on the floor. Judge Soronato drew his sword, pointing it toward Brian and Mark. He shone. David put his arms around Tara. She shivered, then sobbed on his shoulder without looking at his face.

"David, you must say goodbye. You must not dance. I... cannot protect you. I must go home, but God won't let me go yet."

"God promised we would dance, my Tara. I will wait. I am yours. I love you. Be mine, Tara."

"No, David. We must defy God. Never dance with me." She sobbed and held him very tightly.

David played with her hair, trying to calm her and the beating of his own heart. He loosened her grip, tilted her head back, kissed her forehead, and whispered, "I will never defy God. You will not either, Tara. Let us get on with your lessons. Come for target practice."

Tara whispered, "I will not be able to protect you, David. I know the bow is holy. It belongs to God. God is going to take you away. I am afraid I will shoot you, David. What will happen if God points the arrow at you? How will I stop God?"

"You will do your duty when the time comes, Tara. It is not today. Become a puppet. Give yourself to God. Be obedient. Come take the bow from the Judge. All is safe. I will give God no cause to aim an arrow at me."

Still, Tara clung to him. Eventually, her sobbing ceased, and her breathing calmed. Soon, David felt the steel determination of one given to God in terror. Letting her go, he felt terrible. He wanted to dance with her. Protect her forever. Yet, he, too, understood that

God had a plan for them both. Calmly, with conviction, David stated, "Tara, we will find a way to face the future." With that, he took her hand and the bow from the Judge.

None watched as he resumed teaching Tara to wield the weapons of God. Tara, with obvious trepidation, followed all instructions. Every arrow found its mark on the target.

"I cannot miss, can I, David? God is aiming, not me. Is that what I was to learn? I think I knew that. I do not like God today."

Tara's sincerity made David want to cry. Without understanding why serving God terrified Tara, he said, "Yes, Tara. We can proceed now. You are wearing the blanket of Koe Sai Serena. You will do only God's work. The bow is holy. Love God. Trust God has a plan, and it will bring about the Kingdom of God."

Natthia insisted Tara rest in her room for half an hour. Telling Tara to think about the arrows while resting, she sent everyone away and stood guard at her door.

While lying on my bed, I did think about the arrows. The arrows were not simply things used to frighten people into obedience. They were deadly weapons, handled with exacting precision and in total confidence of their righteousness in both destroying those who stood against the will of God and supporting the sacrifice of those defending the will of God. Holding and shooting arrows was not a game. It was holy. I did not believe that I had the power to kill, but David had clearly taught me how to aim and shoot an arrow.

When David had insisted that I learn and handed back the bow, I shook in fear. It did not feel like an inanimate object. The bow implied righteousness. It spoke with power. Clearly apparent, it belonged to God. Words, thoughts, and ideas came alive within me. I had no thought of revenge or control. They were holy thoughts, which reached deep into my soul to remind me that I was a servant of the Lord. I knew in those moments that whatever I did with the bow, I would be powerless to control. The bow and the arrows belonged to God. With them, as though a programmed robot, whoever wields them would carry out the will of God.

The bow and even the arrows suddenly reminded me of my own responsibilities. Living carried a great price. God had expectations. Existing was a gift but not freely given. I owed God, my whole soul. I belonged to Him. I had duties that demanded fulfilment.

Thankful to have had the opportunity to rest and clear my thoughts, I asked Natthia to escort me to the Judge's office again.

All rose when Tara entered. She stood at the door and worshipped. Although there was no evidence of the blanket of Koe Sai Serena, all knew God was with the Little Smiler. She lowered her arms. "I am going to sit beside David. He is going to hold my hand. I need his security. David connects me to God. His touch will prevent me from erring."

Tara sat. David sat beside her and held her hand. She looked at him and smiled. Mark sat beside David, Brian beside Tara. Natthia sat next to Mark and Muma Horren comfortably beside Brian. The Judge sat between the two women.

Tara asked them to hold hands and said a prayer for God to guide the conversation. Then she turned into a powerful Cultural Judge.

"Judge Soronato, I must prove Earth is blessed. What proof will you accept?"

The Judge watched Tara for what felt a very long time. She felt as though he was seeing through her. He penetrated her soul.

She stared right back and was suddenly very pleased not to be in his shoes. Finally, he answered, "What proof are you offering?"

Tara said with no hint of remorse without batting an eye, "I have nothing to offer. All I have is my faith that it is true." Frowning, the Judge said, "Who are you?"

"I am insane, Sir. I am nothing but one of the living dead."

"Are you an Earthling?"

"I was once an Earthling, but I am not one now."

"Have you been blessed?"

Tara looked at David and squeezed his hand. He blushed as she searched his eyes, then smiled and nodded. "Yes, Sir, I have been blessed beyond doubt. All today has been a blessing."

"I will accept nothing of today, Tara. Today, you are of the Muki. Your blessings today are our blessings. They have nothing to do with Earth."

Tears ran down her cheeks, and Tara struggled for a correct response. "Love is universal, Sir. You hold no monopoly. Our creation, too, is universal. There is a place for Earth in the Kingdom of God. We only have yet to find it. There is but one kingdom. Are we not all brothers? Do blessings not belong to all of creation?"

"Well answered, Tara. However, I remain steadfast. Today's blessings are not sufficient proof."

"David is the greatest blessing that God has ever bestowed upon me. I fear he is the proof you demand."

"How can that be so, Tara?"

"He recognizes the blessings of Earth in his own faith, Sir. He told you Earth is blessed. Believe him."

"You told David, God sent him to you. Why?"

"Yes, Judge Soronato, God did send David to me. However, when God grants gifts, He does not generally tell me why He has done so. God told me to learn from him. David is my friend."

"What has David taught you, Tara?

"David has filled me with love. He has blessed me. He is my future."

"That does not answer the question. Try again."

"David is the answer, Sir. He is the proof you are seeking. Listen to David's first lesson. Understand what he has told me."

33

DAVID'S FIRST LESSON

I REMEMBER THAT SEPTEMBER DAY AS though it was yesterday. I had just met David. I brought him a glass of water, and we played in the mud, in the cold, and fell in love. It was the right kind of love. Because God ordained it, it was holy. With David's help, Judge Soronato, I will give you David's first lesson and tell you what I have learned from it.

"David took me among the trees, stepped off the path, and said: "In the very beginning, there was nothing. Not even a void. There was no space. There existed no definition upon which to build. There was nothing upon which to experience. One would be correct in saying there was no existence. There was no God. 'What was there was a yearning. Aware, it was raw. Demanding expression, the yearning gained power. It knew it required experience. However, it had no way of defining the meaning of experience. Therefore, it yearned. The yearning gained wisdom. Focusing, it perceived and defined itself and finally recognized it was empty and nothing."

"That was the very first concept to be born. All concepts come from that realization. As nothing, the yearning created itself as consciousness. Out from the depth of the depression, the yearning then concluded with nothing, all was possible. Like understanding the concept of zero, the yearning understood the total of itself was zero, but unlimited possibility could exist as parts of a whole.

"The yearning filled with elation. Free to create, it could express.

Through the idea of expression came the discovery that it could create an experience. Furthermore, that was the beginning.'

"David had said, 'Close your eyes, Littl'un. Imagine pure power. Describe it as vibration. Let it flow and perceive it creating a wake. That wake became void. Like a stage, the vibration achieved a backdrop upon which to experience all that was possible. It was a miracle.

"What the yearning created was the Voice of Life. Without sound, the Voice of Life screamed. Without shape, it wreathed. With determination, anger, and frustration, figuratively speaking, the Voice took a breath. That breath broke the void, and the breath of life drew back a reflection of the wake of the void and achieved balance. Forever, the wave of void will expand, and as it does so, it reflects life. The yearning experienced delight. That, too, was a miracle."

"I remember David grabbing my hands and smiling as he rubbed mud all over them. He laughed. I believe that moment, Judge Soronato, was when I first understood that David owned the future. I recognized him as God. In shock, I felt boundless. I felt terror. David must have understood, for he lifted my chin with muddy fingers and said, 'Littl'un, have you ever watched a single drop of rain fall into a puddle?'

"I may be insane, Sir. I have no words to do justice to what I experienced at that moment. I will swear that I did see a drop of rain. It fell into what must have been an imaginary puddle in the space between David's and my eyes. Perhaps the puddle was in his eyes. Is that a possibility? It was dark in the trees, Judge Soronato. Then, I really struggled to comprehend what I was experiencing. Perhaps, it was simply David sharing a vision with me. However, I concluded David was the universe.

"I realized I had been holding my breath, so I exhaled, and as I did so, the puddle reacted to the drop of rain. I felt ecstasy. This feeling was beyond anything I had ever felt before, even during the numerous times I had known I was in the presence of God. It was not like immersion in creation when I worshipped with David on Snowshoe plateau or when we cleansed. It was... indescribable. Raw, it was untamed emotion. A wave on the puddle radiated out from the point of impact, reached the edges of the puddle, and, as I inhaled, reflected. Overcome with a sense that I had just been born, I was fully alive. Truly connected to absolutely everything, I felt as though I, too, was God."

I could feel the vanity and arrogance of those words and sought comfort and forgiveness by hiding against David's chest. I waited for the beating of David's heart to calm me. There was not a sound in the room. The silence, too, was comforting.

I sighed and looked at Judge Soronato. So many visions and emotions were coursing through my thoughts that I could not grab coherence in my own soul, let alone express them to another. David's lesson had occurred in less than an hour. Yet, its impact was and remains eternal. I said, "Sorry, Sir, I cannot go on. David, help me find words to explain to the Judge what happened next."

David blushed and coughed. "I held her, Sir. I told her she had experienced the emotion of the yearning as it comprehended love and thus generated the Lines of Infinity."

The sound of David's voice gave me courage. Like magic, the turbulence in me settled. No longer overwhelmed, my words were bursting to be voiced. Cutting David off, I continued, "It sounds completely ridiculous, Judge Soronato, but that wasn't all he said. He said I felt the very first shape ever to exist." I closed my eyes to try to recapture that moment. It gave me confidence. I took three deep breaths, and conscious that I was breathing with David, I took comfort in growing security that David and I were one, not two. Looking at David, I smiled. "Thank you, David. I can continue now." I sat up straight. Relaxing my grip on David's hand, I realized I really was calm and confident. I smiled. "David has tried to teach me to understand my own Line of Infinity ever since, but he has been wrong. That was not what he needed to teach me. In that very first lesson, Judge Soronato, David taught me the most important truth. All Lines of Infinity join. There is only one line. There is only one shape, and it is called love."

No one spoke. I felt something hazy and golden descend upon us as God joined us at the table. As I heard the dum dum dump of the beating of the drums of the Muki, I knew I was safe in my mother's womb and felt like singing. Yet, I also knew that none was outside my door, creating the sounds my ears perceived. I stood up, walked to the door, opened it, and proved it was so. I blushed when everyone else smiled at me as I sat back down. Natthia made an urn of cider. We drank the whole urn before anyone spoke.

As Muma Horren cleared the mugs and urn away, all eyes turned back to me. I sighed and closed my eyes to focus upon an event that led me here. "David began making things in the mud, Sir. I struggled to focus on his actions and words unsuccessfully..." I paused, unsure of how to continue. I looked around the table. All were looking at me with encouragement. Understanding the ramifications of this meeting had far-reaching consequences, I was afraid to ask David to continue for me.

"Please accept my apologies because I know I don't have the rest of David's lesson clearly imprinted in my soul. I was terribly overwhelmed. Continually visions flashed before my eyes, and I was not sure where I was. It was as though David's words and actions were in themselves events. I comprehended timelessness. His words lived, moved, and had substance.

"Reflecting on that lesson, I have often considered the possibility that I was high on something or absolutely at the height of insanity. However, I also know that the only explanation that has stood the test of time and reason was that I was in the presence of God and experiencing life at its fullest. Immersed in a holy experience, I existed without constraint. I will try my best to continue." Again, I sighed.

"Filled with emotion, the yearning remained incomplete while struggling to find meaning. It took the first shape and began to mould it. Thereby, the yearning perceived form. There was an action best described as a combination of explosion and implosion, as the yearning demanded the ability to have substance and fractured. It broke into particles of light, and God was born.

"What was the event? Was it time? Was it a change? It is

indefinable. The Muki call it, Deplukador. Personally, I think it was the first combination of judgement and movement. It was the first solid. Concrete, it bound us in space and time. I like to think of it as the body of God, perhaps more accurately, the image of God. Bound vibration or radiation, solids are the reflection or opposite of light. Infinite but almost too small to comprehend, it is existence, discrimination, and alliance. It gave God the ability to distribute power, learn, and develop. Separating one shape from another, creation conceived.

"The rest is in our Book of Genesis. God's intent is to experience. God's Kingdom arises when all the parts in the heavens recognize they are part of a whole. All must be in harmony and balance. Totaling all that is possible, the Kingdom of God will rejoice in perfection and collapse into a perfect whole... once again, the sum of all possibility: nothing.

"Sir, I am blessed. We are all blessed. Everything that is and all things to come is blessed. David is an example to us all. He is our blessing. His gift to you and Earth is all the proof needed. Although some like to believe God is only those parts that are good, it is not so. David understands and has taught me that even evil is a blessed component of God. It achieves balance. Perfection is the harmonious helix of all opposites held in balance. It is true, Judge Soronato, that every particle of light is precious. Love and hate are precisely the same emotion and are the axes of creation. Like polarity, there can be no existence without both poles. Not only mandatory, both, when balanced, are good. Blessings come from both good and evil. Both are God's weapons.

"Judge Soronato, I remember three specific things David created in the mud. They were a turtle, a bird, and a leaf. The visions I experienced as he moulded and told stories about each model that he held out to me were incredible and too real to be daydreams.

"I watched his hands as he rolled a blob of mud in his palm. It was round when he began each story and demonstration. Picturing it as the formless first shape, I laughed as David flattened it into a drop cookie shape. David brushed the edges like making a pie. He stamped the top with fingerprints. He drew out a head, four legs, and a tail with his thumb and forefinger. I swear a whole universe appeared in David's hand when he held the turtle before me. It stretched its head, looked around, and began burrowing into David's hand with its forelegs. It pushed with its hindlegs. As the turtle's head touched his palm, it withdrew. If you have ever watched a turtle prepare to hibernate, you know how it interacted with David's movement and voice. It paused, hid, and investigated. Its actions emulated curiosity, fear, trepidation, determination, and satisfaction as it slowly submerged below a pile of compost on David's palm.

"The turtle was gone, Judge Soronato. However, I did not feel that David had squashed it. It had merely crawled into the security and warmth within the universe. The universe was within the body of David. The turtle was cold. It was fall. Waiting for spring, the turtle had sought the warmth of his blood coursing through the dirt. "Gently, David began to work the compost, again just a blob of dirt on his palm. Yet, it was somehow no longer the same blob. It had changed. Feeling that the dirt somehow contained the turtle, I thought it could not quite reproduce the first shape. Having form, it was an ovoid egg. Furthermore, I sensed it was warm, not cold, when I tried to touch it. With delight, visions of it being alive fascinated me, and I laughed with glee and pleasure.

"Watching David's hands, I saw an egg crack and open. Lightly drying the new chick with the back of his fingers, David continued to mould it. The chick seemed to fluff up, and ever so gradually, the fluff became feathers. The bird sat on David's palm, preening, and testing its wings as David spoke. He held it out to the sky. I watched. With a sudden flick of his wrist, David threw the bird into the air. It circled and disappeared in the darkness.

"I felt a horrendous sadness. Grief-stricken, tears ran down my cheeks as my whole soul felt broken and lost. I wanted the bird to come back.

"I do not know how David did it, but the next moment I realized the blob of dirt was in the clenched fist of his other hand. I felt security but also comprehended that the bird was trying to get back into the palm from which it had flown. Emotionally, I calmed. A wave of security held me. Safe, I had direction. I knew where I was going and where I wanted to be. Elated, I comprehended the vastness of eternity.

"In anticipation, I focused on David's hands. Curiosity held me. I could not see what he was making. As I guessed, David laughed.

"He said, 'Everything is possible, Littl'un.'

"I believed him. However, I found patience in indisputable confidence that whatever he made, it would somehow complete me. When David lifted his hand away from the other, on his palm was a common broadleaf. He held it out to me. I had very strange visions. I thought I reached out, lifted, and ate it. I closed my eyes to savour it. However, when I felt it sliding down my throat and opened my eyes, it remained on David's palm. I felt nourished, powerful, and without limit. With excitement, I concentrated on the leaf. It appeared to morph into a seed. Roots grew out of it. The root, in slow motion, crawled along the veins in David's hands. I imagined them spreading out inside David and migrating to his heart. A stem also grew, then buds appeared and unfolded. They bloomed as green leaves appeared. It became a huge tree. Encompassing David, it, too, was the universe.

"Feeling a friendly breeze that seemed to whisper to my soul, 'You are alive.' David spread his hands wide apart. Raising horizontal palms upward and outward, and as he sang to the sky, there were two leaves, one on each hand. One showed the underside of a leaf and the other the top. David brought his hands together in front of his face and gently blew on the leaves. A single leaf floated whimsically to the ground.

"My whole body tingled. I wanted to dance, sing, and honestly thought I had become a drop of rain glistening in the moonlight. In desperation, I wanted to grab David's leaf and hold it forever. Understanding filtered through my consciousness as I emphatically summarized that I had to take David's hand to hold it.

"After a moment of suspended time, David broke the trance I was in when he asked me to tell him what the turtle, bird, and leaf represented. I had them mixed up then. However, now I realize what they were at that moment. The turtle is the Voice of Life, hiding from itself. The bird is the Line of Infinity flying through eternity, searching for its egg. Lastly, the leaf is a tree, the only constancy in the universe, change.

"In another moment, they may represent another of five other possibilities. For what they represent is unanchored and really is not what is important. The important thing to comprehend is that they add up to light. Together, they are God.

"The last thing David made of dirt was a figure of a man. The end of David's lesson was to teach that man is God's tool. We are the instruments required to enable God to guide creation. Creation, including humanity, is the physical body of God. We have a duty. Our responsibility is to be tools of God. We must walk in the light on the path of righteousness and mould the universe into something pleasing to God. Akin to chromosomes, God grants humanity the power to carry out the will of God.

"To have, we must give—the more given, the more received. Natthia did not lie to me. To be a slave is to be free! We find what we seek. Therefore, we all must seek unity: love, acceptance, and respect.

"Our duty is to let no cancer grow. Our responsibility is to recognize our blessings. Our souls recognize the blessings of Earth. A cancer holds no blessing and is without direction. It does not hurt the soul, or the spirit, to destroy a cancer. However, the destruction of a blessing unleashes agony... pain beyond comprehension. It amounts to extinguishing light, ending existence.

"I remember, Judge Soronato, how every particle of my being wanted to mate with David. I was filled with a weird combination of emotions, which cumulated in shock and terror. I had to run. Commanded to run, I looked at David with realization first that I was not God and never could be. Second, I understood that David was not either. We were parts of a whole. Oddly, I was equally pleased and disappointed.

"The Muki will always be angels to me, and David, my guardian angel. Without him, I am nothing. With him, I can create the future.

"The conclusion, Judge Soronato, is David knows Earth is blessed. Therein lays the redemption of Earth."

34

TOUCHING SLAVERY

I THINK I EMBARRASSED DAVID. HAUNTED with guilt, I had a feeling I had put David in a very awkward and dangerous position. It was no consolation that I had done so under instruction from God. I got the impression that they had not known David, and I had shared this spiritual experience. I believe they thought he had given me a superficial overview of the foundation of the Muki. For most of that year, David had endeavoured to teach me about the ground beneath my feet, the sky above my head, and the light of God.

Judge Soronato did not tell me whether he accepted my proof as adequate to redeem Earth. I was not sure myself whether I had saved or condemned Earth. The Judge regarded me for several silent minutes. He said, "Proceed." Then he stood up, waved his hand, and uttered, "Dismissed." Moreover, he walked out the door, taking Brian, Mark, and David with him.

Natthia and Muma Horren, completely without expression, rose. Clearly, under guard, they brought me back to my room. Without comment, they helped me change and escorted me to the plane. David, Doug, and Brian joined me there. We flew back to the river, and David walked me home. If David had not kissed my forehead and held my hand, I think I might have screamed. Yet, I did not have any words left myself. Therefore, I was neither angry nor thought their silence strange. It only felt strange after they had left, and I was comfortably at home, in bed, and under my covers.

David's first lesson is my treasure, and I felt everything I did with

David to be connected to it. My comprehension of faith grew as I related all that I did subsequently back to those precious forty minutes. No matter what anyone else said, I had faith. I knew my God. I had a living relationship with my maker. My God was boundless and did not fit in a book. My faith was my weapon against the wrongs of the real world and was the foundation of my Island Kingdom. God charged the Grey Sentry with protecting my Island Kingdom. David, God ordained to let my Kingdom grow. That is what I hoped, anyway.

When I had prepared to meet with the Muki, I had trusted God would guide me and fate would provide all the words I needed to make them understand the will of God for us all. I had not planned to speak of David's first lesson. It was not something that I liked to share. Indeed, I have never shared it in its entirety. It is too intimate. It is holy.

Personally, I felt it was also taboo. I was afraid others would twist it into something sacrilegious, dangerous, and even shameful. Turning to the Bible after that experience with David, I had tried to understand how it fit in my understanding of my own faith. I determined it augmented the Bible without contradicting it. However, I had met with a friend for Bible study shortly after I met David, and my friend got very upset with the small amount of the lesson I revealed. She said, "I was the antichrist and would rot in hell for my blasphemy." Her parents forbade the continuation of our friendship.

The evening I lost my friend, I dreamt I was in a classroom with God. Speaking about the Bible, particularly the Book of Genesis, God reviewed my experience with David. God set my heart at rest in a very comforting and peacefully reassuring fashion. Suggesting belief and incorporation of the living God upon the living word, God told me to shut the book and take His hand. God promised guidance and demanded caution. Subsequently, I refused to speak about anything even remotely connected to David and my experiences with the Muki. I understood my friend and her parent's response was a warning from God. Furthermore, God approved my vow of silence.

I have accumulated a whole lifetime of odd religious experiences. Although they, too, were unacceptable to those proclaiming faith on

Sunday mornings, I had never found God in a church. That truth vindicated me. I found God almost everywhere else. Most definitely, I was not the antichrist. I was nothing. Defiant, arrogant, and stubborn as a mule, I had a relationship with God, period. Sometimes, I prided myself that I could be a slave of God's... at least on occasion.

Whenever I felt overwhelmed or confused by the differences in what the real world was telling me, I would remember an experience God had given me. It gave me confidence and security. The world was not on my shoulders. My role was small and limited. I was only a messenger. I was synonymous with my island kingdom. As David recommended, I would go with it. In the end, although unrecognizable, it might encompass the world.

Lying on my bed at home, I knew I was at peace. I was not upset. I simply had no words. Looking at the stars behind the waving leaves of the tree outside my window, I began wondering whether I had served my duty.

When I was quite young, God had spoken to me while I was rocking my big rubber doll out in the front yard. God described a small wooden box to me. Then God instructed me to make one. With delight and confidence, I had jumped to do precisely as requested. I was afraid I would forget the instructions if I even paused long enough to put my doll and its paraphernalia back in my room. Overcome with urgency, I understood there would not be time later. I had to put my life in order.

Generally, I followed a ritual in how I treated my things. Hastily, I bundled them together as though just toys and cast them into my closet. Then, I ran down the stairs and went into the basement, where my father kept an assortment of wood under the workbench. I looked at the wood, trying to locate appropriate pieces to construct the box for God. I did not know or even wonder why God wanted the box.

I simply wanted to please God with obedience. As I reached for a piece of wood, I felt God's presence.

Suddenly overcome with shock and shame, a thought entered my consciousness and demanded action; Jesus was a carpenter. He would never leave his workshop in such disarray as the room before me. To build the box for God, I had to put the shop in order. In the presence of God, I pulled pieces of wood from under the workbench, carefully sorting them into various piles.

When the wood was cleared out from under the bench, I heard God call from somewhere to my right and, turning toward his voice, stepped forward and tripped. A nail punctured through the palm of my right hand. The nail stuck all the way through my hand, with only a peak of stretched skin remaining on the top of my hand to prevent me from seeing the end of the nail.

I looked at it bathed in the golden light of God. I touched it. Lost in thought, I rubbed the skin that had stretched unbroken over the end of the nail under it. Marvelling at the amount of stretch in my skin, I wondered why God had not sent the nail all the way through by breaking this last layer of skin. Then I thought of Jesus. God had allowed man to nail him to a cross. I felt comforted because I had always thought of the nails in Christ's hands as the reverse of what I saw in my own hand. I whispered, "You want me to be Jesus?" God laughed. I love God's laughter. There is no mock in God's laugh. It is thrilling to hear. Without shame, I blushed in embarrassment at my own arrogance. I felt warm and comfortable as God said, "I want all my children to emulate Christ. However, child, one son of God is enough."

I asked, "What do you want of me?"

"Be my messenger."

Although I heard no more words, God did not leave me. I felt God shared my thoughts while helping me find comfort in what messenger meant. I concluded I was to be like an angel who foretold of the coming of someone like Moses. I was to deliver a prophecy. Content the job was small, insignificant, and would occur in the background, I accepted God's request. I imagined I was the box God had asked me to make. Like an envelope, God would fill me with something good, write directions upon me, and eventually mail me at the correct time. God was putting me together.

Suddenly, I was extremely pleased the nail did not break the skin on the top of my hand. Stamped, I had a destination. Like my skin rolling over the top of the nail, it left play in the formula. I felt freedom retained to decline at the many stages waiting in the future. There was no urgency. It would take a long time to build a box for God. I could relax and be content that all I needed would be in place when required.

When I pulled my hand off the nail, I was surprised that it had left a hole. My hand began to swell a moment later, and a fountain of blood issued forth with every beat of my heart. Thumb pressed firmly over the wound; I went for medical help. Although it upset my mother, who quickly wrapped my hand in a towel and instructed me to keep pressure on the puncture while she rushed me to the doctor, it did not bother me. It did not even start to hurt for hours. My mind was on the incredible future God had offered. It is very hard to explain, but bleeding made me think of extending life, not diminishing it. Does that make sense, or am I just crazy?

Sighing, I went to sleep, hoping that my speech had been the message I was to deliver. David may not be mine to keep. However, I relished the thought that he might belong to Earth. If that were the case, we would be together for a lifetime. Not quite as comforting, nevertheless satisfying was the idea that my message had been for the Muki. They needed to find the answer to their questions within the context of their own faith. David was one of them. They believed in David. They only need to make a leap in faith. They needed to recognize and believe in his faith.

The only indication of the consequence of my speech was an increased presence of the Muki around David and I. Brian, Doug, Mark, and Loren accompanied us as soon as we were a few blocks away from my house. I often felt the presence of the Muki around me regardless of where I was. Occasionally, I would even see them. However, it made me feel safe, not tracked. I felt accepted as Muki, at least conditionally. Neither David nor I mentioned their visit to my castle. We discussed neither why I remained under guard nor why he was no longer alone with me. Instinctively, we knew why. They were ensuring our safety but also preventing us from dancing. Continuing to marvel at the perceptiveness of the Muki, I loved how they were able to give David and me privacy without needing to sneak away or deceive them. They were truly good friends. They were there to join in the fun but were inconspicuously absent during lessons. I honestly believe they never eavesdropped on our conversations. When we arrived at a destination, they would go one way while David and I went another. It would happen unconsciously.

David and I did discuss dancing, though. I would go to university. When I was nineteen, I would introduce David to my family. We would marry and dance... maybe forever.

Clinging to the belief that God was in control and had promised time would allow David and I to dance, I tried to understand the bows and arrows of the Muki in a new way. That they were powerful was not the issue. It no longer seemed odd that they were also a comfort. However, I had trouble with them not making a lot of sense.

Being a slave when carrying God's weapons appeared natural. I could not fathom God's wisdom with a bow in my hand. Life of my own was infinitesimal and sadly insignificant. My hopes and dreams had absolutely no consequence. How could that be true? When the bow was not in my hand, the enormity of the power, the bow held overwhelmed me. At all times, I fully understood that an arrow shot with it was deadly. Therefore, it would kill whatever it struck and was not something I wanted to hold.

In those moments, I had been an inanimate robot, innocent of the consequences of all resultant action. Innocence is soothing. Like cupid's arrows, God's arrows deliver love. Understanding that, I found the images generated delightful. My wanting the ideal of cupid's love arrow to be synonymous with my arrow hitting David's heart was thrilling and comforting. Belonging to each other, we would become a single entity and boundless. The thought was romantic. The arrow would fill us both with love.

Yet, I was not stupid. I also sensed David would be dead, and I would not see him. I would only remember him. The nagging reminder that God had told me David was not mine to keep tore my soul apart. As though I was a combination of two separate things, a soul and a spirit, I felt broken as my soul cried in agony while my spirit soared with purpose and direction.

My spirit was thrilled with the prospects opened before me. It was wonderful to serve God. My service would result in miracles descending upon all of Earth, not just me. We would grow. We would serve the Lord graciously and willingly. Our righteousness would expand, and so would our horizons. As in a song David translated for me, becoming unlimited, we would flow through time on a film of molybdenite. With the strength of scheelite bound with living clay within a shield of magnetite, we would slip, slide, and skip across the universe touching heaven under the command of God. Boundless weapons of God, we will uphold the righteousness of God rather than of man. The idea sparkled with light. It beckoned the future. Wanting to be God's slave, I wanted a part in the scheme of God. Blindly, I would follow the will of God.

The arrows I shot at target practice were absolute in their meaning. My hands would hold the bow that unleashed arrows into David's heart. Even if innocent, I would be responsible for David's death. Indeed, the three arrows I shot at target practice had already done the deed. I fully understood it was a fact they would do so when I collapsed in my room at the base before picking up a bow.

Accepting the future and me as Muki, Muma Horren understood, and the words she hummed brought me peace. Forgiving me, she helped me comprehend David's lessons about God knowing no time. I prayed David and I had a lifetime together. We were both slaves. Enabling the Kingdom of God to grow, sometime in the future, our love and sacrifice would redeem Earth.

David and I walked whenever we were together, and often speech was unnecessary. It did not matter where we were, but we both liked to be outdoors, in lonely, awe-inspiring places. Indeed, our hearts felt akin and knew our future was lonely, frightening, and absolute.

One day sitting on a mountainside, looking out into a valley below us, David and I talked about the arrows. The Muki believed when God shot arrows; there were always three of them. The first arrow was to stop, the second to end, and the third to forgive. David asked me to explain what that meant.

I was aware stopping was more complex than getting one's attention. Yet, it was similar. I thought it was like insisting one was on the wrong path. It was a warning to change direction or speed. Saying think again, something is not quite right. The obvious is saying your existence is on the line or knowing a police officer has shouted, freeze. Time, motion, and even creation are suspended. I imagine this is when God starts playing with the stage, remoulding, shaping, and sculpting to bring all into a new alignment.

The question I could not answer was whether the result was metamorphic or final. Does stopping kill? Does it merely allow for the tweaking of circumstances in suspended animation? More puzzling was who did the tweaking? David said it mattered who shot the arrow from the bow. Why did it matter? Apparently, the answer connected the action to the consequence. We are independent. Each being has a contribution to the coming of the Kingdom of God. Equally true, we all have a unique vision of the Kingdom of God. Therefore, the consequence connects to the one holding the bow. Possibilities are as vast as are the parts of the whole. The objective is to experience. When the arrow flies, it insists on the consequence demanded by the intent of the one holding the bow. It is dependent on an individual's dreams for the righteousness of the situation. It is about the birth and death of thought and ideals. Hold that thought.

The second arrow is the conclusion. It is the realization of the consequence. It seals fate. Playing out the destiny of both the one holding the arrow and the one whose heart it pierced confirms the result. It is like making out all the reports and filing them appropriately. Concrete and solid, it is a raw fact.

Finally, my understanding of the third arrow is forgiveness. Resurrecting peace, the third arrow allows forward movement. It renders justice served. In summary, the three arrows are initiation, comprehension, and acceptance. They boil down to living with thoughts, actions, and reactions.

David said the arrows were like synapses of creation. The first arrow both opened and closed doors of possibility, thus confining the future. The second arrow presented passage through doors confirming present and locking past. Last, the third arrow releases the future into a new realm of possibility. The bow permitted God to guide the arrows. It was the interface between God and Her tools. In short, the bow and arrows of the Muki enforce walking upon the path of God. It was about making righteous choices.

Sometimes, I struggled to fathom the connectedness of all ideas. When I was with David, I could clearly say and understand things and ideas that they would hold no doubt and no error. Conversations felt absolute. When I was alone, my mind began playing with the lessons. Strange what-ifs and could it be speculations arose so that I would ultimately lose the lesson. It was frustrating. David and I laughed at my inability to comprehend the constant movement of the lessons he taught. There was no stone in them. They were dynamic.

David always emphasized life was dynamic and not static. Lessons grow. He laughed when I said they did not stay still long enough to capture. Then he discussed Deplukador, and it usually went right over my head. Often, I threw up my arms and said, "You said I had a lot of Deplukador in me. My conclusion is Deplukador is full of confusion and chaos."

David sighed and emphatically answered, "Creation is not chaotic, Littl'un. It is not confusing. It is extremely well-ordered. If you recognize and follow the will of God, the Kingdom of God approaches." Then, after doing something to make me laugh, David either assumed a different tact to help me understand or changed the topic completely.

"I do not like change, David. It confuses me," became a commonly uttered phrase.

Just as common was David's answer, "If too much stays the same, Littl'un, it gets stagnant and stale. It becomes a cancer preventing growth and development. It signals a lack of options in the pursuit of possibilities. It becomes redundant. Caught in a rut, it self-destructs."

David and I talked about civilization, technology, and philosophy as though they were intricately connected. It always came down to opening and closing the right doors in the movement of energy. We, and all the things we did, were synapses in creation. Within every cell was a whole universe, whether speaking about something simple and minuscule or the known universe itself. Everything was part of something else. Everything mattered tremendously.

It was too complex for me to grasp. At least I could make David laugh when he spoke of things that were way over my head. The Muki had a handle on how the universe worked!

35

AN ERROR IN TIME

I COULD NOT FIGURE IT OUT. For example, on the day I pretended the base was my castle, I could worship with instantaneous results. I had God's ear, so to speak. David tried to teach me to recapture the state of mind to open a door at will to God, regardless of my location. I could not do it. I lost consciousness, my balance, or my concentration. Often, I found myself daydreaming or bursting out laughing, singing, or crying about our surroundings or some thought that popped up out of nowhere. Frequently, David got cross with me for being content to just waste time listening to his heartbeat. I teased him that it took him long to realize I was doing so because he liked me listening.

I tried to cooperate and be an attentive student, but I seemed to be failing more and more frequently. Just being close to David filled me with such joy and a sense of freedom that I was not any good at focusing on his lessons. I treasured my time with him and thought I had opened the perfect door and wanted to stand in the doorway - unmoving, just savouring the blessing God had given me in David. Maybe subconsciously, I was afraid of learning how to worship because Natthia had said doing so would complete my lessons.

Late February is an unpredictable time of year. The weather can do odd things. I do not know what people call it in the Caribou. Called a Chinook on the east side of the Rockies and the Pineapple Express on the Pacific coast, it is an unseasonable wave of warm moist air that makes one think it is spring. Regardless of its name, it was delicious weather. It was well above twenty degrees Celsius. The wind was light and breezy. While I was supposed to be clearing my mind to hear God, I kept thinking God was pulling strings to delight me! Furthermore, I was delighted. The world was perfect. Although I was trying hard to focus on learning to worship, too many thoughts insisted on filling my mind.

It was an incredible day. David had taken me to a big lake in the middle of nowhere. There was no snow left on the ground along the shoreline. The ground was brown and muddy. Under the trees, there were piles of leaves, which reminded me of autumn. Disappointingly, they did not crinkle and snap when I walked on them. They were too wet. The ice on the lake had melted sufficiently to leave a four or five-foot gab between its edge and the shore. Ice was breaking up. As the wind blew, the ice would sing a melody of pops, crinkles, tinkles, and chimes as it broke into incredibly perfect hexagonal crystal cylinders. Like a huge floating plate, the wind pushed the ice onto the shore. The wind teased me. The sun shone brightly in a clear blue sky. Our location was awesome.

It was approximately a month after I had been to the base to meet with Judge Soronato, Natthia, and Muma Horren. Trying to teach me to worship, David was sitting on a rock up the bank from the shoreline, watching me. About twenty feet away from him, I stood on an outcrop stretching out into the lake. Imagining I was on an island in heaven, I tried very hard to let my mind go blank to hear the voice of God.

Occasionally, I glanced at David. He sat so still. Even when I was not looking at him, I would see him in my mind's eye. Unfortunately, David would sense my gaze, sigh, and say, "Concentrate on nothing, Tara. Banish your thoughts. Open your mind to only God. Sometimes, counting helps. Try that."

"Stand behind me, David," I begged to no avail. I had to do it on my own. Giggling to myself, I waited for David to realize he filled my thoughts to overflowing. He would give up hoping that I would focus on God and talk to me. The harder I tried to succeed; the sooner David would give me a break. I really did try. It was peaceful. However, my mind just insisted on flashing from one scene to another. David was in every scene. The events appearing before my eyes sent shivers of delight through my whole body. I smiled and started talking to him. The truth was I loved David. Being around him was like being in heaven. Honestly, I could not imagine any time more blessed than the times I spent with David.

Eventually, he sighed and took my hands. "Come sit with me, Tara. Tell me what is on your mind. Perhaps if you share your thoughts, I can help you find peace. Worship is not about us, Tara. It is about God and what God wants us to do."

"You will get angry with me, David. I really am trying. Memories surface. I follow your instructions, focus on a single picture, and file it into my heart. I can even imagine putting the memory in a file folder and setting it in a drawer. I see the drawer closing and feel the lock turning. Feeling incredibly blessed and peaceful, my body tingles, and I have to dance."

"Tara, you cannot dance."

"I know that, David. I banish the thought by letting another memory surface or counting."

"We agreed to wait until you are nineteen, Littl'un. It is not so far away. Time goes quickly."

"I'm not asking you to dance. I am trying to seek God's will. It just doesn't work, David. Maybe, you need to find Brian and Mark. Maybe you are too close."

"I did that for you last week. When I came back, you were hysterical. It took an hour to calm you down. I will not leave you. Besides, Tara, you told me you have tried every day all week."

"I did."

"What happened?"

"I could stay calm and quiet for a long time, David, but got lonely and cried. Then I laughed as memories took over my whole existence. It makes me smile just thinking about special moments."

"Share them with me, Tara."

"Promise not to get mad at me."

"I promise, Tara."

"I dance in my memories, David."

"We have not danced. You cannot have memories of dancing with me. Those are dreams. Tell me no dreams. I will listen. Try not to tease me, Littl'un."

"When I try to worship, I always see the same scenes. Remember when you took me on the glacier? We had climbed for hours. I wanted to get to the next wave. You said it was too dangerous."

"I remember that you ran ahead of me. In a panic, I had to crawl after you."

"When you yelled, I stopped, David. I still do not believe the snow would have caved. The ice bridge was thick where I stopped. I thought you were being silly."

"I was not silly. You saw the open crack."

"Yeah, but God was holding me. Powerful and alive, I knew I was safe. Obeying you had been so hard because I did not want to lie down. It would be cold. I wanted to jump to prove I was safe. However, God got angry. He said, "Listen to David. Do exactly what he tells you." Then I was too frightened to obey you. I watched you lie down and crawl up to me. You told me to crouch down very slowly and do a backward summersault. When my hand was within reach, you grabbed and pulled. Sliding around like a whip, my feet slipped out from under me. Lying on the ice beside you, I saw the opening. It was at least fifty feet to the left. Creation is incredible. The edge of the ice bridge was a sparkling blue arch. It got thicker as it curved along the fissure. I got mad at you for scaring me, and you looked so frightened. I felt awful guilty. Pointing to the right, you whispered, 'Look that way.'

"All colour drained out of your face, Littl'un. Clinging to me, you shook like a leaf. For a long time, you were silent. After a long, drawn-out sigh, you thanked me."

"You saved me, David. The fissure opened less than ten feet to the right. It was open for thirty feet or more, and then the ice bridge covered it again. However, it looked thin. I guessed it was less than four inches thick. The fissure was wide, too. I could have fallen into it. I might have died."

"Yes, you brat, my own heart took its time regaining a normal rhythm. Realizing how easy it would be to lose you, I did not want to let go of you. I wanted to protect you, forever."

"We stayed on the ice until we were freezing. I discovered how fast goosebumps burn." I reached over and took David's hand. He put his arm around me. A breeze softly brushed our faces, and the ice tinkled, creating a perfect moment. Our eyes locked.

David smiled and quickly moved away but remained holding my hand. "We came down so slowly. Every shadow had to be investigated." He whispered as though he did not want the moment to disappear either.

"After a couple of hundred feet, we relaxed and started to play on the slope, running and sliding. Then we held each other's hands, leaned back, and swung each other round and round. We went so fast."

"I worried we could not stop."

"We got dizzy."

"That is a wonderful memory, Tara. I am glad we shared it."

"We wanted to dance."

"Yes, Tara. I panicked. Remember, I told you to follow behind me."

"You gave me strict instructions to stay more than ten feet behind."

"I had to sing to keep my eyes focused on the path. This is a dangerous discussion, Littl'un."

"I told you my thoughts would upset you. I knew you would get mad."

"I am not mad. I am nervous. I should go find Mark."

"On the way down, I found a slippery rock. Remember? You took it from me, and while you held it, you sang a song about slipping through time on a film of molybdenite. Sing it for me, please."

"No. I should never have sung it for you. Judge Soronato was furious."

"Do you tell him everything?"

"Only when we need to do damage control," laughed David as he calmed down again. He ruffled my hair. "I sometimes forget you are not Muki, Tara. Emotionally, I feel like I am jumping out of a pot of boiling water and landing in a frying pan. I, too, struggle with being the right kind of friend. I need help from Jarrock frequently. Fear, shock, and worry are good weapons at times."

"I really do not try to tease you, David. However, you are right. I had never heard your fairy tales before. I thought your song was a recipe for making a spaceship. It worked. I stopped teasing you right away. Demanding to know more about the Muki, I badgered you with questions for hours afterward."

"I was too busy trying to unsay my explanation of the song to think about dancing. I have so much fun with you, Tara. If I could, I would take you to the stars. I would build you..."

"Be quiet - I am pretending you are not an alien. Be my angel. I can comprehend angels."

David laughed, and we sat beside each other, listening to the ice and the silence between the gentle gusts of wind. "I liked that memory, Tara. It is a good memory. Can you tell me another one, hopefully, one of which I am not a part?"

"August rain," I said and smiled before becoming lost in thought.

"Share it with me, Littl'un. What about August rain?"

"I think it is the closest I ever got to worshipping that was not when I was terrified."

"Alright, this may be the key I can help you turn. Tell me about August rain."

"August rain is a name I give to a thunder and lightning storm that comes late in August. It is a special storm. The air gets thick and heavy, and I can feel the storm coming hours before it arrives. The world seems to get very quiet as it gets dark, and the birds stop flying. The lightning gets closer, and the thunder booms almost overhead. It starts to rain. It does not just rain. It pours. The sky opens and the rain, often starting with hailstones, pounds the ground. The raindrops are huge and bounce off the ground. In seconds, if outside, the rain drenches through all your clothing, making you dripping wet, but the rain is warm, not cold. It demands dancing.

"Last August, I was at work when the rain started. It was almost quitting time. My boss laughed at my excitement. Many others offered me a ride home. Of course, I declined all offers. They thought I was crazy. Afraid the storm would pass by before I could leave, I watched out the window. Itching to get out into the rain, I could not concentrate very well. When quitting time finally arrived, refusing offers of umbrellas, I asked for a plastic bag for my shoes. They were my favourite shoes, and I did not want to wreck them in the rain.

"Slightly embarrassed by others watching me, I slipped into the washroom to take off my shoes and pantyhose. I stuffed them in the bag. Leaving the snickers behind the door, I ran out into the rain. Running, skipping, and twirling, I headed down the road as fast as I could to get away from the gawking eyes following me. When the rain really pounded the road, I stopped, raised my arms out to the side, leaned my head back, opened my mouth, and caught raindrops on my tongue.

"I have always thought of the rain as a shower from God. It refreshes the world. Everything smells clean and new after a rain. Like a cleansing, pain, sorrow, regrets, and sins wash away. New, unencumbered by the past, I felt sufficiently blessed to hold me safely until the next August rain. I felt full of promise. Was I worshipping, David?"

"The Muki calls such activity cleansing. Yes, Tara, you were worshipping."

"I don't think about God much while dancing in the rain. I think of it as a celebration. Feeling alive, I live in creation. Surreal, I create visions and act them out in dance. Does that make sense?"

"Those are the thoughts which allow direct access to God. Does God speak to you? God's voice does not require sound. It may be visions, ideas, thoughts, or feelings. It can be as simple as an overwhelming conviction to do a particular thing."

"No, David, that could not be right. If it is, then I worship all the time. I succeed in opening the door to God so often that I don't think the door is ever closed."

David laughed. Putting his arm around me, he whispered that he loved me. "What has God been telling you?"

Whispering very quietly in David's ear, my face getting redder with every syllable, I said, "God has been telling me to dance with you, David."

David did not move. Tears ran down his cheeks. After a long time, he stood up, pulled me into his arms, and held me close. When he stepped back, he held my chin and looked into my eyes, and I knew exactly what he was going to say. Together, in perfect synchronization, we said, "We will when I/you am/are nineteen." We laughed.

Running along the shore, we released tension and gained comfort in God knowing no time. David took off his shoes and socks, rolled up his pants, and stepped out into the ice-cold lake to fetch two ice crystals. We returned to David's rock by the shore. Sitting beside each other, we sucked on the crystals.

It was fun. They were so cold. We had to hold them in our mouths to warm up our hands. Then our mouths would freeze. The crystals were about eight inches long and over an inch around. If we held them the right way in the sun, they made rainbows. Laughter, silly songs, and games occupied all our attention. We were truly comfortable in our blessings.

Mark and Brian came back, and we ate lunch together. We played tag after lunch and then talked. Brian asked Mark to climb some cliff he had noticed on the way to lunch. They left.

David asked if I was willing to try to continue my lessons again. He asked me to focus on the present. David was looking for external proof that God was with me when I worshipped. How I wished I could shine like the Muki. I know I had gained a slight glow last time I was at the base. I like to call it my visit to my castle. Attributing my glow to be a reflection from off the Muki, I guess I simply did not believe I could shine.

"My people do not have the gift of Koe Sai Serena, David. I do not know if I will ever be able to prove the authenticity of my worship. You will have to accept my word."

David smiled. Scowling, I said, "Please do not make fun of me, David. I want to please you."

"That is your first mistake, Littl'un. Do not worship for me. Do so for yourself."

"When God wants something from me, God has always told me. I have never searched for God. It just happens. Why should I waste God's time? It makes me feel guilty and selfish. This is dumb."

"It is easy to misunderstand instructions, and it is wise to present your availability and willingness to seek God's will. Before you act, it is also wise to seek God's approval."

I sighed. "It is arrogant, David. Besides, my experience is that talking directly to God is terrifying."

"Why?"

"God never asks what is easy to do. There is always a catch. God tricks me by letting me believe one thing when it turns out I am doing something else entirely. It is generally something that I would never do if I had understood what I was being asked to do."

"What do you do when God terrifies you?"

"Obey."

"Why?"

"God leaves no option. God will make me do as I am told."

"Obedience is always your own."

"No, David. It is not. God put my hand on the branch and held it there when I fell out of a tree, and God threw me off a train. I didn't willingly jump."

"Tell me about the train, Tara. It is a tale you have not told me before." Chuckling, David ruffled my hair.

I scowled at him. "You are not supposed to make fun of me. It was a few months before I met you. I jumped the wrong train. It was stupid of me. Usually, I jump trains as they are being put together. The engine pulls the cars forward then backs into a different line to pick up other cars. It goes back and forth along the main track quite a few times and never gains much speed. However, on this day, I boarded a train pulling out of the station and heading north. I was not ready at the place I usually dismount. I was not too worried, though, because I was sure I could get off at the corner by the farm. I could not jump. The train continued to gain speed. By the time I passed the mills on Two Mile Flat, I was terrified. I kept imagining horrible thoughts. It might be headed to Prince Rupert, but I figured it would probably turn east at Prince George. It might not stop for days. Speed increasing, the train chugged. I panicked. I cried. I exhausted my search for options. I could not get into a car from the ladder on which I was perched. When I looked at the top, I was too afraid of falling off to get on the roof of the car. Feeling stupid, I asked God for help. Following instructions, I prepared to jump. Eventually, God said, 'Jump,' but I froze. God said soothing words. Without bawling me out, God continued to encourage me. God told me to jump on three and began counting. I was terrified. When I did not jump on three, God literally threw me off the train. I should be dead, David. I do not think the train was up to full speed, but it was going fast. I landed on a grassy slope and rolled head over heels a long way. I crashed through weeds and bushes and came to a stop after rolling into bulrushes on the edge of a pond. My pants had ripped, my knee was bloody, and I had multiple scrapes and scratches on my arms, legs, and torso. Limping for the first few ties, I headed back to town long after the train disappeared down the track. Feeling incredibly blessed, I thanked God.

God laughed at me. I would have preferred God chastising me. Finally, I smiled up at the sky and sang. It was so good to be alive. Miraculously, I stopped limping. It was a long walk home. I concluded I owed God big time."

"You are very fortunate, Littl'un."

"I know, David. God stayed with me all the way home. It was well worth all the fear, as I like walking with God. The whole world is so much more alive when God is beside me. Nothing could be more perfect."

"Did God talk to you while you walked?"

"Yes, David. God teaches me lessons just like you do. I did not understand most of what God taught that day. Nevertheless, looking back, God was preparing me for your arrival. I even think God had something to do with me being on that train in the first place."

"That is very arrogant of you, Littl'un. It is not wise to test God."

"I do not believe I was testing God. I believe God was testing me. Proving I needed help, God forced me to pay attention and understand.

I fight with God, David. It is in my nature. What confuses me the most is that God likes me the way I am and instructs me to maintain my defiance. It does not make sense. Regardless of how confused I get, I would not change for the world, David. I live to hear God's laughter and feel God's hugs. I feel very special, and God forgives my arrogance."

"Are you going to tell me what God told you about the Muki?" asked David with a look of both curiosity and fear.

"No, I will not tell you all my secrets. However, I will tell you that you are all and more than God promised. I think the point might be that I must trust God in all things. Terror is not an excuse to disobey God. Whatever my duty is to God, it is not necessarily pleasant. The plan is complicated. Furthermore, I do not believe God intends it to be pleasant at times. All I know is that when it is over, miracles will have happened. Without me needing to understand, the future will be golden. God's will will be carried out. One day, I will go home. Besides, David, it is not my job to understand, just to play some small part. I do not have to be brave or strong."

"I love you, Tara. God gave you a blessed destiny. I feel blessed to know you."

We sat silently for a few minutes, each lost in our own thoughts. The wind teased us. The sun shone down so brightly, that I thought God had joined us. I thought about the past. So much had happened over the last two years. Watching David, I really did comprehend how fortunate and loved I was to be able to have him as part of my life. Realizing the future was not in my hands, I tried to fathom the agony and terror that was welling up inside me.

David was not mine to keep. Time was running out. I wondered what all the messages I had been receiving today meant. Slowly, I formulated a plan. Then I prayed for God to give me success and not let me stray from His path. I smiled at David and said I was going for a short walk. I asked him to stay where he was rather than accompany me.

After a few steps, I turned back to David and said, "David, I just need a moment to make sure I understand what has been happening today. I think I know what I have been doing wrong. Then, I am going to try worshipping again."

I walked among the trees and stopped behind a bush. David watched me. Tears fell down my cheeks as I tried to comprehend how I had been so fortunate to be given the opportunity to love David. "Do not watch David. I need to go to the bathroom," I shouted. To myself, I whispered, "I just need to be terrified, and the door to God will open. Be brave." I took a deep breath and undressed. Remembering Natthia, I set my clothes in a neat pile. Thinking the water would be awful cold, I ran into the lake. The many ice crystals near the shore swirled around my legs. The water was deep surprisingly quickly. I had taken four steps, and the water was up to my hips. I gasped. It was so cold. I told myself that people did the polar bear swim on New Year's Day and survived. I counted. By the time I counted to five, my legs were numb.

David called. His voice sounded frantic. I turned around to look at him. He was pulling off his clothes. I laughed.

"Hey, David, you don't wear underwear!"

"Please come out, Tara."

I locked eyes with him and raised my arms to the sky. A breeze was picking up. As I lowered my arms to the horizon, I felt the ice pushing against my legs. Having enough time for only a single thought, I marvelled that such a gentle breeze was strong enough to move the huge sheet of ice floating on the lake. The ice pushed my legs out from under me. I fell backward. With the ice crinkling and snapping all around me, I lost track of time. Slowly, I slipped under the ice. It was unbelievably cold. Yet, I was not afraid. The sun looked so pretty, and the ice was like a blanket. It was hard to move, but I did not care for some reason. God was with me. Marvelling in the beauty of my surroundings, I was ready to go home with God.

The next thing I remember, I woke up in David's arms. My head was under his chin, arms crossed on my chest, and hands tucked into David's armpits. David rubbed my back and then my legs while he held his sweater draped across my back with his knees. My skin was blue. However, the golden touch of God was also shining on my skin. Afraid to move, I closed my eyes and enjoyed the heat seeping into me as David vigorously massaged my body to warm me up. Realizing I was cold, I started to shiver. David hugged me. Our eyes locked. I smiled. David kissed my forehead. He called me a brat, and I danced with David. David tried to stop me, but I said, "God may know no time, but God knows when it is time."

I was afraid that David would refuse to dance with me. I closed my eyes and gave myself to God. What I experienced was heavenly. It was holy. God handed a gift of incredible worth to me. Knowing I will love David forever, I lay with him for a long time. Basking in the sunshine on our naked bodies, a warm breeze drifting across my back, I was in heaven. I looked into David's eyes and knew without a doubt that I was loved. Then very slowly, God withdrew.

We shivered. David, white as a ghost, uttered, "What have I done?" Then he pushed me to the side, sat up, and vomited. Realizing I had raped him, I started crying. David held me again, whispering that he loved me and then wondering aloud how he would protect me. We dressed and then sat very close, waiting for Brian and Mark to return.

They knew as soon as they saw us. Realizing I did not understand the Muki culture at all, I got terrified and confused. I thought David would fight his best friend and his own brother. He was almost mad with an inconceivable urge to protect me. Mark and Brian did not act normally either. They assumed David would kill them. They did not know where to look or what to do. David held me behind him with one hand, threatened with the other, and all of them stared with unmistakable defence.

God returned. I gave myself to God. Words came out of my mouth, which I did not even understand. However, they understood my words, and very slowly, the aggression was replaced with a sense of calm. I took Brian's hand and put it in David's hand. I held onto

David's other hand and took Mark's hand. It felt odd that my own fear of Mark had vanished. I felt safe again. However, I was on the verge of hysteria. I started to sing the Deplukador song. They laughed at my poor pronunciation, and the spell was broken. God left us again.

We walked up the trail to the truck, singing all the way. By the time we arrived at the truck, I had thought everything was back to normal again, even though we had fallen silent. It was a quiet trip back to town.

As usual, I slept against David's shoulder most of the way into town. Tension in the air woke me as we went past Quesnel and headed west. Worried, I watched David. He was pale but extremely serious. His whole expression said not to mess with him. Turning to Mark and Brian, I tried to figure out what was going on. Beside me, Brian looked as frightened as I felt. Oddly, although Mark was fidgeting and shaking, I felt safe. Usually, Mark terrified me. Feeling terribly guilty, I was confused. This was not normal. I thought I knew the Muki, but it was blatantly obvious that I did not know anything. Tears fell as I wondered what I had caused. Sighing, I tried to smile at Brian.

"I guess I am just plain trouble, Brian. Please do not be so worried. God was with us. I did as God instructed. I love your brother. God must know what He is doing."

Without a word, Brian put his hand on mine. I felt loved, but David tensed. I put my left hand on his leg. A very strange feeling filled me as Brian's hand began to glow. Barely speaking above a whisper, I asked David to pull over and stop the truck. He started to object; I lifted Brian's hand, "Look! Stop the truck."

David looked at his brother's hand. He gripped the steering wheel so tightly his knuckles turned white. Afraid we would have an accident as David accelerated, I yelled, "Please, David." David turned blue as Mark, with obvious authority, ordered David to stop.

I looked at Mark. He blazed with a bright shimmering light. I had to squint. I thought of pictures of Christ. Without thinking, I said very calmly, "Oh Jarrock, help me."

From out of thin air, I heard, "Touch David, Tara." It was not an order. Those words entered my consciousness with such calm and peace that for a moment, I felt frozen. Marvelling that the world was filling with wonder, I gave all my attention to David. Letting go of Brian, I touched David's cheek. He shook like a leaf in a breeze. I thought of the breeze that touched us so gently by the lake. Then, I remembered it had the strength to cause the ice to knock me off my feet. As I wiped the tears off David's cheek, the world disappeared. I saw only David. Completely overwhelmed with love for him, I drew his tension and fear away. It is hard to describe how it happened. David's blue light flowed onto my fingers and turned into shimmering white light. As David slowed down and pulled over, the shimmer on me seemed to turn around and flow back onto David.

Brian waited for only seconds before he leaned over, breaking our focus on each other. He took my right hand and David's left hand and held them together between his own hands. He said, "What God has joined, let no man take asunder. Jarrock protects you both, and so do I, my brother."

"And, so do I, friends," added Mark.

I smiled and felt so giddy and loved that a shiver crawled along my spine. God truly was blessing me. I closed my eyes very tightly. I wanted that moment to last forever. However, I wanted to see the light on us all. With an audible sigh, I said, "I am Muki now." Even though no one answered me, I knew it was true. Finally, I belonged.

Being Muki meant belonging to God. At that moment, I did. It was a wonderful feeling. Worth more than anything else in the universe, that feeling of connectedness to God invoked indescribable feelings.

As our lights faded and David started the truck again, I savoured the peace surrounding us. The future was not going to be easy. The Muki were angels, and arrogantly, I felt a feeble hope that I could be an angel as well and silently pledged my obedience to God. As I concluded my oath, I realized I was also an imperfect human guilty of sin.

Feeling that mating with David was a holy act, carried out according to the will of God, I understood that it had universal implications. It was not important for me to understand. Perhaps one day I would, but I felt God's pleasure upon me. I had not sinned. I had obeyed. Mark and Brian accepted the truth. I hoped Judge Soronato, and especially Muma Horren, would understand. Brian and Mark's acceptance was very reassuring. Perhaps, I was not about to die today.

The atmosphere would have been perfect had David not had a blue sheen flickering on his flesh. I wondered what it meant.

Realizing it was almost dinnertime when David turned onto an old overgrown logging road, I wondered if I should ask David to take me home. However, I was afraid of the answer and remained quiet. As we bumped along the trail, David, Brian, and Mark talked, but they spoke in their own language, and I could not understand them. When we stopped, Brian and Mark immediately jumped out and ran ahead. David asked me to lie down on the seat and not to make a sound. David opened his door and got out. I obeyed. I could hear David pacing back and forth in front of the truck. Again, I asked for Jarrock's protection. Although I heard no words, I felt a shield of peace descend.

Brian and Mark must have returned because I heard footsteps and talking. David opened the passenger door and invited me out. When I got out, David held me behind him as Natthia had when David came into my room at the base. Peering around him, I saw both Brian and Mark were armed. They had arrows mounted and looked very serious.

Nervous, David nodded to the others, and we walked forward, with Brian and Mark slightly ahead of us. Doug and Loren appeared. Immediately, arrows aimed at them. They went pale and stood still. Without any idea what I was saying, I began to sing. I must have been speaking their language because David let go of me, stepped back, and listened.

Loren and Doug nodded very slowly and then walked past us. They were carrying weird poles. Although I wanted to inquire what they were doing, I continued to sing. Brian and Mark put the arrows back into their quivers. Handing their bows to David and me, they removed their quivers. Brian adjusted the strap on his and helped me put it on while Mark handed his to David. Then they started pulling branches off the bush beside us. My song ended. I asked David what I had said, and he started laughing. I blushed.

With a sense of urgency, David instructed me to load my bow. Deadly serious, David and I faced down the trail with bow and arrow pulled taught. I felt frightened again. Curiosity got the better of me as I watched Doug and Loren back up the trail toward us.

They were waving the poles back and forth in front of them. A strange shimmery yellowish glow appeared to be swirling around the ends of their sticks. Leaves, twigs, dust, and even rocks were bouncing and hovering in the air a few inches off the ground. The turbulence continued across a swath about ten feet wide and maybe two feet deep. The further in front of them I looked, the more settled the dust bowl looked.

Still laughing, David said they were covering our trail. David and I just moved aside as they approached. They did not even glance at David and me when they backed into the truck. They headed to where Mark and Brian were continuing to move bushes. There was something shiny behind the bushes. Loren and Doug started putting the bushes around the truck. I was amazed at how natural the clump of bushes looked and how hard it was to see the truck. I would never guess the bushes were not a natural, growing feature beside the trail. No tire tracks were visible. In fact, the trail looked as though nothing had used it for a very long time.

Slightly frightened, I reluctantly looked at the shiny thing they had uncovered. David lowered his bow and put his free arm around me as I turned.

Before me, sat a slightly squashed pencil-shaped machine. A haze wavered around it. As David stiffened, we both turned back to Doug and Loren. Automatically, my arms reacted to a danger, which I failed to understand. I held the bow, drew an arrow out of my quiver, and aimed at Doug. If he moved, I knew I would release the arrow. There was no doubt that it would fly true, and Doug would die.

I appealed again to Jarrock. I calmed as I felt a tingling in my skin. I began to glow. Glancing toward David, I saw that he, too, was glowing. The calm descended. I felt a smile creep across my face and lowered my bow. I said something. Loren's and Doug's expressions changed, but they remained nervous. Doug took a short oblong flat object out of his pocket and started waving it around in front of the big pencil. I heard the familiar sound of the plane's door opening. I began to shake. My glow turned blue. I handed my bow to Loren, took off my quiver, and let out the strap before handing it to him as well. David put his arrow back into his quiver.

David whispered, "It is okay, Littl'un. I will protect you."

I watched the glow on my hands fade. I felt cold and alone. Then when I looked back at David, I saw an alien rather than an angel. Suddenly hysterical, I became overwhelmed. Not understanding, I felt an urge to escape because nothing around me was right. The sights and sounds were wrong. Thinking I had betrayed Earth, I started to run.

Confused and insane, I wanted to pretend I was dreaming. Today could not have been real. It had to be a fantasy.

Jarrock commanded me to stop. Powerless not to obey, I froze. With the sting of an arrow aimed at my back, very slowly, I turned around. A gasp of dismay escaped my lips. David, deadly serious, was pointing an arrow at me.

My world tumbled down around me. David was incredibly powerful. His authority seemed to emanate from him. My soul calmed. David ordered me to get into the transporter. My mind kept saying, "you mean the plane." I yelled, "Doug, where is the junk on the plane. Put it back. I need it back."

They all laughed. Doug said, "I cannot do so, Tara. This is a different transporter. I was not expecting to take you to the base today. You will like this one better. Go ahead, Tara. Get in."

Something still was not right. Doug was teasing me. I scowled. Determined, I headed toward the plane. After a couple of steps, I found myself on my bottom. Something had pushed me with significant force. I heard laughter. Then David's voice stopped all sound. "Open the door for her, Doug. Now!" Immediately, Doug's features became very serious again. Stepping forward, he started waving the thing in his hand around again. I remembered the odd dance I sometimes saw them do before entering the plane and tried to relax. "But, David, the door is already open."

Simultaneously, I heard laughter and felt a jolt. Something grabbed me and threw me into the plane. It was not David. He had always thrown me into the plane. I fell. Angry, David dropped the bow. Tackling Doug, they rolled onto the ground. A moment later, David tossed the 'thing' to Brian. Brian waved it around. Then David and Doug landed beside me inside the plane. David pinned Doug to the floor. There was a tense moment before both Doug and David began laughing.

I started breathing again. I watched Brian waving the thing around Loren. Fingers of pulsing golden light flickered out from the edge of the door. They swirled and bounced. Sometimes they disappeared, and I could see nothing. The haze got bigger and surrounded Loren. Then when it pulled back, Loren landed inside the plane.

I watched Brian. He waved at me and walked out of sight. Concentrating on remaining calm, I refused to use the word transporter to describe the plane. I hung onto David, insisting to myself that he was my angel.

Our glow identified our service to God. It was not alien. It was a symbol. It had to be so because dancing was just a fancy name for having sex, albeit a holy kind of sex. David and I had mated before God. The whole experience was incredible and blessed. I knew that to be true.

My only concern was why David had turned pale, covered his face, and cried, "What have I done." Then he had thrown up. It marred the precious event and made me feel guilty. I feared I had raped him, which tore me between believing God or David. I had always connected David to God. All my memories of activities with David had previously meshed with everything God told me. I often thought David was God. The discrepancy in the meaning and holiness of our lovemaking confused and frightened me. How can a dance make me Muki? Why is God so close now, especially if I had tricked David into obeying my command to dance with me? Why does David feel I betrayed him if it was God's command? Yet, I was delighted that I could shine. Nothing added up.

Where was Brian?

Brian returned carrying straps before I could ask David what his brother was doing. He waved the thing around again and quickly landed inside the plane. Loren jostled his way to Brian, and Brian helped him into a harness and buckled the straps onto hooks in the sides, ceiling, and floor of the plane. He could barely move. Brian had even strapped Loren's head against the interior. I laughed.

David said, "There are only four seats, Tara. This is not funny. Check the straps again, Brian. Make sure they are tight. Loren, do you feel secure?"

I could detect the fear in David's voice. I had always felt safe in the plane, just a force holding me firmly during takeoff. My voice cracked as I asked, "David, where are we going?"

Thankfully, David chuckled as he reassured me we were only returning to the base. I sat where David directed and watched as he strapped me in. I was familiar with the lap belt. It was like an ordinary seatbelt, except it went over both shoulders and around my waist. The seat had a headrest, and David tightened a strap across my forehead. I could move and be comfortable, but I thought the countdown to launching into outer space would be next on the agenda. I tried moving around while David, Brian, and Doug strapped themselves into their chairs.

As there was no cockpit, I wondered how Doug would pilot the plane. I could not see any instruments at all, except a small plate with a bunch of buttons on it. When I strained to see beyond Doug in case the instrument panel was on the other side of him, my seat moved.

Experimenting, I could make the chair tilt forward, backward, and to the sides. If I pushed on the floor, it rose higher. It was a neat chair. I asked David how to make it go down again, and he said, "Just pull up on your armrests."

While I was laughing, Doug pushed some of the buttons. The door closed. The plane tilted almost straight up and took off. There was absolutely no sound. It was eerie. We levelled off, and I grabbed David's hand. Windows opened in front of me. I could see the sun and a lot of sky. I wanted to lean against David, but the seat would not let me, so I closed my eyes. David hummed a song to me, and I slept.

The sound of the door opening woke me. Fumbling with the straps, I tried to undo them. David told me to wait. It was crowded. I would have said there was insufficient room for four, let alone five people. I stayed still while David unbuckled me, and the others jostled about. Realizing they had all picked up their bows, I got frightened again.

David spoke to them again. I wish I could understand what he was saying. He was obviously in charge, though. The others nodded, and Doug pushed some keys. The door opened. Looking out, I relaxed. We were at the base. All except David and I exited. They did not jump as they had from the transporter when it was dressed up to look like a plane. They stepped out, hanging onto the doorway, braced themselves, and then sort of leaped as they let go of the doorway. While David instructed me, they drew arrows and stood guard. I threw up after David landed beside me. Doug laughed when I told him that although I liked riding in the transporter, I would rather get out of the plane he had brought me in previously. They all laughed. I wondered why we were under guard but refrained from asking. Everyone was too serious.

David asked me to worship with him. By the time our arms lowered to the horizon, I felt God's presence. The tension gave way to confidence as we headed down the path to the camp. Both David and I shone. Others backed away as we approached. No one spoke. Without incident, we entrered the door in the cliff. David took me to his room. We entered, and David closed the door. He gently touched my face with the tips of his fingers. It felt wonderful. When I reached to touch his face the same way, David pulled me close to him and said, "I will find a way to protect you. I love you, Tara."

I believed him. I let him undress me and watched him undress. He lifted me onto his bed and lay down beside me. We held each other. Then he kissed my forehead and told me to sleep while he spoke to Judge Soronato.

Panic engulfed me. I grabbed his hands and would not let go. "Leave me with Natthia, David. Do not leave me alone."

When David promised to take me to my own room and wait there with me until Natthia joined us, I let go of his hands and watched him get dressed. He dressed very formally. He even put on the sword Judge Soronato had given him the last time we were here. I asked him what I should wear. David searched through his closet, handed me a blue shirt, and helped me put it on. With tears in his eyes, David asked me to dance.

I blushed and touched his face. He closed his eyes. I hugged him. Then we waltzed in his room. I was so tempted to take his clothes off him that I could not dance anymore. Smiling and full of confidence, I said, "It is time for you to see the Judge, David. Take me to Natthia. We must be careful. This is not really my castle. If you let me make you believe it is, the blessing God granted us will be destroyed. It is too dangerous for us all." I did not know about what I was talking, but David let go of me, and everything about him became serious and powerful. When he opened the door, Brian and Mark snapped to attention. The hall was deathly quiet. We crossed the hall and walked to my room. David asked Brian to fetch Natthia, and we went into my room. It felt very strange, as though it was not mine anymore. To David, I whispered, "I belong in your room, don't I?" David nodded and smiled while we stood hand in hand waiting for Natthia.

Maybe I was beginning to understand. Life with the Muki was very different. Every move seemed to speak with a voice of its own. We were slaves. All we did was immensely important. It had meaning far beyond the two of us. It was imperative we do not err.

I soon recognized Natthia's knock. David held me behind him and nervously opened the door. With tears of uncertainty and concern in her eyes, Natthia hugged him. Stepping between us, she instructed David to leave.

When David looked afraid to obey, Natthia said, "If arrows fly, I will take her arrow for you, son. I will keep her safe for you.

Brian will guard the door."

David kissed the back of my hand, tucked me behind Natthia, opened the door only wide enough to slip through, and quickly closed the door.

Natthia hugged me and asked me to turn around for her. She said, "You look good in blue, Tara. Come let me examine you. I do not think the Judge will keep David long. I will make sure Josh helps you find a castle. Do not worry."

While she slowly turned me around, I felt Natthia's scrutiny. I blushed many shades of red. Natthia said I could not get any bluer. Then she told me to have a shower. She scrubbed me very hard and thoroughly. I love Natthia. After drying me, she helped me put on David's blue shirt. We sat quietly on the edge of my bed, talking quietly. Natthia told me I was now officially Muki.

A heavy burden settled on my shoulders, and I feared the wisdom of God in choosing me for this task. I was not worthy. I could feel defiance welling up from the depths of my soul. Unable to stay and refusing to believe the words Natthia said, I suddenly needed to go home and opened the door. Brian aimed an arrow toward me, shook his head, and smiled as he pushed me back from the door and pulled it shut.

Telling Natthia I was a child, I sobbed. Natthia tucked me under the comforter on my bed, then massaged my back, and Natthia sang to me until I calmed down. I felt God surround me again. Calm, I waited silently for David to return. While Natthia held my hand, I realized how privileged I was to have her as a friend. When David returned, the Judge accompanied him. Brian opened the door and stepped back, but David blocked the doorway. Putting his hand on the hilt of his sword, David denied the Judge entry into my room.

Without a sound, the Judge drew his sword and pointed it at the hilt of David's sword. With his eyes locked on the Judge, David slowly drew his sword. Natthia stepped between them. Brian called Mark. There was the noise of running feet, and everyone was pointing arrows.

As I stepped around David, some pointed them at me as well. Instantly, Brian and Mark shoved me against the wall and stood in front of me. They were so close that I could hardly move. Barely able to breathe, I demanded David and Judge Soronato relinquish their swords, and my words seemed to hang in the air as silence resumed. Ignoring the arrows, I very cautiously forced myself some space, raised my arms, shifted one foot in front of the other, leaned back, bent my knee slightly, and let my arms fall to the horizon. With relief, I felt the light flowing down my arms and swirling around my head.

Hearing bows tapping the floor, I looked at the people I loved so dearly. They were so serious and so frightened. I did not think they knew how to handle my presence because their culture did not allow the situation in which we found ourselves to arise.

Then, I heard a door opening and watched Muma Horren step into the hall. Even I knew to make only very slow and deliberate moves. As Muma Horren stepped toward us, I braced for a lecture but smiled because she was unarmed. As she approached, she started humming, and I pried my way out from behind Brian and Mark. I stepped around them. Everyone seemed frozen. I slowly let my arms lower to my side. I raised my palms before me then pushed them out and down. Instantaneously, as though they recognized God's authority upon me, everyone in the hall lowered their bows.

Mark and Brian lowered their arrows, too. Turning to David and the Judge, I touched their blades. Gently pushing them, I nodded my head. Both raised their swords, swung them through the air, and placed them in their sheaths, causing a sigh of thanksgiving to be uttered by most of those present. Taking David and Judge Soronato's hands, I pulled to increase the space between us until Muma Horren held Natthia's hand between her own.

In a calm, firm voice, Muma Horren asked, "Do you take responsibility for Tara's actions, Natthia."

Natthia answered, "I do."

Tears fell down the Judge's cheeks as he slowly nodded.

David shook his head and drew his sword. He pulled Natthia behind him and held her there. Staring at David, Muma Horren continued to hum while I stepped between them. David pulled me back against him while thrusting his sword forward until Muma Horren stopped humming when the end of the sword was almost touching her chest. Reaching up, I wrapped my fingers around the sword. Although I was being careful, I cut my finger. Blood dripped onto the floor.

As calmly as I could, I said, "Put your sword away, David. The sun has set. You need to take me home."

"This must be our castle. You must stay here."

"This is not my castle. I did not dance here," I answered emphatically.

"Where did you dance, if not here?" indignantly demanded Muma Horren.

"I danced on Earth. Earth is my castle," I confidently responded. With a shocked expression, Muma Horren frowned at me. Blood continued to drip, but I did not let go of David's sword. As Natthia began humming an odd tune, she took my other hand. Other than knowing I was over my head; I did not know how to get out of this stalemate. However, I could not let Natthia remove my fingers from the sword, and I did not even know why I could not. In desperation, I said, "Brian, protect Natthia."

Muma Horren let out a heart-wrenching sob and stepped back. Brian stepped in front of her. In anguish, David said, "Tara, let go. I will lower my sword."

When I let go, David did as he had promised, but the Judge immediately put his hand on the hilt of his sword. Leaping forward, I put my bloody hand over his. After a scrutinizing moment pondering my motive, he let go of his sword and put his arms around me, rendering me oddly secure. He knelt at my feet, put his head on my shoulder, and cried. His sobs were lonely and full of pain. Putting my arms around him and wishing my finger would stop bleeding, I worried about the blood I was getting on him. My tears refused to stay in my eyes. Whispering to Jarrock, I begged for help to get us all safely out of the mess into which I had gotten us all.

Jarrock said, "You are doing just fine, my child."

Feeling cheated because nothing was fine, and everything was wrong, defiance filled me, and I got angry. With all the fire I could muster, I ordered everyone to go to their rooms. Surprisingly, all except David and Natthia rose to do so. A firm hold on the Judge was all it took to have him remain in my arms. Wondering why Judge Soronato had granted me such authority, I took Muma Horren's hand and held it while watching for the last door to close. As an afterthought, I called for Brian to wait. Softly I whispered to the Judge, "Come, Judge Soronato, I need to borrow your office again." Although surprisingly calm and honoured, I prayed for Jarrock's guidance. Muma Horren had warned me not to dance, and I had danced anyway. Therefore, my guilt meant I had to establish a course of action to keep all of us alive and whole. Attributing my calm to shock, I was determined to succeed in restoring a sense of peace and order.

Natthia took over when we entered the office, washed my hand, and put something on my finger. It stopped bleeding. She washed my blood off Judge Soronato's hand, cheek, neck, and hair. Then she told us to sit at the table and brought us a drink of hot apple juice, which we sipped very slowly. When the teapot was empty, Natthia nodded to me.

Cautiously praying I knew enough of the culture of the Muki to respond appropriately, I stood up and walked slowly around the table. Starting with the Judge, I rested my hands on his shoulder and stood silently behind him. Without knowing what I was waiting for, I stood there trying to impart comfort and security. Although I did not understand how to do it, I focused all my concentration on willing Jarrock to use me as a conduit between God and the Muki. The Judge put his hands over mine and said, "Bless you, child. Jarrock protects you. Tell us how to react. Our culture demands both your and David's execution. This is too new."

"Jarrock demands your love, not your wrath, Judge Soronato," I answered as a wave of reassurance engulfed and filled me with confidence.

"The law requires -"

"The law is wrong, Sir. We need to celebrate."

"How?"

"I suggest we dance."

Indignantly, as though what I suggested was improper, he lectured, "I cannot dance. I am not fit. Brian is unlicensed and too young. David should have waited. You are too young and have no castle. Natthia and Muma are too old and no longer fertile."

The strength of my conviction in the righteousness of my suggestion grew with each word as I answered without hesitation, "We are never too old or too young. Everyone is fit to dance. You have all danced every evening I have been here. You dance under the stars before the campfire."

"That is not dancing. It is singing praises to God."

"It is dancing to me." I leaned over the Judge and kissed the small bald spot on the top of his head. He patted my hands. I moved behind Natthia.

Holding my hands, Natthia said, "This is David's Doleran. He has obeyed God. Tara is correct. We should celebrate. There is time to allow the Panel to determine the meaning of the meeting with Tara last month and the activities of today. God is with Tara. I will stand with her. My position has not changed, nor will it. All of you must accept it, including you, Josh."

Tears fell again down the Judge's cheeks.

I did not understand what Natthia was saying. Nevertheless, I felt thankful for her support, and I moved further around the table. Touching Brian, I immediately felt his love. Tears came to my eyes as I stood behind him, waiting for him to speak.

"Muma Horren, Judge Soronato, thank you for allowing me to be here. I have learned so much. I have pledged my life to protect Tara and my brother. I will do so. I do not care what the Panel recommends. I have faith in David's faith. This land is blessed. God sent Tara to teach us that we are human. To err is to be human. To love is to be holy. There is time to let the future unfold. I like what Tara promises. We should dance now. There will be time to judge and to cry tomorrow. Jarrock leads us all. Let us take his hand and follow." Brian then silently nodded to me and sat down.

When I touched Muma Horren, she burst into loud sobs, then stood up, and hugged me. Soon regaining her self-control, Muma held my chin up and spoke quietly to me. "I warned you, child. When I first laid eyes on you, I recognized you were Muki. Believe me, foreseeing what was going to happen; I did not want anyone else to recognize you. You did not listen to me. Now, it is too late. You danced. You have no castle. David has no chance of upholding his responsibilities. You have failed us all, Tara. Your child will be born on alien soil. A freak, he will have no home. His existence has thrown both our homes into turmoil. To what end, Tara? How will you live with the future you have planted? God is testing us all. Dance for us, Tara. I will give you the time Jarrock is demanding. The future is on your shoulders. I pray you can carry the weight. Give us God's message. Then send us home with a clear judgement."

"The love of Jarrock will protect us all, Muma."

"You are naive, child. I command you to prove my visions wrong." Muma Horren sat down.

As Muma Horren continued to glare at me, I felt cold while visions flashed before my eyes. Unwilling to accept her visions, I sought condolence from Jarrock and defiantly said, "God gave me a tiny job. I just try to do as commanded by God. It is hard, Muma. I am not in control. I try to be, but God catches me off guard, and things just happen."

Choking back tears, I moved to David. Fear gripped me as I reached to touch his shoulders with tears pouring down my cheeks. I was overcome with the sorrow I foresaw in the images Muma Horren had sent me. I was afraid to touch David. Jarrock said, "Prove her wrong, Tara. Love him. Hold and reassure him."

I opened my mouth. A lot of noise came out of it, but none of it was coherent. Yet, somehow, David understood, stood up, and held me. I whispered, "I am sorry, David. I had to do as God commanded. Please forgive me."

David ruffled my hair. Then he wiped the tears off my face and said, "Come with me, my Tara. It is time to sing our praises to God." As he led me out into the hall, the others followed, a bell rang, and the rest of the residents joined us before the campfire. As Brian beat his drum, David led me out by the fire and shouted, "Dance with me, Tara. Dance with me, forever."

We danced until we heard all the drums join in song. The heavens sang with us, and Jarrock sent blessings down among us. When David kissed my forehead, reading each other's minds, I curtsied before Brian and asked him to dance. He turned so red I had to laugh until he smiled and, taking my hand, stepped out to dance. David took Muma Horren's hand, and they danced beside us. At the end of the dance, I kissed Brian's cheek. He bowed and took me to the Judge. I felt like I was dancing with my father, and it was special.

As I watched David dance with Natthia, it was easy to see he loved her very dearly. Wanting to cry but without jealousy, I craved the kind of love the Muki shared with one another. Filled with sincerity, it touched the heart and demanded time to stand still. I could have watched Natthia and David dance forever. After a very short time, I realized how old Natthia was and how precious she was to David and the Judge. Having Natthia as a friend was priceless. Suddenly torn with a sense of guilt, I walked with the Judge to dance beside them. Emotions running rampant, I traded partners. The tone of the background drums changed dramatically. We all watched Natthia dance with Judge Soronato. Personified love, their dance sent shivers up the spine. If any feeling could be perfect, the minutes passing while they danced fit perfectly. Without a doubt, they demonstrated love was eternal and, oh, such a blessing. To David, I said, "Promise me you will love me like that."

He answered, "I do, Tara. Truly, I do."

As his eyes begged me to allow him to take me back to his room, wanting to stay, I hugged him, and if God had not spoken, I would have succumbed to temptation. Filling with urgency again, I whispered, "Take me back to Quesnel, David. God forbids my staying here. Know that if it were my choice, I would hold you forever."

We stood in front of the campfire, crying. I wanted so desperately to defy God. However, I could not do so. David, too, understood, probably better than I, our destiny demanded us both to follow the will of God. Muma Horren thanked us for dancing and told me before I could leave, I needed to dance with Mark. She would dance with David.

Realizing the unmistakable symbolism of her request, I stared at Muma Horren. The next dance would seal our fate. Could I prove to Muma Horren that I could embrace that future with gratitude and thanksgiving? When I was near Mark, he reminded me our worlds were alien, and our cultures did not mesh. The Muki were real, and we were phony. Earth was one big contradiction, and our relationship meant danger. Together, Mark and I were like dynamite, apt to blow up at any moment. Thinking Muma Horren was being cruel; I nodded despite knowing this was not the right dance to end the evening. Filled with guilt, sorrow, and foreboding, this dance would make me face facts even though I wanted the fantasy.

While the drums rolled, I listened carefully to the beat. Wondering how the drummers knew the meaning of this dance when I felt so lost, I curtsied before Mark. I might be Muki, but I remained lacking the gifts of Koe Sai Serena. God may have given me light when I was serving God, yet it was blatantly clear to me that I did not understand with God's understanding. An inanimate robot in His service whenever required, I could only grasp at straws around the edges of events too complicated and cosmic to comprehend. Mark bowed, and everyone watched us intently. Like dancing with David early in the afternoon, this dance would have far-reaching consequences.

Unprepared, I circled Mark, and he turned as I turned. Trying to figure out whether I could influence tomorrow, I reached for his hands, but Mark was reluctant to take mine. Understanding far more of the future, he hesitated. As tears welled up in my eyes, I comprehended the right response and smiled. Stepping closer to

Mark, I raised my hands, and thankfully Mark grasped them and raised his own as well. Noticing how much taller than David Mark was, I let my hands slide down his arms as I stepped ever closer until chests touched. I leaned my head back. Mark smiled, nodded, and leaned back as a wave of calm and peace surrounded us. In time with the beat of the drums, we let our arms fall to the horizon, God joined us, and I gave myself to God. Destiny had trapped Mark and me in roles that neither of us wanted. With arms waving from side to side, turning, and brushing lightly against each other, we created a vision of our cultures melding as we danced.

As time progressed, I embraced the future, and blessings descended upon Mark and me, leaving me feeling fortified and confident that we would carry out our parts in a scheme only God directed. Mark and I would rage war for peace and future growth, and our worlds would burn in a torch of love. Love truly was the greatest weapon imaginable. Come what may, I would forever more love Mark. His role was every bit as painful as was mine. Our dance promised survival to see the war through to the end.

On the way home, David told me Mark and I swayed like a flame of blazing white light. He laughed when I said I would like to have seen it but had kept my eyes shut the whole dance. I had been a robot held in my maker's control.

Saying goodbye was incredibly difficult. I watched David walk away and then run after him. Hugging him, I begged him to be the grey sentry. He laughed and gave me the look that I loved so much.

He said, "Tara, you are my island kingdom. I will stand guard and mould the future. He held me close, and I whispered that I was his mud.

36

PANIC

Wanting to stay with him wherever he went, I almost followed David back to the plane. When he left, he immediately began singing, and I stood in the bush listening to him until I was convinced that the sound that I was hearing was only my imagination because he was too far away to be heard. Lonely, I started walking along the trail.

Imagining I was juggling balls, I headed home. Frantically, I caught each ball and threw it back up. They were my life. Life had become too complicated. Panic seized me as I examined each ball as it landed in the palm of my hand. What could I say to my parents? Nothing could possibly explain the truth. I could give them no explanation. I stepped up to the door, and all the balls hit the ground and rolled down the basement stairs.

Cautiously, I gripped the handle and opened the door. My mind went blank as I hung up my coat, and I cringed as I heard my mother's voice.

"There you are. Just where do you think you have been, young lady? I have been worried sick..."

I searched for words. I felt like saying, "I have been to the very edges of time, touched the fringes of heaven, and felt the depths of hell. Where have I not been?"

That would have been terribly disrespectful and rude. Therefore, I said nothing. Well, what was I supposed to say? I danced with an alien. I am trying to save Earth from destruction. I am waging war to keep all I love together and breathing. By the way, I am going to have a baby. Your grandson will be a freak. Like an electric eel, he will shine with a light of his own. You could sit in the dark and use him as your lamp. On top of that, I dropped the balls. They rolled into the dark. How am I going to get them back?

Get real. I stood in front of my mother and imagined seeing my parents' faces drop. No. I could say nothing that would make any sense at all. Tears rolled down my cheeks as I whispered, "Nowhere. I have been nowhere at all. I am tired and am going to bed."

"Go to your room. You are grounded. Wait until your father gets home. You have not heard the end of this."

I wanted to stop, hug my mother, and reassure her that everything was fine. However, it was not fine. Absolutely everything was far from fine. I felt guilty and helpless. Then my mind's eye saw David walking away, singing. Smiling, I stopped on the landing and called, "I am sorry for worrying you, Mom. I did not mean to be late. I just lost track of time, but I am home now."

When I fell onto my bed, I cried. Wiping my tears, I started saying goodbye to everything in my room. Picking up my big rubber doll, I whispered, "I have really done it now, haven't I? Rocking my doll back and forth, I told myself I was not old enough to be a mother. I touched my belly and thought, Natthia cannot be right. How could she know? Does it not take time? With empty wishful thinking, I begged, "Should it not take more than once?"

With a sigh, I remembered Natthia saying, "Tara, you danced before God. What did you think would happen?" I had not answered Natthia either. However, words had formed clearly. They were absolute. "I expected a miracle." Natthia had said, "Well?" Then I had laughed. Filled with joy, I had danced in the room while Natthia clapped a beat and hummed.

As I touched my doll's face, gently tracing the shape of its head, teardrops fell onto it. I whispered, "How am I going to protect this child?"

God answered, "I will hold this child."

As though the world held no cares and worries, I felt a wave of peace surround me. Putting my doll away, I peacefully went to sleep because God would take care of tomorrow, and I needed to worry about nothing.

I think my father avoided finding out about something he would rather not know. My mother was too busy with the final arrangements for my sister's wedding to have time to push me into making up a story to account for my absence. Although we avoided each other, I was thankful.

The next few days, I spent carefully sifting through and savouring all the experiences I had lived through on that wonderfully blessed day. As I carefully wrapped every detail in strings of gold, I put them in folders and tucked them in the very center drawer of the cabinet in my heart. There, they were safe from all harm. I thanked God for the feeling of peace that accompanied me throughout the week. I snuck out to meet David next Friday, and he had come alone. He said he had decided, for today at least, that was safest for everybody. I laughed. We walked. Life would carry on. At the walky-talky tree, we sat on the lowest spot and made plans. Our plans were immature, but they gave us confidence. I would say nothing about my pregnancy to anyone. David and I would continue learning from each other. As though we had not danced, we would be careful to act appropriately whenever together. When my pregnancy became obvious, David and I would run away. We did not know where and concluded that detail was not important. Our time together, we would just treasure. If we felt strong, we would discuss the meaning of our dance and all that followed it. Otherwise, we planned to play and just enjoy each other's company as though no future existed.

It did not work. Emotionally unstable, I had difficulty concentrating on the world around me. When I sought assistance from Jarrock, I calmed and received amazing lessons. Although I treasured the lessons, I felt I had lost myself. My fear of God grew to astronomical proportions. I really did not like what I knew of the future. It held far too much pain.

Pretending the future was a fairy-tale just made everything appear hopeless. There was no happily ever after. No glory waited in the future. No one ever needs to know about it on Earth. The whole event would be anonymous. My knight in shining armour was destined to pay a terrible price for believing in us. I was just a messenger. I would be empty when the message was delivered. The future was hopeless.

I wanted God to keep the message and let me have a happily ever after fairy-tale. I wanted David forever to be mine. I did not want to give him back. I thought God was cruel and a cheater. When Jarrock said, "Child, you have been blessed. Treasure memories, they are your own," a bucket of guilt poured over me.

True, I could not imagine never having met David. I certainly did not want to give up all my time and experience with him. David had become my life, and I valued my time with him and the Muki and loved them enough to carry my burden. Guilty and selfish, I could not even imagine never having known them. However, I did not want to be alive.

I really could not understand the difference between success and failure. The result, either way, was not pleasant. It certainly was not happy. All about sacrifice, it was a unique kind of love. Our love was a weapon. Because it might even be a wasted effort, David or Jarrock telling me that our sacrifice was for the future hurt me.

The visions I had were terrifying, and I had horrible nightmares. Sometimes I honestly believed Earth was not worth saving. I lived in moods alternating between ecstasy and deep depression.

The first hurdle I had to face was my sister's wedding. My sister was a lot older than me and had moved back east after graduating from university, and I had not seen her for a long time. Unsettled, I did not feel like celebrating. The wedding was in Vancouver and meant that I would not see David for two weeks and was not sure I could survive that long without getting to hold his hand and recharge my survival batteries.

I remember standing in the reception suite feeling totally out of place. I had not met my brother-in-law before the wedding. Overwhelmed with unfamiliar emotions, I felt bombarded with terrifying thoughts. It was not that I wished the newlyweds bad luck or even disapproved of their marriage. I simply felt jealousy and resentment. My sister was the oldest. She got to do everything first. Everything she did was wonderful. She was popular, the prettiest, and the smartest. On top of that, she did everything right. It was not fair. It should be David and I getting married. I did not want anybody calling our child a bastard. I kept reminding myself God had orchestrated, not merely witnessed the creation of the child I carried. That, too, was too terrifying to ponder.

As I do not like being in crowds, especially strangers, feeling claustrophobic, I looked for an escape but could not find anywhere to hide. I wanted this for David and me, but a wedding party would never happen for us. That hurt and crying would not change the truth.

Hating myself for feeling jealous, I tried to refocus. I picked out people, one at a time, and imagined David and I were tracking them. Going through the checklist, I assessed the significance of their outward appearances and the conversations in which they engaged; what I saw and heard shattered my jealousy. With a shudder, I affirmed I would trade nothing for my time with David and the Muki.

However, I concluded there were many very special people in this room and chuckled at all the odd images generated in my thoughts. Some of the older women reminded me of Natthia or Muma Horren. There were even people whose continence reflected the essence of Judge Soronato. Thrilled, I felt the familiar guilt people watching invoked. However, imagining David was here with me, I carried on with satisfaction and mischievous glee. Wanting to be a child, I let go of reason and caution.

Focusing on my brother-in-law, suddenly shocked, I was taken aback as I pictured him as a thief disrupting the continuity of my definition of family. How dare he take my sister away? Who did he think he was? She was my sister. He was upsetting my view of the world. I do not like the ramifications of change. I was crazy. Relationships were supposed to be predictable, stable, and constant. I did not know this person. I laughed as I imagined Mark saying, "David is my friend." Then I pictured Brian. Seriously, he said, "Yeah, Tara, David is my brother." Blushing, I whispered, "Oops."

My thoughts drifted into a daydream. I laughed and then blushed and looked at the floor as a few people stared. Okay, so I am crazy. Who cares? A voice inside my head said, "A lot of people care. You better start caring, too." I went to get a glass of juice. All the way there and back to my spot near the door, I lectured myself about calming down before I got hysterical. I realized I needed time to get a grip on myself. I told myself to gather up the juggling balls. Get them in balance and stop being stupid. Having a nervous breakdown was completely unauthorized. I could not afford the consequences, which could result in an examination by any doctor. Remember what they could find out, I chastised myself.

Slowly sipping on my juice, I told myself I was drinking hot cider in Judge Soronato's office. The Muki calm their emotions by silently sipping on a drink while organizing every minuscule fibre of their existence to focus on a single task.

When my drink was half-finished, I sighed as I admitted once again that the Muki were not a figment of my own imagination. They were not fantasies allowing me to escape reality. The problem was that they were real, and I had to keep them secret. That was the only way to preserve their security. Furthermore, I had to act in a way that maintained my child's security. The Muki could hide at the base. I think they could evacuate quickly if need be. I could fade into the background as the weird little sister, but again, the child that I carried could not. I had to protect him. I began wracking my brain to establish a safe course of action. I did not want to create a scene. This was a special event. If circumstances had been different, I could have invited David to come as my guest. That would have been wonderful. If David had been here, just touching his hand would have calmed all these rampant emotions, and I would have been fine. If I had been at home, I could have sneaked out of the house to meet him.

I shook my head. Taking three deep breaths, I told myself to practice calming techniques, even to count until I could do my duty as a little sister at her big sister's wedding aught perform. After a while, I shrugged. I really did not know what my duty entailed.

This was my sister's day, a celebration, and I wanted to be part of it, supporting their belief in the future she and her groom were embarking on. There must be some lessons the Muki had taught me that would define my function.

I began by smiling. Smiling is usually right in most circumstances. At a happy event, it would certainly be appropriate. As I relaxed, I concluded my approval was required. After all, I wanted my family to approve of David someday. I would want my sisters to say, "Little sister, I can see you love each other. Your future will be bright and golden. I grant prayers for all the best life can offer and a long, happy and exciting future together."

Inwardly crying, I begged God to let me keep David, at least a little longer. Pain throbbed in my soul as I heard an echo of God reminding me that wishing could not change the future but focusing on finding a better and brighter future for us all – God, creation, the Muki, Earth, David, our unborn child, and myself. Choked, I admitted it was a lot for which to pray, knowing that only the right actions for every moment and situation would reflect my image of the future onto reality.

Did I approve of my sister's marriage? I did not know that answer. The teachings of the Muki demanded honesty. I endeavoured to find the answer. I looked for my sister and could not locate her. Continuing to people watch, I searched for evidence of blessing on this event. I permitted game playing and refused to be guilty of spying. I was analyzing the event as a cultural judge. After all, I was officially Muki. In a way, it was my duty to prove there were blessings on my sister's future. Her safety was my business because she was family.

Very quietly under my breath, I whispered, "Jarrock, may I please look at the blessings around us? I want to approach the gifts of Koe Sai Serena. Just to observe. Can I without shining or anything that will cause trouble?"

Blushing in my own embarrassment, I giggled. At that moment, I wanted to have power. I wondered if I was sinning. Was my request using the gifts for my own purposes? I hoped not but figured I was sinning big time. I shook and apologized for my arrogance and vanity, with rampant emotions welling up again.

I am nothing. I know I am nothing. I do not even know why I am Muki. Sometimes, I do not even know what being Muki means. It is too scary and serious. Realizing I did not want any power, I said, "I did not mean to ask. Please erase that thought. I must be powerless. Let me out of here. I am insane. Help me."

Jarrock said, "Calm down. Close your eyes. Open them when you are ready to see them. Be still. Touch nothing."

Although I calmed immediately, I was afraid to open my eyes. I heard laughter, smiled, felt a tingling in my hand, lost my fear, and opened my eyes, knowing I was walking with God. Deaf, I could hear nothing. The room was all blurry, and I felt disconnected. As I looked around, strange flashes of light bounced off blobs wavering in front of me, and my eyes started to water. Blinking them, I worried that I had embarked on a dangerous journey. (Being childish always got me in trouble.) Like a child in a toy store, I knew not where to look and began hearing myself arguing about what I wanted to see.

Delightfully, I figured it out. Before me were threads of the Lines of Infinity which were ripe for exploring. Closing my eyes again, I pictured my brother-in-law. I saw him in my mind's eye. I opened my eyes again. Scanning the room, a tunnel opened in front of me, and I focused on him talking to someone across the room. This was cool. Although everyone else remained out of focus, I could see him clearly. However, I did not see the point in what I was doing. Now, what do I do? My eyes hurt. I closed them, and an odd film started to play in my head.

There was a hollow wall, and a person, dressed in a black suit with a big brown leather apron on top of it, was seriously working on the inside of the wall. There was a whole bunch of tools in the pockets of the apron. Meticulously inspecting the wall, adjusting here and there. I tried to figure out whether he was building or dismantling the wall. Would it make sense to say he was doing both? Yes, I think he was. He was very confident and serious about what he was doing. Delighted, watching him made me smile.

Quite suddenly, there were sounds near the top of the wall. The man looked. He shook his head then resumed working. The sound occurred again, but this time it was behind him. Making some quick adjustments, he climbed the wall and looked around. Returning to his work, he walked back and forth, picked up a different tool, and redid parts of the wall. Sometimes it was easy to see that he was pleased to have the interruptions. Appearing to affect the pace and style of his work, it was as though the outside disturbance influenced his mood. This sequence continued. If it remained quiet for a long time, he stopped and listened. In anticipation of the sound, he climbed the wall and looked around or made big changes in the texture of his work while scanning the wall. If he ignored the sound, a blur came over the wall and made some change, like polishing a section, turning a block, or messing with the tools. His reaction was a bit unpredictable. Sometimes he frantically undid the change, and other times he admired it and carefully polished it. Occasionally, he chased after the blur. It was like a dance. Making me smile and laugh, I liked the vision.

As though the film was receding into the distance, I heard more sounds and gained more awareness of the room and activity around me, and soon recognized my sister's laugh. Seeing her peer over the top of the wall and remembering what a tease my sister was, I thought, poor guy, as I recognized her husband as the man in the wall, "You do not have a chance. She will have you wrapped around her finger, and you will not know whether you are coming or going." Yet, the same would be true for my sister. She would have to follow his rules. Their life would proceed according to plan. All deviation would be subtle. The relationship was solid and correct.

I looked at the wall. Long and narrow, it stayed on a very clear path. Realization hit me. They are both eldest children. Made for each other, they would be successful. They would give each other freedom but remain solidly a couple. It was a neat film.

I hoped it was more than my imagination. Regardless of whether it had any real meaning, it spoke loudly to me. Moreover, without any doubt, I concluded I approved. As I looked down the tunnel, the wall disappeared. The newlyweds were standing together at the end. It seemed so perfect that I felt blessings. I honestly wished them all the best for a long joyful future without jealousy or resentment.

Satisfied that I had fulfilled my duty as a sister, I wondered what else I should do and then focused on other individuals and watched various short films. Although I wondered if I was being rude or snoopy, I did not think I was prying into the personal lives of the people around me.

I thought the films were like intuition or first impressions and was only guessing at their meaning. The gifts of Koe Sai Serena were like a set of tools to see the world differently. Often, I thought they opened doors to hallucination. In a sense, I thought they gave me freedom but never seriously tried to lift and wield them. Doing so was unthinkable.

It might sound strange, but I strongly resisted anything with the potential of extending involvement in any further schemes of God. Call it terror or cowardice, but all I sought from God was comfort. Thankfully, God delivered on every request for peace and freely handed blessings out to me. Chuckling, I said, "Natthia is right. Slavery does have its advantages." God laughed along with me. I was fortunate, not condemned.

Some films were comforting and enjoyable, and I let them play. Others I had no interest in pursuing. Having no idea what it all meant, I decided to enjoy myself and would ask David to explain their meanings when we next met. My only understanding was that there were patterns to the films. The kind of activity correlated with what I knew of the person's position within siblings. The eldest children tended to work on or in walls. The walls were straight and blunt. The youngest children tended to work around their walls as though they had more leeway than elder children. Their walls had more curves and were neither as straight nor uniform as those of oldest siblings. Whether born first, last, or in the middle, the fabric of one's line of infinity visually identified it.

For the first time, some of David's lessons about the Lines of Infinity started to make some sense. I was the youngest and found reflection in the lines of other youngest children appealing as though somehow, we shared a kindred soul. Delighted, I thanked Jarrock for this lesson. Just as David told me, I now understood souls were dynamic. They did change and adapt. I found that fact comforting.

Soon everyone left, and I escaped into sleep. Sighing, I took comfort in having survived another day. Only two more, and I would be able to refill my batteries by holding David's hand.

I admit I struggled with saying goodbye to David every time he left, but I also had memorable events. One evening we had made plans to go for a hike with Brian and Mark. Forgetting that my parents were hosting a duplicate bridge game, I had agreed to meet them. It was the first time that I could not escape. When the time for our rendezvous came and went, I still was in my room, sitting on my bed crying. Noticing irregular and unusual shadows on the wall, I looked out my window. The tree was waving and shaking very unnaturally. Leaning closer to the window, I glanced around, searching for the cause below, and David waved to me. I laughed as he signalled for me to join him. As it only had shutters, my window did not open. After signalling hopelessness, I got an idea, opened the shudder, and carefully pulled out the winter insulation. Although it was a struggle, I managed to get the screen to move. Hoping I was skinny enough to get through the small opening, I yanked until the screen slipped into my room. Although it was heavy, I managed to put it on the floor without dropping it. The boys laughed as I struggled to squeeze myself through. I kept telling them to be quiet. Luckily, my brother was not home. His window was right under mine, and he would have seen us. Mark tried to take my foot by climbing on the fence at the end of the house and leaning over, but he could not reach me. I did not want to scratch the stucco off with my feet. If I slid down the wall, I knew it would scratch something terrific. Finally, Brian stood on Mark's shoulder. With David helping them maintain balance, I lowered myself out the window until hanging by my fingertips. Leaning on the wall, Brian hung onto my legs and helped me slide down the wall. Just as I predicted, the stucco had scratched my arms and hands.

In the light of the streetlight, I examined the stucco but, thankfully, I saw no obvious damage. I said, "You would not happen to have that track remover along with you, do you?"

They shook their heads and laughed. David said, "How am I going to get you back in there?" David would not leave until we had a couple of options worked out. We could not get a ladder out without making too much noise. They figured they could use the stilts to lever me up. Failing that, we would make a human pyramid. I made David angry, laughing at his seriousness. My worry was not so much getting to the window. It was being able to manoeuvre to get through it. I went through contortions to get out. However, I kept my mouth shut.

We went on a gorgeous hike in the moonlight, and it was wonderful to have all of us together again as I had missed seeing Brian and Mark. All too soon, our time was up. David wanted me safe inside before the bridge party ended. Sharing many laughs, we used the stilts to lever me up to the window. Although very wobbly, they managed to get me high enough to slip a leg into the shutter opening. Using the stilts for support, I discovered it was easier to get in than it had been to get out. However, David vowed never to let me come out that way again. I guess the near falls had scared him. I had merely assumed they would not let me fall and had trusted them implicitly.

Perhaps preoccupied, my mother did not say a thing, but I was sure she knew I had snuck out through the window. I double and triple-checked both inside and out but saw no evidence that would give my secret away. My grandmother was coming to live with us and could not handle the stairs anymore, so my mom asked me to move to the basement. Delighted, I could not have been happier. Wondering if God had something to do with it, I could not wait to tell David.

After everyone went to bed on future outings, I would get up and unlatch the basement door. David would come in, lay beside me for hours before, near dawn, he would leave, and I would close the door behind him. He used to bring one of those poles, used for removing tracks, with him. If it snowed, he could get rid of his footsteps. Thankfully, we never got caught. We did have a narrow escape, though.

One night, my mother came down to tuck me in. She did not often do that anymore, but she must have thought I needed loving that night. David always folded his clothes neatly in a pile and set them out of sight in my closet. When the light turned on in the basement, David moved incredibly fast. He slipped off the bed, smoothed the blankets, and tucked himself under the bed before my mom reached the bottom of the stairs. He even reached up and flipped the pillow. I felt very guilty.

Mom looked around suspiciously before she sat on the bed beside me. She stared at me and ran her fingers along the edge of my face. I felt incredibly loved but ashamed of my deception and worried she would notice David. I assured her that everything was all right. She stayed a while longer and then kissed my cheek and left. I do not think I had succeeded in setting her mind at ease. She was worried about me.

Neither David nor I moved for a long time. We listened to the grandfather clock ticking in the room above us. I joined David under the bed. Then, he dressed and left. I cleaned all the cobwebs and dust bunnies out before going back to sleep. Poor David, he had been really squished under my bed. In fact, if mom had walked around the bed, she would have seen him because most of him were not even under it.

I shuttered, thinking what might have happened if she had discovered the truth. David and I would have made a run for it.

After that, David did not stay nearly as long as I would have liked. Those hours beside David were special. We rarely talked unless I was alone in the house, which did not happen nearly often enough. We just held each other.

Thinking back to those months, I know God was blessing us.

There were moments of peace and many blessings to remember. I do treasure them. Feeling privileged, I spent more time thanking God than blaming him for my fears and guilt. I avoided thinking of the future.

David stopped being completely possessive, and relationships with Mark and Brian became relaxed and friendly again. I felt I had three friends. They were true friends. The kind of friendship that lasts a lifetime formed between us all. They were all that mattered in the world. I missed going to the base. Other than that, I thought life, under the circumstances, was good. I did not feel pregnant. There was no evidence that I was when I stood naked in front of a mirror. It was easy to tell myself the child was imaginary when I was awake.

When I was asleep, it was another matter entirely. I had recurring nightmares. I would be giving birth in a hospital. Delivering him, the doctor would turn him over to put him on my belly. Rather than cry like an ordinary baby, he would suddenly blaze with bright light, blinding everyone. The doctor dropped him, and he fell onto the floor. The light would go out, and I saw him twitching in a tiny pool of blood. I choked and woke up.

In another nightmare, authorities took him to a big children's hospital and subjected him to scary tests while they interrogated me. He screamed in pain. Sometimes he shone in the unmistakable terror of blue steel. They let me cradle him in attempts to calm him, and he was so dark I thought he had turned to ebony. I tried to escape with him, but there was nowhere to go. My milk would not let down. They gave me a needle as I became hysterical, and I lost consciousness yelling "No." I would wake up in bed frantic. I would lay awake shaking for hours.

In the third nightmare that haunted my nights, the church demanded the right to raise him. They insisted he was the second coming, and they didn't believe me that his father was human but alien. He was not holy, I said over and over. He only had the gifts of Koe Sai Serena. Men in white uniforms would put me in a straight jacket and lead me away. Kept in a cell, visions flashed before me. My son hid in a corner, rocking back and forth, crying. He neither talked nor socialized. His eyes looked hollow. Accusingly, he glared at me, saying, "How could you do this to me? Why do you not love me?" I knew he wanted me to release him. I would picture picking up an arrow and a quiver with three arrows. I would awake, gasping in tears.

When David was beside me, he rubbed my back and shared my tears. We developed a soft bluish glow, and Jarrock reminded me of his promise to hold this child. Defiant, I rubbed my belly gently, promising to protect him somehow. If David was not there, Jarrock remained silent, but my room filled with soft golden flickers of light. Oblivious to all else and knowing I was loved, I remembered nothing of the rest of the night.

David never tried to convince me that God had a good plan. He just loved me with his whole soul. I could not have loved him more. With every ounce of my being, I wanted to defy God, prove him wrong, and keep our baby and David safe and alive. Sometimes, I yelled at God, calling Him names and refusing to grant recognition of His wisdom and affirmation of His power. Often, I told God that He was a figment of my imagination and no more real than the mythical gods of the past. While God soothed me, I felt the weight of my guilt and blasphemy and promised to repent and try harder to understand. Supported by David and the Muki, I filled with guilt and struggled to find the strength to carry on and bare my responsibilities with grace, honour, and fortitude.

Destiny is absolute and inescapable. One day, not feeling very well, I looked forward to seeing David after gym. I landed wrong on the uneven parallel bars, and it really hurt. I told my instructor I would be fine, and that it was just cramps, but I left class early and slowly walked home. Seeing David made me feel better even though he looked so worried. I tried to laugh it off and told him I thought it was time to stop going to gym. David insisted on staying with me. Telling my mom that I had cramps and was not hungry, I went downstairs. After letting David through the basement door, we sat on my bed. David tucked me in and rocked me until I fell asleep before he snuck out the door.

I felt better in the morning. Instead of a walk, we went for a drive on Saturday. Only Brian accompanied us. Although they treated me as though I was about to break, I felt loved and worked to cheer them up. That was the first time I realized David was afraid of the future. Furthermore, so was Brian. David asked me if he could give me a device to summon him. Brian went pale. I searched their eyes. David was obviously sincere but also extremely nervous. Brian looked torn. I thought half of him wanted me to nod, but his eyes said it was not safe. Therefore, I refused to let David give me anything. I was inquisitive, though, and sure I would have liked it, would have loved to be privy to a bit of their technology.

Before he took me home, David had me promise to go to the tree on the edge of the cliff at the top of Vaughan Street if I wanted him for anything at all. He said he or someone else would always be there. Someone would be watching for me at the corner near our old house on Wilson Street during school hours. With tears in his eyes, David said, "Do not ever feel alone or afraid, Littl'un. I will be available if you need me."

"I am okay, David. I feel better. Really, I do. Thank you. I'll remember."

Honestly, I did feel better. I got tired easily, but that was the only change I noticed until the middle of the next week when I tried to put on my favourite jeans. I could not do them up. I gave up when even lying on my bed and sucking my stomach as flat as possible did not help. Crying, I put on a different pair that I did not like because they were too big and was shocked that they were now tight.

Cleaning my room, I wondered whether I should pack anything but decided I should not do that because it would prove I had run away. I needed to create an illusion that would set my parents' minds at ease because I neither wanted them to worry nor look for me. I sat on my bed with a notebook and pencil and tried to figure out how I could say goodbye without saying it. It was a difficult twenty minutes of staring at a blank page. When I arrived at school, I was late and daydreamed the day away while looking forward to Friday. Confident David would have a plan. Although frightened, I was pleased that my parents were going out of town on a business trip. I could miss gym and maybe not even go home. Yet, if David wanted me to get anything, the house would be empty, and I could easily take him there. I cleaned out my school locker before going home.

I could not get comfortable on Thursday evening. I thought I had the flu. I had diarrhea and threw up. I said goodbye to my folks early in the morning on Friday. Waving as they drove away, I figured it was just nerves. I decided I had time to have a bath before school. It was a good idea. I felt much better afterwards. I even ate breakfast. As going to school would help pass the time until meeting David, I went.

As the day progressed, I got more and more uncomfortable. I had cramps. I was miserable. I left school at lunchtime and headed over to Wilson Street, hoping David would be there. I was disappointed when I did not see him when I got to the corner. I sat under the tree in front of the house my father had built and cried. David came up to me and said, "Hi, little girl. Do I know you? Are you alright?"

Despite how awful I felt, I laughed. I said, "I sure hope so. I am sick. I need your help desperately." David offered me his hand, and we walked up the road to where he parked his truck. We headed out of town.

Brian and Mark had always told me that David drove like a maniac. I did not believe them. When I was in the truck, David had always been a model driver, except on the day we danced. When we had gone snowmobiling, David had always been the first to arrive at our meeting spot, but we were always at the end of the line after I climbed on behind him. He used to tease me that I slowed him down. David was going too fast now.

"I am not that sick, David. Where are we going?"

"I am taking you to Natthia."

"You cannot, David. I will not go to camp. It is not safe for us. You know we cannot go there."

"You need Natthia, Tara. She is a doctor."

I had such a bad cramp I could not answer. I cried.

It did not take very long to get to camp. David carried me into my room. I was surprised that my brown dress was still in the closet. Smiling, I felt at home. Brian and Mark had walked in front of us with arrows pulled taught across their bows. Doug and Loren had followed us, also armed. David sent for Natthia and instructed Brian and Mark to maintain guard duty at the door. David helped me undress and tucked me under a comforter on my bed. I laughed. "I guess I will sleep here in my bed tonight."

David laughed, but it was a strained odd sound. I apologized. David sang to me after telling me to rest. Finally, comfortable, I relaxed completely. I slept the rest of the day, but I did not let go of David's hand.

When I woke up, David and I talked. Natthia examined me, and no amount of shaking my head changed the fact that I would lose the baby. I hugged David as the cramps returned with a vengeance. Natthia had brought a narrow bed into the room. After I had thrown up and said I was desperate to use the bathroom early in the morning, David helped me up onto it. It had stirrups for my feet. I cried and shook. Natthia brought me warm blankets. I tried to be brave. David delivered our son. He did not cry. As small as a kitten, he fit in the palm of my hand. I looked at him, realizing he was not ready to be born. To this day, I will swear that I saw him move. Surrounded by a heavenly golden haze, I felt loved and safe. A split second later, I screamed at Natthia to take him away. "Protect him, Natthia," I yelled. While Natthia took him, I cried in David's arms, whispering, "I want to remember him alive, David. Can Natthia keep him alive for us? The Muki can do things, David. Please ask Natthia to take him to the sky."

David delivered the placenta, checked my vital signs, and wrapped me up in a warm sheet. He took me to my bed and lay down with me. Delirious, I kept muttering, "His eyes are golden ebony, David. He is the future." I soon stopped shivering and snuggled against David. I slept knowing I was held in the arms of the most precious gift in the universe. David shone. I recognized him as love personified. Before I closed my eyes, I carefully wiped the tears off his face. Aloud, I prayed, "Jarrock, please let me keep him for just a little longer. I really need him."

I woke up when the sun shone across my bed. I lay on David's chest, listening to his heartbeat until he woke up. Muma Horren brought me a drink. It tasted awful, but she insisted I drink it all before she left. David and I had a shower together. We danced in my room, wet and naked, but we acted appropriately. Neither of us was thinking about sex. We were just silently storing each other in the golden cabinets within our hearts. David asked Brian to bring his sacred chest, and we celebrated a thanksgiving ritual.

At the end of the ritual, we both shone. In delight, I danced around David, barely touching him. The visions, sights, and sounds created by our lights contrasting each other were holy. Having incredible hallucinations, I watched while we relinquished our existence to God. No longer separate, David and I belonged wholly to each other because our ebony child had tied us together. We were boundless but firmly anchored to the future. Realizing the child was a gift, I felt only gratitude for the privilege of having been able to serve God in doing my part in a scheme I could not comprehend. I did not think of our child as dead but rather as a promise, and I felt blessed and thankful instead of regret and sadness. For some unexplainable reason, I felt calm and at peace with a firm conviction that our child was safe and secure in the arms of God, while it was David who required my thought and attention. Seriously and sincerely, I carefully gathered my light and spread it all over David. He stood like a statue while I did so. With the last wisp of my light, I wiped away the tears on his cheeks. We worshipped.

Muma Horren knocked on the door. David opened the door a crack. Muma Horren told David that Judge Soronato wanted to see me in his office. After nodding, David closed the door. With tears rolling down his cheeks, he stood hugging me but said nothing. He just cried in my arms for a long time before he fetched my brown dress from the closet and helped me put it on.

Trying to raise his spirits, as he struggled with braiding the sleeves, I said, "Natthia has always helped me dress, David. Ask her to help."

David choked and pulled me close. I backed away from him with shock, realizing Natthia was gone, shaking my head. As I panicked and cried, David held me tight. I told him I was taking the dress off because I did not want to wear it and would not be Muki. I screamed that nothing was fair. David stepped back, held my head firmly in his hands, and, clearly ordering me, commanded, "Tara. Be silent."

He said it with such authority that I froze immediately.

"This is your castle. You made it so. You will wear this dress. You owe the Judge this courtesy. Do your duty. Now let me help you braid your sleeves. Be patient. I have never dressed a woman before."

"I should be able to do it myself."

"You have not sufficient practice. I have two hands to use. It is easier to let me do it for you."

"I owe it to Natthia to at least try."

"Please grant me this honour, Tara."

His eyes begged me not to be defiant. I stood against David, closed my eyes, and entered heaven. David was not merely braiding panels of cloth. He was shaping me because I was his mud. Although it sounds odd, my dress symbolized the water necessary to make me malleable. Like the glass of water that I had handed to him seemingly ages ago, with every touch, I felt a fountain of love pour into every crevice of my being and gained affirmation that I was alive.

Savouring our intimacy, we stood in my room, listening to each other breathe. I will swear our hearts beat together as one. A knock on the door broke the moment. I instinctively stepped in front of David. Holding him behind me with one hand, I opened the door with my other. Brian stared at me. Turning several shades of red, he took my hand, saying, "Tara, you are beautiful. Thank you for granting this expedition success. I shall treasure the lessons you have given me. You are a true friend. I have brought clothes for my brother. Here." Brian pushed a bundle of clothes into my arms and pulled the door shut.

David reached to take them from me but I smiled, and clung to them tightly. "No, David," I said, "Let me dress you. I have never dressed a man."

Whispering, "I love you," David nodded.

I chose the paisley shirt from the bundle. It felt like silk. It was mostly pale blues, but it had some darker blues and a little bit of green and gold. I found a nondescript creamy tunic that felt soft and light. I decided against tights. His belt was black. I dressed David with all the tenderness I could muster. As I wrapped the laces of his sandals around his calf, I marvelled at the smoothness of his skin. Because he had no hair follicles other than on his head, his skin felt like an infant's skin. With tears welling in my eyes, I thought he was more human than me. He was innocent. After hugging him, I stood back to admire him, and I did not want to leave the room.

Taking his hand to head out the door, I was surprised at his resistance. Without moving, I looked at him. He said, "I will wait for you here. I have no authorization. I cannot accompany you this time."

I hugged him again, kissed his cheek, and tentatively opened the door.

Brian and Mark looked past me at David and made comments that made me laugh. Mark said, "You are dressed very appropriately, David. You look good."

Brian nodded. Then he looked at me.

I ordered, "Guard him."

Mark pulled the door shut, raised his bow, and he and Brian stood guard. Seeing power and authority emanating from every particle of their beings, I wondered if they would let me back into my room but felt assured of David's safety. An ominous echo accompanied my footsteps while I walked directly to Judge Soronato's office. Feeling alien, I reached for the doorknob and instantly realized I was neither an Earthling nor Muki. I belonged in neither world, and opening this door would slam the door to the Muki. I was nothing and no longer existed.

37

BEFORE THE JUDGE

WHEN I WALKED INTO THE room, Judge Soronato rose and put his arms around me. I hugged him back. The air was thick with agony, and the pain was overwhelming while I debated the merits of both running back out that door as fast as I could and stamping my foot to banish the pain from the room. I could not run because the man clinging to me forbade it.

I took deep breaths. Stepping back from the Judge while maintaining a firm hold on his hands, I stamped my foot as hard as I could. The sound broke the silence. The Judge and I gazed deeply into each other's eyes. Letting go of his hands, I raised mine above me, sincerely hoping to open the sky above us and touch heaven. Without breaking eye contact, the Judge also raised his arms as I went as high as I could onto my tiptoes before lowering my arms, twisting them around so that my palms faced upward. Lights danced around us as we tilted our heads back and lost eye contact. I closed my eyes and waited for the golden light of God to flow through my heart. Eyes open. Smoothly, we brought our arms down and forward until they stretched in front of us. We bent our elbows to bring our palms before our eyes while straightening our necks to look at each other again. Carefully turning our palms upward, we pushed the heavy weight of sorrow up to the sky. I could feel it rising. It swirled in the lights like a helix of stars getting wider as it blended into the heavens. Bringing our palms together, the Judge wrapped his fingers around mine. I felt incredibly peaceful.

Putting his arms around me once more, the Judge smiled. "Oh, our precious little Tara of Earth, I thank you. Let us sit awhile. I shall make an urn of cider."

I sat and watched him prepare the urn. Oozing respect for all things, every movement, every pause was symbolic. I loved how the Muki conducted their lives. They displayed their sincerity in all they did. When they returned to the sky, I would miss them dreadfully and hoped they would leave a little of heaven behind them. For, if anything was certain, this base was part of heaven. Being here was a great privilege.

I enjoyed the comfort of the liberty of sipping cider in silence. It was good simply to absorb the tranquility of sharing space with another human being. People on Earth do not, as a rule, conduct themselves in a manner allowing such luxury. We tend to fill in the silence with needless but copious rhetoric. I found the peace and tranquility far more rewarding.

An incredible amount of intimate communication takes place listening to the beating of another's heart. When engaged in conversation, one tends to miss expressions and small habits that speak volumes. Patience expands the comfort zone and opens the door to understanding. Thoughts float through the air, and eventually, one discovers they are in harmony with another. In my opinion, such action nourishes the soul. Sitting across the table from a powerful man, I felt blessed. Surrounded by love, acceptance, and peace, I wanted the urn to never empty. I could spend eternity basking in these moments.

As demanded by the laws of God, the urn did empty. The Judge rose, cleared away the urn and our mugs. He returned to the table and sat beside me rather than across from me. He held my hand and spoke calmly and honestly.

"Tara, I want you to know how honoured I am to have made your acquaintance. Unwavering, you have carried out your responsibilities with fortitude, determination, and wisdom. Thrust into situations far beyond comprehension, you rose to every challenge and surpassed expectations of us all. Congratulations on a job well done, child.

In the coming months, you will begin to reap the results of your efforts. I wish to discuss some events waiting on the horizon and touch on those which have occurred today. In my experience, well-seasoned Cultural Judges would ordinarily have been granted the work you and David have undertaken. Only God knows why She chose you two rookies. Often the fallout of our work has a greater impact on our souls. Our spirits can sing praise and feel the righteousness of all that God asks of us. Our souls, however, can flounder in shock and incomprehension.

David has the training to help him cope with the meaning of all that had occurred on this expedition, and I believe he understood what he was volunteering for before he applied to be part of my team. You, though Tara, appear to have been dragged into universal events unwillingly and without any forewarning of consequences. Please accept my offer to assist you in coming to grips with the path you have set us upon. I am willing to play any role you require."

"Thank you, Sir. I appreciate your offer. I feel as though I can close my eyes and avoid the world as though it does not exist. While Jarrock holds me, my mind will remain blank. When I try to sort out events and feelings, I quickly get overwhelmed and too terrified to accomplish anything. However, things continue to happen. Lost and without any control, there is only pain around me.

"Our time together this morning has truly been a blessing. Since I entered your office and stamped my foot, I have been calm and content. Just being here comforts me. Should I begin to think about what is happening, I will crumble into an insane babbling idiot. I am afraid of making things worse and understand nothing. I want to be nothing. I am looking for a hole to crawl into until the end of time."

"Being in your situation is a very difficult place to be, Tara, and I do not envy your position. I have been in such predicaments myself. Isolating events and responses often help."

I reached for the Judge's hand. He laid his hand over mine and rubbed it gently. I concentrated on his facial features. Closing my eyes, I imagined Judge Soronato as my anchor and knew I was safe. He would protect me from my terror but not deceive me. I could trust the Judge.

Barely above a whisper, I uttered, "I don't know where to start."

"That is a very good place to begin. All possibilities retained. From that point, there will arise a beginning."

Laughing, I watched lights dancing in the Judge's eyes. Imagining him being a fairy godfather, I wanted him to touch me with a magic wand. If he did so, I was confident all the balls I was juggling would line up.

"Would you like to share the joke?" asked the Judge with a chuckle in his voice.

He laughed at the image I described to him. "I like that idea. Close your eyes. Imagine my hand is my wand. I shall wave it. When it touches you, one of the balls will land in the palm of your hand. The others I will have sent to the corner of the room. My wand will hold them there, and they will circle in an orbit as I have commanded. Safely trapped, you do not need to worry about them. Ready?"

I nodded.

"I am waving my wand. Without opening your eyes, tell me when all the balls are circling in the wave of my wand."

As the Judge waved his arm about in front of me, I could feel the air moving. Disappointed that his movement did not become a predictable pattern, I imagined him trying to round up my errant juggling balls. I felt a shiver play down my spine. Giggling, I let myself enter the fantasy the Judge had created for me. Watching the balls, I felt the draft of his wand swishing. "Ah, you almost got one!" I uttered in excitement as the fantasy became real, and I ran a commentary as he captured the balls. Gradually, they spun in a pattern above the wand. I knew they were there. In a surprisingly short time, I said, "That is the last one."

With my eyes still held tightly closed, I watched the balls as Judge Soronato took over the commentary as he propelled the balls into a holding pattern in the corner of the room. A huge weight lifted off my chest, as I confirmed all the balls were behaving themselves, as all juggling balls aught behave. I saw a net come out of the end of the wand travelling in the opposite direction of the balls. It created a web with sparks of light, shooting the balls up one at a time as they fell. There was no doubt that every ball was going to stay in line.

I shuddered.

The Judge said, "Talented, aren't I. Are you satisfied they are all under control, Tara?"

Relief resonating in my voice, I stated, "Of course. I work with the best magician in the land. You cannot fail. It is written in the books of magic." I laughed.

"Shall I release one?"

My nervousness returned to haunt me. My finger began twitching.

Noticing immediately, quietly, he whispered, "Just watch them for a bit; see if you can find one that is the right colour."

Thinking about colours, I watched. Excitement filled me as the juggling balls brightened with colour. I marvelled that I had not previously noticed they had any colour. As I pondered how he was influencing my daydream, I wanted to open my eyes to look at him. After all, it was not real.

"Relax. We both know you are fantasizing. There is no magic, Tara. I am not a magician. I am simply paying attention. I have had a lot of practice paying close attention to many people and tasks. You can trust me to stay with you. What color would you like? Tell me when the wand is about to throw it up, and I will send it to you."

Immediately, I knew the ball I wanted. With my voice cracking, I said, "The ebony one, please." Tears formed in my eyes, but I watched an ebony ball circle.

"Do I have the right ball?"

Although I did not answer, my finger twitched.

"Catch it, Tara."

I felt the ebony ball fall into the palm of my hand, and the Judge put his hand firmly over mine. I knew he was holding that ball in my hand. I would not drop it. I was not alone because he was sharing the burden. Letting my tears fall, I leaned on him and let him hold and rock me. I felt so loved. Safe, I wiped my tears with the back of my free hand and opened my eyes.

Lightly tapping my hand, the Judge said, "Listen to the ebony ball. It wants to speak. Give it your voice."

I looked into his eyes. He was sincere. Slowly, I realized he had given me a command and felt shocked. Then words began to crowd into my head, and I began mumbling.

The tapping on my hand slowed. So, did my thoughts. "Did I kill him? Did I shoot a holy arrow? Please, sir, I need to know."

"First, answer my questions. "Where is he?"

"He is at home in heaven with God," I answered with absolute confidence and no hesitation.

"Is he happy?"

I pictured a baby in a cradle rocked by the hand of God. He was peacefully sleeping. Reaching out, I touched him. Filled with awe, I traced his face just I traced my doll at home and remembered how loved I felt when my mother traced the features on my own face. I smiled. Images from my nightmares, with all their pain and horror, broke as though a ripple of wind had dispersed them, as though they were dust from off a mirror. Drawing a single breath, I knew the child was where he belonged and filled with a sense of relief and even gratitude.

"Yes. He is content. Fully accepted, he belongs and feels loved. I love the arms of God, Judge Soronato. I would have gladly stayed every time I have had the privilege of being in His arms. There is no better place to be. I want to be in God's arms."

I was quiet, deep in thought. Judge Soronato offered such security that I had to shake my head to stop a fantasy that he was God. Just for a second, I had thought I was in God's arms. I lifted my head off his shoulder and admitted a strange revelation.

"Judge Soronato, am I jealous of my son?"

"It is human to want to be with God, child. Your turn will come. We are all destined to climb into the arms of God. Moreover, when the time is right, we will do so."

"I saw him move. He was not dead."

"We can never die. Jarrock gave us eternal life."

"I asked Natthia to take him home."

"Yes. She was honoured to do so. Look carefully. Natthia protects him."

I tightened my grip around the Judge. I felt him tense. I knew his pain. I felt a heavy weight descending. I had ordered Natthia to protect him. I sobbed, "Natthia took him home? She is gone." As comprehension filtered through my consciousness, I whispered, "I killed her, too?"

"Natthia waited a long time for today. She was sick and old. Everyone wants to be with God, Tara. Natthia is no different. Thankful to carry out her duty to God, she carried him all the way when your son opened her door into heaven. He will never be lost because she will guide him through eternity. You delighted Natthia, and she loves you."

"But you are hurt."

"It always hurts to be left behind by the ones you love. I will miss her until I meet her again. When it is time for me to go home to God, she will open the door for me."

"You make it sound like I gave them both a gift."

"You did, Tara. You gave your son and Natthia the most precious gift that can be given. More precious than birth, death is the greatest gift of all. Making them whole, you completed them. They are free to experience all that is possible throughout eternity."

Thoughts floated randomly through my consciousness as I settled snugly against his chest. Without conviction, I gave a few thoughts a cursive glance. Fleeting, they avoided capture. I could feel panic welling in the depths of my soul.

Gently, the Judge rocked me. "Have patience, child." Drawing his arm down my back, he said, "Calm."

Closing my eyes and picturing his arms lowering, my panic also lowered. My state settled into a gentle simmer like water boiling in an open pot. I grabbed a thought and held it. Feeling so incredibly loved, how would I survive when the Muki left me behind? I loved the Judge and felt incredibly safe. Letting my fingers slide down his cheek, round his chin, and up the other cheek, I let tears fall.

Before I knew it, defiance welled up like a brick wall. I stiffened as a picture of David formed in my consciousness. Standing and backing toward the door, I yelled, "I will not cooperate. I hate God. I am keeping David. I want him with me. Why can I not go with him? Take me to the sky. David is my life. Let me break the arrow."

The Judge stood. Without condemning my actions, in a matter-of-fact tone, he said, "That would be very selfish of you."

I stared at him. How could he be so calm? Although I tried to get my voice to sound civilized, it was too loud and shaky. "Of course. I'm selfish. I'm human. I seek control. Wanting the world for myself, I strive and search for happiness and fulfillment. I want to watch my son grow up. I want to dance secretly in my room with Natthia. Sitting on my bed beside her, enjoying laughing and giggling about serious and frivolous things, I want it all. I want them beside me: now, today, and for all my tomorrows. It is not fair. And I'm keeping David! I won't let God take him."

"Acknowledge yourself, Tara. Are the tension and defiance making you happy and fulfilled?"

In shock, I glared at him. My mind froze. No words formed. I was blank. I cried again. I shouted, "Then, they were selfish to leave me behind." Ashen, I sat back down.

Wrapping an arm about my shoulder, Judge Soronato sighed, "Perhaps."

"But they are blessed."

"Yes."

"Selfishness is a sin."

"All emotions have two sides. They are bipolar. They are both good and evil."

"I do not understand."

"As you instructed me, Tara of Earth, look to David's first lesson."

I blushed. To exist, all creation had to be broken. If that is so, then what is the point? "Judge," I said, "It does not matter what I do. Regardless of what I do, I will die when it is time for me to do so. I will receive eternal life. Forgiving all my sins and omissions, God will hold me for all of eternity."

"That is true."

"Then what is the point? Why does it matter? Why can I not have David with me throughout my life?"

"You will not forget him. He will be even more precious as a memory."

"That is a horrible thing to say. I do not want him to go."

"Your arrow said otherwise. Think, child. You know the answer to your own questions."

Pondering him and his words, I was quiet for a long time. The Judge went to make another urn of cider.

"It is about the Kingdom of God, isn't it?"

"Yes."

"I have the power to contribute to the coming of the Kingdom of God. The thoughts and ideas I have influence possibility. My actions reflect what is in the Kingdom of God. Everything I do and think opens and closes doors of possibility. It all boils down to what I want the Kingdom to look like."

"Yes, Tara. You have built your own island kingdom to reflect your vision of the Kingdom of God."

"Is that wrong? Natthia said it was wrong. She said I was taking life but not giving it away. I was destroying the Kingdom of God by allowing it to be a fantasy to escape the real world."

"I believe you have begun to give life away, Tara. You have chosen a noble path. By becoming a tool of God, you have offered to fulfill your duty to bring about the Kingdom of God. Your island kingdom is a vision. It is possible to realize it. Keep it before you. Judge every action you take as to its potential to help the island kingdom grow. You asked David to be the grey sentry. Thank him. Appreciate him. Make his sacrifice meaningful.

Insist on doing your part to make the island kingdom grow. Insist that it encompass all of Earth because Earth is an island in God's kingdom.

Do your duty to God. You owe no duty to mankind. However, you will find serving God is the ultimate gift you can offer mankind. Serving God grants us all a future and lets us continue. Following our own will results in extinguishing the light. It amounts to ceasing possibilities for continued existence."

"It won't do any good."

"You do not really believe that, Tara. Your actions have proven I am correct in believing that fact. You may approach God with trepidation and fear, but you are obedient and loyal."

Rubbing the scar on my palm, I refrained from speaking. I remembered my blood shooting out with the surprising strength of each beat of my heart and smiled. I did have power. If I am brave enough, I can give life away. I could serve God. At least, I could occasionally, provided I figured out how.

I lost myself in previous lessons while we drank more cider. I laughed. The mugs of the Muki were so tiny. They sipped cider, relishing every drop. It was not about consuming. It was about savouring. I wanted to savour life. Most assuredly, I wanted to contribute to the growth of the Kingdom of God. Wanting to fulfil my destiny, I craved being in the arms of God. Regardless of the sacrifices, doing and being exactly what God asked of me, would feel righteous. Judge Soronato was proud of me. So were Muma Horren and David. But how did they know I was on the right path? Why did I feel so torn?

While I wondered if I had been thinking aloud, I listened to Judge Soronato answer a question I had not asked aloud.

"When your soul and your spirit are at odds, there is never any doubt that the voice of the spirit is righteous. Beneath the turmoil is peace and goodness. The spirit belongs to God and comprehends far beyond the present. Unencumbered, it lights the path most pleasing to God. The result, as a rule, is greatest when we have chosen the harder path through life. The soul feels the pain and sacrifice of following God. To overcome it and persevere brings peace, thankfulness, and everlasting comfort. Doing what is right remains right eternally. As time progresses, the things our souls have sensed to be good grow brighter and stronger. Time fades what we misinterpret as good and reveals its evil. Only when we walk the path of God are we contributing to the building of the Kingdom of God. All other times, we are, in fact, destroying it. God needs all our obedience.

David is correct. We must all seek the will of God with respect, love, and obedience."

"Judge Soronato, are you here to judge Earth?"

"That is another question to which you already know the answer. Do you wish to hear it?"

I nodded. "Are you going to let loose holy arrows?"

"This is only the sixth judgement. I will observe and present recommendations. I seek evidence of the will of God."

"To whom are your recommendations presented?"

"I will present them to a Panel of Judges recognized as the holiest among us. Through debate, we will seek and carry out the will of God."

"What are you planning to recommend?"

While Judge Soronato paused, he searched my eyes. I waited, afraid of the answer. He wiped a tear as it escaped my eye. In a very quiet whisper, he said, "That depends on you, Tara."

The colour drained out of my face. Shocked, I shook my head and insisted, "I am only a messenger."

"Yes, Tara, you are the messenger. Tell me the message. Has Earth any redeeming features?"

I rose to run. Judge Soronato put his hands on my shoulders and sat me back down. I shook. He handed me a bowl. I threw up, but he helped me wipe my face and brought water to rinse my mouth.

Still, he silently waited while I stared at him, begging him not to make me answer.

Hugging me, he said, "It is a hard question to answer, Tara. You need to find no words. I can hear them clearly in your silence. I see the answer written on your face. I am sorry. Go to David. Let him comfort you."

When I continued to sit like a statue, the Judge rose, went to the door, and opened it. In a loud voice of authority, without emotion, he said, "Dismissed."

That word was so final. As a zombie, I stood. Believing there must be something I could say, I continued to grope for the right words.

"My island kingdom needs time to prove its worth."

"You have had centuries. Read your Books of God."

"God told me to close the book and take His hand."

"Did you?"

"I took David's hands. I held Natthia's hands. I danced with you all, Sir. I danced for the future with Mark. Did you not understand? I debated with you for hours. I tried to redeem Earth. I tried to prove God's blessings were upon Earth. Why do you not believe me?"

"Because, Tara, you do not believe. You cannot make another believe what you do not believe yourself."

"I am nothing. It matters not what I believe. David believes. Believe him. Recognize him."

The Judge sighed. He bowed, smiled, and said, "You are dismissed, Tara."

Reluctantly, I took steps toward him. He stopped me before I walked through the door and, hugging me, said, "I love your fire, Tara. I want you to understand that I want you to succeed. I want desperately to redeem this land. You are a treasure of immeasurable value. God has entrusted you with the gifts of Koe Sai Serena. Lift them and use them to the glory of God. Know that God loves you. Rest with David. This evening, I invite you to witness a Merchairsta. Natthia requested your attendance."

He gave me a loving squeeze and nodded. Worried, I returned to my room. David was working at my desk. He quickly gathered up his things, put them in a briefcase, and handed it to Mark. He offered me another glass of the stuff Muma Horren had given me. I drank it without complaint. Even if it did not taste appealing, it was nourishing. It satisfied not only my hunger but also fed my soul, which desperately needed feeding.

As though inspecting me, David walked around me. Then he wrapped me in his arms, saying, "The Judge terrified you. Do not pay too much attention to what he has told you. He likes to make us too afraid to fail. He hounds me all the time. The standing joke with our team is that the harder the Judge is on you, the more highly he thinks of you. By the looks of you, I will bet you are his favourite Cultural Judge. He loves you. Do not ever lose sight of his belief in you. I will wager he told you the universe rested on your shoulders. It does not. God hands you a task knowing you will succeed. Then God guides you every step of the way, delighting in your tenacity and willingness to achieve unattainable perfection. The more of yourself given to God, the greater is God's pleasure. I will be your grey sentry. I will not let you fail, my Tara."

"You mean I can redeem Earth?"

"His favourite saying is: Redeem this land, Judge David Miskenack. I will hound you until you do."

"He scared me. I fear he is God."

"He is a great judge. In my opinion, he is one of the best. God dwells in him often. He has a theory that terror makes you open the door to invite God to use you, Tara. He will frighten you into God's arms, not to stay, but to act."

"He certainly terrified me."

"I know precisely how you feel. Let's have a rest."

"Tell me about a Merchairsta, David. Judge Soronato invited me to witness one this evening."

"Oh, Tara, it is a ritual funeral pyre. Are you sure you want to attend?"

"Natthia asked that I be invited. She must have wanted me to be there."

David nodded. We undressed and went to bed. I tucked my head against his armpit and listened to his heartbeat. I basked in the safety he radiated, confident he would not let me fail, nor would God. I felt surrounded by God. No. Not God, but God's tools surrounded me. I chuckled. If God needs me, I will be an instrument. After all, David told me, we are the body of God, each singularly and especially when acting together in unity. Humanity is God's slaves. Together, wherever we are in the universe, we will build the Kingdom of God. Only our obedience will guarantee the construction of a kingdom pleasing to God. As David often proclaimed, "Like Jesus is a carpenter, and Jarrock is a mason, we are all builders."

38

HOLY FIRE

WE SLEPT MOST OF THE early afternoon away. After a very serious conversation about safety, David convinced me to go for a walk with him. Despite his assurances, I was worried. Afraid someone would let an arrow fly, I insisted Mark and Brian accompany us. We had a frank discussion about the meaning of being Muki. I listened very carefully.

The Mukis were unfathomable. To be charged with wielding a bow was considered a great honour. Members on expeditions to alien places generally assigned someone to shoot them if they endangered the expedition or proceeded with actions unblessed by God. If God were displeased, regardless of intent or circumstance, automatically, and with no personal control, the one charged with the honour would carry it out. No one would ever accuse them of murder. However, the person would be questioned. If it was demonstrated God's will had been carried out, the person would be considered a hero. This generally meant they shone when the action was reported. In the event where they could provide no evidence, another would likely shine, draw an arrow out of a quiver and shoot the shooter. Not only expedient, the Muki also had total faith in its righteousness. It bothered me. I asked David whom he had charged with his execution.

"It is not polite to ask. What will you do with the information if I tell you?"

"I am just curious, David. I would want to know how that person felt about it."

Mark answered, "It is a great honour to be asked, but it carries a heavy load of responsibility. Requiring judgement, one chooses his best friend to carry out the task of guarding behaviour. When situations are extremely sensitive, a person will choose an enemy to hold the honour in the hopes that it gives him the right incentive to exercise appropriate caution. The objective is to protect the Kingdom of God from our errors. One chooses to ensure maximum security to the future of righteousness, not our own hides.

"Does a person ever ask more than once to perform the honour?"

"Yes. Sometimes, the whole team watches each other. Even you asked Muma Horren, Brian, and me to guard your activities. There were many tense moments, remember?"

"Are you still protecting us, Mark?"

"Of course, I am, Tara. I will continue to do so to the very end."

"Thank you, Mark."

"You are most welcome."

"I want to protect you, too. You will not let me err either, will you?"

"No, Tara. None of us will let you err. Too much rests on your shoulders."

"You had better be quiet now. You are starting to sound like Judge Soronato."

"Why, thank you! That is a very gracious compliment. I am honoured."

I reached to take Mark's hand, but David's response was so immediate and negative that I apologized and moved away. Mark winked and smiled. David scowled. Brian laughed.

I said that some things about the Muki were too confusing. They all laughed.

Tensions rose again as we neared the camp. Most people turned their backs to us as we came close. However, they were not shunning us. They teased David, speaking mostly in their own language, but some said things in English. They pertained to how he was dressed. Some asked where his sword was. Others questioned whether I was carrying a bow. Occasionally, I heard the words "Tara's castle" before the speaker would change languages. David would blush, and although smiling, both Mark and Brian held their bows firmer. I felt better when David and I were back in my room.

David gave me another of those drinks and then sang me to sleep. I think I was emotionally exhausted. He fetched his briefcase and worked while I slept. I hope he ate supper. I was not hungry. There must have been strong medicine in the drink he gave me because I felt like I had eaten well. I was pleased that I was no longer bleeding, had no cramps, and felt physically healthy. Only my breasts were sore.

David kissed me to wake me. The sun was setting, and it was time to go outside to sing praises to God. I always loved to join in their evening activities but was unsure about this occasion because, unlike usual, it seemed frightening and formal. Trying to relax and trust in the reassurance David had offered, I watched for clues from those around me and bravely followed. David took his sword. Even I was armed. The Judge met us at the door to my room. He, too, was armed. Taking my arm, we walked in front of David while Mark and Brian stood on either side of him. Two people I did not know walked behind him. Unarmed, Muma Horren circled us. When we took our seats before the campfire, Muma Horren took my bow and sat across from us.

Everyone put their bow down when Muma Horren laid her bow across her lap. Overwhelmed with a sense of security, I looked around at the crowd of people assembled around the campfire. Their culture was still so alien and incomprehensible. The drums rolled, and I automatically settled in to share in another holy experience among the Muki.

The beat of the drums was like a sword thrusting through your heart. It was agony. There were tears in everyone's eyes. The voices consisted of moans and groans of despair and sorrow. The depth of pain portrayed was very real, and my sobs blended in among the Muki. The campfire dimmed and almost went out.

Muma Horren stood up and lifted two long poles, which looked like bulrushes, and brought them forward, dancing in the shadows of the few flames left in the campfire. I could not help but think of

Native American dances. The movements were blunt and rhythmic. Full of meaning and symbolism, they opened the doors to heaven, and the air became thick with spirits. It was not like a fog or mist. It was just a feeling of other world presences. I felt drafts, tingles, and itches on my flesh. However, they were comforting, not frightening. Muma Horren paused in front of Judge Soronato and me and began tapping the poles on the ground. In response, others stamped or clapped to the beat of the tapping poles. Soon there was a single sound booming all around the circle. Muma Horren stopped tapping and nodded. Stepping back and folding over, she leaned on the vertical poles with outstretched arms, looking both uncomfortable and unnatural. It was scary.

Signalling me to rise, Judge Soronato lifted my elbow. I had had no preparations for this ritual. David told me to pay attention and follow instructions. Other than reassuring me I would do fine and need not fret about it, he refused to say anymore. I stood and mimicked every move of the Judge. We circled Muma Horren stamping our feet to the beat of the thunderous drums and vocals. We fell to the ground and crawled around Muma twice before touching the poles. We crouched and slowly worked our hands up the poles until we were in the same awkward position as Muma Horren. In perfect unison, all sounds ceased. No one moved. Intently watching the Judge, I was afraid of making a mistake. When he raised his head, I followed suit. Muma looked at him, nodded, and he nodded back. Then Muma looked at me and nodded. I nodded back. Muma Horren jumped back and screeched. David leaped up and drew his sword. Muma screeching, leaping backwards, and wavering from side to side continued in staccato bursts of movement. Each movement froze for several seconds. While Muma was frozen, David leapt toward her, thrusting his sword within inches of her chest. Before I heard any other sound, they went around the campfire twice. Then standing halfway between the campfire and us, David raised his sword high above him, swung it, and yelled a blood-curdling howl with his back toward us. A deafening silence fell again and lasted a long time. David sliced the air with his sword in a smooth motion, first one way and then the other. The sound of the sword cutting through the air was powerful and terrifying. Then he swung the sword forward, turned it, and replaced it in its sheath. David and Muma Horren then walked back-to-back in a shuffling reluctant dance to a stack of branches near the start of the trail out of camp. They picked up two more poles like those held by the Judge and me. They separated and handed the poles to someone else in the circle. Both held the poles until, in unison, they lifted and pounded the ground before letting go of the pole. Those who received a pole took it to someone else. They repeated the lift and pound. Then, the two continued to pound the ground with one pound to every fifth step of the other four. The four then returned in the reluctant step of the dance to the pile for more poles. The beat continued. When the four returned to hand another set of poles to more people in the circle, they skipped a pound. They handed them to someone else, and all six went back for more poles. Those who had received a pole passed them to another, and now fourteen went to fetch poles. Both who received the poles and whom they passed the poles onto appeared random. When someone received a pole, he tapped the ground. Pleasing to watch, this repeated in a very orderly fashion. The sound rapidly increased in volume and intensity, filling the air with expectancy. Soon everyone had a pole, the tapping stopped, and there was a hushed silence. The silence was so complete that I was reluctant even to breathe.

Judge Soronato and I dropped our poles down by pushing them over as far as we could before letting go. The bulrush end pointed toward the campfire. The other end stayed by our feet. Alternating to our right and left, the others laid their poles similarly all around the circle. The pace of placement increased, creating an ominous thunderstorm sound. We went to the pile of branches by the trail, picked up a handful of small branches, brought them back to the campfire, and placed them on opposite sides of the campfire as though we would start two more fires next to the one burning. Retrieving our poles, we thrust the bulrush into the fire. They burst into flaming torches. With the torches held before us, we returned to our places in the circle and sat down. Simultaneously, the campfire light went out, while those next to us went for more wood. Gradually building a huge bonfire, each person set their wood onto the fire pile before returning to their seat and sat, tapping a rhythm with their pole. Some returned more than once to the woodpiles, and they each appeared to have a specified but unequal amount of wood to bring. Others supervised the placement of the wood and the erection of a set of poles providing support for two racks. Although loud, the whole process was solemn, sincere, and filled with meaning and symbolism, and I wished I understood and could explain the sense of comfort and security that it evoked. Gesturing for me to stay put, Judge Soronato with David, Brian and three other men left. A group danced. Repeatedly, the drums rolled, then fell silent.

The men returned with Natthia. She lay on a stiff canvas, or leather skin stretched between two long narrow tree trunks. They looked the size of my stilts. The men supported the poles on their shoulders, three on each side. Initially, I was shocked that Natthia was naked but then filled with a feeling that it was incredibly beautiful and symbolic. I remembered Natthia as a holy person: sparkling clean, fresh, and natural. She had no sins to hide behind and her nakedness, even in death, testified that it was so. Her hands lay crossed over her heart, and something was tucked under her hands. Immediately, I knew she held our baby. Pleased there was little light, I tried not to look too closely. Raising the platform on strange, hooked posts, they lifted it above the prepared bonfire and slid the ends of the poles into the racks at either end.

Then they walked back to their places, picked up their poles, and sat down. The drums began beating. Slowly at first, but the tempo increased as everyone took turns dancing and coming before Judge Soronato and me to light his torch. The whole circle looked like a dancing fire by the time everyone had lit a torch.

Again, David drew his sword. He held it before us as we solemnly stepped forward and together thrust our torches into the base of the bonfire. When we returned to our seats, David stood behind us. Holding his sword high above us, David sang. It was a beautiful melody. Although I did not understand a word he sang, I felt it and knew the meaning of the emotion it evoked.

When his song ended, a swoosh sound came from the depths of the fire. Flames erupted on the pyre. Everyone began screaming and dancing except Judge Soronato, David, and me. Throwing them like javelins, they added their torches to the burning blaze. The heat soon drove everyone back to the seats. The material on which Natthia lay appeared to stretch while it melted rather than burned. Encased within it, Natthia and the baby slowly descended into the center trough at the bonfire's top. A moment later, I could see nothing but flames. There was nothing gross. I did not see a single flame touch their bodies. The fire was beautiful, warm, and oddly peaceful. Soon all the torches were within the bonfire, and the dancers were merely moving shadows before the fire, as though echoing memories of the dead. Dancers with rakes or hoes kept lifting burning material from the edges and putting it onto the center of the fire. Even their movements were part of the dance. They signalled a calm matched by the sounds emitted by the drums, which gradually slowed and emanated peacefulness.

Then, like new life awakening, the beat of the drums became full of life. Even the dances became lively. Soon I could hear laughter. In less than an hour, the campfire had burnt down to look like the campfire I had sat around so many times before. The dances and songs also became familiar. I tried to join the Muki as they sang praises to God.

I looked at David, now seated. His sword was properly sheathed. Taking his hand, we went to my room, changed into normal Earth attire, and left the base. David took me home. We went into my house through the backdoor, walked down the stairs, and went to bed. David stayed with me all night long. I made him breakfast, and we ate at our dining room table. When the grandfather clock struck ten, we went for a walk planning to part again in the early afternoon so that I would be home to greet my parents on their return.

When I kissed David goodbye, I knew that he was safe for the time being anyway. I would not return to the base, but David would continue to come to me. I was still under guard and, therefore, safe on Earth.

It would take me many years to fully appreciate what I had witnessed, but I slowly internalized an appreciation for death as a wonderful and gracious gift to the living. I sincerely believe the Muki philosophy that death renders one whole, and like them, try to live well to die as complete as possible when the time comes. After all, living is about making connections and decreasing the brokenness of creation – uniting and reflecting an ever clearer and more concise image of God.

39

MY VERY OWN CASTLE

THE SUMMER AND FALL OF that year were hard. David and I spent most of our time walking. I missed going to the base and seeing Judge Soronato. My respect for him had grown immensely. Hoping I could learn to be like him, I asked David to teach me how to be observant. From the way David held me, I knew he did not believe he could, but he tried anyway. Conscious of a limited future, he attempted to cram his knowledge of Judge Soronato's lifetime of training into rare teachable moments.

Although there are magical moments in life, there really is not any magic. All magic exists wrapped in coincidence, point of view, and the mood of attitudes. I did yearn for the fairy-tale, very desperately. However, I could not wish our child back to life. Nor could I resurrect Natthia. I caused David immeasurable pain by teaching me how to both let go and hold them close.

Only dreams connected us to our wee baby. The only vision David suggested I hold onto was the moment before I screamed at Natthia to take him. At that moment, I had felt his life.

He was too tiny. His features had been somehow not correct. Recognizing him as a human was not the issue. With a head obviously too big, a non-existent neck, and arms and legs too thin, he seemed out of proportion yet perfect. Although mostly wrapped in wax, his skin was so delicate and transparent that I could see his unopened eyes were truly made of ebony...

Polished ebony, his eyes had reflected the universe. Speaking volumes, those two tiny eyes, far too large for the size of his head, had held a universe full of love. Refusing to believe I imagined his heart beating in the palm of my hand, he wiggled so slightly. It was probably a shudder. I was filled with a sense of his tenderness. I knew he had touched the future. I could almost see his heart beating, but his lungs were too tiny to raise and fall. His color, even through the wax, had turned ebony. Thus, the light of God reached down. In a simmer of gold, the tip of God's hand had touched him.

It was then that I had screamed. That remains the most precious moment. At that moment, I recognized the ebony child as a gift. He was a message.

Without a doubt, that was also an extremely selfish moment. Intuitively, I knew at that moment that he was safe. He was in the hand of his true Mother. My son was Muki and neither an Earthling nor mine.

Having racked my brains and the depth of my soul, I still cannot fathom why I demanded Natthia's life accompany him. I could see the pain I caused David as he guided my observation of those moments. When Natthia took him and left the room so swiftly, I felt a wave of incredible love, while David felt terror. That fact, too, imprinted itself indelibly upon my soul.

Observation stinks. At that moment, I had cheated David when my intention had been to have cheated God. My guilt is so intense that David did not have to teach me to observe the memory closer. Every particle in my soul knew I had traded Natthia for David. Every ounce of David screamed his betrayal. He held me so tightly. Every time we got to that point in my lessons, David would hold me securely as I would try to observe and comprehend that moment. Cruel, I was also forcing him to observe it as well.

Not capable of understanding, I constantly ran away. All I would admit to David, and indeed to myself, was that the implications of that moment were cosmic.

While running, I lost control of all my juggling balls. Filled with questions, I felt the sensation that I was nothing. I had no arms to reach out to the balls and no eyes to see them. Devoid of senses, I would yell in desperation to David, "Find me!"

Surrounding me with his love and presence and ruffling my hair, his eyes brightened with delight as he laughed and emphatically said, "Oh, you are boundless. You are Tara. I always knew your name was Tara."

An unidentifiable voice formed within me. The words were crisp and precise. "I am a messenger. My message has been sent. Thus, I am empty." Only an envelope, I pictured landing in the rubbish bin.

I recalled I was just a box God asked me to build and desperately needed to be recycled. It had been awesome to be full of the will of God. Caught by the ultimate addiction, I wanted to continue being a slave. Overcome with sorrow; I craved becoming filled once more. Although neither loud nor frightening, the voice I heard within me commanded, "Seek God."

God descended while I clung to David, bathing us in soft golden light. Feeling like a drop of rain falling in the moonlight onto the surface of a tranquil ocean, I felt blessed. Indeed, I comprehended David's touch being the touch of God. Intuition told me he was Jarrock. Thus, I needed to see him as Jesus.

I could not. My defiance would rise with full force. Desperate, I wanted to separate David from everything holy. I wanted him to be an alien. As an alien, he could return to the stars, whole and alive, with plenty of time for me to build a spaceship and join him again on the Land of the Butterflies far above me in the sky.

Nevertheless, David was not mine to keep. Even with all the dreams in the world, I could not change that reality.

Hating God, bitterness filled me as my soul cried that it was not fair. Insanity gripped me. Knowing not whether laughter or tears were appropriate, I groped for something intangible while wishing I would land in the sea. If I landed in the moonlight, a wave would initiate and fill me with the light of God and make me whole. Crumbling, I whisper to David, "I must seek God."

Backing away from me, his faith evident, David gave me the look I loved so much and advised, "Worship."

Worship was such a simple word, yet its strength was infinite. Doing so was unattainable because, despite wanting to worship, I could not do so. As when I reached to touch a bow, I felt too dirty. I had to cleanse before I could touch God. Caught in a quandary, my arms would not rise to the sky, and I remained a drop of rain. The ocean I craved and required was both behind and ahead of me. In the word, worship, I observed I could conceive neither present nor direction.

When my lesson ended, we walked in the silence of intense pain, knowing we were one. Another memory needed to be stored in the ebony file holding a child. A child none knew. Although too young for life, his life was infinite with implication and meaning. His sentence was short and absolute. He existed.

Avoidance could not stop the truth of what I observed. David and I had packaged a gift together, but Natthia would deliver it.

Furthermore, there was no guarantee the gift would be received. Where would she take him? To whom would she hand him?

What did he mean?

In solitude, walking or sitting beside David, not touching one another, I repeatedly experienced a vision. I opened my hands, palms upward, preparing to worship, but elbows held firmly against my sides. Looking down at my hands, I understood they were missing something. My left palm did not connect with my right hand because my right palm held a scar. It was just a tiny v in the very center, but it filled me with turmoil. Captivating my gaze, the scar turned into the hole I remember fascinating me when I was just a little girl. Its depth was amazing. I felt it sucked me into the universe. Immense pleasure filled me as I appreciated the significance of the unbroken skin that I knew existed on the top of my hand. Illogically, that pliable, wonderfully stretchable skin at the bottom of the hole proved to my soul that the universe had no end. It was eternal. The dark well within my palm filled with ebony life. Moreover, I perceived being ebony, that it too, was eternal. I would smile in comprehension that the vision was a memory.

Opening the memory while remaining within the vision, I saw

myself in the same position. Captivated by a clot swelling within the hole left by a rusty old nail, I waited to be delighted. My hand became a volcano. Swelling turned my hand into a shapeless blob prior to issuing forth a fountain of lava. Every pulse filled me will ecstasy. A fire of blood streamed and splattered, filling the air with sparkling red-hot ash. The hole in my hand had reflected life.

A calm, absolute thought filled my consciousness. I was alive. Completely, without a doubt, I knew it was true. I watched the volcano erupting so perfectly in rhythm with my beating heart. Reluctantly, recognizing the lava was blood, I pressed my thumb over the hole. Dripping and falling away from me, it was life, taking part of me away with it. Torn, I wanted to both lift my thumb to feel the thrill of experiencing ultimate freedom and holding it pressed firmly to keep fully in control of my existence.

I wanted to give all of myself to God, but my soul screamed there had to be a better way. Time existed. Using it and demanding success, I was arrogant and believed I could create possibility. With the same defiance, I held my thumb over my palm. I determined to take hold of all I knew and put a stopper into the letting of blood.

Feeling God smile, the vision ended. Ashamed, I shrunk in the reality of my own insignificance and powerlessness. I had to let go of David. Yet, without him, I could not succeed. I was only a messenger.

Convinced David was my thumb, and Earth was my palm; I had no hands with which to work. If I let go of David, Earth would bleed, experience Armageddon, and result in the end of the world. If I held onto David, I could not initiate a better way and held stasis, the future would remain unrealized, and existence would cease in its entirety; the Kingdom of God, not just Earth, ends. Without sacrifice, there is no glory. Without change, there could be no growth. Without growth, there is no experience. Without experience, there is no kingdom. Without a kingdom, there is no God. Irreversibly broken, the yearning shatters and collapses.

I cried as I saw David's mud symbols. The turtle had nowhere to hide and nowhere to go. The bird had no wind to support its flight and no hope of finding its egg. The tree withered. Because there was no yearning, all were dead.

Often sharing my bed at night, David comforted me. We left lessons behind, finding thoughts to lighten the day. We clung to faith that there was still time to figure it out. Judge Soronato reassured David that this expedition was only the sixth judgement. He, in turn, reassured me. The ebony child had joined us. We acknowledged time would tear us asunder. We endeavoured to do all necessary to enforce the delivery of the message and the full impact of its meaning to reflect the glory of God.

Judge Soronato guided David. David guided me, and we both concentrated on discovering the right way to enforce the righteous meaning of our friendship. It became clear that it was even more imperative that there be no sin in our relationship. We were friends, ordained by God to be the right kind of friends. Whenever I thought that we should try to create another child and tempted David by dancing for him, he got angry and said goodbye. Likewise, I would run immediately when his actions caused the desire to dance to well up inside me. I would use any weapon attainable to ensure escape. Three things were clear to us both soon after I left the base for the last time.

First, we had already sent our gift. The ebony child was the gift. Our actions would demonstrate his meaning. We wanted it to mean redemption for both our homes. David had condemned his home with a thesis he had written in defence of Earth. I condemned Earth by failing to prove to the Judge that it was blessed and, therefore, redeemable. Having faith in our eventual success, Judge Soronato would continue to hound us until we did succeed because failure was not an option.

Second, we both understood the creation of the child was contrary to universal law. His existence clearly tampered with the Kingdom of God. The Great Books of God held by the Muki were clear. The Muki were under the direction of God as Instruments of Creation. As such, they had the power to wield the gifts of Koe Sai Serena. However, the Panel of the Muki were duty-bound to judge all activity undertaken by individuals and expeditions. Their Judgement needed to confirm to the best of their ability that David and I had used the gifts of Koe Sai Serena righteously for the glory of God, not man. Faith in the ability of the Judgement to stand the test of time required confirmation within the context of known law. The writing of new laws required support from accepted prophesies and faith in following logically from the known laws.

The Muki were humans and, as such, recognized they had the power to abuse the gifts and destroy the coming of the Kingdom of God. Confirmation that David and I had danced according to the will of God was unconfirmed by the Panel. Without the support and approval of the Panel, there would remain a possibility that we found our belief only in the deepest depths of our own souls and our spirit's conviction it was ordained merely fantasy.

The Law was absolute in demanding our deaths. To succeed, we had to die. However, God clearly demanded our survival, actively prohibiting harm from approaching us.

Third, no one likes destruction assignments. The stakes were very high. It was imperative that the evidence of all ten of the required judgements be clear and indisputable. The approval of God was required to be evident, preferably in applicable precedent. If unorthodox, the judgement must logically result from applying acceptable interpretations of known law, albeit novel in approach.

It was the responsibility of Judge Soronato to produce a judgement worthy of presentation to the Panel. Thus far, he was confident God had blessed the actions of David based on recognized and supportable prophecy. Judge Soronato believed all my tales and activities preceding dancing had demonstrated blessings, well-grounded in the standard interpretation of known laws, upon me. The presence of God in granting me the gifts of Koe Sai Serena was obvious, direct, and indisputable. Both prior to dancing and becoming Muki, David and I had clearly received direction through prophecy, also received by other members of the expedition. Although there was no precedent, that I, as Muki, fell under the apron of the Laws of the Muki, followed logically.

The trouble with trying to interpret the meaning of recent events was that David and I were guilty of breaking the law. I had no right to dance neither under the laws of the Muki nor those written in Books of God held by Earth and the laws developed by the country within which I lived. I had no castle. David was unauthorized. God responded by taking the child as expected according to known Law. Natthia, as clearly predicted by prophecy and direct interventions by God died in Tara's place. Only David was unsure of the meaning of Natthia's death. He feared Natthia had died in his own place and was therefore confused about the righteousness of his own existence and feared failing to protect me as commanded by God.

David believed our gift would not reach its destination if he lived. Without both our cultures upholding the righteousness of our deaths were not upheld, Earth would be condemned, and the Judge forced to conclude in favour of destruction.

All agreed the verdict was not clear. Evidence obviously pointed toward destruction, and only David and I could change the verdict. The Judge insisted the verdict was on my shoulders alone because David was the grey sentry, and his duty entailed protecting my island kingdom. I had to prove the island kingdom held the blessings of God and would, in fact, grow to encompass Earth. Other than understanding I had to succeed, I did not know how to prove it. God continued to insist that David was the proof I needed them to recognize.

God permitted none to harm us. The Muki turned their back on David but worked behind the scenes to assist him whenever possible. Everyone wanted the expedition to succeed.

As summer progressed, I saw less and less of David. Always tired and smelling of sawdust, he came to see me for very short visits. We stopped trying to find answers and put our trust in God because God had always opened the path before us at exactly the right time.

I loved David. Treasuring the brief visits, I savoured the smell of sweat on his body, the evidence of grease under his fingernails, and the constant presence of sawdust in his clothing. I was fully confident he, honestly, was the proof demanded by God. I understood the grey sentry. He was alone but full of faith in a bright future. I did not know how he would succeed, but my faith in his success was absolute. David would save Earth. Supporting him by loving him, I needed to do no more.

Early in November, David took me for a drive. We went by logging road and trail to an isolated trail near the Quesnel River canyon. Tucked against the back of an outcrop in thick wild forest terrain, David had built a small cabin.

He picked me up and took me inside. It was beautiful. Every detail spoke of his sincerity and dedication. David had built this cabin for me. Excited, David connected the location, the construction, and the meaning of every detail of the cabin to the places and things I loved and had shared with him. It was his vision of my castle within my island kingdom. Overwhelmed with love for him and the world he created for us, I cried. It was perfect in every way.

I pulled the curtain around a traditional Muki toilet. While I used it, David changed into traditional attire, complete with a sword. I was shocked. "David, you cannot bring evidence of your ancestry out of the base. You know that is illegal and unsafe. You must take it back. The security of the Muki is at stake."

"This is your castle, Tara. You are of Earth. Your land permits freedom to follow your destiny. Your destiny is to be Muki.

You may live as the Muki live. If you will have me, I will be your Sire. Here, together we will plant the seeds to grow the Island Kingdom. I will continue to teach you to mould the mud. We will create the future out of the failures of our ancestors."

Not able to respond, I continued to stare at him. He blushed. "I will change if you ask me to change. I am the grey sentry, and I refuse to fail you."

I watched him change back into his jeans and smelly shirt. He stood barefoot before me and took me in his arms. "I love you. Marry me."

"God has already made us one, David. Yes, I will be your wife. I already am." I clung to David. I wanted to stay in his arms forevermore. With tears streaming down to my face, guilt welled up within me. "God promised there was a time for all things. We must wait, David. God will lead us. If we touch here now, we will become the living dead and destroy both the Muki and Earth. I am no longer Muki because my visions forbid me to worship. I cannot touch the future without worship, and the ebony child will be lost. Natthia will be unable to deliver him. He must belong to both our worlds. Both our worlds must accept him. When they do, God will open heaven, and we shall dance forevermore."

Remaining in each other's arms, we cried, desperately wanting to dance but realizing we could not do so righteously. I needed him to smile and confirm he knew I had spoken truthfully. Wiping my tears, David whispered, "Remember, I will be your Grey Sentry, regardless of all the future God brings. I remain yours. I love you, Tara."

I hugged him. We wiped our tears, and I knew I would fail if I did not immediately run. I stepped back. With all the fire I could muster, I demanded, "Take me home to Quesnel immediately."

David took my hand and led me down the trail in silence, although I dragged my heels. I did not want to go and needed David to make me continue. Every step was agony. Even the sunshine reflecting off the snow could not bring joy into my heart. I needed David. I loved him. I feared I had pushed him away and might not be able to get him back.

I was late getting home but pleased it was a long weekend and promised to see David the next day. Before leaving, he hugged me as though he was saying goodbye and left without speaking. In a panic, I ran after him. He washed my face with snow, kissed my forehead, and said, "Thank you." Then he turned and, humming the Deplukador song, walked down the trail. Content and relieved, I went home.

At bedtime, I unlatched the basement door hoping David

would return in the night to lie beside me. In the early hours of the morning, I awoke from a nightmare in which David had died. Driving too fast, he had slipped on the ice. The truck had rolled, killing David instantly. I lay shaking in bed, listening to the tick of the grandfather clock. The clock chimed midnight. Then it bonged one in the morning. I was anticipating it chiming the hour at two when I heard a tap on my window instead of the chime. Mark and Brian were there. Intuitively knowing David had really died and my nightmare was real, I immediately signed for them to come in the basement door.

Perhaps it was shocking, but I had no tears. When God told me of David's impending arrival, I think I knew his presence was temporary from the beginning. Numbness settled upon me; that was almost relief. No matter how much I loved David and wanted him to stay with me, I felt that I had been living through a hopeless battle to change reality ever since the ebony child's conception. Finally, it was over. Just as David promised, his death opened the door to a future that shone with promise. Mark and Brian's presence woke visions of David's laughter and reassurance that he would remain with me in spirit, and I wanted to express my thankfulness for having the privilege of having known him and the Muki.

Hastily dressing, I went barefoot up the stairs to meet them. The cold hurt my feet as my big toe reminded me of dancing barefoot in the snow. Refusing to cry, I asked Brian and Mark to dance barefoot in the snow with me for David. I said I promised to dance tomorrow on red-hot coals. Tomorrow, I will dance at David's Merchairsta. They made a chair of their arms and carried me into the bushes where David had given me his first lesson. Mark and Brian clapped and hummed while I danced barefoot in the snow for David.

Brian held me while Mark warmed up my feet and promised to pick me up later in the morning. They carried me to the basement stairs. Pulling the door behind them, they told me this was my castle, and they were unauthorized to enter. I burst into tears. With the utmost respect, I turned the latch on the door, stamped my foot as loud as I could, and returned to bed. Unable to think or feel, I slept as though God held me.

40

ONLY A CATALYST

LIFE PLAYS TRICKS ON YOU. I was prepared to join David on the funeral pyre. Nothing in the world made any sense to me. I was in shock and pain. Nothing went right. Remembrance Day should never have been made a holiday. I recall it always being a stressful day.

My father had fought in the Second World War. His tours of duty had cut his soul, and memories were difficult to endure. Remembrance Day is steeped in pride, sorrow, and unbelievable horror. Scenes imprinted so profoundly on my father that my mother tried to escape Remembrance Day. It held sorrows for her as well. War is not pleasant. It remains full of pain for all those old enough to have been there.

When I went to breakfast, my folks announced we were leaving on a driving tour to Alberta that day. We would go to the hot springs at Miette, travelling the new Yellowhead highway from Prince George to McBride, circling back through the Rogers Pass. I did not want to go. Unable to convince them I had made plans; I was the height of the impetuosity of a sullen teenager. Miserable, I sat in the backseat, fuming, and shedding tears.

I missed David's Merchairsta.

The world jarred me. I could not comprehend the joy and excitement relayed over the radio of a football game while memories and events were tearing my world asunder. For the first time in my life, I resented the joy and indifference of the world in which I lived.

I recognized with all my heart and soul that Earth was doomed. Wrapped up in needless rhetoric and fantasy, it was not real.

I had lost the grey sentry; I had failed God and my fellow Earthlings. I was sick.

In the misery of the backseat, I alternatively threw away my juggling balls and searched in a total panic to recover them while feeling terribly lost.

God sent the sunshine into my pain, and Jarrock whispered words of peace and hope. God demanded fortitude. Wiping my tears, I gave myself to my memories of being among the Muki and pledged to do all within my power to live up to the standards and expectations of my island kingdom. I owed success to my ebony child, his father, and my friend, Natthia. Their sacrifice, I would not allow to be in vain. My soul and spirit in harmony would simply not permit it. Having loosed my three arrows for God, God was pleased. Whether I understood why or how was not relevant. God knew what they meant. That was all that would ever matter.

Guilt and deception summarized the last three years of my life. I could share my joys and sorrows with only God. I had erred. All I loved was paying a terrible price. Having taken a life, someday it would be time to give it away. I concentrated on focusing on appreciation and thanksgiving for all my blessings. Without raising my arms, I set my soul free and worshipped my God. Easing my agony, God spoke to me, reminding me that I had sent my message. Confident and faithful in its eventual delivery, time would continue to unfold. With God's blessing and permission, I could rest and play in the fantasies of the real world until hearing my name called across the wind.

Relinquishing my future to Her, God rocked me and soothed my pain, inferring that one day I would understand my lessons and, eventually, know what to do with them. God had blessed me, and I owed my salvation to Jarrock and my duty to Koe Sai Serena. I would not fail because the ebony child would light the way. The grey sentry would stand guard for all of eternity. Natthia would forever sit upon my shoulder, whispering that slavery was the route to incredible freedom. Laughing and full of joy, I would smile and dance. Basking in the dark, I would feel the presence of the Muki. The drums would roll. The reflected light of the heavens would speak to me across the expanse of the universe, ever reminding me I am alive. I would follow the plans David and I dreamed of. Forever touching the future, I would one day pick up some mud, rub it carefully in the palms of my hand and begin to shape the world one grain at a time. I would do it for David, the Muki, and Earth. I would share David's first lesson and initiate change. I was nothing more than a catalyst. I had played a part in setting the stage for tomorrow. Faith told me it was golden.

The next weekend, Brian and Mark picked me up early in the morning and took me to my very own castle. I had never seen so many transporters as there were sitting on the trail. I could not see them well, but I knew they were there. There is a comforting haze surrounding the spots where a transporter is hidden. It whispers to the soul. 'Come! I will take you across time on a film of molybdenite. We will slip, slide, and skip through the universe with a shield of magnetite. Strengthened with the dormant light of scheelite, packed safely in a blanket of living clay and potash, I will give you the future. With the secrets held within my leaden box filled with the power of Deplukador wrapped in tears of gold, I will lead you on a carpet of possibilities. Approach me with caution and a noble heart. Pledge to leash no harm upon the Kingdom. Stand for inspection. I will approve. Come! Carry out your duty with me.'

If I had known how to get the little stick to let me board one, I would have stolen one that day. I would have headed straight up. The thought was comforting. Sighing, I admitted I could not steal anything more from the Muki. I had caused them enough pain. Besides, I had no clue how to make a transporter go or where to find the little stick.

There were many people on the trail as we approached the cabin. I noticed guards with bows held peacefully at their sides. They stepped out on the path to hug me. Hugging them back, I felt blessed. They returned to their duties without a word while we walked past the cabin without pausing or entering through the door. Four or five people carried containers in and out the door as I watched. Others were pacing around the perimeter of the cabin waving odd-looking sticks. Tears fell freely down my cheeks.

Judge Soronato joined Brian, Mark, and I. He took my arm, tapped my fingers, and said, "I am very proud of you, Tara of Earth. Thank you and congratulations for a job well completed."

I cried. Mark and Brian stopped while the Judge comforted me. "Let me hold your juggling balls for you, Tara. I will give them back when you leave."

With gratitude and relief, I closed my eyes and symbolically sent my balls to the waving hand of the Judge. He kissed my cheek and held my hand. The four of us stood by the rushing violence of my favourite river, talking about David and his Merchairsta. I said I wished I had been there.

"Unable to risk you being there, I forbade it, Tara. I had visions of you dancing in flames and climbing onto the platform to lie down beside David. God approved. Our Lady sent you to the mountains to remind you of worship on Snowshoe Plateau."

Smiling, I squeezed the Judge's hand. "Life hurts something awful, Sir. I want to be with David."

"You are, child. David wrapped his soul around yours at your castle. Try to remember the dance. Be calm, breathe deeply, and you will feel his presence."

They stepped back as I stood before the river, while I worshipped. God descended. Satisfied that I remained his mud, I heard David instructing my every move.

A loud grinding noise broke the silence. Looking for the source, I saw the crumbled remains of David's truck. Admitting I could no longer pretend that his death was not real, I choked and ran toward it without knowing what I was thinking or what I would have done if Brian had not restrained me. As the sound of finality crushed my agony, I watched a film in my head. The splash of David's truck landing in the river fell back to Earth. Seated behind the steering wheel and smiling, David revved the motor and headed for the sea.

Clearly, I could see him towing my island kingdom. The river closed over the truck. Reaching down, I lifted a handful of sand, kissed it, and threw it out to David, whispering, "Take me with you, David. I am coming, too!" After an agonizing moment's silence, Brian led me back to Judge Soronato and Mark.

Mark held out David's sacred chest. He said, "Do you want it to float or sink?"

Stunned, I stared at Mark. Tears came to his eyes. I wondered if David had died in the truck. I knew Mark had been charged with protecting the security of the Muki from David should he err. I also knew David had endangered the Muki by building my castle for me. I had wanted to lift Natthia's hands at her Merchairsta to confirm my suspicion that there were three arrow holes on the flesh above her heart. My fear that she held the ebony child under her folded hands had prevented me from the action.

Searching Mark's eyes, I smelled danger. A vision blinded me. With David standing behind me, I was at the base camp, and the target had been set up. Drawing back the bow, I aimed at a child standing stoically in front of the target. My arrow entered his heart. He smiled up at me, faded into a haze of golden sparkles, and understood I had stopped the present. While Natthia stood humming and beckoning me to shoot, I drew another arrow, shot it, and sighed as the child stepped out of the hole in Natthia's chest. With eyes sparkling with delight and innocence, he laughed. Natthia's spirit danced as a fountain of pleasure before echoing the essence of a much younger woman than I remember Natthia being. Happiness welled up within me; I had ended the separation of the heavens. Earth and the Muki were connected. I knew it was so as Natthia's spirit took the child's hand and they stepped to the side together. Following the direction of Natthia's pointing finger, I saw David. He stood so tall and elegant as he worshipped. Then turning, he faced me and nodded. I let the arrow fly, and all was forgiven. The door to the future flew open, and the past was etched in stone. Taking hands, all three stepped into the future. They would wait for me there. It was true because I saw a tendril of their Line of Infinity wrap tightly around my own line. Part of me, they would light my way.

Holding onto a feeling of security, promise, grace, and thankfulness, I stood wishing I could remain in that moment forever. However, Mark waved his hand in front of my face and repeated his question.

Desperately, I grabbed Brian and begged him to explain Mark's request.

"David's ashes are in his sacred chest, Tara. He is the grey sentry. Where do you want him to grow? How fast do you want his roots to spread? Mark needs to know. If you want him anchored here, you should add stones. His journey will be slow, but his roots will be strong and deep. If you wish him to float on the surface, put no rocks inside and seal the lid tightly. He will grow quickly into a vine spreading along the river to dance in the currents and tides of this land."

"I want him to be safe. Which is the safest?"

"It is your island he is shaping, Tara. All paths have benefits and risks. Sinking, he could become stuck and crushed by time. Floating, he could be plucked out of time to disperse on the wind. You must make the decision. No one can do it for you," Brian answered kindly. His pain was evident, but he was putting on a brave face.

Determined not to cry, I stammered, "Spreading ashes is not part of your culture, is it, Brian? You keep them in the castle. Brian, my castle is Earth. No matter where David's ashes go, they will be at home."

As he hugged me, Brian let tears fall. "I offered to take his place, Tara. I would have gladly done so if the Judge and David had permitted it."

"So, would have I, Brian." I nodded to Mark, and he, too, nodded back. We were in this together. It is good to be part of the schemes of God and feels good to contribute even though it is hard to understand our sacrifices. "Brian, I want the Island Kingdom to retain David's strength, but I need the island to grow. It must not grow too fast, or it will produce not much more than shock. However, it cannot be content to stand still and silent like the snag on Beaver Pond. It must be brave enough to move forward, gathering grains of sand along the way. David is already strong, and I want him to be able to dance. He was always too serious and needed some freedom. Please put enough rocks inside the chest to make it touch the bottom as he leaps in the current. He would like that. It was always important for David to keep the ground securely beneath his feet."

Carefully choosing rocks, Mark sought my approval before setting them in the sacred chest. Satisfied, he asked, "Do I leave it unlatched, or shall I close it tightly?"

Without hesitation, I smiled and asked him to leave it loosely latched. "I want David to be able to dance in the moonlight over the river with me, Mark. I want it to be easy for him to find me."

When Mark handed the chest to me, I wanted to keep it. Running my fingers across the top, I thought of all the sacrifices made to have arrived at this spot in the universe. I knew very little about David's family because they were not something he spoke about. However, I understood he was a long way away from home. I thought of my own family and realized I had begun to understand a few things about the Lines of Infinity. There were many sacrifices to create me. Visions came to mind.

The soldier sitting on the narrow bunk in a room lined with bunks. He looked very thoughtful as he wrote a letter. He understood his future. Willingly, but with a certain amount of fear and trepidation, he performed his duty. Coming home was not part of his destiny. I owed my existence to his sacrifice. My mother would have married him rather than my father.

The women looked upon their newborn sons, but neither would watch them grow into adults. Strange rituals of culture would cheat them out of a future. Their sacrifice, too, opened a line of infinity for me. Their husbands remarried my grandmothers so that my parents were born. Even to this spot on the river, I owed my existence. Hanging onto a piece of a broken raft, God had held my own father in His arms here long before I was conceived.

Protecting my ancestors from harm, God set up my future, and even my own existence is an act of God. A broken condom was orchestrated just for me. So many strange visions fill my soul. I am a descendant. My line is long and rough. There are echoes of sacrifice followed down through the years, highlighting experiences filled with a touch of visions of faces attached to my line through memorable events, circumstances, and trauma. With delight, I see the twists tied around my line. They are new and come from far away. My line of infinity has broken off the planet, the solar system, and beyond. I cross the heavens, linked to places unimaginable. With delight, I realize that I belong to the universe.

This box connects me there. Most of the connections are echoes, but the knots are solid and strong. I hold them tightly bound because I shared my soul with the Muki. The ebony child exists and will dance along the line. His echoes will touch all I touch. How satisfying! Ever watching for him, with pleasure, I await the future.

The present is not so easy. There is ice forming here and there in the river. The river roars and thunders. Rocks roll deep in its heart. Fearing it is too rough, I resist setting my precious chest here and search along the river for the perfect spot. My mind hears a voice in the running water, "Just around the bend."

I head there. Brian and Judge Soronato accompany me. Mark stayed staring out at the river. I thought of my pictures of David, which I held in the files of my heart. I watched Mark. Fate had touched him as deeply as it had touched me. With content, I carefully stored the picture of Mark before me beside one of his soulmates.

I loved Mark, too. I hoped this was not goodbye but admitted it might be and took another picture. The way Brian looked at me wrenched my soul. Yes, indeed, he was the little brother. I said a prayer to keep him safe. Picking up a leaf from the ice-cold water, I kissed it and handed it to Brian. Brian bowed and kissed the leaf as well. When he dropped it into the river, we watched it swirl and dance away. Brian took my hand. I stepped into the water, leaned down, and let a treasure go. Brian pulled me out of the water and tried to wring the water out of my jeans. Oddly, I did not even feel cold but numb and full of fleeting and inconsistent emotion as reruns of special moments flashed through my aching soul.

I stepped to Judge Soronato. A tune Natthia used to sing popped up in my mind, and I had to hum it. Putting my arms around him, I felt Natthia awaken within me and realized I had been unaware that she was there. I was delighted. The Judge held me, and I let her hum a song for him. He cried and patted my hands. Aware his touch carried no blame or resentment; I felt loved. When the song ended, he thanked me and begged me to keep Natthia alive in me.

The three of us stood beside the river, making memories until I felt a wave of warm air. It was magical. Turning around to look up the bank and shocked by the brilliant red and yellow flame wall before me, I saw David's cabin was burning. A strange sound escaped my lips as I choked. Brian put his arms around me and held me until there were only embers. I was amazed the cabin could burn that fast. The finality of life hit me hard. It was time to go.

I asked Brian to take me home. As we began walking, the Judge called, "Wait, Tara! I have something for you."

The Judge handed me David's bow and quiver of arrows. There were three arrows in the quiver. I said, "Do you mean to keep or to shoot?"

The Judge laughed. "They are for you to keep, Tara."

"These came from the land in the sky, Sir."

"Yes."

"Did I earn them?"

"Yes."

"Were they David's?"

"Yes."

"Am I Muki?"

"Yes."

"I need to charge a soulmate with protecting the Kingdom of God from my errors. Am I correct?"

"We will be leaving, Tara. It is not necessary. You may keep them."

"No, the friendship and protection of the Muki stretch across the universe without boundary. I may err. I need a friend, a soulmate, to protect the Kingdom of God."

Judge Soronato smiled.

Turning, I sincerely held the precious gift out to him, "Mark, would you please take this bow and quiver? I trust you to stop me if I put any at risk. Please feel justified in your service to God." I hoped Mark would shoot me immediately, but he did not.

He bowed, put on the quiver, and held the bow. "I am honoured. Please take my arm, and I shall escort you home with Brian."

I took his arm. I felt no fear and smelt no danger.

It was going to be hard to live without the Muki.

The Judge walked with us.

41

RECEIVING PROPHECY

THEY DID LEAVE.

Life became one big empty hole. I would not say that I was depressed for, automatically, a memory would arise within me to cheer me up. Often, it was a vision of an opening cabinet. Rising of its own accord, a folder would open like a flower blooming to reveal a treasured moment. I would sigh and feeling ever so blessed, a smile would spread across my face. The cosmic winds of God would stretch out to encompass me. I would look to the future and know it was golden.

Sometimes it was hearing my mother's words echo across time, "This, too, shall pass."

I sometimes lied that I was special beyond and above all others. I would say the privilege of having performed a task for God was worth every single drop of agony. However, it was not true, and I would fill with guilt. Being no more special than was anyone else, I hated my arrogance and wished to be ordinary.

The innocent wish upset me. I did not want to be ordinary, and defiance would well and overflow. I refused to be ordinary.

Calming the turbulence, I screamed to the sky, "Alright, I am insane." Laughing near hysteria, I would think and do the strangest of things. Being crazy gave me the liberty to survive.

Thus, another year passed. Moreover, so did another one. I alternated between loving and hating God. The only constant within me were the echoes of the souls of Natthia, David, and an ebony child shining in the golden haze of eternity. I loved them. Nothing, not even the agony within me, could ever tarnish the overwhelming honour to have had even a single moment to share with them.

Thinking often about being Muki, I tried to establish meaning and appropriate responses to all I did in life. Ever aware of the sacrifice of Koe Sai Serena, I feared her story and its meaning. I rarely summoned the courage to understand the strange shiver that sometimes ran up my back inviting me to do something good. It terrified me, and I ran. I did not care where, if I was moving and not near a situation requiring intervention by an instrument of God. I had learned my lesson well.

One evening, while on the upper field of the high school heading home, I saw the Northern Lights. They are not, as a rule, very spectacular in Quesnel. It is too far south. However, sometimes they are visible. I watched them. I felt that shiver and giggling, said, "Make the streetlights go out. They interfere with seeing the Northern Lights."

There came a terrible boom like thunder, and the lights went out. I stood still watching the Northern Lights and soon danced across the field. There was a whiff of burning flesh as I approached a street light pole near the edge of the field. There was something on the ground. Upon investigation, I discovered I had killed a raven. His body ripped from end to end, one wing almost severed. Coincidence, I asked?

God, devoid of expression, answered, "There is no such thing as a coincident. All things happen for a reason. Why did this happen?" I knew the answer. I had taken the gift of Koe Sai Serena and abused it. An innocent creature paid for my arrogance with its life. After that incident, I always ran when I felt that shiver up my spine.

The only good thing about such moments was the comfort and peace following them. God soothed my soul and filled me with acceptance.

Often going for walks, I had taken to walking the bridges. I would head down Kinchant Street to the highway and walk to the old Fraser River Bridge. It was now a pedestrian bridge. Old and wooden, it had a certain dignity that I loved. Perhaps it was history, as the bridge knew things. Stepping onto and off held a sense of foreboding but being on it felt delightful, as though the bridge gave me power. I smiled and sang snatches of the songs I recalled from the Muki. I danced. There was so much room on the bridge. Feeling the bridge was mine, I let it be magical. Freezing time, I plucked ideas and made them live. I only acted normal if others were on the bridge. I am a very fast walker when I am escaping human contact. Unfortunately, despite wishing it did, the bridge did not span the universe. Suddenly shocked by reality, I had crossed to the other side.

I was not comfortable in West Quesnel. I stepped up my pace and went by the quickest route to the New Fraser River Bridge. It is long and curves to align with the roads at either end. It has no top. Without character, it simply crosses the river. It does, however, offer spectacular views. To the south, the clean cold Quesnel River joins the muddy Fraser. There is a war for supremacy before the Quesnel must surrender to the expanse of the mightier water. Reflections from the streetlights of the town and the dances of the moonbeams on the water are hypnotic. On the west side, Baker Creek also empties into the Fraser. Mostly out of sight, Baker Creek cries, "Do not forget me. I am here. I am significant." Eventually, I laughed, called the creek vain, and carried on my journey.

Looking north, across the flat pavement and through the railing, was the old bridge, full of character and cutting the river in two. It made me think of Rearguard Falls, far to the north and east. There the Fraser is not so muddy, but it defeats even the salmon. The Fraser looks like the Quesnel, excites my spirit, and thrills my soul.

True, looking at the old bridge from the new filled me with unexplainable sadness, and I did not like to look that way. My pace increased, and I passed the peak on the eastern approach.

Usually, I would turn to the railroad tracks and head across the railway bridge crossing over the Quesnel River. If I decided to cross it, I would put my ear on the rail and listen. I would daydream while imagining delicious journeys and deadly thrills. If I heard even the faintest vibration, sadly and reluctantly, I turned away. Even if I heard no indication of a train, I would run across the bridge, carefully and awkwardly adjusting every step to the unnatural spacing of the ties. At every side platform, I would stop and put my ear back to the rail. I would watch the water through the holes between the ties and get dizzy, looking at the moonlight and shadows dancing below me. Walking the railroad bridge demanded I search my soul. I would cry. Then I would run to the next platform, disappointed a train was not coming. If I did hear one, I would panic and run to the closest end of the bridge. I had no intention of dying.

The other route was to walk along the tracks to the old Quesnel River Bridge. I could walk the rails all the way. I was afraid to use the rails on the railway bridge because the spacing between the ties seemed large, with the river visible so far below. There, I thought my foot could fall through. If it did, I would be as likely to break an ankle or a leg as to gain a covering of grease and creosote on top of the scrapped ankle that tended to accompany falling off railroad tracks.

In those days, I wore mini shirts called hot pants. They were very short dresses that had matching shorts or underwear-type bloomers. There was nothing to protect my anklebones wearing pantyhose and flat oxford-type shoes. Falling off the ties would be painful. I walked carefully, even if I could move quickly. Pantyhose was expensive, and even rubbing soap on the damage could only stop the runs from getting bigger. Vainly, I really did like my clothes and certainly did not like the thought of getting them greasy. I rarely fell but was not willing to risk ruining my clothes falling through the ties on the railway bridge. One had to have priorities.

Racing on the ties, I played games on the railway bridge. During that portion of the journey, I was always a spy. I listened to the wind surrounding me, the water gurgling below me, and the sky whispering above me. It spoke volumes whether the sky was dark and cloudy or clear and bright with a full moon. Yet, it was kind. It gave only what I could handle and leaped through concepts in a mystery demanding to unravel.

I would be disappointed if I was not brave enough to cross the railway bridge. I captured the same mood on the rails. Pretending the rail was the route to discovery, I wove complex challenges into the progression along them. I had to rub the grease off the soles of my shoes after a set number of paces, dance certain steps, and weave across the ties at precise moments to attain the security of the other rail. Thus, I controlled thoughts and responses to ideas that boggled, terrified, and stunned both the spirit and soul of my existence. The game interacted with the concepts I permitted entry into my consciousness. I know; it sounds like I was crazy. I will never deny it. I survived. I had knowingly destroyed all I loved. I was coping with those years, not living them. My journey continued.

Whether I crossed the old Quesnel River Bridge or walked to the Johnston subdivision side of it after crossing the railway bridge, the meaning of the portion of the walk was the same. I just walked it. I shut down completely. I did not hurry or worry about my safety. I let the evening settle. I might stop and dance for the moon or howl and chant. Mostly, I just put one foot in front of the other, basking in the reality of living in a very beautiful and peaceful place.

My only discomfort would be from traffic or other pedestrians. People made me very guilty. I had let them down. I had failed. Especially at night, I envisioned them carrying a bow. They stood in the shadows but continued to come toward me. They knew where they were going and what they were doing. Whether catching up to me from behind or coming toward me in my path, they would draw an arrow, fit it in the bow, and aim it at me.

My guilt overwhelmed me, and I walked tall and proud to meet my end. In silence, in turn, they passed me. Filled with sorrow and disappointment, my anticipation would sink, leaving a huge emptiness. Feeling cheated, I would calm my broken heart and whisper songs of the Muki until I could regain the mood the people's presence stole. Sometimes I would laugh at the croak in my voice to banish it.

It was a long way to the next bridge.

I liked to take a shortcut over the bank at the end of the park onto the field stretching along the river. There was a pond just as I walked out of the trees and before I reached the open grasses of the field. In the pond were bulrushes. In most seasons, there would be crickets and frogs. Certainly, there were bugs. The snow would sparkle in starlight in winter and contrast the grays and blacks of last year's rushes.

Relief filled me when I arrived at the pond. The eerie loneliness of the park and the impenetrable darkness of the trail through the forest terrified me. This spot meant salvation. Even without moon or stars to guide me, the lights from town would be sufficiently bright to see my way. From only a few hundred or so feet further, I would be able to make out the bank I would climb to gain access to the highway and enter the last bridge. Crossing the new Quesnel River Bridge, I would cross the highway to walk home by streetlight or venture under the bridge to regain the railway tracks and the trail up the bank to the top of the alley beside my house.

Being spatially handicapped, I do not judge distances well. Nevertheless, it was a long walk. My guess is about seven miles door to door, but it might have been ten miles. The only guarantee was the knowledge I would be late, arriving home far beyond my curfew. To me, it was measureless and a journey through time extending across the universe.

A railway bridge did exist to service the new pulp mill built above the sandbars on the east side of the Quesnel River, but I never crossed it. I hated it. I felt ownership of that section of the Quesnel River. I resented the 'no trespassing signs and industrial development, marring my connection to significant events of my life.

In a sense, the bulrushes were the end of my journey across the bridges, and I had to pause there. It was hard to continue from there as well. I always cried. Furthermore, I always treasured the moments I stood before the bulrushes. This was where I left the past behind and picked up the present without concern for the future. Like the third arrow, the bulrushes brought peace and forgiveness that would last until the next journey.

Once, I had determined that all factors were perfect for an adventure on the way home. The weather was perfect. Dry, there was no dew or frost. The moon was shining, but it was just shy of a half-moon. Bright, but not too bright, the moon lit the night with a flicker, calling, "Reach to the sky." It was a weekday. I had seen no people, not even the headlights of an occasional car. Instead of walking across the bridge in the pedestrian lane, I climbed the railing and went up over the top of the bridge. I was disappointed at how easy it was. It was not slippery. The bolts and their covers were in a regular, predictable pattern. I could almost walk up with no hands.

The view from the top was magnificent. Just do not look down. Looking down made me dizzy. I had to crouch and hold on with my hands to calm down and regain equilibrium. The trouble did not occur until I was on the downward slope past the peak. There was too much down. Like an idiot, I turned around and backed down the bridge using both arms and legs. It was not fun. Having concluded it was better just to walk home from the pond, I never did it again.

Years later, my brother told me he ran across. There was no glory in having done it first. Unfortunately, I found that disappointing.

Anyway, on this night, I encountered trouble. A gang of boys saw me enter the trail down from the park and followed me. I did not get to soothe my soul at the pond. Pausing only a moment, I set a steady pace across the field while they jeered and harassed me from a distance. Although I walked even faster, the lead boy picked up a stone and threw it. Others also threw stones. I could hear them landing behind me or to either side until one hit me on the back of the neck. While falling, I thought my neck was broken. There were all these hands grabbing at me. I tried to get up and run but only got a few steps before the lead boy grabbed my breast with such force that I suspected he had torn it off.

The world changed. It went golden. The boy let go. I saw my belly floating in the sparkling waters of the Quesnel. Head down, searching for a lost treasure, legs pushing fruitlessly to do a backwards surface dive to the bottom. I was dead.

In the shock of realization, I looked back. God's arms, palms forward, clearly screamed "Stop!" with undeniable authority. The gang stopped. The lead boy took a couple of steps before he, too, stopped. God brushed my cheek and whispered, "Run!" I stared at the boys. I turned toward the bank up to the highway so very far away and froze. God put a hand on my shoulder and yelled, "Run!" I ran.

Whenever I slowed, God pulled me forward. I am not a runner and dislike running. However, I ran more than a mile. That was a Friday night. I should never have walked the bridges on a Friday night. It was stupid. God does not chastise, and I would have felt better if She had.

Although my neck and breast hurt, I was not angry with the boys. They were just stupid, sad dead kids who did not know how to enjoy life. It was the vision that bothered me. That was the first time I seriously admitted I wanted to be dead. With all my soul, I screamed at God, "Let me go. Let me find David. I hate you. Never help me again. Please."

God, silent, soothed my aching soul. I stood on the top of the cliff above Vaughan Street, watching the moonlight on the river far below. I picked up the rope tied to the tree on its edge. I swung out. God sent a hint of the Northern lights. They danced in the sky before my eyes. Although I imagined letting go, I did not. Swinging back to the cliff, I dismounted as normal. I sat on the cliff after retying the rope and cried. I had no choices. I went home confident David would wait for me but hating God for making me wait. God laughed. I slept.

After that event, I took to riding bikes. Every day when I got home after school, I grabbed my bike and headed off around Dragon Lake, a fourteen-mile round trip. I know because I passed the sign saying Quesnel, seven miles, when I got back onto the highway. For weeks on end, I rode around that circuit searching for David in places we had walked. I cursed God and fought exhaustion and anguish.

I could ride all the way up the two-mile hill from the river to the turn to Dragon Lake. I could come down exceeding seventy miles an hour. (A guy stopped at the bottom one day. He had driven beside me halfway down and told me he had clocked me.) In the summer, I had ridden to Barkerville and tried several times to ride the circuit from West Quesnel to the Alexandria ferry and back by the highway. Something always happened, and I would turn back without meeting my goal. I think it was too close to the logging roads leading to the spot where the Muki stored a transporter. I tried to find it even though I knew it was no longer there.

Fighting with God one day, I was furious. The whole ride around the lake was full of tears and frustration. I did not understand my past, and I struggled with the lessons God continued to offer. Coming down the highway, I crouched down against the frame and peddled furiously. I was going too fast.

God descended and forced me to slowly straighten up. The increased resistance brought my speed down dramatically. With defiance dominating my thoughts, I screamed at God to stop hinting and teasing. "Show me your face," I demanded.

The guilt of my arrogance served to make matters worse. I tried to lean down again, and immediately my eyes began to hurt. I had to slow down because I was losing vision. Squinting and blinking, I tried to refocus. I was terrified. God still surrounded me. I knew I was safe but felt helpless, and, in a panic, I whispered, "How am I going to stay on the highway?" Immediately, with determination, I instructed God to leave me be.

I felt stupid as God laughed and steered my bike for me. Constantly slowing me down, my defiance died as I thanked God.

I was humbled. I still could barely see. The vision was strange. I could see the highway below me, part of the front wheel but nothing else. Pumping my handle brakes, I finally stopped at the intersection leading to the pulp mill. Clinging to my bike, I walked it across the highway, following God's instructions to guide me to the edge of the road to Johnston Subdivision. Standing on the edge of the road, feeling both awe and embarrassment, I looked up at the face of God.

God is infinite, while I was so small and insignificant. In shame, I hung my head. Ever so tenderly, God touched me under the chin and kissed my forehead. I pictured David doing so many times previously. I was filled with an indescribable emotion.

God told me a prophecy. Just ten words, they were not even hard or unusual words. The only thing I understood with absolute certainty was the meaning of those words was not as simple as they sounded.

I said, "I do not understand."

God answered, "You will."

I asked, "How?"

"You will study them. I will send opportunities for you to decipher."

"I cannot say them; it would sound stupid. No one would listen."

"When you understand, it will be time to say them, and you will say them."

I shook my head. "I do not trust you."

God answered, "I know, but you will. Remember, I will always be here, especially whenever you have a need."

"Thank you," I said. As an afterthought, I added, "I am not going to do it for you. Get somebody else."

"No. You will do all I ask."

"How do you know?"

"You are mine. You have proven your obedience. You are Muki."

I felt God receding while an echo from the past sang in my heart. It echoed down from the sky in a shower of peace as angels sang with my heart.

> Jaca! Jaca! No a see.
> Con moe a lay my,
> Keshena a coat knee.
> Jaca! Jaca! So a Muki!

Letting a sigh escape my lips, I smiled. Yes, I know it is so deep in my heart. I am Muki. My destiny will continue to unfold. I am no longer an empty box.

God had planted a seed. It will fill me with the comprehension of ten simple words. I will savour the light dancing on every shred of growth throughout the future. Satisfied my past has given it a strong foundation. It is firmly rooted in love.

Forevermore, I will watch as the grey sentry guides the budding of every leaf. Praying for strength to lift the gifts of Koe Sai Serena, I will take David's hand. No longer will he wait alone. I will stand beside him. Watching the horizon, together we will hear the coming reinforcements thundering over the horizon.

With delight and impish glee, I will do my part moulding a tiny piece of the universe. My island kingdom will stretch. It will touch the future, and I will leap across heaven into the waiting arms of David. Together we will lift the ebony child. He will laugh and dance. Then rolling the drums, he will invite David and me to dance.

Someday, I will unlatch the box.

The grey sentry will snap to attention. Raising his sword, he will point to the sky. With the sound of thunder, he will stamp his foot. Following his gaze, our hearts will fill with wonder. Delivering prophecy, we will watch for evidence of a coming miracle.

Epilogue

September 5, 2008

Well, my friends, my tale of receiving prophecy has ended. Only a few years would pass before God would allow me to board a bus to the sky. Without hesitation, I climbed aboard. Unlike my fellow travelers, I knew where we were going. Although I knew none of the people who took us there, I would eventually read the sixth judgement of Earth while being educated in a castle on the Land of the Butterflies. I would rant and rave in anger, disgust, and defiance. Reading David's diary and submissions hurt. Sometimes they delighted me. Other times they shocked me, but I gained insight I would otherwise have not known. I would laugh and cry, spending hours alternating between reliving significant events through another's eyes and applying my own memories to the ethos of an alien culture. My insistent demands to meet again with Judge Soronato, would result in meeting the Prophet York Sabastin. However, that is another tale.

For many years, I watched and listened. With determination, I have faced my lessons. I often think of them as my juggling balls, but usually they line up almost perfectly.

Come join me another time. We will sit comfortably

sipping cider. Hopefully, I will be able to impart the lessons I have learnt trying to understand prophecy.

Love Tara.

Coming Next

Tales of Prophecy Vol. 3
Kotoada
Understanding Prophecy

The Tales of Prophecy continue with Tara of Earth's journey to the Land of the Butterflies. After boarding a bus to the sky, Tara finds herself in much more than a spaceship. She resides in a place where nothing is real but where her every thought and dream will reflect reality – somewhere, for someone, sometime. Recognizing she is in a place the Muki call "Katoada", she travels outside of space and time. Tara undergoes a spiritual journey leading to understanding prophecy.

Tales of Prophecy
By S L Bergen

Volume 1
The Land of the Butterflies
A Prelude to Prophecy

Book 1 Preparations
Book 2 Lakker
Book 3 A New World
Book 4 Merse

Volume 2
So A Muki
Receiving Prophecy

Volume 3
Katoada
Understanding Prophecy

For further information
Please contact the author at:
Tales of Phophecy.com or laurie@lasqueti.ca

9 781955 177757